◁ P9-BYW-081

**Praise for #1 *New York Times* bestselling author
Sherryl Woods**

"Sherryl Woods writes emotionally satisfying novels
about family, friendship and home. Truly feel-great
reads!"

—#1 *New York Times* bestselling author
Debbie Macomber

"Woods is a master heartstring puller."
—*Publishers Weekly* on *Seaview Inn*

"Woods knows how to paint a vivid picture that
encourages the reader to feel the emotions of her
characters...everyone will be able to relate to this
book."

—*RT Book Reviews* on *Catching Fireflies*

**Praise for *New York Times* bestselling author
Allison Leigh**

"[Allison] Leigh has a natural ability to draw a
reader into a story."

—*RT Book Reviews*

"Two endearing yet genuine characters along with a
solid plot make this story hard to put down. A truly
delightful read."

—*RT Book Reviews* on *Once Upon a Proposal*

With her roots firmly planted in the South, #1 *New York Times* bestselling author **Sherryl Woods** has written many of her more than one hundred books in that distinctive setting, whether it's her home state of Virginia, her adopted state, Florida, or her much-adored South Carolina. Now she's added North Carolina's Outer Banks to her list of favorite spots. And she remains partial to small towns, wherever they may be.

Sherryl divides her time between her childhood summer home overlooking the Potomac River in Colonial Beach, Virginia, and her oceanfront home with its lighthouse view in Key Biscayne, Florida. "Wherever I am, if there's no water in sight, I get a little antsy," she says.

Sherryl loves to hear from readers. You can visit her on her website at SherrylWoods.com, link to her Facebook fan page from there or contact her directly at Sherryl703@gmail.com.

A frequent name on bestseller lists, **Allison Leigh**'s high point as a writer is hearing from readers that they laughed, cried or lost sleep while reading her books. She's blessed with an immensely patient family who doesn't mind (much) her time spent at her computer and who gives her the kind of love she wants her readers to share in every page. Stay in touch at allisonleigh.com and on Twitter, @allisonleighbks.

#1 *New York Times* Bestselling Author

SHERRYL WOODS

ONE STEP AWAY

⬥HARLEQUIN®BESTSELLING AUTHOR COLLECTION

If you purchased this book without a cover you should be aware that this book is stolen property. It was reported as "unsold and destroyed" to the publisher, and neither the author nor the publisher has received any payment for this "stripped book."

ISBN-13: 978-0-373-01018-9

One Step Away
Copyright © 2015 by Harlequin Books S.A.

The publisher acknowledges the copyright holders of the individual works as follows:

One Step Away
Copyright © 1994 by Sherryl Woods

Once Upon a Proposal
Copyright © 2010 by Allison Lee Johnson

Recycling programs
for this product may
not exist in your area.

All rights reserved. Except for use in any review, the reproduction or utilization of this work in whole or in part in any form by any electronic, mechanical or other means, now known or hereinafter invented, including xerography, photocopying and recording, or in any information storage or retrieval system, is forbidden without the written permission of the publisher, Harlequin Enterprises Limited, 225 Duncan Mill Road, Don Mills, Ontario M3B 3K9, Canada.

This is a work of fiction. Names, characters, places and incidents are either the product of the author's imagination or are used fictitiously, and any resemblance to actual persons, living or dead, business establishments, events or locales is entirely coincidental.

This edition published by arrangement with Harlequin Books S.A.

For questions and comments about the quality of this book,
please contact us at CustomerService@Harlequin.com.

® and TM are trademarks of Harlequin Enterprises Limited or its corporate affiliates. Trademarks indicated with ® are registered in the United States Patent and Trademark Office, the Canadian Intellectual Property Office and in other countries.

 HARLEQUIN®

Printed in U.S.A. www.Harlequin.com

CONTENTS

Also by
#1 *New York Times* bestselling author Sherryl Woods

Chesapeake Shores

Willow Brook Road
Dogwood Hill
The Christmas Bouquet
A Seaside Christmas
The Summer Garden
An O'Brien Family Christmas
Beach Lane
Moonlight Cove
Driftwood Cottage
A Chesapeake Shores Christmas
Harbor Lights
Flowers on Main
The Inn at Eagle Point

The Sweet Magnolias

Swan Point
Where Azaleas Bloom
Catching Fireflies
Midnight Promises
Honeysuckle Summer
Sweet Tea at Sunrise
Home in Carolina
Welcome to Serenity
Feels Like Family
A Slice of Heaven
Stealing Home

The Devaney Brothers

The Devaney Brothers: Daniel
The Devaney Brothers:
Michael and Patrick
The Devaney Brothers:
Ryan and Sean

Ocean Breeze

Sea Glass Island
Wind Chime Point
Sand Castle Bay

Rose Cottage Sisters

Return to Rose Cottage
Home at Rose Cottage

Trinity Harbor

Along Came Trouble
Ask Anyone
About That Man

Don't miss Sherryl Woods's
Willow Brook Road
Now available from MIRA Books

For a complete list of all titles by Sherryl Woods,
visit sherrylwoods.com.

ONE STEP AWAY

Sherryl Woods

Chapter 1

Vermont! In winter! It was the last place a once fanatical California surfer had expected to wind up.

It was also the last place anyone would look for him, Ken Hutchinson decided as he reached for the phone. And that was all that really mattered.

Hesitating, he fingered the business card in his hand. It was printed on some kind of heavy paper that reminded him of fancy wedding invitations. Embossed in gold, no less. Classy. Expensive.

What the hell! He could use a little class in his life. He could certainly afford to pay for it. After more than ten years in professional football and quarterbacking the Washington Redskins to two back-to-back Super Bowls, he had a bank account about a million times bigger than his worried parents had anticipated during all those years when they had wondered if they would ever get him off the beach long enough to finish high school, much less college.

Thanks to a degree in finance and continuing education classes during the off-season, Ken had determinedly learned how to manage all that money wisely. He had slowly and methodically assembled an investment portfolio that paid outrageous dividends. His financial success had earned him the kind of respect usually reserved for smart mutual fund managers. He had even run an off-season financial-planning seminar for his teammates, trying to keep them from falling prey to some of the shady advisers who latched on to football heroes hoping to cash in on their fame.

More than likely there would never be a chain of Ken Hutchinson restaurants or Ken Hutchinson auto dealerships or Ken Hutchinson surf shops, for that matter. His ego didn't need to see his name flashing in neon from every street corner. His investments tended to be carefully discreet, disgustingly sound and, on those rare occasions when he did take a risk, wildly lucrative. The only attention he craved these days was from his broker.

The truth was, he had just about had his fill of notoriety. Thanks to a strong arm and quick feet, he had had the kind of fame many men would envy, along with enough commercial endorsements to pay for his seven-year-old daughter's college education, right on through a Ph.D., if that's what she wanted.

Unfortunately, at the moment Chelsea seemed to be having difficulty mastering second grade. Lately she'd become unruly, inattentive and, according to the nearly hysterical teacher who called him at least once a week, destined for juvenile hall. Despite that rather dire prognosis, Ken thought she was just about the smartest, spunkiest kid he'd ever met and he was damned lucky to have her.

By most people's standards, he had it made, all right. At least, he had until that second Sunday in August, barely into the exhibition season, when his knee had been shattered by a bone-crunching tackle, pretty much ending his football career. The surgery had been considered a success but at thirty-two, he wasn't masochistic enough to believe that even the most arduous physical therapy could put him back on the field for one or two more outstanding seasons. If he was lucky, he might salvage a year as a starter. Then he'd start the slide to backup and finally he'd be lucky to wind up as third string quarterback on a team going 4 and 12. He had too much pride to set himself up for that. He would have preferred to go out in a blaze of Super Bowl glory one last time, but at least he was leaving in the midst of a winning season with his per-game passing yardage records intact.

He supposed it was somehow fitting that the injury had come only a few weeks after his wife had announced that she wanted out of their ten-year marriage. She had added that she would be flying to some Caribbean island he'd never heard of for a quickie divorce that same afternoon if he would sign the papers she had all ready for him. She had even handed him the pen.

Looking into Pam's cold, blank eyes, he had seen a stranger and suddenly realized that the marriage had really ended long ago. Hell, it probably never should have happened in the first place. She had never wanted to leave Los Angeles and her dream of becoming an actress. For ten years she hadn't let him forget what she had given up to follow him to the east coast.

Recognizing that there was little point in prolonging the inevitable, Ken hadn't seen much reason to fight her, except for Chelsea. He had been adamant about his daughter staying with him. If Pam was going to throw herself wholeheartedly into the Hollywood rat race, she wouldn't have time to give Chelsea the attention she needed. Pam hadn't even bothered to argue. She was too busy planning her long-delayed acting career to worry about the impact her leaving would have on her daughter.

So his days of football glory were over. His marriage was dead. He couldn't bear the thought of going home to California where he would suffocate under all that well-meant parental sympathy. He figured those were valid enough reasons to move to some quiet little backwater town in southeastern Vermont.

With luck, no one there would have ever heard of Ken Hutchinson. Or, if they had, with typical New England discretion, perhaps they would simply leave him the hell alone, anyway. He and Chelsea could both start over. Clean slates and no memories, if such things were possible.

He had visited Berry Ridge, Vermont, a few years back at the invitation of Chester K. Mathias, a blustery, good-hearted sporting goods manufacturer who'd been courting "the decade's greatest quarterback" for a commercial campaign. Ken remembered the town, not all that far from Woodstock, had been isolated and picturesque. At the time, the only activities had been watching wildflowers bloom and long walks. All that peace and quiet, combined with Pam's constant complaints of boredom, had made Ken restless as a caged lion. Now it lured like the aroma of homemade soup on a wintry day.

Despite the fact that that very costly commercial campaign had lost a considerable percentage of its value with the shattering of Ken's knee, Chet Mathias had been the first to call and offer help after the injury.

"You need anything, son, anything at all, you call me," he had said, and Ken had heard the ring of absolute sincerity in the older man's voice.

When Ken had mentioned that he'd wanted to get out of Washington, to settle someplace where he could take a good hard look at his future and his options, Chet had wasted no time in getting the business card for Berry Ridge's best real estate agent to him. Ken studied it again.

According to Chet, Beth Callahan not only handled the finest properties in the Berry Ridge area with brisk efficiency, but she was also willing to coordinate dozens of extra details, the kind of things that left Ken bemused. What did a guy who had spent most of his personal and professional life outdoors know about wallpaper, for example? And he knew more about AstroTurf than he did about carpet.

Pam had tried to get him involved in selecting the decor for their home in a pricey Washington suburb and had finally given up in disgust when he hadn't been able to tell the difference between the dozens of white paint samples she had spread out on the coffee table. Worse, to his wife's way of thinking, he hadn't cared. He seriously doubted he would be any better at it now. Whatever her consulting rates were, Beth Callahan sounded like a godsend.

From Chet's description of her limitless virtues, Ken pictured a mousy, intense, middle-aged woman wearing sturdy shoes and tweed, with bifocals perched on the end of her narrow nose and her fingers permanently affixed to the top of a calculator. He didn't care what she looked like, as long as she could get him settled with a minimum of fuss and maybe teach him to bake chocolate-chip cookies before Chelsea staged a rebellion. At the moment, his culinary skills ran to barbecuing steak on a grill. With a foot or more of early snow on the ground in Vermont last time he'd checked, he'd freeze his buns off unless he developed a more varied cooking repertoire.

Was he making the right decision? he wondered, struck by an unexpected attack of anxiety. For all the interest Pam had shown in her lately, Chelsea had virtually lost her mother. Even so, he wondered if his daughter would be better off in California, where she would at least have her grandparents for emotional support and an occasional whirlwind visit from her mother. Maybe what threatened to be suffocating to him was exactly what Chelsea needed in her life right now. But how the hell was he supposed to know with any certainty?

Suddenly the whole prospect of single parenthood took on daunting proportions. Up until now, he had been mostly an absentee father, at least during training camp and football season. Now he was essentially all his daughter had. There was no counterpoint to his decisions. There was no sharing of responsibility. What if he made a royal mess of things and damaged his daughter irreparably? Was that something this Beth Callahan could fix, as well?

No answers flashed with laser clarity on the opposite wall. No advice hummed through the air. Just like all those Sunday afternoons when he'd had to make a last-second play call at the line of scrimmage, the decision was his. He would either be a heavy or a hero, but the clock was ticking and he had to do something. With a heavy sigh, he picked up the phone and dialed.

For better or worse, it looked as if he were going to Vermont. In winter. Heaven help him!

It was absurd to fall in love with a house, Beth Callahan thought as she stood in front of the Grady place just as she did almost every afternoon, but this house seemed to epitomize her shattered dreams. The big, faded white Victorian with its gingerbread trim practically cried out for the pounding of children's feet across the wide sweep of porch and for the echo of their laughter. A swing hung from a branch of the old maple tree in the front yard. It required all of Beth's resistance and several reminders that she was a professional and a grown-up, not some daredevil kid, to keep her from trudging through the snow for one quick ride in that swing.

She sighed. It wasn't just the swing ride she regretted. It was the fact that she would never live in this house, that she would never fill its five bedrooms with children of her own. Once, that had been her most cherished dream—a marriage, children, happily ever after.

It had almost been within her grasp, too. She had fallen deeply, irrevocably in love with a young widower with two children, a girl and a boy. She had been fascinated with the idea of a ready-made family. In retrospect, she wondered if Peter's biggest attraction hadn't been those two adorable children whose pictures he carried in his wallet.

When Peter Wycroft had finally introduced her to Josh and Stephanie, she had been impressed with their intelligence, charmed by their polite manners and more than ready to be their friend, if not their mother. She had been totally undaunted by all the tales of failed stepfamilies. Hers would not become one of the statistics, not if she had anything to say about it.

Unfortunately, Peter's two children had had other, unspoken ideas about her future as part of the Wycroft family. Both had been about to enter adolescence, both had resented her intrusion into their lives, both had remained determinedly loyal to their mother. And though they were silently sullen in their father's presence, when they were alone with Beth, they had done everything possible to discourage her.

That had been Beth Callahan's first experience with deliberate, malicious animosity. She had been faced with fighting a ghost, a woman whom young memories had rendered perfect. In her dismay, Beth had jumped through hoops trying to win Josh and Stephanie over. Nothing she tried—from kindness to outright bribery—had worked. She hadn't even dented their stubborn resistance. And with each failure, she had lost a little more of her self-confidence.

Everyone had said they would come around eventually. There was practically a textbook timetable for these things, if one survived the stages in between.

Peter had been so certain of that that he had insisted they go ahead with their wedding plans, despite the objections of his children. Beth had been nagged by doubts, but with one last burst of faith, she had dismissed them. She had believed with all her heart that, given time, she could succeed in earning the love of Peter's children. Hadn't everyone always said that Beth Callahan was meant to be a mother? And no two children had ever been in more desperate need of a mother's love.

Beth's faith had suffered its first blow when Stephanie refused to allow Beth to attend parents' night at school along with Peter. It had cracked a little more the first time Josh ran away, blaming her for his not wanting to live at home anymore. It had taken a nosedive when Peter undercut her attempts at discipline time after time.

There had been incident after incident, some small, some large, chipping away at Beth's belief in her own maternal instincts and keeping the household in constant turmoil. For three years she felt as if she were living in an enemy camp with no reprieve in sight. Of all the roles she had ever envisioned for herself, wicked stepmother had never once been among them.

The final blow to the marriage had come when Peter had refused to consider having a child of their own, blaming the tension in the family entirely on Beth. "After all, you're the adult here. If you can't handle two teenagers, how on earth do you expect to deal with an infant?"

His decision, which he had declared irrevocable, had destroyed not only the marriage but the last of Beth's already tattered self-esteem. She had left with little pride and no self-confidence, but had accepted a tidy settlement that had enabled her to move as far away from California as she could get. She had firmly declined alimony, but that lump-sum payment for three years of hell had allowed her time to get her real estate and interior designer's licenses and to open her specialized agency.

Her wildly successful one-woman operation offered everything from the property itself to choosing wallpaper for the client rich enough to customize a country house but unwilling to spend the time and energy it took to do it right. Beth didn't want it to appear that the sale of a client's home hinged on the buyer accepting her additional services, so she optioned her chosen listings herself at a fair market price. She kept only a select few homes on this basis but they were the cream of the market. Each project required patience and dedication, something a good many of the buyers lacked and which Beth had in abundance.

Of all of her select listings in Berry Ridge and the surrounding countryside, the Grady place was Beth's favorite project. She almost hated the prospect of giving it up when it sold. And though she could have afforded to keep the house herself, she had no desire to rattle around in the lonely rooms or to look longingly out the window at an empty swing. She wanted to see the house occupied by the large, happy family it deserved.

Her particular dream for the old Victorian made the call from Ken Hutchinson somewhat disconcerting. He had been referred to her by a satisfied client who had since become a good friend, Chet Mathias, so she knew this Mr. Hutchinson could afford not only her pricey listings, but her additional services, if he wanted them.

But in their brief conversation on the phone yesterday, he had made no mention of a wife, much less children. He'd simply asked what she had available, then picked out three houses based on her detailed descriptions without giving anything away about his own requirements. He had made an appointment to see them all this afternoon, starting with the Grady place.

As a result, Beth had taken an instinctive dislike to him on the phone. He had set her teeth on edge with all of his cool, businesslike questions about plumbing and wiring and heating. The questions were reasonable, but the fact that he'd concentrated on those issues more than any other told her a lot about him. He certainly hadn't sounded like the kind of man who'd bring much liveliness into any house. In fact, he had sounded like a crotchety old bachelor, who had grown more set in his ways with every passing year.

As she waited, shivering just a little in the icy air and watching the sunlight catch on the old rippled glass of the glistening windows, she was almost tempted to break the appointment. Only her pride in her professionalism kept her from doing that. At the very least, though, she would steer Mr. Hutchinson to another property, one that was smaller and more austere, to suit his personality.

Her first clue that she might have misjudged her client was the swirl of powdery snow that rose as an expensive, deep green sports car tore up the lane. The driver was apparently recklessly oblivious to the icy conditions. He was bouncing over the ruts carved by last spring's rains as if they were no more than a minor nuisance. The driver swerved with the skill of an Indy 500 competitor, never once slowing his speed. She had to struggle to reconcile this image of Ken Hutchinson with the stodgier one already formed in her head. It wasn't easy.

But if that was difficult, seeing him emerge from that mud-streaked, highly impractical two-seater was enough to send her into shock. This was not the crotchety, middle-aged man she'd envisioned. If, in fact, this was Ken Hutchinson—and she had what she considered to be reasonable doubts about that—he was definitely more hunk than Hitchcock.

Tall and lean, he had a long, purposeful stride that occasionally caused him to wince, as if he'd been recently injured and was still not used to the slowing down that required. His sun-kissed brown hair was a shade too long and beguilingly tousled. As if that weren't intriguing enough, he had the sort of engaging smile that probably left most women speechless. Beth hated to include herself among those ranks. Unfortunately, though, she could barely form a coherent thought.

"Ms. Callahan?" he said.

He spoke in that brusque, no-nonsense tone that had so irritated her over the phone. In person, his crooked smile took the edge off it and the glint of amusement in his gray eyes replaced coolness with warmth. No doubt about it, he was a charmer. Which suddenly raised all sorts of images of wild parties and raucous nightlife in her beloved house.

She just couldn't do it. She couldn't sell the Grady place to this man. He would spoil her vision for it. As costly as it would be, she would keep the place herself before she would let that happen.

Beth drew in a deep breath and prepared to do something she had never, ever done before. She was about to lie through her teeth to a prospective client.

She smiled, hopefully matching his grin in warmth

and charm and convincing sincerity. "Mr. Hutchinson, I'm terribly sorry for bringing you all the way out here, especially with the roads such a mess."

Wariness immediately replaced the warmth in his eyes, turning them from glimmering silver to the shade of granite. "Is there some sort of problem?"

"Not a problem exactly. It's just that I've made a dreadful mistake." She drew in a deep breath. "You see, this house isn't available after all."

Chapter 2

Ken studied Beth Callahan's face with its model-perfect cheekbones, wide, innocent green eyes and generous mouth and wondered why the woman was brazenly lying to him. She'd planted herself in the middle of the snow-dusted front walk—right next to the prominent For Sale sign—as if she were an armed guard single-handedly responsible for the safety and preservation of a national treasure.

From where he stood, her stance wasn't justified. The house looked a little too fussy for his taste and definitely in need of fresh paint. Half the boards on the sagging porch were probably rotted through, as well. Maybe this was her sales technique, he theorized. Tell him the place wasn't available, just so she could get him into a bidding war with some nonexistent would-be buyer. Fat chance.

Still, he was intrigued about what had happened between yesterday afternoon and today to get her to take this house off the market. Surely it hadn't been the sight of him, though now that he thought about it, she had regarded him and his car with a certain aura of dislike. It was not a reaction he was accustomed to. Football heroes—even recently fallen heroes—generally had their pick of the female population, whether they wanted them or not. Oddly, though, there hadn't been the slightest glimmer of recognition in this woman's eyes, just that faint expression of disdain.

He studied Beth Callahan's sturdy, low-heeled brown shoes, her tweed blazer, slim brown skirt and the beige silk blouse with its prissy high neck. Ironically, the outfit was just about what he'd expected.

She, to the contrary, was most definitely not. He wondered why an attractive woman no more than thirty had deliberately gone the fashion route of a spinster librarian. She'd even pulled her rich, chestnut brown hair into a severe style, though it hadn't managed to tame all the curls. A few tendrils had escaped to brush against her cheeks. The flush of color that tinted her face as he continued his slow, deliberately impudent inspection and the wariness in her eyes added to the almost virginal aura about her.

Of course, those pink cheeks and wary eyes might also have been due to the fact that she wasn't used to lying. He supposed that would be a lousy trait for a woman whose career depended on her credibility. He had no doubt at all, though, that she'd suddenly veered away from the truth. The way she was unconsciously twisting her gloves into a knot was a blatant giveaway.

"Sold, huh?" he said finally, watching her closely. Some of the color seemed to drain out of her face.

"Um, not exactly," she said, avoiding his gaze.

Ken held back a grin and barely resisted the urge to murmur "Gotcha!" Instead he nodded soberly and strode up the walk, trying like hell not to favor his injured knee. The brace he was supposed to wear had been giving him fits, so he had left it off. Now, between the long drive and the cold, the damn knee ached like the dickens.

He glanced back and saw that she was still rooted in place. "Come on, Ms. Callahan. Let's get a look at the house. No deal's final until the money's in the bank."

Despite his encouragement, he noticed that the reluctant Ms. Callahan was still lagging behind. With his hand on the doorknob, he beamed at her. "Is there a problem?"

"No," she conceded. "I suppose there's no harm in looking."

As she joined him on the porch, he tested a couple of the boards with his weight. "Rotten," he muttered. Probably termite infested. It was just as he'd expected. The house was a money pit.

Rather than being offended by his remark, she seized on his critical comment as if he'd tossed her a lifeline. In fact, a smile spread across her face. That heart-stopping smile made his blood hum in a way it hadn't for some time now. It was a good thing, too. It was damn cold outside.

Moving a little faster now, she stepped toward a sagging shutter and fingered it pointedly. "You're right, Mr. Hutchinson. It really would take a lot of work to fix this up right. Perhaps we should move on. I think you'll find the other houses more suitable." She glanced quickly toward his leg, then away again. "Besides, there are a lot of steps inside."

Ken bristled at the display of sympathy. She had unwittingly fueled his stubborn determination to see this house. "So?"

She winced at his tone, but faced him bravely. "You might find that troublesome."

"I can handle the damn steps," he retorted irritably. He turned to look her directly in the eye. "Ms. Callahan, you have a reputation as the best real estate agent in the area, am I right?"

She murmured assent, that delightful pink tint back in her cheeks again. Whether it was due to pleasure or embarrassment or the blasted freezing wind, he couldn't be sure.

"Then you wouldn't have told me about this house unless it was something special, right?"

She evaded his gaze. "But it's difficult to tell if a house is right for someone until you've met them."

Bingo! "So you don't think this house and I are well suited?"

To his chagrin, she didn't hesitate. "No." She studied him worriedly. "Sorry. I didn't mean to sound rude. Actually, I have a place in town that would be just right," she said with enthusiasm. "It's small, completely modernized, well-maintained. I'm sure you'd be much happier with that. It would be perfect for entertaining."

"Ms. Callahan, I don't do a lot of entertaining."

Her spirits deflated as obviously as if he'd poked a pin into a balloon.

"Oh," she said.

"Now, let's just pretend for a moment," he began in

the tone he used when telling a story to his daughter, "that you think this house is suitable for me. Cut to the chase. What are its selling points?"

She regarded him with obvious disapproval. "Mr. Hutchinson, buying a house isn't like investing in a stock portfolio. It's not the bottom line that's important. You should have a feeling for a house. It should reach out to you."

That sounded like heresy to him. Ken knew quite a lot about investing in stock portfolios, but he had to admit buying a house was new to him. He'd figured the strategy was the same: buy low and eventually sell high. Judging from the expression on Beth Callahan's face, that wasn't going to work for him today. He was beginning to get a vague inkling of the problem.

"This house reaches out to you, doesn't it?" he said, throwing her own phrasing back at her.

She nodded, suddenly looking younger and more vulnerable. Appealing, in fact. He wondered why she worked so darned hard to hide her physical attributes.

"Ridiculous, isn't it?" she admitted with a self-conscious shrug that he found downright charming.

"And you don't want me to have the house, because you want it for yourself," he suggested, finally understanding her dilemma.

"No. Actually, the house is mine. That is, I bought it for resale. I want to see it sold to the right people," she blurted out, then groaned. "Sorry. I didn't mean any offense."

Ken had to admit he was intrigued by her notion of who the right people would be for this dilapidated monstrosity. He normally didn't like wasting time on fanciful nonsense, but he was in Berry Ridge overnight, anyway, and he had promised Chelsea he'd come home tomorrow with pictures of their new house. He was hoping to spark some enthusiasm for the move she'd been resisting from the minute he'd mentioned the possibility.

"Tell me what you see in the house," he urged. "Room by room."

As she listed its attributes, which were a wide stretch of anybody's imagination as far as he could tell, Ken began to see it through her eyes. He could also begin to imagine Chelsea clattering up and down the stairs, sitting in the window seat upstairs on a rainy day with a book, swinging from the branch of that maple tree—once the worn-out ropes had been replaced—and Chelsea and him baking cookies in the old-fashioned oven, which probably had about another fifteen minutes of life left in it.

"Sold," he said when Beth Callahan had toured him through every room, delivering her sales pitch at last with unchecked enthusiasm. She looked stunned...and adorable.

"But..." she began, then apparently lost her tongue.

"What's the asking price?" He kept his gaze pinned on her face to make sure she didn't inflate it outrageously.

She started to give him a high figure, then met his gaze and blinked. She sighed and named a lower one.

He countered by offering fifty thousand less. It was the first time in his experience he'd ever seen a real estate agent look utterly defeated at getting a firm offer that was clearly above the property's appraised value. He'd checked it out the day before and knew it was worth less than what he was offering to pay for it, according to the tax assessor's office.

"Are you sure?" she asked, casting one last wistful look toward the house.

"Absolutely."

She held out her hand. "Then I suppose we have a deal, Mr. Hutchinson. I hope you'll enjoy the house. The papers will be ready as soon as you can arrange financing."

She added the latter with the air of someone clinging to a last desperate hope that he would be disqualified for the mortgage. He dismissed an instant's guilt for robbing her of her treasured house, then announced cheerfully, "That's taken care of. I deposited cash in the bank here this morning. We can take care of all the details first thing tomorrow, if that suits you."

She looked as if she might cry, and suddenly Ken had the oddest desire to pat her consolingly on the back. Or maybe kiss her until she smiled again, which, he decided, was a very bad idea. Still, to be fair, he would give her one last shot to stake her own claim on the house. "Are you sure you don't want to keep this house for yourself?"

"No," she said unconvincingly, her gaze pinned on that swing. "I hope you'll be very happy here. Berry Ridge is a nice community."

She said it in a flat, unemotional tone, as if she thought this sale had just caused the town's property values to plummet, rather than just the opposite.

"Do we *have* to move to Vermont?" Chelsea demanded later that night when Ken called home.

The question had him rubbing his head, which was

starting to pound. It seemed nobody today wanted him to buy this house. He held back a sigh. "It's for the best, Shortstuff. You'll love the house. It's like something out of a storybook."

"But, Daddy, I like *this* house. I have friends here. I like *my* school."

"Your report cards aren't much indication of that," he countered dryly.

"I'll do better. I promise. *Please.*"

Even though the tearful plea cut straight through him, Ken kept his own voice firm. "We're moving and that's that."

"But you didn't even discuss it with me," she said in that grown-up way that mimicked her mother.

Forgetting that she was seven, not twenty-seven, he kept the argument alive instead of asserting his authority and putting an end to the debate. "I told you exactly what I had in mind before I left to come up here."

"You *told* me. You didn't *ask* me. That's not a discussion."

"Don't you want to make new friends? You can learn to ski here. There's already snow on the ground."

"I hate snow!"

This from the child who'd practically caught pneumonia the year before when she'd built an entire snow family in their yard, then snuck out of the house after dark in an attempt to spend the night with them.

"You know that's not true," Ken replied, clinging to a last shred of patience. "It's just that this is something new. I know you've already had a lot of changes in the past few months, sweetie, but this one will be for the best. You'll see. Now put your grandmother back on the line."

Pam's mother had pitched right in when her daughter had run off and abandoned them after the divorce. She had come over every day to be there for Chelsea after school, had left dinners for the two of them in the refrigerator and hadn't even hesitated when he had asked her to move in to baby-sit while he made this trip. She was all alone since her husband had died and she enjoyed helping out. Delores Jensen possessed all the calm stability that her daughter had lacked. Ken genuinely loved and respected her.

When she had taken the phone from Chelsea, he asked, "How is she really feeling about this move?"

"It's not the move she's fighting. Not really. It's all of the changes. She'll be fine, once you're settled in up there."

"Are you sure?" he asked, oddly in need of reassurance.

"Ken, you're doing the right thing. A new start will be best for both of you," Delores said firmly.

She muttered a curse he hoped Chelsea wasn't still around to hear.

"Honestly, when I see the disruption my daughter has caused this family, I could just shake her," she said.

"You can't blame Pam for going after what she wants," he soothed with more goodwill than he realized he held toward his ex-wife. "She probably should have done it years ago. Instead, she married me and tried to be satisfied with being a wife and mother. She wanted to be on the big screen, not in some amateur little theater."

Delores sighed. "I suppose you're right. I suppose I can always hope she'll be a better actress than she was a wife."

"Hey, she's bound to be. She fooled me all these years into thinking she was happy."

His ex-mother-in-law chuckled at last, just as he'd intended. "She didn't deserve you, you know."

Ken laughed at that. "The truth of it is, she probably deserved something better. If you believe all the tabloids, I wasn't anybody's idea of a perfect husband, Delores. I just hope I can make up for that by being a decent father."

"You always have been. Nobody who knows you ever believed all that junk the tabloids printed about you being a playboy. You never looked at another woman once you and Pam got married."

"You sound so sure of that," he said, grateful for her faith in him.

"I know you. Now, tell me about the house. Will there be room for me to come visit?"

He laughed. "The place has five bedrooms."

She gasped. "Oh, my! I thought you wanted something small that wouldn't require much upkeep."

"I'm afraid I got caught up in the excitement of the moment."

"Meaning the real estate agent was either beautiful or incredibly persuasive."

"Neither." He thought of Beth Callahan's generous mouth and thick, curly hair. "Not exactly, anyway. She didn't want me to have the house."

"Why on earth not?"

"I think she found me lacking in some way."

Delores Jensen chuckled. "She must have been blind."

"You're prejudiced."

"Hey, I saw that calendar you posed for, remember. I'm not too old to recognize a hunk when I see one."

"I don't think it was my physique that turned her off."

"Then what was the problem?"

Ken recalled the way Beth Callahan had talked about the house, the way her eyes had lit up when she'd described how suitable it was for a large family. "I think she was hoping for that TV family. You know the one. With John-Boy."

"The Waltons?"

"Yeah," he said with a slow smile. "That's it."

"Doesn't she realize they're just make-believe?"

"I doubt it. Something tells me that Beth Callahan has some very old-fashioned ideas about family."

"I see," Delores said, sounding as if she'd just made an intriguing discovery.

"Forget it," he said hurriedly.

"I didn't say a word."

"You didn't have to. Your reputation as a match-maker is legendary. Half the bachelors on the team refuse to even meet you since you fixed up Claude Dobbins and practically escorted him all the way to the altar."

She ignored the gibe. "Beth Callahan, huh? I can hardly wait to meet her."

"Don't hold your breath," he muttered to himself.

"I heard that," she said, laughing. "Will we see you tomorrow?"

"I may stay on a couple of days to get the renovations under way. Is that a problem for you?"

"Of course not. You know I love staying with my baby."

"Then I'll call you tomorrow and let you know my exact plans."

"Sure you don't want me to drive Chelsea up?" she teased. "I'd be happy to. Maybe I could give you a little advice on decorating…or anything else that might come up."

"Good night, Delores."

"Is that a no?"

"That is definitely a no."

The very thought of his ex-mother-in-law getting a look at Beth Callahan sent a shudder down his spine. He hadn't been joking about her penchant for match-making. What he hadn't said was that she seemed determined to choose the most incongruous people to pair off. Somehow, though, the pairings worked. Right now, he couldn't imagine a more unlikely couple than prissy Ms. Callahan and the reportedly daring, reckless play-boy of the Washington Redskins. It would probably be a challenge Delores couldn't resist.

Chapter 3

The next morning Beth was still astonished by her uncharacteristic behavior. She wasn't particularly proud of herself. In fact, she couldn't imagine what had gotten into her. She'd taken one look at Ken Hutchinson, made a judgment about what kind of man he was and completely lost her head. She had not only been downright rude to a man who had done nothing to deserve it, but she had been totally unprofessional in a way that could have destroyed the good reputation she had worked so hard to attain in a tight-knit New England community that wasn't won over easily.

Every time she thought about her actions, she shuddered. Never before had she tried to talk a client out of buying a house. Nor had she ever boosted the price in an ill-considered attempt to block a sale. And all just because she didn't think he deserved to own it. Her license could have been yanked if he had wanted to make an issue out of it.

There was no question that he had known exactly what she was up to. She had been able to read the awareness in his expression. If she were lucky, maybe he would just chalk it off to momentary lunacy. Or, more likely, he would make her pay at some point down the line.

That was probably it, she decided with a sudden flash of insight into the man who had battled wits with her the day before and won. He had struck her as an advocate of the don't-get-mad, get-even school of retribution. That hard glint she had detected in his eyes definitely didn't suggest he would be the type to forgive and forget.

Yet his rare flashes of humor that she had observed were at odds with her overall impression. In many ways, the evidence of a wry wit was even more disconcerting because it had almost tempted her to like him. And in liking him, she would underestimate him, she realized belatedly. It was probably one of his more successful business ploys.

The man apparently also had a streak of stubbornness equal to her own. The harder she had tried to foul up the sale, the more insistent he had become about concluding it. She wondered if he even wanted the blasted house or if he'd just enjoyed sparring with her. She supposed she would know for sure when it was time for the final papers to be signed in—she stole another furtive glance at her watch—about five minutes.

As she sat outside the office of the Berry Ridge bank's president, waiting for her client's arrival, she couldn't help glancing at the time every ten seconds, hoping that Ken Hutchinson wouldn't show up. Maybe even now he was on his way back to wherever he'd come from, having a good laugh at her expense. The humiliation would have been worth it just to keep him out of the Grady place and to keep her from having to face the oddly conflicting feelings she felt in his totally, undeniably masculine presence.

Naturally, however, he strolled through the door right on time. His punctuality grated, even though she knew she ought to be grateful he hadn't kept her waiting, prolonging the uncertainty.

As she took a good long look at him in his tight-fitting jeans, flannel shirt and heavy winter jacket that would have made him a solid candidate to model for the L.L. Bean catalog, her heart thumped unsteadily. She blamed it on disappointment at the now inevitable loss of her favorite house.

The truth was, though, that some seriously deranged part of her found the man attractive, despite the way he'd run roughshod over her the day before. She would hate to be up against him in a cutthroat business negotiation. She had seriously underestimated both his skill and his determination. Under other circumstances, she would have admired those very traits in him. As it was, she floundered unsuccessfully for any logical explanation for the odd, fluttery sensation he caused in the pit of her stomach. Nerves? Maybe. Fascination? All too likely, she decided ruefully.

As Roger Killington, the stuffy, middle-aged president of the Berry Ridge bank, invited them into his office, she tried to gauge his reaction to the area's newest prospective resident. Roger was also president of the Chamber of Commerce and cared a great deal about maintaining the town's upscale serenity. She doubted if that vision included wealthy playboys. Berry Ridge had been gentrified, not turned into some Aspenlike ski resort for the jet set.

To her bemusement, however, Roger was beaming at Ken Hutchinson as if they were old friends.

"The minute you told me yesterday that you were working with Beth, I knew you'd find exactly what you were looking for. She's the best," Roger told him. He beamed at her with almost fatherly pride, which belied some of the battles they'd had about the town's future.

Beth managed a weak smile.

"She does have a way about her," Ken conceded, turning that impudent grin of his on her. His eyes sparked with another display of that humor that warmed her when she least expected it.

Oblivious to the byplay, Roger asked, "So, what did you choose?"

Ken glanced at Beth. "What did you call it? The Grady place?"

Beth nodded.

Roger's expression lit up. "That's terrific. I'm less than a mile away. Maybe we can put together a touch football game in the meadow once the snow melts in the spring. I know half the men in the area will get a big kick out of playing with one of the best. Maybe you could get a few of your teammates up here. We could raise some money for charity."

Roger was so caught up in his plan, he apparently didn't notice Ken Hutchinson's reaction. The man's handsome, chiseled face had turned gray, even though he managed to keep his expression bland. What was going on here? For the first time Beth began to wonder exactly who Ken Hutchinson was.

She didn't have to puzzle over his identity for long. With what was for him an unusual lack of tact, Roger was oblivious to Ken Hutchinson's discomfort. He pulled what looked like a football program out of his desk drawer.

"I knew I had this someplace. Found it at home. Would you mind signing it? My son will be thrilled. He's a huge fan. Hasn't stopped talking about that terrible game back in August." Suddenly he wound down and his voice faltered. An expression of sympathy spread across his face. "Jeez, I'm acting like a jerk. You'd probably like to forget all about that day. How is your knee?"

Although she was hardly a sports fan by anyone's definition, Beth was beginning to piece together the clues. She added what Roger had said to the faint limp she'd detected as she'd watched Ken Hutchinson going through the house the day before. She decided her client must be some sort of football celebrity who was recovering from a serious injury. She glanced into Ken's expressionless face, then met his eyes and realized the torment this conversation was putting him through. Even though she didn't understand the details, she jumped in to try to ease the awkward situation.

"Roger, as you just said yourself, I'm sure Mr. Hutchinson would rather talk about something else," she said firmly. "Perhaps we should get down to business."

Roger looked taken aback by her sharp tone, but his innate diplomacy finally surfaced. "Of course.

Sorry." He slid the unsigned program back into his desk drawer. "I have all the papers right here."

Arrangements for the transfer of the title took less time than it took to select a ripe melon this time of year. Beth had to swallow hard as she took the pen in hand to sign the papers. And with her client's steady gaze pinned on her, her signature was disgustingly shaky.

When the deal was closed, it required all of her will to keep the ridiculous resentment she felt out of her voice as she congratulated Ken Hutchinson on his purchase. She drew the keys to the house from her purse and handed them to him.

"I hope you'll be very happy here," she said in a voice so low and unenthusiastic she drew a surprised look from Roger. "If that's all, I'll be on my way."

"Whoa!" Ken Hutchinson said, latching on to her arm with a grip that had probably served him well on a football field. "Trying to run out on me?"

Beth lifted her startled gaze from the hand resting on her arm to his eyes. "Is there a problem?"

"We haven't discussed the renovations. It's my understanding that you can handle those for me. Chet said that was part of any deal you made."

Dear Heaven, this wasn't a twist she'd anticipated. Even as she started to speak, guilt sliced through her. "Really, Mr. Hutchinson…" Catching the warning look in his eyes, the guilt won. She allowed the protest to die on her lips and hoped she could come up with something really good before she was forced to continue to see this man who so unexpectedly and unfortunately stirred her senses.

"Ken," he insisted.

"Mr. Hutchinson," she repeated stubbornly.

His eyes sparkled with mocking laughter as he matched her stubbornness. "Ken."

Beth gave up that fight, saving her energy for trying to make him see reason. "Fine," she said agreeably. "Ken. As for the renovations, I'm sure you have your own ideas about what you'd like to do to the house."

He smiled blandly. "Nope. I don't have a clue."

"But surely…" Her voice faltered.

"I was counting on you."

The look in his eyes threw her. There was nothing innocent about it. Rather, it was warm and very masculine, almost speculative. It took her a minute to gather her thoughts and remind herself sternly that he was interested in her professional skills, nothing more. It still struck her as a bad idea.

"Well, of course, I can recommend local men who are qualified to do anything you'd like with regard to repairs," she offered as a compromise. "As for the interior, I suspect our tastes are very different."

"Afraid I'll want AstroTurf in every room, Ms. Callahan?" he inquired cheerfully.

She could feel the rush of blood into her cheeks. "No, of course not. It's just that—"

"Look, let's cut to the chase," he interrupted with that more familiar brisk tone that didn't make her pulse buck. "I can give you whatever budget you need and carte blanche to make whatever choices you think best."

"I can do anything I want?" she repeated slowly, not quite believing her ears. Temptation rose to crowd out all of her logical arguments.

"Anything," he confirmed.

"Pink marble and lots of velvet?" she suggested, testing him.

He swallowed hard, but nodded. "If you think that's appropriate."

She found herself laughing at the brazen lie. "You must figure you're safe on that score. Choosing pink marble and velvet to decorate a house for someone like you would ruin my reputation forever."

He grinned back at her. "I was counting on that."

"I'm sure you were," she said dryly. "Okay, exactly what do you want me to handle?"

"Everything."

At the prospect of working closely with this man for the weeks, maybe even months it would take to complete renovations on the Grady place, alarm bells went off in her head. Still, it was the opportunity she'd dreamed about to restore the house to the country-style showplace it must have been around the turn of the century. And she'd just about run out of graceful ways to try to turn the job down.

She glanced at Roger and had to smother a laugh at his expression of bemusement. No doubt he couldn't imagine any sensible businesswoman saying no to an opportunity this incredible.

"You realize it could take some time to get everything done. When will you want to move in?"

"As quickly as possible. If you can make a couple of bedrooms livable in the next week or so, the rest can move along at a slower pace."

"Two rooms in a week?" she repeated with disbelief. "That's not possible."

"Sure it is," Roger said hurriedly. "You're a miracle

worker, Beth. You know you can get the guys in town to do anything for you."

"For a price."

"Pay the price," Ken said without hesitation. "After experiencing firsthand what a tough negotiator you are…" He allowed his words to hang in the air for one pointed moment before continuing. "You have my complete confidence that you'll get the best possible deals to get the work done in a timely manner."

Given what had transpired the day before, that was quite a statement. It also signaled the catch she'd anticipated. He was willing to forget all about her unprofessionalism. In fact, he intended to turn her questionable tactics to his advantage. Beth sighed. She should have known he would win this round, too.

"How hard can it be?" Ken prodded. "A little paint. A couple of beds to start with. The rest can come later."

The comment showed exactly how little he knew about what the project entailed. Maybe when he saw the price tag for doing it her way, he'd back down and let her off the hook. She could always dream.

Once more, she slid her gaze to Roger's. Damn him, he was watching the two of them with the evident fascination of some paternalistic matchmaker. She could just imagine what he'd have to say about the entire exchange at the next Chamber of Commerce meeting. Roger did love to gossip. With a football hero involved, the story would be too juicy for him to pass up.

"Do we have a deal, Ms. Callahan?" Ken asked.

"Do I have a choice?" she muttered under her breath.

He grinned. "Was that a yes?"

She pulled out her leatherbound notebook and jotted a note on it for the following morning. Then she managed her coolest, most professional smile. "I'll have your estimates for you in the morning. About ten, if that's okay?"

"I'll have a pot of coffee waiting in my suite at the inn."

Beth hesitated. She hadn't counted on a meeting quite that private. She'd been picturing someplace nice and public. Maybe the steps of the town hall. Or the inn's small dining room, at least.

"Is there a problem?" he inquired, that challenging glint back in his eyes.

"No problem at all," she lied blithely. The only problem would be keeping her unexpectedly rampant hormones in check and she hardly intended to share that dilemma with a man who probably took such reactions for granted.

Back at home, Beth shed her fancy boots and traded her carefully selected, oh-so-professional suit for sweatpants and a stretched out, faded T-shirt from a long-ago visit to Disneyland. She made herself a cup of orange spice tea and settled behind her desk, which she'd placed so she could look out the bay window in her living room.

This house was about a fourth of the size of the Grady place—correction, the *Hutchinson place*—but it suited her well enough. She'd chosen it for the bright, cheerful rooms and the view from this one window. She could see the Green mountains in the distance and the birds up close. She'd hung several bird feeders from the bare branches of the trees and scattered seeds across the snow for the birds each morning, which assured plenty of activity. In the spring there were bluebirds and blue jays, robins and woodpeckers. There were fewer birds now, but they were no less fascinating to watch. Every now and then a couple of ducks wandered up from the iced-over pond to get their share of the bounty. She'd even spotted a white-tailed deer early one morning at the edge of the woods. She'd remained perfectly still for several minutes, awestruck, then sighed as the deer had moved back into cover.

In the spring, which seemed to be later and later in coming, the snow gave way to a profusion of daffodils and tulips. She'd planted more bulbs just last month.

She took a sip of her tea and watched the birds until the morning's disconcerting encounter with Ken Hutchinson began to fade into perspective. This was a job, she reminded herself. And doing it well would simply add to her already impressive credentials. Besides, she owed Chet Mathias for sending her a client. She didn't want to offend a friend by botching the job.

With that in mind, she decided to take Ken at his word and pull out all the stops. She'd been dreaming about the Grady place from the first time she had set eyes on it. She knew exactly how every room would look if she spared no expense, from the design of the wallpaper to the patterns for the upholstery. Like a child furnishing a beloved dollhouse, Beth had combed antique shops from New York to Maine locating pieces she would buy, if only the right client came along. She'd kept notes on everything from washstands to brass beds with snapshots attached.

Assembling her price lists and samples took the rest of the day with time out only for a quick sandwich. She spent an hour calling the half dozen trades people she used regularly for everything from electrical wiring to plumbing and painting, checking on their availability. All were currently on other jobs, but every one of them promised to meet her at the Grady place at seven the next morning to give her price quotes for the needed work. Because she paid on time and well, she didn't even have to mention the bonus she would be willing to pay to get them to squeeze this job into their schedules before the hectic rush of Thanksgiving and Christmas holidays. She was a steady enough employer that they were willing to work miracles for her.

At six-thirty she sat back in her chair with a small sigh of satisfaction. So, she thought, she was going to get to fix the Grady place up exactly as she wanted to.

But she still wouldn't get to live there.

Unless, of course, the glint of interest she'd detected in Ken Hutchinson's eyes on more than one occasion turned into something more.

She dismissed the wildly improbable idea as soon as it arose. A man as attractive and eligible as he was would eventually want marriage and children. She had no intention of trying her luck again with either. She'd failed too miserably the first time around.

After all the heartache, she had finally found a sort of contentment. She intended to hang on to it with everything in her. She was alone, but not lonely. At least, most of the time. And even if there were occasional bouts of middle-of-the-night blues, that was better than asking for the trouble a new relationship would bring.

No, her life was fine just the way it was, she concluded decisively.

Unfortunately, she couldn't help imagining a pair of laughing gray eyes mocking her firm resolution.

Chapter 4

The Berry Ridge Inn had been built in the late seventeen hundreds as a gentleman's farm. The house itself sprawled this way and that, thanks to additions tacked on by the generations of Hopewells who had lived there. Increasing taxes and decreasing family size had forced the most recent generation to turn the house into a cozy inn, known for its blazing fireplaces, early American antiques and excellent gourmet cuisine. The rates were exorbitant, but the service was impeccable. And the view from every window was spectacular: snow-shrouded, pine-topped mountains and a glistening lake that was often dotted with ice skaters.

Ken had taken a suite that included a sitting room, which he'd set up with the laptop computer, printer and facsimile machine that went everywhere with him. The hour or two he spent checking on his investments by modem was every bit as stimulating for his brain as his rigorous exercise regimen was for his body.

He glanced around the room, his mouth curving into a rueful grin. All of the high-tech equipment looked totally incongruous amid the flowery fabric and the eighteenth-century furniture. Still, there was something almost comforting about sitting back in a wing chair in front of the fire with a glass of brandy at the end of the day, the tools of his trade nearby. He decided to mention to Beth that he would like the office in his new home to resemble the makeshift one he had created in the inn. Otherwise she would probably set him up in some chillingly sterile glass-and-chrome decor suitable for the bachelor she apparently thought he was.

The realization that she had him pegged as a jet-setting, single jock had come to him only last night. Though his single status was true enough, the rest was garbage. He hadn't quite decided yet whether to fill her in on the desire for seclusion that had brought him to Berry Ridge or to allow her to continue spicing up her apparently dull life with her wild imaginings.

Beth Callahan puzzled him. Though she seemed to go out of her way to present herself as a staid New Englander, he'd seen intriguing flashes of temper, wit and vulnerability that belied the image. Maybe this morning's meeting would give him some more insight into what made her tick. The challenge of unraveling the complex puzzle she represented lured him more successfully than provocative clothes or seductive perfume ever could have. It gave him something to look forward to over the coming months of self-imposed isolation, far from friends and family.

She was due any minute with her first set of plans

for fixing up the Grady house. He had given her a week to do something with the two bedrooms, hardly expecting her to agree to the impossibly tight timetable. He had done it just to test her, and, to his satisfaction, aside from an almost perfunctory objection, she had barely even blinked. She had just jotted something down in that damnable notebook of hers, topped him by saying she would have plans for the whole renovation ready by this morning, then marched briskly out of the bank to get busy.

In most business associates, Ken would have considered such cooperation and equanimity to be worthy traits. In Beth Callahan, he found them disconcerting, two more pieces of the puzzle. He couldn't help wondering how she had ended up in this small rural community. Was she seeking solace from the past, just as he was?

"A fine woman," Mr. Killington had said to him when she'd gone, his expression shrewd.

"If you say so," Ken had replied, wondering why such a fine, efficient businesswoman managed to get his juices going, when far sexier women had tried and failed in the weeks since the demise of his marriage... and before, for that matter.

Maybe it had something to do with the fact that Beth Callahan was totally oblivious to him as a living, breathing male. In true macho form, that made him want to do something—*anything*—to awaken her responses. Perversely, he wanted to see her unruffled, calm demeanor shattered by an explosive climax. His body stirred as he envisioned stripping away those deplorable, boring clothes of hers to discover the woman beneath. He didn't doubt there was one, because he'd seen the unmistakable evidence of dark, smoldering passion in her eyes whenever he had challenged her in some way. Yes, indeed, Beth Callahan would definitely relieve any boredom that set in once he was settled in Berry Ridge.

He poured himself another cup of coffee and sat back with the *Wall Street Journal*. He'd barely scanned the front page when he heard the sharp tap on his door. Glancing at his watch and confirming it was precisely ten o'clock, he grinned. That was one of Beth Callahan's traits he admired most. She might not like the situation he'd put her in, but she was obviously planning to bravely muster through.

"Come in."

The door opened at once. Again, no hesitation. He smiled to himself. A fascinating, complex woman, no doubt about it.

"Good morning, Mr. Hutchinson," she said briskly, her arms laden with samples, which she allowed to tumble onto the room's sofa.

"Ken," he reminded her as he studied the way she looked in what she no doubt considered her less formal work attire: red wool slacks, a soft winter-white sweater, a navy blazer and a jaunty scarf knotted at her neck. Though the outfit was more intriguingly feminine than that unfortunate tweed he'd seen her in before, he still longed to see her in satin and lace with her hair tumbling free of that ridiculously prim knot she'd twisted it into.

To his amusement she barely noticed what he'd said or the way he was studying her. Totally absorbed in her own agenda, she shed her coat and pulled her notebook from her crammed-full leather attaché case. Perching on the edge of the chair opposite him, she tapped a pen against some notation in her notebook.

"Now, then, I have met with the trades people, gone over my figures, and I think we've come up with a reasonable plan, except for furniture. I wasn't sure what you might already have." She finally glanced up at him, her expression expectant.

"I'm bringing nothing with me," he said. "This is a fresh start."

She didn't bat an eye. "I see. Did you have an amount in mind for the furnishings?"

He shrugged. "Whatever it takes."

Her gaze narrowed. "Could you be more specific? I don't want to send you into bankruptcy."

"There's not much chance of that," he said dryly. "Unless you're planning on solid gold fixtures and rare art for every room."

Serious green eyes blinked at him. "Mr. Hutchinson, perhaps it would help if I knew a little more about you."

He grinned. "You want to know just how rich I am?"

"I want to know something about you," she corrected. "Your likes. Your dislikes. That sort of thing. I gathered yesterday that you play football."

Ken's ego had an instant's pause at the realization that she didn't have a clue who he was. Then he decided that was all to the good. She wouldn't waste much time pitying him. And she obviously wouldn't be catering to him because of his celebrity. A rare sense of calm stole over him at the realization that with Beth Callahan, he could be whatever he chose.

"I used to play football," he corrected. "My career ended in August."

"I'm sorry."

With a sudden lack of bitterness that surprised him, he shrugged. "It happens. I had a great career. How many people can reach the top of their profession by the time they're thirty-two? What about you?"

She looked disconcerted by the question. "I love what I do."

"It shows."

"Oh?"

"Your face glows whenever you talk about your houses."

"You'll probably think I'm nuts, but they're a lot like people," she confided with an oddly wistful expression. "They each have a distinct personality."

The admission didn't surprise him, but it did make him wonder if she had more feeling for these projects of hers than she did for actual people and why that would be so.

"And what about Mr. Callahan? Does he share your affection for real estate?"

"There is no Mr. Callahan."

"Ah," he said knowingly.

She frowned at that. "I was married," she said. "It didn't work out."

She said it with a note that might have been defiance or raw pain. Maybe some combination of the two. At any rate, he flinched at the tone that conveyed far more than her actual words.

"Sorry," he said automatically, though some part of him appeared to be rejoicing at the news that Beth Callahan was available.

"If it hadn't happened, I wouldn't be doing this," she said with a more cheerful air.

"I guess the saying is true, then. Every cloud does have a silver lining."

She grinned suddenly. "You just have to be careful you don't get soaked while you're waiting for it."

Ken chuckled, as much at the unexpected wit as at her determined show of bravado. Obviously there were even more layers to Beth Callahan's personality than he'd initially guessed. It was definitely a toss-up whether it would be more fun to peel them away or to strip her down to the fashion basics to see if she wore serviceable cotton or delicate, sexy lace.

"Mr. Hutchinson? *Ken?*"

Her voice finally cut through the pleasant fantasy he'd been having about her. He regarded her guiltily. "Sorry. I just remembered a call I should have made this morning," he improvised.

"Do you need to take care of it now? I can wait. I'd really like your full attention when we go over this."

He moved his chair a little closer. "Now is fine. And I can assure you that you have my undivided attention."

Apparently something in his voice alerted her that his attention just might not be all business. She shot him a puzzled frown. He grinned and leaned back. "Bring on the samples."

Ken was prepared to be bored to tears, just as he had been when his ex-wife had laid out all those look-alike paint chips. Instead, though, he soon found himself caught up in Beth's enthusiasm. He also began to appreciate the subtle differences in fabric texture and color, especially when he considered whether Beth Callahan's skin would feel like the silk she was proposing to use for a fancy window treatment and whether the shade of material she'd chosen for his office furniture was any deeper or richer than the color of her hair.

In fact, he was gazing intently at her hair when she cut into his thoughts again.

"You're not paying attention," she accused.

"Oh, but I am," he disagreed, and rattled off the costs she'd quoted for various alternatives. "I like this shade of brown for your hair, but not for my office. Your hair catches the light. The fabric doesn't. It's dull and lifeless."

Her startled gaze shot to his. Her fingers lifted automatically to smooth a stray tendril into place. "My hair? What does my hair have to do with anything?"

"Just a color comparison to prove I was paying attention."

She seemed more than ready to accept that innocuous explanation. "What about the gray then? It's very businesslike, especially if we throw in some colorful accents."

He shook his head and gestured around them. "I like this."

She took in the flower-patterned upholstery of the sofa and the wing chair in its complimentary solid blue fabric. "This?" she repeated doubtfully. "Flowers? Wedgwood blue?"

"It feels...comfortable. Homey. Don't you think so?"

Her expression brightened. "Yes, of course. It's just that I thought for your office you'd want something more..."

"Businesslike?" he offered.

"Masculine," she said.

"This isn't clothes. I don't expect the room to make

the man. I want a room that's cheerful, that anyone, male or female, would feel comfortable in."

"No game room with pool table and felt-topped card tables?"

"You sound disappointed. Do you play poker or pool?"

She grinned. "Afraid not."

"Do most of my neighbors?"

"I have no idea."

"Then I guess there's not going to be much call for them. For the moment, I just want to get the repairs done, get a couple of beds in and then we can decide what's to be done with everything else." He extracted the estimates she'd drawn up from the pile of papers and samples that had accumulated. He made a few calculations of his own and decided the deals she'd managed to pull together in barely twenty-four hours were more than satisfactory.

"How soon can they get started on this?"

"They promised to get a crew together as soon as I give them an okay."

"Do it."

"Just like that?"

"Are these figures going to change if we debate them?"

"Probably not, although I suppose there's always room for a little negotiation."

"Beth, one thing you should know about me. I know exactly what I want in life and I go after it." He fastened his gaze on her and saw the color rise in her cheeks. "Also, I don't waste time trying to nickel and dime a man who's just trying to make a living. These look like fair prices to me. I see no need to haggle over them.

And I want to get moved into this house as quickly as possible. Do whatever it takes to make that happen."

"Will you…?" She swallowed hard. "Will you be moving in alone?"

He was amused by her apparent embarrassment. "No," he said, and left it at that. He could be just as closemouthed about his personal life as she was about hers. He wondered if the flicker of reaction he'd caught in her eyes was dismay.

"Well, then," she said, all brisk efficiency again. "I'd best get busy. I'll call the workmen as soon as I get back home and make arrangements for them to get started."

"Do it now," he said. "And then we can have some lunch."

She stopped in the midst of trying to stuff all her papers back into her attaché case. "Lunch?" she repeated as blankly as if she'd never heard of the meal.

"Lunch. Maybe some clam chowder. A salad. A veal chop. Whatever you like. The food is excellent here." He deliberately dropped his voice to a seductive whisper. "And I understand the chocolate mousse is downright decadent."

She ran her tongue across her lips, as if they'd suddenly gone dry. Ken watched that delicate movement and felt his heart buck. Damn! What was it about this woman's every movement and gesture that got to him? He hadn't stopped thinking about sex and seduction since the moment he'd met her. The irony was that he'd never known any woman more determined not to stir lascivious thoughts in someone of the opposite gender.

"You said you wanted to get to know me," he reminded her. "To help you choose the furnishings.

Here's your chance. I'll have to go back to Washington first thing in the morning. It may be a few days before I get back up here."

He made the lunch sound as businesslike as possible. He figured once they were settled comfortably in front of the fire with a glass of wine or two, he could twist the conversation away from himself and toward Beth Callahan. Instinct had made him entrust his home to her. Now, like the rational businessman he was purported to be, he wanted the facts to justify his actions.

Or so he told himself. The truth was, he just wasn't ready to say goodbye to the first woman in a decade who didn't seem to give a damn that he was a football hero. Maybe, just maybe, Beth Callahan would see the real man.

And maybe, by looking into her eyes, he'd begin to figure out who he really was now that the phrase "record-setting quarterback" would no longer automatically be said along with any mention of his name.

At some point between the clam chowder and the chocolate mousse, Beth began to relax and enjoy herself. As she sipped a cup of cappuccino while Ken took a call from a business associate, she found herself leaning back and studying him with more objectivity than she had in the past.

This entire meeting had surprised her. She had known from the first that he was intelligent and shrewd. She had even recognized his quirky sense of humor. What she had failed to see was that Ken Hutchinson was not the arrogant, egotistical man she had built him up to be. Even though he hadn't hesitated to disagree with her, he had been consistently respectful of her opinions. She had expected him to be condescending to her or, worse, to overrule her at every turn, simply because she was a woman or because it was his money they were spending. Instead he had treated her as an equal, as a professional, she admitted with a sense of amazement.

Not that he hadn't noticed her as a woman. She had caught his speculative surveys, the occasional lingering looks that would have turned her insides to complete mush if she hadn't hurriedly looked away. There was enough electricity humming through the air to provide power for his new house through the entire icy Vermont winter. And on some level she couldn't afford to indulge, she was enjoying it, even if his enigmatic response about moving into the new house with a companion had disconcerted her more than she cared to admit.

Suddenly she felt the sensation of his gaze on her again. She glanced up and caught him grinning.

"What were you thinking about?" he asked.

"Plumbing," she said, grasping at the first thing that came to mind.

He regarded her with obvious amusement. "Remind me to check out the plumber, if he can put a glow like that in your cheeks."

Beth almost laughed as she considered his reaction to the portly Chuck Wilson, whose pants tended to scoot dangerously low as the day wore on. She doubted if the grandfather of ten was anybody's idea of a sex object, except perhaps Mrs. Wilson. At any rate, he was hardly in Ken Hutchinson's league and Ken would know that at first glance.

"Worried about the competition?" she asked without thinking, then wanted to die right where she sat.

"What if I am?"

The tone of the inquiry was bland enough, but the implication was very dangerous, especially coming from a man who might very well be committed to someone else. Beth tried to still her suddenly erratic pulse. "We have a business relationship, Mr. Hutchinson. Nothing more," she said, then added emphatically, "Not now. Not ever."

"The plumber's that fantastic?" he said, his gray eyes skeptical.

"The plumber has nothing to do with it," she said briskly. She stood and began gathering her things.

"Don't run off just when things are getting interesting," he taunted.

"You're not my only client," she informed him.

Judging from his expression, he clearly didn't believe that was the reason for her hurried departure. Still he didn't argue as he walked her to the door. She thought she'd made a clean getaway when he said quietly from the doorway, "Just remember one thing, Beth Callahan."

Swallowing hard at the quiet command in his voice, she turned back. "What's that?"

"I may not be your only client, but from this moment on I'm the only one who counts."

She opened her mouth to argue, then snapped it shut as the door was closed softly right in her face. It was probably just as well, she thought even as she fumed. With the money he was currently proposing to spend, Ken Hutchinson really was the only client who mattered. And despite that gauntlet she'd thrown down as she'd exited his suite, the truth of it was, he was the *only* client she had.

She warned herself that she would be very wise to change that situation in a hurry or she would find herself hip deep in the kind of trouble she'd been trying to avoid ever since her disastrous marriage. Right now, it was just a darn good thing Ken Hutchinson was leaving town for a couple of days so she could reclaim her equilibrium and muster her previously well-honed defenses.

If she had any doubts about the need to get a grip on her emotions in a hurry, his admission that he wasn't moving into the new house alone ought to be enough to convince her to keep her distance. The very last thing she needed in her life was a flirtation with a man who obviously didn't take commitment of any kind very seriously.

Chapter 5

"I hear you just sold the Grady place to a man who is drop-dead gorgeous and rich as that king with all the gold. What was his name?" Gillie Townsend said to Beth the following morning, right when Beth was doing her best to put the man out of her mind.

"Croesus," Beth supplied, since she had no intention of discussing the other man.

"Yeah, right," said the thirty-year-old mother of two seated across from Beth in Berry Ridge's one and only coffee shop, which doubled as the town's bakery. The scent of bacon and eggs vied with freshly baked pastries and pies and the aroma of freshly perked coffee.

Gillie propped her chin on her hand. With her blond hair caught up in a ponytail, she looked about half her age.

"So, tell me everything," she insisted.

Beth scowled at her. "Have you and Daniel been married so long that you need to live vicariously through me? If that's your plan, you're going to have a very dull time."

"Obviously you don't understand just how tedious laundry, dirty dishes and conversation with a couple of pint-size hellions can get. Your life is definitely exciting by comparison. I'll bet you've even eaten a meal out that didn't come in a bag."

Beth recalled the clam chowder, chocolate mousse and conversation she'd indulged in the previous afternoon. Apparently something in her expression gave her away.

"You have, haven't you?" Gillie said triumphantly. "I knew it. Did he ask you out to dinner? Where? I'll bet it was at the inn. I heard that's where he was staying, in a suite, no less. What did you have? What did you talk about?"

Beth chuckled despite herself at her friend's enthusiasm. It was definitely time for Gillie to go back to work. Being room mother for her second grader's classroom was not nearly challenge enough for a woman who had once handled mega-bucks advertising accounts in New York.

"It was lunch, not dinner," she told Gillie. "Yes, it was at the inn. We both had the clam chowder. And mostly we talked about fabric samples and plumbing."

"You didn't talk about him? Didn't you find out anything? Is he married? When are you seeing him again?"

"I don't know if he's married, but someone is moving into the house with him."

"A woman?"

"He didn't say. If it is, she's apparently moving into

a separate bedroom," she said, suddenly recalling the request of *beds,* plural not singular. She couldn't ignore the relief that suddenly spread through her. "As for the rest, I don't know when I'm seeing him again. He said he'd be back in a few days."

Gillie shot her a disapproving frown. "How could you not find out if he's married, for heaven's sake? What's wrong with you? Was he wearing a ring?"

"I didn't notice," she lied. Actually, she had. He wasn't. She didn't intend to tell Gillie that, though. It would only fuel this absurd fantasy she was hell-bent on inventing. Besides, a lot of married men didn't wear rings. The lack of one was an indicator of status, not a guarantee.

Gillie sighed. "Okay, let's back up. What's his name?"

"Since you obviously possess the detecting skills of Nancy Drew, I'm surprised you haven't found that out already."

"Paula Redding, who heard about him from Denise Winston, who saw him with you when she was driving by the Grady place, said she didn't know any details except that he was built to die for and he drives an outrageously expensive, very classy emerald green sports car. So, give. What do you know?"

"He's some kind of ex-jock. A football player."

Gillie's eyes lit up. "No kidding. What's his name?"

Beth told her.

Her expression turned incredulous. "Ohmigosh," she whispered. "You're kidding? Wow! Wait till I tell Daniel. Ken Hutchinson! Drop-dead gorgeous doesn't begin to describe him."

"You know who he is?" Beth said, then remembered that Gillie and Daniel drove to Boston for football games practically every single weekend of the season. Of course she would know who Ken Hutchinson was. "Tell me about him."

"He's only the greatest quarterback to hit the National Football League this decade! Or he was," she said, her expression filled with sympathy. "He was injured during the pre-season. They say he'll never play again."

So, Beth thought, he had been telling the truth about that. No wonder he'd looked so pained by Roger's tireless goings-on about football. No wonder he'd seemed a bit startled when she hadn't recognized him. He was probably far more used to Roger's behavior than hers.

Gillie regarded her with amazement. "You mean, you really didn't know who he was?"

Beth shrugged. "I didn't have a clue. I don't watch football. He was really great?"

"The best. Not only that, from what I've read, he's really a nice guy. Does a lot of stuff for charity. Of course, he also has a reputation as quite a playboy, according to the tabloids, but who believes them?"

Beth could imagine that there might have been at least the tiniest little kernel of truth in the reports. He'd wasted no time in engaging in a mild flirtation with her. She sensed it had come to him as automatically as breathing, something he probably couldn't quit if he tried.

Gillie apparently regarded her continued silence with suspicion. "You did notice he was gorgeous, didn't you?"

"I noticed," she admitted under that penetrating gaze.

"Good. I guess there's hope for you yet."

"I am not looking for a relationship," Beth reminded

her for probably the hundredth time since they'd started getting together for coffee at least once a week. "Been there. Done that."

Gillie waved off the protest. "There are some forces in nature that are just too powerful to fight."

A few days ago Beth would have argued vehemently with her about that. Then she'd met Ken Hutchinson. Now, no matter what she said aloud, she wasn't nearly as certain of anything as she had been. Okay, so maybe there was a wildly passionate fling in her future. She could go along with that. But more? Not a chance.

She looked Gillie straight in the eye. "Ken Hutchinson and I have a business relationship and nothing more."

"Sure," her friend said agreeably.

She didn't look any more convinced than Ken had when Beth had said those same words to him. Beth wondered if either of them realized how irritating their reactions were.

Ken spread the pictures he'd taken of the new house on the dining room table for the benefit of his daughter and his ex-mother-in-law. Delores, he had to admit, was more enthusiastic than Chelsea.

"I love it!" she said at once. "It has fantastic possibilities." She glanced at her granddaughter. "Look, Chelsea, it already has a swing in the yard."

"It's a dumb swing. Besides, I have a whole swing set here," she said, her lower lip set mutinously. She glared at her father. "With a slide!"

"You can have the exact same set there, if that's what you want," Ken said, feeling absolutely helpless. He was convinced this move was best for both of them, but his daughter was hell-bent on making it difficult. She'd been glowering at him from the minute he'd walked in the door. He was trying his damnedest to be patient with her, but it was getting more difficult by the minute.

"I want to stay here with Grandma," she said. "You go live in that awful place."

"Sorry, Shortstuff," he said mildly. "That's not an option."

Tears welled up in his daughter's eyes. "I won't go. I *won't*," she screamed at him and ran from the room.

Ken sighed. He looked into his ex-mother-in-law's sympathetic eyes.

"This won't last," she promised him. "She's just scared."

"What the hell do I do in the meantime? I don't want her to be miserable."

"Get her involved. Let her choose the things for her room. Let her help to make it her house, too." She picked up the snapshots of the bedrooms. "Let her choose which room she wants. Take her to a furniture store to find the right bed, ask her about colors and curtains."

"I thought that's what I was paying Beth Callahan to do."

Delores smiled at him. "I'm sure she won't be distraught if you take one room off her hands. Besides, whose feelings matter more? Chelsea's or the decorator's?" She studied him intently. "Or is she already becoming important to you, too?"

"Don't be ridiculous," he muttered. "I barely know the woman."

"When are you going back up there to supervise the work?"

"I was going tomorrow, but I suppose I'll wait until the day after so I can spend the day shopping with Chelsea tomorrow."

A triumphant expression spread across Delores's face. "So you are interested."

He regarded her irritably. "I didn't say that."

She patted his hand consolingly. "You didn't have to. The fact that you're rushing back up there says volumes. If you weren't interested, you'd wait and go back when the job is finished."

"She's spending a fortune of my money," he countered reasonably. "Are you suggesting there's something unusual about my wanting to oversee the work?"

"How many shares of that electronics stock do you own?"

He scowled at her. "Quite a few. What's your point?"

"When was the last time you felt a need to visit the factory?"

"It's not the same thing."

She grinned happily. "Close enough," she said as she headed for the kitchen. She stopped long enough to wink at him. "I can't wait to meet her."

"Don't hold your breath," he muttered in the direction of the closing door.

"I heard that," she called back cheerfully.

Before he could think of anything to counter her convictions about his interest in Beth Callahan, the phone rang.

"Yeah?" he growled.

"Hey, buddy, you okay?" Claude Dobbins asked

worriedly. "You didn't go and break something else on that ice up in Vermont, did you?"

"No, you just caught me at a bad time. I was considering strangling my ex-mother-in-law." He figured Dobbins, an all-pro offensive lineman who'd been the target of Delores's matchmaking efforts himself, would understand.

"You touch a hair on that sweet woman's head and I'll personally break your other knee," the three-hundred-pound man said.

"Since when did you start taking her side?"

"Since I realized that marrying Harriet was about the smartest thing I ever did and it wouldn't have happened if Delores hadn't given me a shove."

"I don't recall your having the same attitude when we were trying to get you into your tux before the wedding. Making a fast getaway to Tahiti was mentioned more than once."

"I've wised up since then." He fell silent and Ken could hear him taking a deep breath. "Besides," he blurted out, "Harriet and me, we're gonna have a baby. That's what I called to tell you."

Ken felt the unexpected sting of tears in his eyes. Though Claude had claimed to disdain marriage and everything associated with it, he'd spent his off-the-field free time working with half a dozen children's charities. He was a natural with the kids, sick or well, rich or poor. "Hey, man, that's just about the best news I've ever heard."

"Good enough that you'll be the baby's godfather?" he asked, an oddly hesitant note in his voice.

"You name the time and place."

"Thanks," he said, his relief evident. "We couldn't

think of anyone we'd rather have. Think Delores would be godmother? Harriet's got her heart set on it."

"She's right here. I'll let you ask her yourself. When's the baby due?"

"Next May."

"Smart move. It won't interfere with the football season. That'll keep the coach happy. Let me get Delores, so you can tell her."

"Wait one sec, buddy. What's this I hear about you buying a house *and* finding a new lady in Vermont?"

Ken groaned. "I'm going to strangle my ex-mother-in-law, after all."

"No house or no lady?"

"There is a house. Plenty of room for the soon-to-be-enlarged Dobbins family to visit. As for a lady, Chet Mathias introduced me to a woman who is going to handle all the renovations and the decorating. That's it."

A sudden vision of Beth Callahan flashed through his head. His pulse automatically kicked into over-drive. The reaction made his voice less emphatic when he added, "Don't go listening to everything Delores says. The woman has a wild imagination. It comes from those romance novels she reads all day."

"I heard that," the woman in question hollered from the kitchen.

Dobbins was chuckling in his ear. "Oh, brother, I can't wait to see how this scene plays out. I'm gonna get me a front row seat and laugh my head off, just like you did to me."

"Go to—"

"Tsk-tsk. You shouldn't let a little innocent teasing get to you. Isn't that what you were always telling me? Now let me talk to the finest woman in the western hemisphere."

"Only if you promise you won't start conspiring against me."

"The only promise I ever made was to keep the defensive tackles from nailing your sorry butt on a football field," Claude informed him. "And if I hadn't been sidelined for that one damned play back in August, you'd still be the best quarterback in the NFL. I'm never going to forgive myself for that."

Ken had heard the self-accusations long enough. "Stop it. They dislocated your shoulder, for God's sake. It's the only play you've missed in the entire ten years we were together."

"And just look what happened," he said miserably.

"Claude Dobbins, if you don't knock it off, I'm going to start praying that Harriet has quadruplets. You won't sleep from May right on through next season's Super Bowl."

"Look, man, I know you don't blame me, but you can't deny that if I'd been in there, things would have been different."

"Maybe. Maybe not. There's no point speculating. Believe it or not, I'm okay with this. It's not the way I would have chosen to end my career, but it sure as hell beats spending an entire season getting intercepted or sacked on every other play and winding up fired." He glanced up gratefully as Delores came back into the room. "Now, here's my ex-mother-in-law."

She shot him a puzzled look, but accepted the phone.

While she talked to Dobbins, Ken drew in a deep breath and tried to put aside all the memories his friend had stirred up. He picked up the photos from the new house and headed for Chelsea's room. The important thing now was to think of the future. For both of them.

Despite the teasing of his ex-mother-in-law and his best friend, Ken headed back to Vermont two days later. To his astonishment, he was suddenly looking forward to studying wallpaper samples and choosing paint. Maybe he'd go completely off the deep end and do some of the remodeling himself, especially if Beth Callahan would pitch in and work by his side.

He tried not to let himself worry too much about Chelsea's uncharacteristically stubborn behavior. She had professed no interest in looking at furniture for her room or in selecting a color scheme. She wouldn't even go to the store to look at swing sets. Her teacher had called again yesterday afternoon and asked if there was anything going on at home that might explain why she'd gotten into a fight on the playground and another in the lunchroom. Despite the fact that he was uncomfortable with airing his problems to anyone other than family, he had to tell the woman about the impending move. He couldn't say for certain, but he was almost sure he'd heard her utter a sigh of relief. He'd left for Vermont feeling frustrated and angry and uncertain.

Delores had suggested grounding the seven-year-old for her rotten behavior, but he hadn't been able to bring himself to do it. He'd kissed her goodbye this morning and tried desperately not to notice the accusing expression in her big gray eyes.

When she'd shouted after him, "I hate you. I want to go live with Mommy," Ken had thought his heart would break. If he had thought for an instant that letting her live with his ex-wife would put things right, he would have let her go.

But Ken knew better than anyone that Pam didn't want their daughter in Hollywood with her. Because of that knowledge and the terrible guilt it stirred in him, he vowed to make allowances for Chelsea's behavior. She would get over it soon enough and be back to her sunny, normal self. He hoped.

He was still worrying about his daughter when he drove down the deeply rutted lane to his new house. This time he'd come in his four-wheel-drive wagon, a far more practical vehicle for these roads than his sports car. He figured he might as well get it to Vermont. He'd bring the sports car later. Maybe the different car explained why Beth didn't spot him at first. Because she was totally absorbed in her conversation with the roofer, he had time to study her and try to analyze why she, of all the women he'd met, made his heart thump unsteadily.

She was wearing the snug-fitting jeans he'd hoped to catch her in one day. They curved over an enticing bottom and slim hips, then smoothed over perfect thighs before being tucked inside high, sturdy boots. A bulky, fur-lined jacket disguised the shape of her torso, but Ken found he remembered it well enough just from the hints he'd gotten from the fit of that soft sweater and tailored blazer she'd worn the last time he'd seen her.

The collar of her coat was turned up around her ears and a knit cap was pulled down to meet it, leaving only stray tendrils of brown to curve against her glowing cheeks. Even from where he sat observing her, he found it amazing that her hair could catch the sunlight and shatter into so many different shades from sparkling gold to radiant red, all deepened by the basic brown.

She blew on her bare hands to keep them warm as she talked. It was so cold, her breath was visible. He suddenly had the strangest urge to march across the yard and snatch her gloves from her pockets and insist she wear them. Or, perhaps, to just take those frigid hands in his own until they were warm again. He couldn't help wondering if they'd be soft or if there would be calluses from the work she pitched in to do.

Where had this crazy attraction come from? he wondered yet again. He wasn't sure whether he was drawn to her physically, whether he was attracted by her competence, or whether he was intrigued by the vague hints of vulnerability she so rarely allowed to show. It would be easy to dismiss it as simple, straightforward lust, but the truth was, she'd engaged his mind almost as quickly as she'd taunted his hormones. Too few women had ever done that.

Given the flurry of activity inside and outside the house, Ken was suddenly oddly hesitant about intruding. Beth looked thoroughly at home amid the chaos and the workmen. He felt as if he'd suddenly grown an extra pair of hands as he stood awkward and uncertain beside his car. He told himself he might have left, satisfied that there was progress being made, but just then she spotted him and made leaving impossible.

"Hi, there! I didn't expect to see you back here so soon." Her boots crunched over the ice-topped layer of snow as she walked over to join him.

"I told you I'd only be gone a few days. Come here and get in the car where it's still warm. You look frozen."

She laughed. "I'm used to this. It'll have to drop another thirty degrees before it really bothers me."

"It's already below freezing."

"It'll get colder. Trust me."

Ken shivered. "I'll never get used to it. I think I still have California blood."

"You're from California?" she said with a look of surprise.

"Los Angeles."

"That's amazing."

He grinned. "Not so amazing. It's a big city. Lots of people are *from* there."

"You don't understand. That's where I'm from, too. I've only been living here a couple of years now."

Ken suddenly felt yet another invisible thread tying them together in a way he couldn't explain. "I guess that means we should have dinner tonight and talk about old times."

A sudden wariness flashed in her eyes. "I can't do dinner tonight."

"Can't or won't?"

"Not used to being turned down, are you?"

"Not for long," he said mildly. "Okay, you don't have to say which it is, can't or won't, as long as you agree to breakfast tomorrow instead."

"Sure," she said readily. "Seven o'clock?"

Ken couldn't remember the last time he'd been awake at seven, much less functional. "Seven?" he repeated doubtfully.

She grinned. "You wouldn't want me to report late for work, would you? The crew here starts at eight."

"I admire your dedication, but couldn't you be late, just this once?"

"What kind of example would that set?" she chided.

He sighed. "Seven o'clock. Just don't expect me to be coherent."

"Don't worry, Mr. Hutchinson. I don't expect much from most men." She glanced toward the crew she had working. "Unless, of course, I'm paying them to do a job."

Ken watched her stroll back into the fray with an increasingly familiar sense of bemusement. Despite the humorous tone she'd adopted, he suspected there was a very real trace of bitterness in her comment about men. He wondered who had hurt her and how high the wall was that she had built around her heart.

It didn't matter, he decided. He'd been climbing over everything from backyard fences to the hulking linemen of opposing teams his whole life. A few shaky feminine defenses shouldn't pose any kind of real hurdle at all.

Chapter 6

Beth wasn't sure what had made her insist on a 7:00 a.m. breakfast meeting with Ken. It was obvious the man didn't consider that a civilized hour for social chit-chat or business talk. Maybe she was hoping to catch him while his brain was still a bit muddled. She liked the prospect of having the upper hand for once.

Or maybe she simply wanted to see him when his hair was still provocatively tousled from sleep, so she could let her imagination conjure up images of being beside him in bed. Gillie, who had taken one psychology class in college and considered herself an expert on human behavior, would have a field day with that one.

She had dressed with care. She had chosen a soft green sweater the shade of spring leaves to wear with her jeans. She'd slid her feet into a pair of flats and left her more practical boots and heavy socks in the car for the trip to the work site. She'd also caught herself taking extra care with her makeup. She had added a rare touch of eye shadow and mascara, even as she scolded herself for being ridiculous. She'd debated leaving her hair down, but at the last second she had wound it into a knot atop her head. As if to punish herself for her absurdity, she'd twisted it even tighter than usual.

Now, as she stood in the hallway outside Ken's suite, her stomach felt as fluttery as a teenager's on a first date. Only when she had spotted him beside his car the day before had she realized how much she had looked forward to his return. She was anticipating this breakfast even more and that terrified her. She knew where this breathless, edge-of-the-precipice feeling could lead—straight to heartache. Damn her lack of control over her own emotions and damn Gillie Townsend for encouraging her to risk everything on a man whose personal life was essentially a huge question mark.

She clutched her attaché case more tightly, reassured that there were enough papers inside to keep any conversation focused on business for the hour she had allotted for this meeting. Satisfied that for now she had her emotions and the next sixty minutes under control, she finally rapped on the door.

"Come on in. The door's open," he called from somewhere deep inside the suite.

Beth stepped through the doorway, then hesitated. Ken was nowhere in sight, which meant he was in the bedroom. Or perhaps he had just stepped out of the shower, his body still slick with water. Her blood sizzled as she considered that possibility. Heat climbed into her cheeks just as he poked his still-damp head around the door between the rooms.

"I'll be right out. Breakfast's on its way. Sign my name, if I'm not out when it gets here, okay?"

With her gaze fixed on the tiny sliver of bare chest she could glimpse through the partially closed door, she nodded. Unconscious of the gesture, she ran her tongue over her suddenly dry lips.

When she realized with a start that Ken's eyes had locked on her mouth, she blinked, then looked hurriedly away. She heard his deep chuckle as the door clicked shut. The man, blast him, obviously knew the effect he had on her. In fact, he probably deliberately set out to provoke her responses.

Fortunately, breakfast arrived just then, a rolling cart laden with fresh fruit, scrambled eggs, bacon, pancakes, toast, orange juice and coffee. She was still staring at it with open-mouthed amazement when Ken joined her.

She glanced at him. "Expecting an army?"

"I wasn't sure what you'd like. Besides, I always have a hearty appetite in the morning."

Unbidden, an image of his probably very busy nights filled with steamy sexual encounters flashed through her head. "I can imagine," she muttered.

He grinned, as if he had guessed the very wicked direction of her thoughts. He pulled out a chair for her at the table that had been set up in front of the window. As she sat, his fingers skimmed her shoulders, sending shock waves ricocheting through her. Such an innocent gesture to stir a response that was anything but innocent, she thought. To regain her equilibrium, she reached for her attaché case. Ken's hand closed over hers. Her heart thundered.

"Leave it," he commanded, his voice a whisper

against her cheek. "Doing business over breakfast is bad for the digestion."

"I thought that was what power breakfasts were all about," Beth countered. "Besides, we don't have much time."

"Sure we do," he contradicted. "All day, in fact. I'm planning to come out to the house with you when we're through here."

"You can't," she said without thinking. How would she ever get anything done with him in plain sight, when she had barely been able to get him out of her head when he'd been in another state?

"Oh?" he said, regarding her with more amusement than offense.

She scrambled for an argument he wouldn't see straight through. "I mean, won't you be bored just standing around in the freezing cold watching other people work?"

"You do it all the time, don't you?"

"Yes, but it's my job."

"And it's my house. Besides, I intend to do more than stand around. I thought I'd pitch in."

She regarded him as if he had just announced an intention to build a skyscraper single-handedly. "Can you do that?"

"Depends on what needs doing, I suppose," he said cheerfully, his gaze challenging her to argue. He held out the platter of bacon and eggs. "Care for some?"

Beth shook her head. "No, the fruit and toast are just fine."

"That's not enough fuel for a cold day like this," he said, and plunked a spoonful of eggs and two strips of bacon on her plate. "Protein is essential."

She eyed the tempting but long-ago forbidden food warily. "Protein, maybe, but this is pure cholesterol."

"When was the last time you ate bacon and eggs?"

"I can't remember."

"Then you don't have to worry about the cholesterol just this once, do you?" he said, looking disgustingly pleased with his triumph. "Now, tell me how you ended up in Vermont."

With a faint sigh, Beth conceded to herself that she had completely lost control of this meeting, after all. Worse, she was beginning to relax under his patient, teasing questioning. And she knew what lay at the end of that road—trouble.

At the very least, she needed to put some distance between them. She had no intention of telling this man her life story. She kept her reply brief and unemotional.

"I had been skiing nearby one year," she said, avoiding any mention of how disastrous the trip had been with her stepchildren sulking the whole time and Peter blaming her for ruining the vacation.

"When I decided to leave California, I remembered how charmed I'd been by Berry Ridge when I'd driven through it one day."

She didn't add that she had taken the car for a ride while the rest of the family stayed at the ski resort. It was during that drive that she had reconciled herself to the fact that the marriage would never work. In fact, it had been over a cup of coffee and one of the Berry Ridge bakery's huge, warm cinnamon rolls that she had vowed to call it quits.

What had convinced her to move here was the fact that Lou Pulanski, the bakery's owner, had brought her the roll and refilled her coffee cup half a dozen times without any hint that she had noticed the tears streaking down Beth's cheeks. Oddly, Beth had found comfort in that quiet attention that had been offered without any attempt to intrude on her pain.

Now that she knew Lou better, she knew that the older woman would have been more than willing to lend an ear or to dispense advice, if asked. But she would never be so indiscreet as to suggest by word or deed that a customer might be in need of sympathy.

"Some folks just plain like to keep quiet about their troubles," she'd told Beth later. "If that's their choice, then I got no business not respecting it."

"What?" Ken said, interrupting her memories.

She regarded him blankly, unwillingly drawn back to the present.

"You were smiling. What were you thinking about?"

"How different Berry Ridge is from Los Angeles."

"You don't regret leaving the warm weather and sunshine for this?" He gestured out the window where more snow was falling against a leaden sky.

"It was a trade-off. No earthquakes, no traffic, and lots of serenity. What about you?"

"I've been on the east coast playing ball for more than ten years. I've gotten used to the cold. Chet Mathias had me up here one summer. I wasn't wild about the solitude at the time, but when I realized I was facing a long recovery from this injury, this seemed like the right place to do it. I figured maybe nobody around here would bother me." He shrugged. "I suppose it's too soon to tell if I'll like it enough to stay on."

Beth was surprised by the wistful note in his voice. She would have expected him to crave the recognition and adulation he'd had as a star quarterback, but she could definitely relate to his desire to keep to himself and recover. Perhaps they had more in common than she'd guessed. Both of them apparently viewed Berry Ridge as a haven, far from the turbulent life-styles they'd previously led.

"I guess Roger put an end to that notion right off the bat," she sympathized. "I'm sorry he was so tactless."

Ken shrugged. "He didn't mean any harm. Hopefully, though, he'll lay off those plans for some kind of football charity event."

"Fortunately, it will be months before the snow melts," she reassured him. "He'll probably forget all about it by then. Roger's enthusiasm is legendary in these parts, but he's fickle. He comes up with something new almost every day. If the town wants to follow through on one of his ideas, the mayor turns it over to a committee. Even the Chamber of Commerce, of which Roger's president, manages to snatch the reins away from him if it really wants to implement one of his ideas."

She glanced at her watch. "Gracious, look at the time. I really do need to be going."

"I'll drive you," he suggested.

"But my car..."

"Will be here when I bring you back."

"What if you decide not to spend the whole day there?"

"I won't."

To her amazement, Ken did stick it out. He even sent out for sandwiches and coffee for everyone at noon. And he graciously signed autographs for every single man before they left for the day. Initial awe and wariness had quickly given way to respect when he had, as promised, pitched in to help with whatever task was asked of him, no matter how menial.

"You've won them over," Beth said to him as they stood on the walkway after everyone else had gone. "You could complete this job without me."

He glanced down at her and the expression in his eyes made her heart slam against her chest. "Not a chance," he said softly. "They'd figure out in no time that I don't have a clue about what needs to be done or how to do it."

Beth seriously doubted the modest claim. He'd required almost no direction before he was handily repairing the molding in the master bedroom. In fact, at the rate the work was coming along, they really would have the repairs done and those two bedrooms ready with the basics by the following week. After that, most of the work would be cosmetic—wallpaper, paint, furniture, and those carefully chosen accessories and pictures that would make it seem like a home.

Still, it would take weeks to finish up. Weeks of working side by side with this man to whom she was drawn as inevitably as bits of metal to a magnet. Dangerous weeks.

She glanced up to find his gaze on her face. She lost herself in the warm expression in his eyes.

"Your hair is just about covered with snow," he said, his voice low.

Her entire body stilled as his fingers reached toward her hair. As light as his touch was, she could feel it all the way to her toes. And when the caress moved on to her cheek, she was convinced her heart would never withstand the thrill.

"Beth?"

"Hmm?" she murmured, her face upturned, her gaze locked with his as the pad of his thumb skimmed over her lower lip.

"Your skin is so hot, the snow melts as soon as it touches you."

She could believe that. In fact, she was burning up. She doubted her temperature would drop to normal until he took away his touch. She couldn't have dragged her gaze away from his for anything. Again her pulse skittered wildly as he slowly lowered his head. A half-hearted protest formed, but never made it past her lips as his mouth covered hers. Warmth spread through her, warmth and a kind of sweet torment.

She'd only had a heartbeat to anticipate the actual kiss, but somewhere deep inside she realized she had been anticipating it, dreaming about it, for days now. She had imagined the smooth texture of his lips, the fiery heat, the gentle persuasiveness. But none of her imaginings were nearly as devastating as the reality.

In reality, the kiss stole her breath, stole her good intentions, stole her powers of resistance. If her resolve and emotions were shaky, her body was alive with almost forgotten sensations. No, she corrected. She had never experienced anything quite like this before, after all. Every fiber of her being hummed... all from just one kiss.

Maybe if it had seemed practiced and assured, she wouldn't have fallen prey to it so easily. But his initial touch was uncertain, just hesitant enough to convince her that he hadn't expected this, either.

And in that instant of awareness, she felt the first faint stirring of trust. That was the most unexpected, most treasured sensation of all.

* * *

It had been seventy-two hours since the kiss.

Ken realized with chagrin that that was how he was beginning to mark time. Every minute, every hour that passed was traced back to the moment when he had lost his head and kissed Beth Callahan.

Damn, he felt as if he'd never kissed another woman before, when that was far from the truth. Not that he'd seduced anywhere near the numbers the tabloids printed. The fact of the matter was that he'd never seduced a soul other than his wife during his entire marriage. The vows had meant something to him, even in the last terrible months when he'd known in his gut the marriage was over.

Unfortunately, that commitment on his part hadn't prevented a lot of exuberant women from planting a kiss on him from time to time. Not one of those stolen kisses, not even the most enthusiastic and darkly sensual of them, had ever held a candle to the sweet surrender of Beth's lips beneath his.

Since the night when they'd stood in the snow, their bodies barely touching, but their mouths locked in a seductive dance, he hadn't laid so much as a finger on her. That resolve to back off hadn't stopped him from wanting to, though. In fact, he was losing patience with himself. He'd never allowed any woman to tie him in knots this way.

Like some randy kid, he had dreamed up excuse after excuse to spend the past three evenings with her. He had questioned prices, insisted on additional samples and, just the night before, had hauled her back to the house for a midnight inspection of some flaw that he claimed had been on his mind.

Standing on the front porch, bathed in moonlight, his body had ached with need for her, but he'd kept his hands firmly jammed into his pockets. He was proud of that restraint, that determined refusal to take what he wanted, not even another kiss. He wasn't nearly as proud of having dragged her out at that hour in the first place.

She had responded to his irrational demands with patience and good humor. In fact, she was so blasted calm and serene, he found it irritating. Hadn't she felt what he'd felt? Hadn't she been as stunned as he was by the force of a desire barely held in check?

Apparently not, he decided as she quietly handed him yet another set of unnecessary figures.

Avoiding her gaze, he decided enough was enough. Once the house was finished, he would avoid the lingering dinners that somehow always seemed to follow their business meetings. In fact, he would avoid anything more than a casual greeting on the street. That would be best...for both of them. He needed to concentrate on his daughter now. Beth needed peace of mind.

In the meantime, every time they saw each other he felt a terrible longing to kiss her again, to loosen her hair and watch it tumble free, to unbutton the top button of her high-necked blouse...and then the next... and the next.

Damn, but he'd better finish the initial redecorating and get an increasingly impatient and belligerent Chelsea up here before he made an utter fool of himself and did something he'd regret. Berry Ridge was too small. He would have to face up to a mistake with Beth Callahan every single day of his life. And she, no doubt, would pay an even higher price for his lack of sensible restraint, especially if things didn't work out in Berry Ridge and he moved away to someplace better for Chelsea.

He glanced down into her green eyes, as luminous as emeralds, and felt his resolve waver. Again.

"I've been thinking," he said, his voice husky with unspoken need.

She regarded him expectantly. "About what?"

"I read that there's a big antique auction this weekend. I thought maybe we should go. What do you think?"

She beamed at him and his heart flipped over. "I have the notice in my purse. I was thinking the same thing."

"Great minds…" he murmured.

"We can stop by some shops, too, and you can see the pieces I had in mind firsthand before you make a decision."

"Sounds perfect," he said. A whole day, alone, together. It did sound perfect.

It also sounded more dangerous than facing down an all-pro line dead set on stripping him of a football and planting his rear on a rock-hard field. To his everlasting regret, he could hardly wait.

Chapter 7

Saturday dawned with cloudless blue skies, relatively mild temperatures in the thirties and endless stretches of snowy landscape. It was the kind of postcard-perfect morning that reminded Beth why all the sub-zero temperatures were worth tolerating.

For once she didn't think about Ken as she chose her clothes: a pair of sturdy jeans, a turtleneck, boots, and a down-lined jacket. Though the auction itself was indoors, many of the places they planned to visit would have items on display outdoors or in unheated barns. She didn't intend to miss anything, no matter how chilly the air or how many filthy things had to be moved out of the way. An antique lover had to be part dreamer, part expert and part intrepid adventurer. She wasn't entirely sure which mattered most. She, for one, liked the adventure of it best.

Until she'd come to Vermont she had never known the joy of discovering a genuine treasure buried amid piles of dilapidated furniture or time-worn utensils. The process of discovery was almost as rewarding as taking some beloved object home. She enjoyed talking to the knowledgeable dealers, learning more with each contact until she was now able to spot quality amid junk. She loved sorting through a clutter of items and imagining the people who'd once lovingly held even the most garish knickknack in their hands. She got a real adrenaline rush from the competitive bidding. Her excitement mounted just thinking about the day ahead.

And that was even before she added Ken into the mix.

She brewed a pot of coffee and poured it into a thermos, then put that into the basket she'd already filled with Lou's bakery-fresh blueberry muffins, napkins and two mugs. That should tide them over through lunch. And the coffee would take the chill off while they were exploring all of the prospective finds at the auction.

She hoped that Ken proved to be a patient companion. She'd been known to linger through hours of bidding just to get her hands on some two-dollar treasure she'd spotted lumped in with an entire lot of pure junk.

By the time her doorbell finally rang, she was already pacing, anxious to hit the road to see what the day had to offer. Basket in hand, cash in her purse, she opened the door and all thoughts of antiques died, driven straight out of her head by one quick glance at the sexy man on her doorstep. Lordy, but he took her breath away—a fact that deeply troubled her.

"Good morning," he said, seemingly oblivious to the impact he had on her.

"Morning," she mumbled when she managed to find her tongue. This wasn't good. If the man could render her speechless just by showing up, exactly what would happen if he ever actively set out to seduce her? She sure as heck hoped he would try soon so she could end the speculation and then get on with her life. Trying to figure out why that one knockout of a kiss hadn't been repeated was tormenting her.

He reached for the basket and drew in a deep breath. "Coffee?" She nodded. "Thank you. You've saved my life. Maybe we should have a cup here before we hit the road," he said, regarding her hopefully.

"No," Beth said curtly, then winced. "Sorry. It's just that we don't want to be late. I want to get a look at everything before the bidding starts."

"You take this stuff seriously, don't you?"

"You should, too," she advised him. "It's your money we're spending." She closed the door and headed to the driveway. "Let's go. You can drink your coffee on the road."

She realized he wasn't following and turned back. "What's wrong?"

"I was just wondering if you ever slow down and have fun."

She grinned at his worried tone. "This *is* fun," she promised. "You'll see. I guarantee that before the day is out you're going to buy something ridiculous that you don't need, just for the sheer thrill of acquiring it."

"Bet I don't," he countered. "Talk to my broker. He'll tell you I'm thoughtful and disgustingly methodical when I look into a new stock acquisition. I have never, *ever* taken an impetuous, uncalculated risk."

"Want to lay odds that you will today?" Beth challenged.

"Sure," he said with supreme confidence. "If I win, you'll spend an entire evening with me. Dinner, dancing, the works. Not one mention of the house or its contents will cross your lips."

She was taken aback by his choice, but she was too much of a competitor to back away. "And if I win?"

"You won't," he said confidently.

"But if I do?"

"You choose."

She thought about what she wanted most at this precise moment on a Saturday morning in early November. "If I win, I want you to come to my place, fix a huge bowl of buttered popcorn, pour some nice white wine—"

"I'm beginning to like the sound of this," he taunted. "Maybe I should let you win."

"Stop," she said, laughing. "I'm not finished." Her expression sobered and she studied him worriedly. "You may not like this."

"Try me," he said, apparently not fazed by her suddenly troubled tone.

"I want you to show me the tape of one of your Super Bowl victories."

He regarded her incredulously. "Why would you want me to do that?" he asked, his voice suddenly dull and lifeless, all the joy drained out of it.

"I want to see for myself how great you were."

"Past tense," he reminded her. "You know who I am now. Why does any of that matter?"

Beth wasn't sure she could explain, short of admitting that over the past few days she had felt an increasing need to know everything about him. Football seemed a safer topic than his personal life.

"Because football was a huge part of your life. It shaped you. I'd like to understand that." Unwilling to explain further, or to admit to feelings that she wasn't ready to put a name to, she met his gaze evenly. "If it's still too painful, I can wait a while longer."

"But you won't just forget about it."

She shook her head. "Afraid not."

Suddenly his expression brightened and he winked. "Or I can just win the bet."

Relieved that her request hadn't spoiled the mood, Beth grinned at him. "Not a chance, Hutchinson. Not a chance. You're too much of a competitor to let anything you want get away."

His gaze caught hers and held, the challenge plain and far more seductive than she'd anticipated. "I hope you will always remember that, Beth."

Her heart climbed into her throat as their gazes remained locked. The bet faded in importance. All that mattered now was the intent of that quiet warning. Ken had just reminded her with a few spare words that there was more at stake in the game they were playing than a few stolen kisses. She trembled at the realization that whatever the stakes, he was a man whose entire public persona revolved around winning.

Ken gazed around the jam-packed auction house with a sense of amazement. It looked to him as if every farmer, every Yuppie, and every slick antique dealer from a two-hundred-mile radius or even farther had turned out.

He stood in line with Beth to purchase a number, chuckling when she insisted he have his own.

"If I'm paying for everything, why can't we share?" he grumbled without any real rancor, loving this light-hearted mood she was in.

"Because when you go nuts and start bidding, I want that number of yours on record so there won't be any reneging on our bet." Suddenly all business, she pulled a notebook from her purse. "Now, are you coming with me or do you plan to look around on your own?"

"Hey, this is all new to me. I'd better stick with my instructor."

She grinned at him. "Just try not to fall behind. We only have an hour to see everything."

"I'll do my best," he promised, trying to keep the amusement out of his voice. After all, there was absolutely nothing in this huge room that could possibly compete with the woman he was with. She was just about the most fascinating person on the face of the planet, as near as he could tell. He loved her whole-hearted enthusiasm for whatever task she was engaged in. More and more, he was wishing that driven intensity would be focused on him. Not his house. Not the furnishings. Not these antiques. Not any of the other myriad things that distracted her. Just him.

His gaze rarely left her as they surveyed a pile of rusty beds. It never strayed as they tried the doors and drawers on a dozen different dressers and cabinets. Most of them had warped wood and layers of paint, as near as he could tell.

Beth definitely held his attention as they edged between stacks of old quilts that, despite their intricate beauty, smelled musty to him. And she was far more intriguing than a bunch of old pictures, most of which couldn't even be seen through the coating of dust on frames and glass.

Then he saw the old-fashioned sleigh. Its runners were rusty. The paint was chipped and peeling. The leather upholstery was weathered beyond repair.

But when he looked at it, he remembered every Christmas card he'd ever seen with a Currier and Ives winter scene. He envisioned that sleigh with its runners gleaming, its upholstery buttersoft and comfortable, its paint a shiny black trimmed with gold and a pair of prancing horses pulling it through the snow.

Chelsea would be entranced, he thought at once. But it wasn't his daughter he imagined bundled up in blankets as the sleigh moved across the pure white Vermont landscape. It was Beth, snuggled by his side on a romantic, starlit night.

"Well, I'll be damned!" he muttered to himself as he ran his fingers over the sleigh and marveled at his sudden flight of fancy.

Two hours later the decrepit sleigh was brought up to the front of the auction house.

Ken listened to the first bid to get an idea of the value. Fifty dollars. He would pay ten times that or more, he decided. He stayed out of it until the price hit two hundred and fifty.

"Five hundred," he called out, holding his number aloft as he'd seen others do.

Beth's head snapped around and she regarded him with wide-eyed astonishment. "What are you doing?" she asked, trying to tug his arm down.

"I want it."

"It's falling apart," she told him in a hushed voice.

"I want it," he repeated stubbornly.

Suddenly a slow, delighted smile spread across her face and whatever argument she'd planned to offer died on her lips. She released her grip on his arm. "Go for it, then."

He bought the sleigh for six hundred and fifty dollars and considered it a bargain. He didn't even want to know what it was really worth. Only when the bidding was over and he'd paid the attendant and gone outside to claim the sleigh did he stare at it with a sense of bemusement. He turned to Beth.

"Now what do I do with it to make it go?"

Her quick peal of laughter rang out on the crisp air and in seconds he had joined in. "Promise you'll go for the first ride with me when it's fixed," he coaxed.

She glanced from the sleigh to him and back again. "You'll be lucky to get this thing cleaned up and usable by next winter."

Ken shook his head. "You're forgetting that I have a miracle worker on my payroll. Consider this your first priority."

Her eyebrows quirked up. "Before the house?"

"Before everything," he said softly. "Except this."

His lips met hers in a quick claiming, then lingered to savor her startled sigh, the velvet-soft texture of her mouth and the warm moistness inside. His entire body trembled with a fierce longing for even more, but he slowly pulled away, shaken by the force of his growing feelings for this woman who had been a stranger only a few weeks before.

His gaze settled on the flashing sparks in her green eyes. "I wish…"

"What?" she said, sounding faintly breathless from an anticipation that he sensed matched his own.

"That we were somewhere other than the middle of a snowy parking lot, someplace cozy and warm and intimate."

Her eyes widened, then darkened with what he was now certain was a desire as powerful as his. He could feel the quickening of the pulse in her neck beneath his fingertips, the slow, unmistakable heating of her skin. "Beth?"

"Hmm?"

"Is that a possibility?"

For an instant he sensed that she was at war with herself. Then a sigh seemed to shudder through her and she slowly nodded. "My place," she said in a voice barely above a whisper.

The answer might have been succinct, a little hesitant, but he knew a commitment when he heard one. He sensed there would be no second thoughts. He pressed another kiss against her lips, headed off to make arrangements for the delivery of the sleigh, then practically ran back to the car, praying all the while that he was right and that she wouldn't change her mind.

He wouldn't blame her if she did. Even if she'd never heard of him before, surely over the past few weeks she'd heard about his reputation for supposedly torrid, love-'em-and-leave-'em affairs. The whole town was abuzz with such gossip and a lot more speculation about him. The tabloid lies were something he'd come to take for granted, but he didn't want Beth believing them, not for one single minute. He wanted her to understand that whatever happened between them would be as rare and special for him as he guessed it would be for her. He wanted her to know, even if he didn't understand how or why it had happened, that she mattered to him, that because of her he was healing, learning who he was again.

If only he could find the words.

All the way back to Berry Ridge, Beth prayed that Ken wouldn't say another word. She didn't want him to manufacture pretty speeches or to make promises that he wouldn't keep. It was enough that right now, at this moment, they both wanted the same thing. They both wanted to explore this wild, reckless longing that had sprung up, unanticipated and unwanted, but undeniable in its fierce intensity.

Ken Hutchinson had somehow sneaked into a heart she'd been so certain had turned to ice. It was enough that there was fire and passion back in her life again, that she felt desirable and alive. She needed this proof that no matter how badly she had failed as a stepmother, she had not failed as a woman. She would deal with the consequences soon enough and she didn't want that process complicated by a longing to believe words spoken in haste. She had convinced herself of one thing—Ken was an honorable man. If he hadn't mentioned a wife by now, one didn't exist. She supposed she should have asked directly, but this was one time she was going to go with her gut instinct.

Ken drove with a sort of savage intensity, his brow knit in concentration as he guided the four-wheel drive SUV over narrow roads with a thin, dangerous coating of ice. The trip seemed to last forever, fraying Beth's nerves more with each mile. She concentrated on the road, because she feared if she thought about the step they were about to take her resolve would falter. She didn't want to be robbed of a chance to experience just once the pleasure of making love to a man whose loyalties and attention weren't divided by other obligations as Peter's had been from the outset of their relationship.

She caught Ken's quick, sideways glance, then felt his gloved hand wrap around her own and squeeze reassuringly. "I could slow down or change direction," he offered, and won her heart completely.

"I'd have to shoot you if you did," she retorted lightly, drawing a smile.

Within seconds his expression sobered. "I'm serious, Beth. This doesn't have to happen today or even tomorrow. It will happen, though."

Grateful for the option to say no, she declined it nonetheless. "Today," she repeated with more assurance, reading into the promise of someday a statement about his availability being uncompromised.

He nodded and turned his full attention back to the slippery road for the remainder of the drive.

It was late afternoon by the time they pulled into Beth's driveway. Low, dark clouds promising a new snowfall and an early dusk hung over the horizon, shutting out the last pale rays of sun.

Inside the house, Ken immediately set about lighting a fire, while Beth tried to settle her jitters in the kitchen. She opened a bottle of crisp Chardonnay and poured it into her best crystal wineglasses. She put a bunch of grapes on a tray, along with a round of Brie and an assortment of crackers. To that she added a fat green candle, scented with evergreen, telling herself it would seem as if they were making love in a forest clearing or in the final, magical hours of Christmas Eve. Then she chided herself for the whimsical, romantic thought.

The only thing she couldn't bring herself to do was to slip upstairs and shed her dusty clothes and trade them for delicate, lacy lingerie. Somehow it seemed as if that would be too calculated, hastening a process that deserved slow, deliberate and ever-more-thrilling seduction.

After setting the tray on the coffee table, she found herself suddenly at a loss. Ken was stretched out on the carpet in front of the fire. The sofa was too far away for any sort of intimacy. It seemed as if even conversation would grow stilted across that chasm. And surely no quiet secrets or whispered words could be shared.

Ending her dilemma, Ken held up a hand and tugged her down beside him.

"I like your house. The warm colors suit you," he told her, brushing a stray tendril of hair back from her face. "It feels like a home."

Beth's breath snagged in her throat, but she managed a shaky "Thanks." Even that much was a struggle with every touch assaulting her senses. She felt one pin come out of her hair, then another and another, until the careful knot she'd twisted on top of her head that morning was undone. Ken's gaze was rapt as he ran his fingers through the curly strands until they had tumbled free to her shoulders.

"It looks exactly the way I'd imagined," he whispered. "Why do you always wear it up?"

Beth shrugged as if the styling of her hair were of no consequence, even though she knew that she had chosen it deliberately because it seemed less feminine, less likely to entice masculine attention. "It keeps it out of my face when I'm working."

He looked doubtful. "Are you sure that's it?"

"What else could it be?" she asked, even though she knew herself that it wasn't the whole truth, but merely as much as she was willing to admit.

"I thought maybe it was like all that bulky tweed and those prim blouses you wore when we first met."

Startled by his perceptiveness, she met his eyes, then looked away in embarrassment.

"So, that was it," he said softly. "Why were you trying to hide? Didn't you realize that no matter what you wore, no one could mistake you for anything other than a very attractive, very sexy woman? Why would you even want to disguise that? Who made you afraid of your own sensuality?"

Beth didn't want to think about the past or the failures that had driven her to retreat from relationships. She only wanted to think about here and now. About this man and being held in his arms. Who better to reassure her than a man who wasn't looking for commitment, a man whose amorous adventures had been bandied around town ever since his arrival? She wanted passion, not love. Or so she told herself.

Without saying a word, she reached out and cupped a hand behind his neck and drew his head forward until their mouths met. As she'd hoped, that gesture was all it took to end conversation, to drive out thoughts of anything else.

The slow, experimental kisses soon exploded into desperate, frantic need. Ken, who up until now had seemed endlessly patient, suddenly indulged only in caresses meant to inflame. The swift, sure strokes of his hands drove out everything except the way her body was melting under his touch.

Clothes miraculously disappeared, leaving firelight to dance across bare flesh glistening with a sheen of perspiration. There was no time to linger over the masculine perfection of his body, because her own was filled with this increasingly urgent demand.

"Do you like this?" he murmured, his fingers slick with her own moisture.

A nod, because there was no breath to speak.

"And this?"

"Oh, yes," she whispered, the words choked.

"Tell me, Beth. Tell me what you need."

She moaned softly and because the words still wouldn't come, she showed him, guiding his hands and then his body until he was deep inside her and the world was spinning, topsy-turvy around them.

It seemed like forever before the spinning slowed and the world righted itself. But even though her senses calmed to something more like normal, Beth knew that nothing would ever be quite the same again.

As impossible as it seemed, as untimely as it was, she had just discovered magic.

Chapter 8

Ken wondered if there was anything more complicated in the entire realm of human relationships than
waking up next to a person for the very first time after
a night of making love. He studied the woman curled
up next to him in the cramped bed meant for two people who never budged all night. They had done considerably more than that, he thought, smiling at the
memories. And Beth continued to look radiant and
desirable, even asleep.

What a delightfully sexy, unexpected treasure Beth
Callahan had turned out to be! He had no idea where
things with the two of them were headed. In fact, if
anyone had suggested just a few short days ago that he
would contemplate an affair, much less anything more
serious, for years to come, he would have argued vehemently against the possibility. Hell, he'd told himself

that in no uncertain terms. But with every day that had passed, he'd become increasingly certain that Beth was too special not to see what the future for them held.

Only days ago his life had seemed too chaotic and unsettled, his daughter in need of too much attention, to bring anyone else into their lives. He had anticipated a long road toward physical and emotional healing for both of them. Instead he suddenly seemed to be looking ahead, not back. The career-ending injury to his knee seemed less and less important except as an inconvenience or irritant. The breakup of his marriage saddened him, but apparently hadn't incapacitated his desire to reach out to another woman, after all.

Quite probably, the very fact that Beth clearly hadn't expected or wanted this to happen, either, had made it possible. After years of being married to a woman who'd manipulated everything, no matter how trivial, finding a woman as straightforward and honest as Beth had broken through his defenses. There wasn't one single shred of doubt in his mind that she wanted nothing from him—not his money, not the reflected light of his celebrity, most likely not even his permanence in her life. To his astonishment, he realized he trusted her more after these past few days than he had ever trusted Pam.

Not that that was saying much, he conceded ruefully. It hadn't taken him long to realize that his ex-wife would use any tactic it took, other than a straight-out request, to get what she wanted. Apparently it was some sort of game for her. A psychologist would probably point out that a woman with Pam's insecurities couldn't believe that asking alone would bring the desired results.

What no one had ever explained to Ken's satisfaction was why a woman as beautiful and intelligent as his ex-wife, a woman who had come from a loving home, would lack self-assurance in the first place. Perhaps he should have tried harder early in the marriage to find out, but he hadn't and it was too late now. Maybe Pam would find in Hollywood what she hadn't found with him—her self-esteem.

Though he knew very little at this moment about what his future held, he did know that the one thing he would not tolerate in a woman again were lies and subterfuge. Beth Callahan seemed incapable of either. Just being with her put him at ease, knowing there was no need to look for hidden agendas behind every word and act.

One thing did puzzle him, though. She had never once expressed any interest in his personal life. Maybe she knew all she needed to know from the tabloids and the gossips in town, but he doubted that was it. If that was where she was getting her information, he doubted they would be in this bed together now.

He wondered how she was going to feel when she discovered he had custody of a seven-year-old daughter. He hoped it would delight her. They hadn't discussed her culinary skills, but he had a hunch Beth could bake those cookies Chelsea pouted about not having whenever Delores Jensen wasn't around to make them for her.

Well, he would know soon enough how his daughter's presence would alter their relationship. Delores was going to bring Chelsea up to Vermont next weekend. Chelsea's rebelliousness was showing signs of fading just as soon as the finishing touches were put on the first rooms in the new house. Beth had promised they would be ready by midweek, which would give him time to move his own things over from the inn. Perhaps they'd even have a night or two there alone. He knew that no matter how things changed, he would never be able to walk through the rooms of his new home without envisioning Beth there, as well.

Of course, why waste time anticipating the future when the present was so intriguing? He slid a hand under the covers and skimmed it lightly over Beth's warm curves. The touch brought a faint smile to her lips. He pressed a kiss against her bare shoulder and earned a soft moan. A caress of her breast brought her eyes open and quickly had them smoldering with re-awakened passion.

Or so he thought, until she yawned and stretched, the movement as lazy and satisfied as a cat's.

"So, you find my attention boring, do you?" he taunted, intensifying his touch until she gasped.

"Never," she whispered, her voice breathless.

"What was that?" he asked again.

Her body arched toward him as he continued to explore. "Definitely...not...boring."

He grinned. "That's better."

She reached for him then and the provocative game immediately reversed, until they were both slick with perspiration, their breath coming in gasps, their bodies demanding a fulfillment that finally came with shattering intensity.

When their heartbeats had slowed and their skin had cooled, Beth stretched out alongside him, their bodies touching from shoulder to toe. Somehow that innocent, trusting contact of two satiated bodies seemed more intimate, more profound than the love-making itself. Ken discovered he was relishing the aftermath of sex as much as the act itself. It was a sensation he'd long forgotten. It had been lost sometime after he'd discovered how deliberately and coolly Pam had used her body to get what she wanted. And though he'd seldom been able to resist, he'd hated himself for the loveless unions.

Whatever happened between him and Beth over the coming weeks and months, he would be grateful to her for this moment, for reminding him of the simple joy of genuine togetherness between a man and a woman who wanted nothing more complicated from each other than to give and receive this incredible, most basic of all pleasures.

"You know, it's a strange thing, my man," Claude Dobbins said to Ken first thing Monday morning. "I called you at this quiet, isolated country inn two or three times Saturday night. Clear up till midnight, in fact. I coulda sworn you told me they rolled up the sidewalks there at nine o'clock."

Ken guessed where this conversation was heading. He attempted a diversion. "Maybe I should be telling the coach about his key offensive lineman staying up past curfew the night before a game."

"Don't you go trying to change the subject," Dobbins said, not taking the bait. "I called you again right before I left for the stadium Sunday morning. No answer. No sign of you downstairs in the restaurant. In fact, do you know what the incredibly helpful dude at the front desk told me?"

Ken could see they were going to play this conversation all the way to the end, no matter what he did.

He decided he might as well relax and let Dobbins have his fun.

"I can't imagine," he said, praying that his friend hadn't shared this speculation with Delores. His goose would be cooked then.

"That man said you'd left on Saturday morning and he hadn't seen you since. He said you had a nice little stack of messages that hadn't been picked up, either."

"Good work, Sherlock," Ken said dryly.

Dobbins ignored the sarcasm. "Now, I know for a fact you didn't come down to see your kid, because I stopped by to see Delores and give her a cake Harriet had baked. She said she wasn't expecting you at all this week. She said she'd be moving Chelsea up to Vermont next weekend and you were busy getting things ready."

"All true. What's your point?"

"Well, I got to thinking. What would keep a man who doesn't know beans about decorating hanging around an empty house? And you know what I decided?"

"I can't imagine."

"I decided it seemed real likely that, despite all of your denials, you do have a thing for that real estate person."

"I thought I explained to you this real estate person is just working for me."

"After hours?"

"What makes you so sure I was with Beth? Maybe I was out with Chet Mathias."

"No way, man. He's out of the country. I called his house, too, and talked to the housekeeper."

"You are one nosy son of a…"

Claude laughed. "Come on, now. Tell the truth."

"About what?"

"Were you engaging in a little hanky-panky with the hired help?"

"Dobbins, my man, I don't believe that's any of your business."

"Me and Harriet weren't none of your business, either. Didn't stop you from messin' with *my* life."

"You have a very short memory. That was Delores at work, not me. I just stood on the sidelines and watched."

"You still haven't answered my question."

"That's right," Ken agreed cheerfully. "Did you have some reason for calling? Other than jerking my chain, that is?"

Dobbins's laughter boomed over the line. "My man, I am not finished with this subject. Not by a long shot. However, I will delay that particular discussion for another time. I called because I thought you ought to know that Chelsea is giving Delores fits. Threw an outright tantrum while I was there on Saturday for a few minutes. Over nothing, as near as I could tell. Didn't want no part of me. Wouldn't touch the cake. Finally stormed off to her room."

Ken's spirits sank. Chelsea adored Claude. For her to display a fit of temper when he'd come to visit was totally out of character. What was happening to his lovely, good-natured daughter? "Delores hasn't said anything to me and I've called there to talk to Chelsea every day."

"She wouldn't. She knows you've got a lot on your mind now. And she thinks this thing with Chelsea will pass once the two of you are settled in Vermont. I'm thinking maybe you ought to bite the bullet and give Pam a call and see if you can't get her to call her daughter."

The very idea of speaking to his ex-wife made Ken's stomach churn. Unfortunately, however, he couldn't argue with his friend's logic, especially since he had a hunch it was advice straight from Harriet, who was a school counselor and very wise in the ways of troublesome kids.

"I assume Harriet agrees with you."

"More like me agreeing with her," Dobbins admitted. "If ever there was a kid missing her mama, that child of yours is it. If you don't want to call Pam, Delores would probably do it, though the way she's feeling about her daughter these days, it doesn't seem to me like that's such a good idea."

"It's not. Besides, it's my responsibility. Thanks, buddy. I owe you for letting me know about this. I'll call Chelsea after school today myself and I'll see that Pam does, too."

"You coming home soon? We got a place of honor for you on the sidelines anytime."

"I don't think I'm much suited for watching the action from the sidelines. Besides, this is home now."

Even after he had hung up, Ken couldn't get the words he'd spoken out of his head. This *was* home now. And in large measure, that was due to Beth's presence. He could only pray that Chelsea would quickly come to feel the same way.

He glanced at his watch. It was barely 7:00 a.m. in California, no doubt a good time to catch Pam. She'd probably be sound asleep and irritable at being awakened. However, it also meant she'd be too muddled to give him much aggravation.

The phone rang half a dozen times before being tumbled off the hook and sent clattering to the floor. He held the receiver away from his ear, prepared for the impending burst of anger.

"What the hell?" she muttered grumpily when she finally had phone in hand. "Who is this?"

"Ken."

Silence greeted him, then a calmer, but no more friendly, "What do you want?"

"When was the last time you talked to Chelsea?"

"Last week. The week before. I can't remember exactly. It's the middle of the night, for God's sake. Ask me again at noon."

"Dammit, Pam. You're her mother. Even if you don't give a damn about her, she misses you. Would it be too much trouble for you to take five minutes to speak to her every couple of days while she's adjusting to all the changes we're dragging her through?"

"What about you? Last time I called, I heard you hadn't been home for days."

He drew in a deep breath and prayed for patience. "Look, I'm sorry. Let's not let this disintegrate into an exchange of accusations, okay? She'll be up here with me by this weekend. I talk to her once or twice a day. It's not me she's missing. It's you."

"Okay, okay. I get the message."

"You'll call her this afternoon?"

"I'm going out on an audition. I'm not sure when I'll have time."

"Make time, dammit," he retorted, then slammed down the phone before he got into a futile shouting match with her despite his best intentions.

When his pulse rate had returned to normal, he sent

a brief gaze heavenward and gave thanks that he was only a few days away from having Chelsea with him, only a few days away from getting a little stability back into both their lives.

On Wednesday afternoon, barely two weeks after they'd started work on the remodeling of the Grady place, thanks to whirlwind activity and persuasive charm, the master bedroom was at least livable, even if the rest of the house was still in disarray.

Though Beth had seen Ken nightly all week long, he hadn't stopped by to check on progress. He'd said the crew was better off left alone to get the job done, rather than training him in the process. She had a feeling, though, that he had suddenly wanted to put at least a little distance between them so they could both examine what was happening with some semblance of rationality.

Personally, though, she didn't want to think. For the first time in a very long time, she was content simply to feel. She could hardly wait for him to see the finished room, could hardly wait, in fact, to join him in the extravagant king-size bed he'd insisted he had to have.

"It's ready," she had told him on Wednesday night as they lay entwined amid the rumpled sheets and quilts on her own bed. "Can you come by in the morning?"

"Make it afternoon and I'll be there," he had suggested. "In fact, why don't you give the crew the afternoon off and we'll celebrate."

Her pulse had skittered wildly at the provocative glint in his eyes, even though it had been only moments since they had made love with so much passion and abandon that her body still ached from it.

With his eyes hooded and his gaze locked with hers, he'd said huskily, "In the meantime..."

As she thought back, a smile tugged at her lips. In the meantime, there had definitely been plenty to occupy their time.

Now, though, as she waited for Ken to arrive, she paced nervously through the debris still littering the downstairs. What if he hated the carpet? Or the wallpaper? Or the antique oak furniture? Oh, sure, he'd chosen it with her, but there was a vast difference between a small sample of something and a finished room. She could envision the end results with no difficulty, but what if he hadn't been able to and was disappointed?

Filled with doubts and anticipation, she took the chilled bottle of champagne from the refrigerator, picked up the two glasses she'd brought from home and carried them upstairs. She was still there, fiddling unnecessarily with the hang of the drapes, when she heard his car pull into the driveway. With her breath caught in her throat, she waited where she was.

"Beth?"

His shout echoed through the mostly empty house.

"Up here."

She heard his footsteps on the uncarpeted stairs. Hampered by his injured knee, his progress wasn't nearly as fast as she would have liked. Hands clasped tightly, she met him in the doorway.

His arms came around her at once, gathering her close. His clothes and his skin were cold against her, but she could feel the warmth radiating from deep inside and knew that within seconds they would both be on fire and the purpose of this visit would fade. Reluctantly, she stepped away.

"Oh, no, you don't," she said. "You at least have to look around first."

"Trust me. I'll see the bed soon enough," he said, reaching for her again.

Beth couldn't recall anyone ever being so hungry for her. His desire was exhilarating. And tempting. The battle to resist was a real struggle, but one she ultimately won.

"Ken Hutchinson, I did not lure you over here just so you could test the bed."

A grin spread across his face. "Okay, I get it. First, I praise your work. *Then* I get to sample it."

"Something like that."

"Then let's get this tour over with."

Beth pulled him into the room, then stood aside. With far more invested in his reaction than simple professional pride, she watched avidly as his expression changed from unexpectant to astonished and finally to delight.

"You're a miracle worker," he enthused, hauling her into his arms and planting a kiss on her forehead.

Beth's pulse bucked with what had become a predictable stirring of excitement, then seemed to skid to a halt. Her gaze flew to his. He looked just as stunned as she felt. His eyes focused on her mouth, then lifted to meet her gaze. Then slowly, ever so slowly, his lips covered hers in a kiss that quickly left her pliant and fuzzy-headed.

That incredible moment lasted for an eternity, then he was reaching for the hem of her sweater and tugging it up, sprinkling kisses across the bare flesh of her midriff. Beth was lost in the sweet, wild abandon of his touch when she heard the creak of the door downstairs. Her entire body froze.

"Did you hear that?"

"What?" he murmured distractedly.

She pushed him away and straightened her sweater. "Somebody just came in downstairs."

"I didn't hear anything."

"I did," she insisted. "Maybe one of the crew came back for something."

He sighed. "You won't be satisfied until we check this out, will you?"

"Afraid not."

He cast a longing look at the champagne, then at the bed and finally at her. "Damn, but I was looking forward to trying out that bed."

She grinned at the plaintive note in his voice. "Me, too, but it will still be here when we come back upstairs."

"You could just climb into bed and wait for me," he suggested hopefully. "I'd like to think about finding you there, naked, anxious."

"Oh, no," she said, forcing herself to ignore temptation in favor of common sense. "I don't want to explain what I'm doing there, if whoever it is gets past you."

"It won't happen, but come along if it'll make you happy."

They started down the stairs together. As they neared the bottom, at a cautionary gesture from Ken, Beth hung back. The position gave her an excellent view of the foyer and the living room beyond. In fact, she was perfectly positioned when a towheaded child wearing a velvet-collared coat, black patent leather shoes and fur earmuffs came barreling through the archway from the living room and threw herself straight into Ken's arms.

Beth watched the smile break across his face, saw him gather the child close and pepper her face with kisses until she was giggling with delight. Beth's heart thudded dully in her chest as she took in the scene with a deepening sense of dread and betrayal.

Maybe she was wrong. Maybe this wasn't Ken's child, a child he had never once mentioned. Maybe, she thought, as the sinking sensation spread through her.

But the gray eyes, the strong chin, the exuberant greeting said otherwise. So did the glow of parental pride and pleasure in Ken's expression.

If those things alone hadn't convinced Beth of the relationship, the child's first comment ended speculation.

"Daddy!" she said, an expression of dismay on her little face as she surveyed the downstairs of the house. "Do we really have to live here? This place is a mess."

Daddy, Beth repeated to herself, more hurt by that single word than the childish disdain for the house she loved. What terrible twist of fate had allowed her to begin falling in love with yet another man who already had a child?

Chapter 9

Holding his daughter in his arms, Ken took one look at Beth's pale, stricken face and wondered what on earth was wrong. He realized that Chelsea and Delores, who must be in the living room, couldn't have turned up at a worse time, but Beth looked stunned. In fact, when she finally shifted her gaze to meet his, he could have sworn what he saw in her eyes was a terrible accusation of betrayal.

Before he could react, before he could offer an explanation or even introduce her to Chelsea, she whirled and ran into the kitchen.

"Who was that lady?" Chelsea demanded.

"That was Beth Callahan. She's the lady who helped me find the house," he said just as Delores came in from the living room, her eyes twinkling, apparently at the mention of Beth.

"So where is she? I'm dying to get a look at her," she teased. "Of course, judging from that color in your cheeks, maybe I should be asking what the two of you were doing upstairs when we arrived and why you didn't have sense enough to lock the front door."

He scowled at his ex-mother-in-law, hoping the look was fierce enough to put an end to that bit of speculation, particularly with his precocious daughter listening in. Unfortunately, there wasn't the slightest sign of repentance in her expression. If anything, she looked even more fascinated by his reaction to the question.

"She went into the kitchen for something," Ken said, glancing worriedly in that direction. He wondered if she would scoot straight out the back door or come back so that she could meet his family.

"I hope you don't mind that we came a day early," Delores said, finally dropping her teasing. "Chelsea was getting anxious. Her teacher told me she wasn't paying a bit of attention in school, anyway."

"We wanted to surprise you, Daddy."

He hugged her. "I'm glad you did, Shortstuff." He just wished they had turned up an hour or two from now. More, he wished that Beth had been more prepared for the arrival.

It was his own damn fault. He should have discussed his situation with her, even if she'd never asked about it. Probably no woman, however much she might like kids, wanted to have one sprung on her the way Chelsea had turned up here today.

It was also entirely possible that Beth was simply embarrassed that his daughter had very nearly caught them in bed together. For that matter, knowing the way she felt about this house, maybe she'd just been incensed by Chelsea's outspoken, negative first impression. He could have reassured her that in Chelsea's present frame of mind, his daughter wouldn't have been impressed if she had walked into an exquisitely furnished palace.

After giving it some thought, Ken decided he liked any of those explanations for Beth's reaction far better than the worrisome possibility that she disliked children. If that was the case, they had a real problem because Chelsea came first with him. He planned to make it up to her for all the turmoil he and her mother had put her through.

He noticed Delores watching him speculatively.

"She didn't expect us, did she?" she guessed. "I don't just mean today. She didn't know about us at all, did she?"

He shook his head.

"Maybe you should go talk to her. Chelsea and I can look around on our own."

"I want Daddy to come with us," his daughter interrupted, her chin set mutinously.

Delores's mouth formed a grim line. "Chelsea Anne Hutchinson, one of these days you are going to have to learn that you can't have everything you want the minute you want it." She plucked the squirming Chelsea from Ken's arms. "Go on. We'll be fine."

He debated doing just that, if only to back up Delores's firm stance with Chelsea, but he figured he owed Beth time to gather her composure. Even knowing his decision was probably based as much on cowardice as consideration, he still shook his head.

"Let's do the tour. I'm sure Beth will join us in a minute."

Delores looked as if she might argue. Finally, she shrugged. "I suppose you know what you're doing," she said, though her tone suggested exactly the opposite.

Ken figured she was probably right to doubt him. He was operating on gut instinct here and something told him there was more behind Beth's unceremonious departure than met the eye, something that would have to be dealt with sooner or later. Not now, though. He wasn't going to do anything to spoil Chelsea's first look at her new home. It was too critical. Beth's questions would have to wait.

Even though he'd set his priorities and was prepared to stand behind them, he felt this terrible weight descending on him. He finally admitted to himself that he had wanted desperately for his daughter and the woman with whom he was becoming involved to like each other. The possibility that Beth might take an instinctive dislike to his child had never occurred to him. And if that's what had happened, he wasn't ready to deal with it just yet.

Chelsea had scrambled out of Delores's arms and stood glaring up at him. "I hate this place," she announced in a petulant tone. "Why do we have to live here?"

Ken barely held on to his already ragged temper. "How can you possibly hate it?" he asked, his tone amazingly even. "You haven't even seen it yet. Let's go up and take a look at your room. It's practically twice the size of the one you've had up till now. You can tell me exactly where you want your bed. The wallpaper we've picked out is supposed to be here on Monday and we can go look for the perfect furniture once you've seen it. This time next week you'll have your room fixed up exactly the way you want it."

He started up the stairs, Delores right behind him. Chelsea lagged behind, but she did follow. Instead of the excited, scampering footsteps he'd envisioned, though, hers were slow and plodding. She refused to come into the room she'd finally chosen from the snapshots he'd taken home. He owed Delores for getting her to do that much. Now, her expression sullen, her lower lip stuck out, she remained in the doorway.

Ken kept his tone deliberately cheerful as he pointed out the already-painted, built-in shelves for her books and dolls, the window seat with its comfortable, brightly covered cushion overlooking the front yard.

"It's ugly," she announced. "And I hate it." Tears welled up in her eyes as she looked up at him pleadingly. "I hate it, Daddy. I hate it. I want to go home."

The tears stripped away his anger and left his emotions raw. He'd never felt more helpless. He gathered her up in his arms.

"Shh, baby. It's going to be okay. You'll see. You just have to give it a chance."

He carried her over to the window seat and sat down. "See, just look outside at all the snow. You'll be able to build a snowman tomorrow. And there's a hill in back. You can go sledding. And you know what I bought the other day? An old-fashioned sleigh, the kind that has to be drawn by horses."

He noticed the first faint stirring of interest in her still-damp eyes.

"Horses?"

"Right. As soon as the sleigh is all fixed up, I'm going to hire two horses and we'll ride all over the countryside in that sleigh. We'll put jingle bells on the reins. And we'll take along hot chocolate to keep us warm. How does that sound?"

She sniffed, her disdain for everything about this new situation beginning to waver. "Okay, I guess."

"And Thanksgiving is only a week away. We'll have a big turkey dinner with all the trimmings. Maybe your grandmother can stay until then," he suggested with a glance at Delores, who nodded. "And we'll see if Uncle Claude and Aunt Harriet can come up. It'll be just like an old-fashioned Thanksgiving."

"What about Mommy? She'll be all alone in California."

"I'm sure Mommy will have friends to be with on Thanksgiving."

"Why can't she be here with us?"

Ken sighed. "We've been all through that. Remember when we talked about people having dreams about what they want their lives to be like? Being in California is something that Mommy always wanted. She wanted very badly to be an actress. For a very long time she gave up that dream to be with us, but now she really has to try to make it come true. It's not fair for us to ask her to stay here, if she's unhappy."

Chelsea's shattered expression told him she didn't understand her mother's abandonment and that nothing he'd said or could ever say would make her pain go away.

"It doesn't mean she doesn't love you with all her heart," he explained, trying futilely to reassure her. "She just needs to do this for herself right now. One day soon you'll be able to go and visit her. And we'll see Grandma and Grandpa in California, too. It'll be fun, kiddo. You love going to see them, remember?"

He glanced up to see tears in Delores's eyes, tears that she hurriedly brushed away. He pressed a kiss against his daughter's forehead. "In the meantime, can't you try to give this place a chance? I really think you'll like it, if you do."

Her little chest heaved with a sigh of resignation. "Can I have a dog?" she asked with a manipulative air that was all too reminiscent of Pam.

They had never discussed pets before. He hadn't even known Chelsea wanted one. He refused to be rushed into such a decision out of guilt. "We'll talk about it."

"But, Daddy..."

"No argument, Chelsea," he said more harshly than he'd intended. Deliberately injecting a calmer note into his voice, he added, "I said we will talk about it and we will."

"When?" she persisted.

"When the house is completely finished."

Her face fell. "But, Daddy, that will be *forever*."

He shook his head. "No, it won't, pumpkin. We have a miracle worker on our side." At least he hoped they still did. "Let's go downstairs and you can meet her."

"I can hardly wait," Delores murmured just loud enough for him to hear it.

"Watch it or I'll banish you," he taunted her lightly.

"You wouldn't dare, Ken Hutchinson. I know all your deepest, darkest secrets."

"You only think you do."

They were still bantering affectionately when they

reached the bottom of the steps just in time to catch Beth trying to slip out the front door.

Pretending he hadn't noticed that anything was amiss, Ken called out too cheerfully, "There you are. We were just talking about you."

She stopped and turned back with painfully obvious reluctance. Her mouth formed a polite smile, but her eyes were desolate. In fact, it looked as if she might have been crying. Guilt sliced through him. The explanations would have to come later, though. There was no time for them now, not with two fascinated onlookers.

"Beth, I'd like you to meet Delores Jensen, the absolute best mother-in-law any man could ever have."

He hadn't thought it possible but even more color seemed to drain out of Beth's complexion. Still, she held out her hand to Delores. "It's very nice to meet you."

"You've done a wonderful job with the house already," Delores told her warmly. "I can see why Ken bought it. Not everyone would see its potential, but I can already imagine how lovely and gracious it will be when it's finished."

Beth's expression softened ever so slightly. "It is an incredible house, isn't it? From the very first time I saw it, I wanted to see a family settled here. Jefferson Grady, the last man who owned it, was eighty-three when he died. He'd lived in it his whole life. I'm afraid, though, that he ran into hard times later in life and he wasn't able to keep it up. His children and grandchildren had all moved away and seldom visited, from what I understand. Every time I drove past, it saddened me to see the house looking so forlorn after years of echoing with children's laughter."

"Well, we're about to change all that, aren't we, Shortstuff?" Ken said, drawing Chelsea over to stand in front of him. "Beth, this is my daughter, Chelsea."

Even though she had to have guessed the relationship, Beth visibly winced at the introduction. "Chelsea, I hope you'll be very happy here," she said, the words mechanical and lacking her usual enthusiasm. She didn't even look at the child as she spoke. As if she'd sensed Beth's displeasure, Chelsea stiffened against the unspoken rejection.

Ken watched the two of them with a sense of despair. How could this warm, gentle woman he'd come to know so intimately suddenly be so cold and distant? And how could she take whatever justifiable anger she might be feeling toward him out on an innocent child? He began to wonder if he knew Beth Callahan nearly as well as he thought he had.

"I really have to go," she said abruptly, still not meeting his gaze.

Even though he could tell it was useless, he tried to argue with her. "Are you sure you can't stay? I'm sure Delores and Chelsea would love to hear about all the plans for the house. Then we could all go to the inn for dinner."

"I have dinner plans," she lied brazenly, obviously fully aware that he knew better. "The samples are all on the desk in your den, if you'd like to show them what we've planned."

"You know I don't know the first thing about all this stuff."

"A couple of weeks ago you might not have, but you're a quick study. Besides, I'm sure you'd like to be alone with your family on their first night in the new house."

The hurt in her voice cut right through him. But before he could argue, she turned and fled, leaving him staring after her openmouthed.

"Seems to me like you've got some fences to mend," Delores said.

"I didn't see any fences," Chelsea chimed in, her expression puzzled.

"Not those kinds of fences," Ken murmured as he listened to Beth's car door slam and the whir of her tires on ice as she sped too quickly away from the house.

Beth cursed a blue streak as she drove away from the Grady place—correction, the *blasted Hutchinson* place. Not once in the handful of meetings they'd had to discuss the house, and certainly not once in all the times they'd lain side by side in her bed, had Ken mentioned a single word about a daughter. Or about the wife that generally came with a child *and* a mother-in-law.

Not that she'd asked, idiot that she was, not even after he'd openly admitted he wouldn't be moving in alone. She hadn't wanted to know the details. She had wanted a few days with him, not an entire future. But somehow, discovering that was all that she would have, changed everything.

She rubbed her hand angrily over her mouth, as if that could take away the lingering sensation of the kisses they'd shared right before her world fell apart. But, she thought hopelessly, if the gesture was a futile attempt to rub out the memory of the kiss, she might as well accept there was nothing on the planet that could strip away all the other sensations they'd shared.

She drew in a deep, determined breath. She just wouldn't accept that. With enough willpower, she could force herself to forget about every single minute they had spent together. Surely there were ways to bury less than two weeks' worth of memories. How indelible could they be?

Perhaps if she thought hard enough about the way Ken had used her, she would want to rip his heart out. At the moment, though, she seemed to be filled with as much self-loathing as fury. How could she ever have fallen for a man who would so blatantly cheat on his wife, a man who had the audacity to introduce his mistress to his mother-in-law and child, for Heaven's sake? Had it been so long since she'd been interested in any man that she'd allowed her judgment to be clouded by physical attraction?

Even if she couldn't wipe out the memories, putting the entire mess behind her would be relatively simple if she never had to see the man again. Unfortunately, she had more rooms to finish in the house. Most of them bedrooms, dammit. And one of them was obviously going to be a little girl's room, which he hadn't mentioned.

To be fair, which she wasn't much inclined to be, they had discussed just one room at a time, starting with the master suite. The subject of what was to be done with those extra bedrooms had never come up. She'd been so caught up in the decor of the master bedroom and her own scandalous imaginings about that king-size bed he'd insisted on that she hadn't given a thought to the possibility that someone else might share it with him.

She lifted her foot off the accelerator and forced herself to slow down and try to treat what had happened this afternoon rationally. First of all, this was a job. She should never once have allowed herself to forget that. Second, he had never mentioned a wife, so maybe she wasn't in the picture. Maybe she was jumping to all the wrong conclusions.

Yeah, right! she thought, chiding herself for the self-delusion. He hadn't mentioned a child, either, and that little girl had definitely called him daddy.

An image of Chelsea came to mind. Beth felt her heart constrict. She was such a beautiful child, her delicate features a softened, more feminine version of her father's. And it had been obvious how much Ken adored her. One tiny part of Beth yearned to be part of such a family, to claim the two of them as her own.

Then she recalled the little girl's derisive remarks about the house, her generally sullen air. Warning bells went off in Beth's head. She knew all about impossible children. It didn't matter that Chelsea had looked like a child right out of the pages of a storybook in her Sunday-best clothes. It only mattered that she was so obviously spoiled by her indulgent family. Her behavior brought too many bitter memories to mind.

Even if the situation weren't impossible, even if there weren't the child's real mother to consider, Beth knew she would never dare to risk involvement in another potentially disastrous relationship. She simply wasn't cut out to be a stepmother, maybe not even a mother. Hadn't she learned that the hard way?

But how had it even gotten this far? Ken might have

committed a sin of omission. Her judgment might have failed her. But what about Gillie, her very best friend? Why hadn't Gillie warned her, rather than encouraged her to get involved with Ken? Surely Gillie's fascination with her favorite sports celebrity must have included details on his personal life. She'd known about his charity work, hadn't she? How could she have missed the fact that the man was married and the father of a daughter?

What a mess, she thought with a miserable sigh. Two years of isolation, two years of hard-won contentment, all shattered because she had foolishly dared to believe that she could separate passion and love, and then, when that had been proved wrong, had dared to believe that love was possible for her, after all.

Well, it wouldn't happen again, she resolved. Never again. She even allowed herself to feel some satisfaction over having gathered her composure so quickly, over making the only possible decision given her track record.

By the time she made her way into her house, she was icily calm. Resigned.

Then she went into her bedroom. The sight of her bed, the sheets still rumpled from the previous night's love making, was her undoing. She sat down on the edge of the bed, drew a pillow into her arms and finally allowed all of the hot, bitter tears of anguish to fall unchecked.

As the emotional storm finally subsided, she was left feeling empty, far emptier than she had been at the end of her marriage to Peter. Because this time she knew, without a single shred of doubt, that this terrible, terrible sense of loss would remain with her for the rest of her life.

Chapter 10

The next morning, just to get herself back out to the Grady place—the Hutchinson... Oh, forget it, she thought irritably—required a stern lecture on professionalism and so much coffee Beth felt sure she could have single-handedly painted half the quaint little shops on Main Street before the buzz wore off.

She ran nearly a dozen unnecessary errands en route to her job. She lingered over one more cup of coffee at the bakery, evading Lou's worried looks and hoping Gillie would turn up so she could strangle her. She had called her periodically the night before, but hadn't reached her. She would, though. And when she did, the woman was going to get an earful.

When Beth finally gave up on confronting the traitorous Gillie, she headed out of town, driving the rest of the way at a snail's pace, far slower than the road conditions called for. She drove miles out of her way to take a look at a house she was considering taking out an option on for her business. She told herself it was because she'd forgotten to note whether there was an automatic garage door opener. She knew better. She was never slipshod in her note-taking. More important, not one thing in the house had been modernized since much after the turn of the century.

Even when she could prolong the painful meeting with the Hutchinsons no longer, she lingered in her car in front of the house while more minutes ticked away. Lethargy seemed to have stolen her will. She couldn't seem to get herself to budge. The sight of a lopsided snowman wearing a Redskins helmet and an old football jersey didn't help. It was too much of a reminder of what she could expect to find inside—a family, of which she would never be a part.

Finally she was able to convince herself that no matter how long she sat where she was, nothing would change. Ken would still have a family he hadn't mentioned. She would still be heartsick and miserable. And she would still have a job to do. The sooner she got to work, the sooner the house would be finished and the sooner she could begin banishing Ken Hutchinson and his devilishly wicked touches from her mind.

Finally she made her way around back, hoping she could slip into the kitchen unnoticed by anyone except the crew working to enclose in glass the previously screened-in back porch. She waved to them as she opened the door and stepped inside, where she immediately came face-to-face with the person she had most wanted to avoid.

"Good morning," Ken said, his expression determinedly cheerful. "I was worried about you. I thought you'd be here earlier."

"I had things to do."

"And last night? I called several times."

"I was…out," she said, stumbling over the lie. In reality, she had unplugged the phone and turned off her answering machine.

Now, standing just a few feet away from him, Beth found she had a hard time clinging to her outrage. For one thing, he didn't seem the least bit guilty. For another, he looked sexy as hell with his cheeks darkened with a faint stubble and his hair rumpled. He was wearing faded jeans and no shirt, despite the fact that the temperature outside had dropped to just above zero the night before. Obviously the heater was very efficient or the man had a metabolism that could have boiled water. She couldn't seem to tear her gaze away from his chest. She wanted—

She stopped her straying thoughts with a sigh. What she wanted she couldn't have.

"Coffee?" he asked, and held up the pot.

Still somewhat taken aback by his cavalier attitude, but determined not to let him see for one instant how he'd hurt her, Beth fell in with his game, whatever it was. She shook her head. "I've already had more than my quota."

"I didn't know it was being rationed."

The quip didn't draw so much as a smile. "Where's your wife?" she inquired bluntly, unable to hold her tongue, after all. "Still in that king-size bed we were about to test yesterday afternoon?"

To her bafflement, he didn't so much as flinch at the sarcasm.

"She's probably on location for some low-budget film by now," he replied without missing a beat. "And, for the record, she's my *ex*-wife."

"Oh." For what seemed like the first time in the past miserable hours, she felt her heart begin to beat again. A tiny ray of hope slipped through her anger.

And then she remembered Chelsea. Wife or no wife, Ken Hutchinson was not the man for her as long as that little girl would be living under his roof. "Are you keeping your daughter, while her mother's working?"

He shook his head, his gray eyes regarding her watchfully. "I have custody."

"Oh," she said again, knowing how dismayed she must sound, but unable to hide her still-raw feelings.

He put down his coffee cup and took a step toward her. Beth backed away and wrapped her coat more tightly around her. He sighed.

"Look, I'm sorry for not telling you I was divorced. I'm sorry I didn't warn you that Chelsea was coming. She and Delores came a day early. I'd planned to tell you last night."

The explanation was too pat to satisfy her thirst for a rip-roaring argument. "There wasn't a single opportunity before that?" she demanded. "Perhaps when we were in bed together?"

Finally, she caught the desired flicker of guilt in his eyes.

"I'm sorry. The subject just never came up. Until just now, I didn't realize you would meet Chelsea and automatically jump to the conclusion that I was still married. That's what put you in such a snit yesterday, isn't it?" He regarded her with obvious regret, then shook his head. "I don't get it. Did you actually think

I would carry on an affair with you, knowing that my wife would be arriving any minute? I thought you knew me better than that."

She decided it was best not to respond to that. Instead she said defensively, "I wasn't in a snit."

"Could have fooled me."

Beth glared at him, her temper rising again. "Look, don't you dare try turning me into the villain here. You're the one who—"

"Daddy?"

The frightened voice came from the kitchen doorway. Beth whirled around and took a step back. Chelsea, dressed in jeans, a bright red sweater and sneakers, looked as if she were about to cry. Beth locked her hands together to halt the instinctive need to reach out and offer comfort that she knew just as instinctively wouldn't be welcomed.

Ken had no such hesitation. He held out his arms to his daughter. "Come here, Shortstuff. Are you warmer now that you're out of all those wet clothes? I had no idea you were going to manage to stuff as much snow inside your jacket as you got onto that snowman."

Perched in her father's arms, Chelsea kept her gaze fastened on Beth. "Why is she here again?" she demanded rudely.

Ken shot Beth an apologetic look. "I explained that yesterday. She's helping to fix up the house. She'll be around here a lot."

"You said the house would be ready really fast," the little girl said accusingly.

"We've already accomplished a lot," Beth told her, trying not to respond to the child's antagonistic attitude even though she was experiencing this terrible sense of déjà vu.

"Chelsea is anxious to have a dog," Ken explained. "I told her we'd discuss it after the house was finished, which means she'll probably drive the crew and you wild until it's done."

"I see." She forced herself to look directly at the child, while trying just as hard to not see her. If she could only manage to stay on autopilot, maybe none of this would affect her. "What kind of dog do you want?"

"A puppy," Chelsea said curtly.

"Obviously the breed doesn't matter," Ken said.

"I had an Alaskan husky once," Beth said before she could stop herself from making the tiny overture to the child who watched her so warily. "She was beautiful. She had the sweetest temperament you can imagine."

"What's a 'laskan husky?" Chelsea asked suspiciously.

"They're the dogs that pull sleds up in Alaska," Ken explained.

"They're black and white and fluffy," Beth added.

Chelsea seemed intrigued. "They can really pull a sled?"

"Absolutely. They're very strong."

"Maybe Beth will go with us when we look at puppies," Ken suggested.

The change in Chelsea was remarkable. It was as if a switch somewhere inside had been flipped, preventing her from agreeing with anything that included Beth. Scowling at the two adults, she countered, "I want a spotted dog. And I don't need any help choosing."

Ken looked taken aback by his daughter's churlish tone. "We haven't agreed you'll have any dog yet," he reminded her sharply. "And if you speak in that tone of voice again, your chances of getting one will get less and less."

Beth watched as tears of shock and outrage pooled in Chelsea's big gray eyes. Clearly she wasn't used to being reprimanded by her father, something Beth considered to be a very bad sign.

"Maybe you'd better go upstairs and think about that for a while," he said sternly, putting her down.

Chelsea stared up at him for a heartbeat, then turned and ran, her sobs echoing through the house.

Beth watched the entire exchange with mixed feelings. She could practically feel Chelsea's pain at being chastised in front of a stranger, but she also felt an odd sense of relief that Ken, at least, had dealt with her quietly, reasonably and immediately. Maybe he wasn't a father who sent mixed signals to his child as Peter had to Stephanie and Josh. No matter how often Peter had told his children that they were to mind Beth, he undermined her decisions at every turn.

She could hear murmured words from upstairs and assumed Delores Jensen was consoling her granddaughter. She couldn't help wondering whether the older woman would provide the leniency that Ken had not in an attempt to make up for the absence of Chelsea's mother. If so, Beth saw little chance for improvement in Chelsea's belligerent behavior.

She reminded herself it was not her problem. She was here to work on the house, not to offer child-rearing theories. She hardly had the expertise for that, she conceded wryly.

Forcing herself to concentrate on the job, she finally removed her coat and edged toward the doorway, hoping to make a quick escape into Ken's den where all the materials and plans had been stored.

"Beth?"

Ken's quiet tone stopped her. She glanced up at him and saw that he was regarding her with a puzzled expression. "I will make this misunderstanding up to you. I promise."

"It doesn't matter," she said. Even to her own ears she sounded unconvincing.

"It does matter," he insisted. "I want you and Chelsea to be friends. I would hate it if it were my fault that you can't be."

Beth drew in a deep breath and tried to squelch the temptation that raced through her. She couldn't—she *wouldn't*—put herself in such a vulnerable position again. It had been too painful the first time.

"I think maybe we'd better clear something up," she said firmly. "You hired me to do a job here. When it's done, I'll be out of your way." She leveled her gaze straight at him and tried to keep her voice just as steady. "As for anything else that went on between us, it was never meant to last."

She saw his eyes widen with shock, but she was too anxious to get away to someplace where she could quiet her own trembling to worry about his reaction. She'd made it no more than half a dozen steps when she felt his hand close around her arm. The next thing she knew she was being spun around until she was crushed against his bare chest, the wind practically knocked out of her.

"How can you say that?" he demanded harshly, his gray eyes stormy. "You know what we've shared the past couple of weeks was more than some casual fling."

Forcing her voice to remain cool, she said, "Maybe for you. Not for me."

She had thought the comment would fill him with indignation or disgust. She had been sure he would release her then. Instead his grip tightened and he studied her even more intently. That slow examination made her increasingly nervous, increasingly worried that she would give away her own tumultuous feelings.

"You're deliberately lying to me," he said with quiet certainty. "What I don't understand is why."

She managed a shrug. "You can believe whatever you like, if that protects your ego. It won't change the truth."

She caught the flicker of anger barely an instant before his mouth came crushing down on hers. It didn't give her nearly enough warning. The hard, punishing kiss practically knocked the breath out of her. There was no mistaking its intent, either. Ken was determined to make a liar out of her.

Beth was equally determined that he wouldn't succeed. She didn't struggle against the sensual assault. She didn't do anything. She kept her mind focused on a list of chores she needed to do and willed her body to remain limp. Trying to stay oblivious to that kiss was the hardest thing she'd ever had to do, but she did it, and a small measure of triumph early on kept her strong enough to continue resisting.

After a few interminable seconds, Ken finally pulled away, looking shaken and confused by her total lack of response.

Beth bit her lip to keep it from trembling and prayed the tears she could feel gathering wouldn't betray her by spilling down her cheeks before she could get away.

"Are you satisfied?" she asked quietly.

His jaw set, he glowered at her. "Oh, no. I am far from satisfied. You can run from me now, if you like, but I will get to the bottom of this. Count on it."

Beth didn't give him a chance to change his mind. She raced toward the den, slamming the door behind her and leaning against it as the tears cascaded down her cheeks. How in God's name was she going to survive several more weeks of this? How long would it be before she betrayed herself by melting beneath one of his kisses? How long could she hide the way she trembled at his touch?

He thought she was only lying to him, when the truth of it was that she was lying even more desperately to herself. She had spent an entire night telling herself she didn't care one whit for this man, when a few seconds in his arms was all it had taken to prove otherwise.

In an act of sheer desperation, she gathered what she needed to do her work for the day and raced for the door. "I'll be working at home if you need me," she hollered to the crew as she passed.

She tossed the invoices and samples into the back of the car, then got behind the wheel. Just as she was ready to pull away, she glanced up at the house. Two pairs of gray eyes watched her. Chelsea's round little face was pressed against the window upstairs. Ken's far more disturbing gaze met hers from the living room window. She could practically hear him calling her a coward, even though his lips never moved.

So what, she tossed back at him mentally. Better to be a coward in this situation than to expose her vulnerabilities. It had taken two long years to begin to feel some measure of self-confidence. She wouldn't let anyone ever shatter that again.

It took every ounce of self-restraint Ken possessed to keep from running out of the house after Beth. He watched her frantic departure with a sense of absolute frustration and outrage.

Dammit, he'd made a mistake. He hadn't committed a felony. There was something going on with her that he clearly didn't understand. He had a feeling it went far beyond any shock she might have felt over discovering he was a divorced, single parent. Unfortunately, that role was all too common these days.

When he had held Beth just now, when he had kissed her, she had stiffened as if he were a stranger. He knew with everything in him how much that effort to remain aloof must have cost her. She had been far too responsive a mere twenty-four hours earlier to be so icily cold now without really working at it. That wasn't ego talking. That was basic human anatomy. What he didn't have a clue about was why she had felt that was necessary.

He looked up at a sound in the foyer. Chelsea had crept down the stairs and stood watching him, an oddly satisfied expression on her face. He wasn't sure he wanted to know what that look was all about.

"I'm sorry, Daddy," she said, clinging to her favorite doll.

He regarded her skeptically. "Really?"

She nodded, her expression solemn. "I promise I'll be really good. Can I stay down here with you?"

He sighed at the plaintive note in her voice. How

could he possibly stay mad at her? "Where's your grandmother?"

"Hanging up my clothes."

"Shouldn't you be up there helping her?"

"She says I just get in the way."

Ken doubted Delores had said any such thing. If anything, he suspected Chelsea had learned that expression from Pam. He had planned to try to put in a couple of hours working, but after reading the forlorn expression on his daughter's face he abandoned that plan.

"Run up and get your grandmother. We'll go for a ride so you can see the town. Tell her we'll stop somewhere for lunch."

A smile spread across Chelsea's face. "And we can look for a puppy."

"Drop that for now," he warned gently.

Her grin didn't waver. "We'll see," she said blithely.

She said it in that adult way that often took him totally by surprise. She was definitely Pam's daughter, all right. Somehow he couldn't find much comfort in that.

"Bundle up," he called after her.

He put on a shirt then grabbed his own jacket and scarf from the back of a chair and tugged on a pair of boots. "I'll be outside warming up the car," he shouted. "Don't be long."

"We're hurrying, Daddy. We'll be there really fast."

Outside as he sat shivering in the icy car, Ken wondered if he dared take them by Beth's house. Perhaps they could persuade her to join them. Then he thought of the possibility she would refuse and decided now was not the time for Chelsea to suffer another rejection. Maybe it was better if they made this strictly a family outing, he conceded, trying to ignore the sense of disappointment the decision sent through him.

The roads had been plowed and sanded since the previous day, making the drive relatively easy. As they passed the house he had learned belonged to Roger Killington, the tactless, but well-intentioned bank president, Chelsea apparently caught sight of a sign he hadn't even noticed before.

"Daddy, doesn't that sign on the tree say Puppies?"

He groaned and wished for an instant that his daughter's spelling skills weren't quite so advanced. "Yep. Very good," he said, and kept right on driving. He caught Delores's smirk. "Don't say it."

"Did you hear a word from me?" she remarked agreeably. "I'm just along for the ride."

By the time they reached town, it was almost noon. The shops along Berry Ridge's main street were about as busy as they ever got. It was too cold to linger on the sidewalk chatting, so most people ducked into the stores when they ran into neighbors. Most places kept a couple of chairs around for these impromptu visits.

Feeling surprisingly at home, Ken pointed out the general store, a gallery of local arts and crafts, an old-fashioned candy store and ice-cream parlor, a model train shop, a combination bookstore and card shop, and the bakery.

"Where's the toy store?" Chelsea demanded.

Knowing she was referring to the kind of superstore that he hated, he gave her a sympathetic look. "Sorry. The closest big store like that is twenty miles away. But several of these stores have toys."

"I'll bet they don't have electronic games," she said derisively. "And I'll bet they don't have Barbie."

"I guess you won't be wanting to look around, then," he said. "We might as well go have lunch."

Chelsea started to argue, then fell silent. Ken had planned to make the twenty-mile drive to the nearest fast-food outlet, but just then he spotted Beth's car half a block from the bakery and guessed she was there having lunch. When a space by the curb opened up just in front of him, he pulled in.

Chelsea shot him an appalled look. "I want a hamburger."

"You can have one."

"But where? I don't see McDonald's."

"Sorry, kiddo. You'll have to make do with the kind they have here," he said, leading the way toward the bakery.

They were almost to the door when he felt Delores's hand on his arm.

"Are you sure this is such a good idea?" she asked.

"What?"

"I'm not blind, young man. I saw her car. I also heard the two of you arguing this morning. This doesn't strike me as the place to try making up. Word will be all over town by nightfall."

Ken recognized there was some truth in that, but he was determined to try to normalize things between himself and Beth, no matter what it took. He also wanted her to spend some time with Chelsea. Perhaps here, in public, there would be the kind of buffer that would ease the situation.

"It'll be fine," he reassured Delores.

She muttered something that sounded like "Men," and rolled her eyes.

The bakery wasn't all that large, but at the moment

it was crowded. It took him a minute to spot Beth in the booth at the back, sitting all alone and looking every bit as dejected as he'd been feeling. Plastering a smile on his face, he determinedly headed her way. He was already shrugging out of his jacket.

"Hi," he said cheerfully as he approached the table.

Her head snapped up. "What are you doing here?"

"We came to have lunch. Mind if we join you? All the other tables are taken," he said, not waiting for a reply before nudging his way onto the seat beside her.

Temper flared in her eyes, but she gave a reluctant nod, probably because she caught the sympathetic expression on his ex-mother-in-law's face.

Once they were all settled, Lou came over to take their order, her observant gaze pinned mostly on Beth. "You want me to hold that order of chowder for you until their food is ready?"

Beth was silent for so long Ken guessed she was warring with herself between politeness and a desire to flee as quickly as possible.

"I'll wait," she finally said with an air of resignation.

With the ordering out of the way and his immediate tactical goal accomplished, Ken was suddenly at a loss about how to proceed. Fortunately, Delores smoothed the way by commenting on the plans for the house. In no time the two women were caught up in a discussion of the appliances needed for the kitchen. Ken listened happily, certain that this was the first step toward a permanent thaw.

Chelsea, unfortunately, was clearly bored by it all. As the talk of refrigerators and stoves and washers and dryers went on, he watched her expression grow increasingly sullen. She picked up her fork and tapped it again and again against the Formica-topped table.

"Stop that, sweetie. We're trying to have a conversation," Delores said.

When that didn't work, she forcibly removed the fork from Chelsea's tight fist and without missing a beat went right on discussing the merits of trash compactors. Ken watched the incident with admiration.

Then, in an action as unexpected as it was sudden, Chelsea hit her glass of cola and sent it streaming straight toward Beth. The sticky, dark liquid splashed over Beth's clothes and into her face. Ken didn't have a doubt in his mind that Chelsea had sent the glass flying deliberately. Neither, if the expression on her face was any indication, did Beth.

Lou came rushing over with a washcloth, which she handed Beth, and a towel she used to mop up the rest of the spill, clucking all the while. "Accidents happen around here all the time," she said briskly. Her kindly gaze fell on Chelsea. "Don't you worry about it. I'll bring you another drink."

"I don't think that will be necessary," Ken said. "I don't believe Chelsea really wanted that one." He met his daughter's gaze. "Did you?"

Her lower lip trembled.

"You might tell Beth that you're sorry," he said more gently when Lou had gone.

She shook her head.

"Chelsea!"

She finally lifted her head and looked at Beth. "I didn't mean it."

"I'm sure you didn't," Beth said quietly.

The comment was gracious, but Ken knew without a

doubt that she didn't believe what she was saying. She and Chelsea watched each other as warily as a couple of enemy warlords meeting for the first time.

Ken suddenly felt like the negotiator who'd forced a meeting and now anticipated being shot...probably twice.

Chapter 11

After an endless weekend during which she'd had
plenty of time to contemplate Chelsea's deliberate spilling of her soft drink, Beth forced herself to go back to
Ken's house. The only way she was going to survive
this ordeal was by taking it one day at a time, one hour
at a time. She felt as if she were in a recovery program.
In those, however, a person was advised to avoid all
contact with the troublesome substance. She was going
to have to face her demon every single day and try
to emerge from the meetings emotionally unscathed.

For the first time since the work had begun, she felt
it necessary to ring the doorbell when she arrived. Delores, not Ken, greeted her, which settled her nerves
somewhat. Then Delores added that Ken had gone out
for the morning to take care of some business. The
only thing that might have filled her with a greater

sense of relief would have been the news that Chelsea had gone with him. Unfortunately, the little girl was standing right beside her grandmother, her expression solemn and distrustful.

"Chelsea and I are going to bake some cookies. Would you like some when we're through?" Delores asked.

"I'd love some," Beth said, keeping her gaze on Delores so she wouldn't have to deal with all of the conflicting emotions Ken's daughter stirred in her.

"With tea or coffee?"

"I'd love a cup of coffee, but don't go to any extra trouble."

"It's no trouble. I brewed a big pot this morning. I can't wake up without it. And when this one gets going," Delores said, smoothing Chelsea's blond hair, "I need to be fully alert."

"My grandmother bakes the very best cookies in the whole world," Chelsea volunteered, startling Beth with the friendly overture. For once there seemed to be no guile in her eyes, no resentment, just a sparkling anticipation of the morning's planned activity.

"I'll bet she does," Beth said, smiling at the childish enthusiasm despite herself. "What kind are your favorites?"

"Chocolate chip. But pretty soon we're going to bake Christmas cookies with red icing and sprinkles." Her expression suddenly turned belligerent. "Just like we did at my real house last year," she said as if to emphasize that this house would never be accepted as her real home.

Delores sent Beth an apologetic look. "She'll adapt before you know it," she said.

Beth shook her head. "Not necessarily," she said.

Apparently something in her voice conveyed far more meaning than the words alone, because Delores gave her a penetrating look. Before she could explore the remark, though, Chelsea tugged on her hand.

"Let's go, Grandma. I want to have lots and lots of cookies for Daddy when he gets home."

"In a minute," Delores began, but Chelsea's expression turned mutinous.

"Now," she insisted, earning a warning glance from her grandmother that effectively silenced her. She retaliated for the rebuke by glaring at Beth.

Delores sighed and gave Beth a look that was full of regret. "We'll talk more later," she said to Beth, obviously intent on keeping peace.

It was a tactic that Beth could have told her wouldn't work in the long run. Instead, wishing that the warm, older woman could become a friend, Beth simply nodded. She had recognized at once that they would never have the chance, if Chelsea had her way. The child seemed ready to do everything in her power to make sure that Beth remained a safe distance from everyone in her family.

As Beth went into Ken's office and tried to get to work, she reminded herself that a seven-year-old who had just been through a traumatic divorce probably needed reassurance that those still around her wouldn't be taken away. Emotionally, she probably required all the extra attention, especially in a new place where she had yet to meet friends. It was probably to be expected that she would view any stranger as a threat.

The generous, caring, rational side of Beth could accept all of the time-honored psychological explanations for Chelsea's behavior. The vulnerable, fragile part of her was terrified to open her heart to yet another child who seemed intent on rejecting her love.

Seated behind Ken's desk, she went over another batch of invoices, comparing them to the prices she'd originally been quoted and to the shipments stacked across the room. As she was shuffling papers, she found a note from Ken asking if there was any way possible the wallpapering in the dining room could be completed by Thanksgiving. He'd promised Chelsea an old-fashioned meal at home and didn't want to disappoint her.

Beth thought of her own plans for the holiday. She'd been invited to Gillie's, as usual, and to the Killingtons' for their annual celebration for family and business associates. Given her present mood, she would be wise to turn them both down. She wasn't fit company for anyone. She couldn't help wondering if she would have felt that way if Ken had asked her to join them for Thanksgiving dinner.

Releasing a sigh, she picked up the phone and called the wallpaper hangers and made arrangements with the owner, Steve Wilcox, to come in on Tuesday to do the dining room as a rush order. The other rooms would be done the following week.

"You'll have that place finished in time for Christmas," he promised.

"Thanks, Steve. You're an angel. Anything you can do to speed things along would be greatly appreciated."

"Remember that the next time I ask you out," he teased.

The man was gorgeous in an offbeat, artsy sort of way, with his thick brown hair drawn back in a ponytail and his chiseled features. He was also funny and hard-working. But he was barely twenty-five, for goodness' sake. At the moment she felt about a hundred years older. "You know perfectly well I'm too old for you."

"That's your opinion, not mine."

She laughed. "You are good for my ego, I'll give you that."

"Oh, my, I've scored two points in one morning. I'd better quit while I'm ahead. Add 'em to my score."

"I wasn't aware we were keeping score."

"I am. I figure there's probably some magical number I'll eventually accumulate and you'll break down and say yes."

"Isn't there some lovely young woman your own age you'd rather go out with?"

"I haven't met a woman in the entire state of Vermont who can hold a candle to you."

"Ah, Steve, you have definitely mastered the fine art of flattery. You're making my head spin."

"That's the idea," he said. "See you in the morning. Eight sharp. You bring the coffee. I'll work on my seduction technique."

"It's a deal," she said, smiling to herself as she hung up.

"Who's the admirer?" Ken said.

Beth's head snapped up. He was leaning against the doorjamb, his posture lazy. His eyes, however, had a dangerous, predatory gleam in them. "I didn't know you were back."

"I got here just in time to hear you tell some man he was making your head spin."

He sounded downright disgruntled about it, too, she thought with a tiny glimmer of satisfaction. "That was

Steve Wilcox. You'll meet him tomorrow. He's the man I hired to hang your wallpaper. He'll have the dining room all set for Thanksgiving."

"Thanks," he said automatically. "I thought it was the plumber I had to worry about."

"All of the guys are buddies."

"Buddies?" he said doubtfully.

She shrugged. "Why not? It is possible for men and women to be friends."

"I suppose."

"Planning a big gathering for Thanksgiving?" she asked, hoping to get off the subject of her social life before he discovered how studiously she had avoided having one up until she'd met him.

"Delores, Chelsea, two close friends from D.C." He paused and waited until her gaze met his. "And you, if you don't already have other plans."

"I've been invited to two parties that day," she said hurriedly, hoping to evade temptation.

He watched her closely. "You said invited. You didn't say you'd accepted the invitations."

"No," she agreed, wishing the man didn't have the perceptiveness of an expert psychic. "But if I go any-where, I should accept one of those."

"Because they asked first?"

She shrugged. "That's what Miss Manners would advise."

"You're not just using that to avoid joining us?"

"Why would I do that?"

"Because you're suddenly uncomfortable in this house," he said, straightening. He walked slowly across the room, then perched on the corner of the desk so his thigh was brushing hers. "I can't tell you how much I regret that."

Even though she knew what was smart, even though she recognized that an honest answer had danger written all over it, she couldn't help admitting, "Me, too."

"Then come for dinner," he repeated persuasively. "You'll really like Claude Dobbins and his wife. They're good people. Delores takes full credit for their marriage. Claude was a confirmed bachelor and Harriet was one very unhappy lady until Delores took charge. They're expecting a baby in the spring."

"They sound really special."

"They are. Claude's my best friend. He'd do anything in the world for me, Delores and Chelsea. It goes both ways."

"It must be nice to have friends like that," she said, thinking of her own best friend, who'd let her walk right into this hornet's nest with a single father even though Gillie knew her background. Gillie had been mysteriously elusive the past few days. Perhaps she'd gotten wind of how things were going between Beth and Ken and had decided to lay low.

"Then you have to meet them," Ken insisted. "I know Delores would love to have you join us. She thinks you're terrific."

She shook her head. "It's too awkward."

"Awkward how?"

"Me, your ex-mother-in-law, your friends," she said, carefully avoiding any mention of the real problem—Chelsea. "Thanksgiving should be for family and friends. I'm an outsider."

"Not with me. And you won't be with them, if you'll give them a chance."

The invitation tempted like the lure of lemonade on a summer day. She resisted. "I can't."

"It's Chelsea, isn't it? She's the real problem."

"I never said that," she said, shocked that he'd zeroed in on it. Even though she credited him with amazing sensitivity, she had assumed he would be blind to anything having to do with his daughter.

"Look, I know she hasn't behaved very well toward you. Don't take it personally, though. She's been difficult for all of us to handle. She threw a tantrum with Claude the other day and she adores him. And I can't tell you the battles she and I have had over this move."

"You can't blame her," she said. "She's been through a lot of changes."

"That doesn't entitle her to behave like a spoiled brat," he said, his expression grim. "I'm not trying to excuse her behavior, but can't you make some allowances for what she's going through?"

"Of course I can." From a nice, objective perspective she actually agreed with what he was saying. Unfortunately she wasn't able to be objective in this situation. Still, because it was the expected reply from an adult, she said, "I understand exactly the kind of turmoil she's experiencing."

Ken's gaze narrowed. "Did you grow up in a broken home?"

"No. I've just done a lot of reading on children who've lost parents through death or divorce."

"Any particular reason?"

Beth wasn't ready to get into her past with him. The present was complicated enough. "Just a topic that fascinated me."

"I see," he said, though it was clear that he didn't.

He sighed and Beth felt certain he'd resigned himself to accepting her decision. Instead he reached over and cupped her face between his hands. Then, while her heart began to thump unsteadily, he slowly leaned down and touched his lips to hers. The heat was there and gone before she could savor its warmth. Just as she was about to utter an agonized plea, his mouth closed over hers again, this time with all of the hunger and persuasiveness at his command.

Beth melted. Her resistance toppled. The only thing in her head was the need to be next to the source of the exquisite heat that made her blood flow like warm honey. When the kiss finally ended, Ken ran his thumb over her swollen lips and kept his unrelenting gaze pinned on hers.

"Say yes," he said softly.

"You don't play fair," she murmured.

A smile tugged at his lips. "I've told you before, I'll do whatever it takes to get what I want. Right now, what I want is for you to come here for Thanksgiving dinner on Thursday. I want you with me on the first holiday I celebrate in this house. This isn't some whim. It matters to me, Beth."

The words weakened her already shaky defenses. And with Ken's vital nearness consuming all of her thoughts, Beth could barely remember why she'd been hesitant in the first place.

"I'll come," she said finally. "But only if Delores will let me help."

"You'll have to negotiate that part of the deal with her," he said, looking satisfied at the relatively easy victory. "I have what I want," he murmured just before his mouth settled on hers one more time.

* * *

After he'd met Steve Wilcox on Tuesday, Ken couldn't believe he had even for a single instant been jealous of the man when he'd overheard Beth on the phone with him. It was obvious the two of them had a friendly, teasing rapport, but he was too young, too laid-back for a woman like Beth.

Still, it had disconcerted him to see her chatting so easily with the other man, touching Steve so casually and with such affection, when it seemed she was doing everything in her power to avoid intimacy with him. The entire experience had rankled until he finally convinced himself that he would be able to find some occasion on Thanksgiving to get her alone for a long, quiet talk…and more, if she'd let him anywhere near her. His entire body ached every time he thought about what they'd shared for a few short days before Chelsea and Delores had unexpectedly turned up that afternoon a week earlier.

Thanksgiving morning dawned with bright blue skies. He expected Claude and Harriet sometime around eleven. They were taking a crack-of-dawn flight from D.C. to Hartford, then renting a car for the two-hour drive to Berry Ridge. Chelsea had been on pins and needles since dawn awaiting their arrival.

"You'd think it had been months instead of days since you'd seen them," Ken said as she ran back and forth between the kitchen where the turkey was in the oven and the living room windows.

"But I really, really miss them," she informed him.

Ken sighed. "I know you do, baby."

She scowled. Before she could say a word, he grinned. "I know, you're not a baby."

"I'm not, Daddy. I'm getting all growed up."

"In that case, I want to talk to you about something. Come over here."

Chelsea approached him cautiously.

"Up here," he said, indicating his lap. "You're not too big for that, are you?"

"No."

She threw her arms around his neck and hugged him, as if to prove it. For an instant he allowed himself to recall what a wonderful, sweet-tempered, snuggly baby she had been. If only they could recapture those untroubled days when Chelsea had felt secure and hadn't needed to be constantly testing the limits of his love.

He regarded her seriously. "Now, then, I want to ask you for a really big favor today. I want you to try really, really hard to be extra nice to Beth." Chelsea's instantly mutinous scowl dismayed him.

"I don't like her," she said at once.

"You barely know her."

"I don't like her," Chelsea said stubbornly.

Ken fought to hang on to his patience. "Why not?"

As he'd suspected, she had no ready answer for that. Her brow knit in concentration and a frown settled on her lips. "Because," she said, apparently hoping the all-encompassing remark would be answer enough.

Ken wasn't about to settle for it. "No, you don't. If you really don't like Beth, I'd like to understand why."

"Because, Daddy, I don't think she likes me."

"That's not true," he said automatically, even though he had no way of knowing if Chelsea might be right. After all, she hadn't made herself very likable. And he had detected Beth's restraint himself. "I'm sure she would love you if she got to know you. You just haven't given her much of a chance. Since you're growing up now, I thought maybe you could try just a little harder."

She frowned. "You're not going to marry her, are you?"

The question took Ken totally by surprise. Not because he hadn't wondered the same thing himself, but because Chelsea had. Out of the mouths of babes, he thought wryly.

"I don't know," he told her honestly.

"I don't want you to," Chelsea said firmly. "I already have a mommy."

"I know you do, Shortstuff. And even if I do decide to get married again one of these days to Beth or anyone else, no one will ever try to take the place of your mommy."

"Are you sure? My friend Kevin has a stepmother and he says she's really mean when he goes to visit. She won't let him do anything. She says she might not be his mother, but she's still in charge when he's in her house."

Ken winced as he considered the problems that family must have. He prayed he could find some way to avoid them. Maybe Harriet, who probably dealt with troubled kids from broken homes every day, would have some advice for him.

"Well, I would never, ever marry someone who would be mean to you," he said for now. "I promise. Okay?" He tugged on the braid Delores had plaited for Chelsea that morning. "Do we have a deal?"

"Deal," Chelsea said, and held up her hand for a high five.

She scrambled down. "You watch for Uncle Claude

and Aunt Harriet, okay? I've got to go see if the turkey's done yet."

"If you keep opening that oven door, it will never get done," he warned.

"I don't open it," she shouted back. "I peek through the little window, just like Grandma does."

No sooner had Chelsea scampered off, than Delores turned the corner and came into the living room.

"Eavesdropping?" he asked. Actually he was hoping she had heard. Maybe then she could offer her own insights into the awkwardness between Beth and Chelsea.

"I was on my way in when I heard the two of you talking. I didn't want to interrupt."

"But you didn't budge, either, did you?"

Ignoring the remark, she settled on the sofa opposite him. "You evaded Chelsea's question about your feelings for Beth," she accused.

"I didn't have an answer for her."

"I think you do. I think maybe you were just afraid she wouldn't like it."

He scowled at his meddling and unfortunately too perceptive ex-mother-in-law. He'd wanted her to talk about Beth and Chelsea, not him. He should have known that would be impossible. "Okay, I didn't want to get her all worked up over something that might never happen. She's not ready to hear my plans." He grinned ruefully. "Unfortunately, neither is Beth. She's turned skittish all of a sudden."

He dropped the light note and looked at Delores. "You've seen Chelsea and Beth together. Do you think Chelsea could be right? Does Beth dislike her?"

Delores slowly shook her head, her expression thoughtful. "I think it's more like she's afraid of her."

"Afraid? Chelsea's a seven-year-old child."

"With the power to come between the two of you," Delores reminded him. "Give some thought to that. I'm going to make sure your daughter hasn't crawled into the oven with the turkey."

Ken might have dismissed Delores's theory without further thought if he hadn't seen yet more evidence of Beth's wariness around his child practically the minute she walked through the door.

She had just stepped into the foyer when Chelsea came racing out of the kitchen shouting for her Uncle Claude and Aunt Harriet. At the sight of Beth, she skidded to a stop, disappointment written all over her face. Beth's smile, in turn, faded, her expression transformed in a heartbeat to uncertainty.

Ken tried to smooth over the moment by explaining that his daughter had been watching for the other guests practically since dawn. Before he could say much, though, the couple in question pulled up outside and Chelsea was racing down the front walk where she was caught up in Claude's beefy arms and swung high in the air. She squealed with delight.

Ken glanced at Beth. She was watching the scene with an unreadable expression. Not until he looked into her eyes could he interpret what she was thinking. The desolation he saw there, though, very nearly broke his heart.

Although he'd been about to follow Chelsea down the walk, instead he stayed where he was and took Beth's icy hand in his own. She glanced at him, clearly startled by the gesture.

"We're going to work this out," he promised her, even though he wasn't entirely sure what needed to be resolved. He just knew that the woman standing beside him desperately needed reassurance of some kind.

To his dismay, though, his promise didn't seem to give her any comfort at all. Without a word, she slowly and deliberately withdrew her hand from his.

"I'll go see what I can do to help Delores." With that she turned and fled, leaving him more confused—and lonely—than he'd ever been in his entire life.

Chapter 12

Beth wasn't sure what she'd been expecting, but it hadn't been the giant of a man that Claude Dobbins turned out to be. The man had to weigh in at three hundred pounds and he looked to be solid as a rock and mean as an urban street fighter.

Until he smiled, which he did a lot. Then his entire demeanor turned from fierce as a lion to gentle as a lamb. The transformation was astonishing. Beth found herself warming to him immediately, especially when she saw the way he treated Chelsea and Delores, sweeping them up in exuberant bear hugs and tickling them until they were both helpless with laughter.

"No, Uncle Claude! No!" Chelsea squealed, her fair complexion, blond hair and petite frame a stark contrast to the huge, ebony man who was teasing her.

"You scared of me, Half-pint?"

"No," she protested, flinging her arms around his thick neck. "I love you."

"Ditto," he said. "Now why don't you tell me what you and your daddy have been doing since you snuck off to the wilderness."

"Don't you go pumping my daughter for information," Ken warned him, his expression filled with tolerant amusement. "That's a low-down, sneaky tactic."

"So what else is new?" Harriet asked, shooting Beth a commiserating glance. "Girl, I hope you have an endless amount of patience, because when these two get together, they are one demanding handful. You can't believe half of what they're saying. I'm thinking of hiring one of those NFL referees during the off-season just to keep Claude in line."

"What makes you think one of those guys can control him any better off the field than on?" Ken said. He launched into a litany of exploits that had confounded the officials and the opposing teams.

"Exaggerations," Claude retorted. "You're making that up, my man."

"Well, what about..." Ken began, describing another incident and then another.

While the others hooted at Claude's increasingly indignant expression, Beth studied his wife. Harriet Dobbins was as much of a surprise as her husband had been. She was tall—at least six feet—and thin, with the regal bearing of someone who'd been made to go through adolescence with a book balanced on her head. Someone had taught her pride and grace, traits not always associated with such height in a woman. And, like her husband, she had a natural, all-encompassing warmth. Beth instantly felt as if she'd known her for years.

Then Claude turned that smile of his on Beth. Brown eyes examined her thoroughly, then gleamed with approval. "Yes, indeed," he said to Ken. "I can see why you'd be willing to freeze your butt off up here."

"Claude!" Harriet chided as she might a wayward child. She shot an apologetic glance toward Beth.

He rolled his eyes. "Pardon me, Beth. My wife thinks I have no couth whatsoever."

"It must come from spending most of your life bull-dozing over men on a football field," Harriet shot back. She grinned at Beth. "Getting paid for his brawn instead of his brain has ruined him for civilized company. You'd never guess this man has a near genius IQ."

Claude scooped his wife up as if she were weightless. "This brawn is what keeps you in champagne and caviar, my dear."

"Put me down, you oaf. You haven't bought me any champagne since our honeymoon." She turned a helpless gaze on Delores. "I hope you're proud of yourself for getting me married to this man."

Delores shrugged, looking unrepentant. "Must be happy enough," she observed. "There's a baby on the way."

Chelsea's eyes widened. "A baby? When? Can I play with her?"

"It's going to be a boy," Claude informed her with conviction.

"Do you know for a fact it's going to be a boy?" Ken chimed in. "Or is that wishful thinking on Claude's part?"

"The man hasn't figured out that he can't just stand

around telling my belly to produce a boy," Harriet said, regarding her husband with obvious affection. "Me, I'm hoping for a girl, just to spite him. Besides, I think it would be kind of nice to see how he handles the boys who come to date his precious firstborn. Or what he does when his daughter decides to play high school football."

All of the talk of babies and families was beginning to take its toll on Beth. She glanced at Ken and saw that he was watching her, his expression thoughtful. A slow smile spread across his face. He came to sit beside her. "Getting ideas?"

"About what?" she asked.

"Babies."

"Not me," she said so adamantly that Ken's expression immediately shifted to a puzzled frown.

"Why not? I'll bet you'd make a wonderful mother."

The well-meant compliment brought the immediate sting of tears. Beth jumped up as if she'd touched a live wire. "I think I'll go check on dinner."

"Beth?"

She caught his worried expression and looked away. "I'll be right back."

In the kitchen, she stood with her hands braced on the counter and battled the tears welling up in her eyes. Memories of other holidays that had never lived up to expectations came spilling back.

She had tried. Oh, how she had tried to make things special for the years she had been with Peter, Josh and Stephanie. She had worked for days to prepare gourmet meals and for weeks before to make sure the house was filled with the right decorations, the right flowers, the right evocative scents or the right gifts.

Not once in all that time had she ever received a word of thanks, not even from her husband. Peter had taken the efforts for granted. The children had been deliberately disinterested in anything she had to offer, even when she had shopped all over town to give them an impossible-to-find present she knew they had wanted. From them she received only disdain.

Even the perfect gift always had some flaw. The color was wrong, or it had an almost-impossible-to-see scratch, or it was what they had wanted last week, but not this. Even the tastiest meal could have been seasoned a little differently. And nothing—*nothing*—was ever as their mother had done it and therefore wasn't worthy of their appreciation or even their simple courtesy.

The terrible thing about today was not how much it resembled all those other disasters, but how wonderfully close it was to the way she'd always imagined a family holiday should be, filled with laughter and shared memories. It was a bittersweet sample of the one thing she would never have on a permanent basis, not with Ken Hutchinson at any rate.

She heard the kitchen door swing open and surreptitiously dried her eyes. If Ken noticed the tears, he pretended otherwise.

"How's the turkey?" he asked, though it was obvious from the concern written all over his face that he was far more worried about her than he was about dinner.

"I was just about to check," she said, and hurriedly did just that. "Looks done to me. Is there a fork around to test it?"

Ken handed one to her.

"Perfect," she said.

He nudged her aside with his hip in a casual gesture that seemed somehow very familiar and very right.

"Let me take it out, so it can cool a bit," he said. "Is there a place for it on the counter?"

Beth saw that Delores had put a thick wooden cutting board next to the already-baked pumpkin pies. "I think the roasting pan can sit right here," she said.

The huge turkey was a golden brown. As soon as the pan was safely on the counter, Ken snitched a piece of white meat and handed it to Beth, then reached for another sample for himself.

"I saw that," Delores said as she came in to join them.

Within minutes, everyone was crowded into the kitchen as side dishes were prepared or popped into the oven for warming. Chelsea was underfoot, trying to sneak a taste of everything. For once she didn't say anything overtly antagonistic toward Beth. In fact, for the most part, she just ignored her. That only hurt when Beth stopped to consider how sweetly the child was behaving toward everyone else.

Thanksgiving dinner was a huge success. Compliments flew, from praise of the food that Beth had brought to Delores's perfectly baked turkey and mashed potatoes and on to Chelsea's neatly colored decorations for the table. The table groaned under the weight of all the dishes, which contained more than enough for a gathering twice this size.

As they ate, Beth felt Ken's gaze returning to her time and again, his expression speculative, as if he couldn't understand why a woman who rarely hesitated to speak her mind was suddenly so silent. If anyone else was aware of how unnaturally quiet she was,

Beth didn't notice it. She saw only Ken's reaction, felt only his bewilderment. Regret stole through her. How could she explain to him that she was terrified to make an effort to fit in, terrified of the awful sense of failure that would follow their eventual and inevitable parting?

"Dessert?" Delores asked when everyone had finally pushed back from the table.

Only Claude looked willing. A chorus of *laters* came from everyone else.

"I think a walk is in order," Harriet said.

"There's a game coming on," Claude protested.

"Can I watch with you, Uncle Claude?" Chelsea asked.

"Absolutely. I can tell you how I would be doing it, if I were on the field."

"You're pitiful," Ken teased. "You're resorting to telling your lies to seven-year-old girls now."

Harriet shook her head and Beth and Delores laughed as the bantering disintegrated into a debate about which man had more talent and more know-how.

"I was the quarterback. Everybody knows that's the brains of the team," Ken challenged.

"And I protected your sorry butt," Claude countered. "My apologies, ladies, but that's the gospel truth."

"Just go watch the game," Harriet said. She looked at Beth. "What about you?"

"I'm ready for a walk."

"Delores?"

"I think I'll stay here and clean up."

"Oh, no, you don't. You leave that for us," Harriet protested. "If you don't feel like walking, then sit down someplace and put your feet up."

"I won't do much," Delores promised. "You two

have a nice walk. Be careful of the road. There are still some icy patches."

Harriet and Beth bundled up and set off along the stretch of road toward town. The icy air froze their breath. The wind cut through the layers of clothes they'd put on before walking outside. For the next few minutes, after the heavy meal, Beth knew it would feel invigorating. Then they'd be ready to dash back inside to warm up by the fire.

They hadn't gone more than a hundred yards when Harriet said, "So, tell me. Are you in love with Ken?"

Beth lifted startled eyes to meet her gaze and felt a rush of blood in her cheeks. Hopefully Harriet would attribute that to the cold. She managed a weak laugh, then commented, "Direct, aren't you?"

"It's the best way I know to get answers. Ken's like family to Claude and me. We've been worried about him since he and Pam split. She was a real piece of work, nothing at all like Delores. I swear that woman must wonder sometimes if Pam wasn't a changeling. Anyway, we've been afraid the whole experience would sour Ken on marriage. Then out of the blue he goes and decides to settle down all the way up in Vermont. I figure you must have had something to do with that."

Beth shook her head. "I don't think so. He seemed pretty set on settling here when he called me about looking for a house," Beth said, avoiding the real issue Harriet had raised. "He hasn't said much about the past."

"And you haven't asked?" Harriet said incredulously. "Isn't that supposed to be the first question a woman asks a divorced man—how bad was it? The answer tells you a lot about what to expect."

"I suppose I didn't ask because the answer didn't matter," Beth said. "I'm not looking for a serious relationship."

"I didn't ask if you were looking," Harriet reminded her. "Seems to me like one found you." She glanced over. "You getting along okay with Chelsea?"

Beth shrugged, wishing she could confide in this woman who was sensitive enough to guess the potential for conflict between her and Ken's daughter. Still, she was determined to keep her own counsel about this. It wouldn't be fair to discuss her relationship with Ken with his friends.

When Beth didn't answer right away, Harriet added, "Chelsea can be difficult."

"I suppose. We don't spend a lot of time together."

Harriet stopped in her tracks. "I must be getting my signals all mixed up here. I could have sworn that the sparks flying between you and Ken were of an intimate nature. Have I been married so long I've lost my knack?"

Beth blushed.

"Aha. So I'm not going nuts. Is there some reason you're fighting the inevitable? Or need I ask? It is Chelsea, isn't it? She's being a brat. Claude said so, too."

"So far the damage is only minor," Beth admitted, trying to minimize the problem.

"Give her time."

"There are some things time can't fix," Beth said bleakly.

Harriet studied her intently. "You've been through this before, haven't you?" she guessed.

Beth wasn't nearly as stunned by Harriet's intuitiveness as she could have been. "How did you know?"

"You display all the signs of the walking wounded. Have you discussed this with Ken?"

"There's nothing to discuss. It's my problem. I'm just not cut out to be a mother."

"Bull—" the other woman began and cut herself off with a wince. "Sorry. I'm picking up Claude's bad habits."

Beth chuckled at her chagrin. "But sometimes those words are just so much more satisfying and to the point, aren't they?"

"You've got that right, girl." Her expression turned serious again. "Look, I'm a school counselor. Prying is my business and I don't seem to be able to turn it off at the end of the day. So you can ignore me if you want to. You can even tell me to hush up, but not before I tell you that you owe it to yourself and to Ken to be honest with him. Nobody comes into this world a mother. It's something we learn to do by trial and error. Whatever happened in the past probably taught you a few things. Chances are you weren't to blame for most of the problems, anyway. I could cite all sorts of comforting statistics to prove you're not alone. Second marriages are very difficult when there are stepchildren involved. Spread the guilt around a little, why don't you, instead of taking it all on yourself."

"But I was the adult," she said, echoing Peter's oft-spoken refrain.

"That's right," Harriet agreed. "You were the *adult*. Not a saint."

Beth was grateful for her directness and her common sense. "Thanks for the advice."

"You going to take any of it?"

Beth sighed. "I just don't know if I can."

Harriet leveled a gaze at her. "Ken Hutchinson's worth it, girl. He's a decent, caring guy, and despite all the garbage that's been written about him, pro and con, he's come out of football with the same solid values he took into the game. Don't go messing up a chance to have a life with him for all the wrong reasons."

Ken had no idea what had happened when Beth and Harriet had gone for that walk, but when they returned Beth seemed more at peace. She didn't even flinch when he brought her a piece of pumpkin pie, then lingered on the arm of the chair next to her.

"I'm glad you're here." He leaned down to whisper in her ear.

A tentative smile curved her lips. "Me, too."

In fact, the den, which had been converted into a makeshift TV room for the occasion, seemed to be filled with warmth and goodwill. It was the happiest holiday he could recall for some time. Pam had always insisted on throwing these perfectly orchestrated bashes, which were incredibly successful but far from homey or intimate.

Just as Ken was thinking how much it meant to be surrounded by family and good friends, rather than an entourage of people he barely knew, Claude lumbered to his feet.

"Come on, Harriet. We've got us a plane to catch."

Chelsea immediately protested.

"Sorry, Half-pint, I've got to get ready to go pound on some bad guys on Sunday. I need my beauty rest."

"But you're already beautiful, Uncle Claude," Chelsea proclaimed, tightening her arms around his neck.

"Don't go. You're my only friend in the whole wide world."

Ken winced at the plaintive note in his daughter's voice. He and Claude exchanged a look, then his friend held Chelsea up in the air. "Now, you listen to me, young lady. I am not the only friend you have. You've already got a brand-new friend right here in Vermont."

"Who?" Chelsea said doubtfully.

"Beth."

"She's Daddy's friend, not mine."

Ken watched Beth's expression when the blunt assessment popped out of Chelsea's mouth. Some of the color drained out of her face.

"Well, that won't always be the case," Ken said hurriedly. "Now that you're all moved in we'll be doing lots of things together."

"There," Claude said. "I told you so. And pretty soon you'll be going to school here and the next time I come to town I won't be able to take a step for fear of squishing some little munchkin under my big, old feet."

Chelsea laughed at that. "You've never squished me."

"That's because you're so noisy, I always know where you are," he informed her. "You're just like a kitty with a bell around its neck." He planted a smacking kiss on Chelsea's forehead and turned her over to her father, then wrapped his beefy hand around his wife's elbow. "Come on, little mother."

Harriet paused on the front steps and looked straight at Beth. "Don't forget what I said."

"I won't."

When the couple was finally out of sight, Ken looked at Beth. "What was that all about?"

"Girl talk."

He grinned. "Must have been about me."

"Don't look now, but your ego is showing," Delores said.

"What's an ego?" Chelsea demanded.

"Something your daddy has way too much of," Delores said. "Come on, Chelsea. You can help me put the dishes in the dishwasher."

"But I wanted to play a game with Daddy."

"After we get the dishes going," Delores said firmly. Chelsea opened her mouth to offer another protest, but her grandmother already had her firmly by the hand and was leading her away.

Ken captured Beth's hand in his own. "Alone at last."

"I really should help with the dishes," Beth said hurriedly.

"Three sets of hands will only get in the way. Believe me, Delores considers the kitchen her domain and it's good for Chelsea to have chores. Now, come into the den with me and relax. We haven't had a minute to ourselves all day."

"Was there something you wanted to talk to me about?"

He grinned at her worried frown. "Talking was not what I had in mind. Today's Thanksgiving. You're one of the things I'm most thankful for. I thought I should demonstrate how much."

A sigh seemed to ease through her, but her expression turned sad.

"What's wrong?"

"Nothing."

"I don't believe that," he said, sitting in a chair

and pulling her into his lap before she could protest. "You've had that expression on your face half a dozen times today. Tell me what it's all about."

"It's just that you're so sweet."

"Sweet, huh? Some guys would consider that an insult."

"Oh, I think you're strong enough to take it," she said, allowing herself the first hint of a smile he'd seen all afternoon.

Ken frowned. "I wish you'd talk to me."

"I talk to you all the time."

He gestured around the room with its remaining piles of wallpaper rolls, paint cans and papers. "About this. Not about anything important."

"This is important."

"*We're* important," he corrected. "All of this is just window dressing."

"You won't feel that way when the wiring goes on the fritz or the plumbing leaks."

"Yes, I will," he insisted. "Wiring and plumbing can be fixed. I'm more worried about us."

"Meaning?"

"I want to get back what we had this time last week. We can't do that as long as you're not being honest with me about what went wrong."

He watched with a sense of resignation as her expression completely shut down. "Beth?" he prodded.

But instead of responding to his question, she visibly distanced herself emotionally, then followed that by physically removing herself from his arms.

"It's been a lovely day," she said in that tight, polite voice that made him want to scream in frustration.

"It could be a lovely evening, as well."

She shook her head. "I really should go. I—I promised Gillie I'd stop by."

Ken knew in his gut that she was lying again. He could read it in her eyes, because she was so damn bad at it. If she actually stopped off to see anyone between his place and home, he would be stunned.

"Are you coming by to work tomorrow?"

She shook her head. "Most of the crew are taking it as a holiday. I thought I would, too."

"Then let's do something together. Chelsea will be starting school on Monday. The next few days will be our only chance to get out and do things just for fun."

He wouldn't have thought it possible, but her expression grew even more distant. "It's important for the two of you to spend this time together," she said stiffly. "She needs you right now."

Ken's temper finally kicked in. "I can't tell if you're truly trying to be unselfish here or if you just don't want to spend time with us. Whichever it is, it's beginning to grate on my nerves."

Her lower lip trembled. "I'm sorry."

He threw up his hands in a gesture of resignation. "Yeah, so am I."

She cast one last look at him, then trudged off through the rapidly deepening snow toward her car. She looked so forlorn he almost went after her, but then he reminded himself that she had made a clear choice. He'd be damned if he'd force himself on a woman who so plainly no longer wanted any part of him.

But that didn't keep him from standing in the doorway and watching until the red glow of the taillights on her car finally faded from view.

Chapter 13

The day after Thanksgiving Ken was still trying to figure out what to make of Beth's abrupt departure when Chet Mathias called.

"Sorry I haven't gotten to you before this, but I've been out of the country," the sporting goods manufacturer explained. "Took my wife on a fortieth anniversary trip all over Europe. I hope to hell I can work until I'm eighty. That's how long it'll take to pay for all the shopping she did. Give that woman foreign currency and she thinks it's play money."

"But you had a good time, didn't you?" Ken retorted.

"The best," he admitted.

"I can hear it in your voice."

"I have to admit I feel better than I have in years. But that's enough about me. You settling in okay? I hear Beth's been helping you."

"She's been a godsend, Chet. I can't thank you enough for recommending her," Ken replied truthfully.

"I thought maybe the two of you…" He allowed the suggestion to trail off, then waited expectantly.

Ken hesitated, then admitted, "We have been out a couple of times. She was here with us for Thanksgiving yesterday."

"Perfect. I knew first time I met you that the two of you would get along. Tried my darnedest to figure out a way to make it happen, but matchmaking schemes aren't exactly my bailiwick and my wife Corinne flatly refused to meddle. Then when you called last month, well, it just seemed like everything was falling into place."

"How much do you know about Beth?" Ken asked.

"Not much about the time before she came here. She doesn't say too much about her past. I've always been a believer in looking at what a person's made of now and not worrying too much about how they got that way." He laughed. "Just look at me. Forty years ago, I was nobody's idea of a good bet. Corinne was the only woman brave enough to take a chance on me. As for Beth, I could see right off that the lady was all class. Maybe a little on the quiet side, but definitely all class."

Ken wasn't about to argue with that assessment, but he needed more. "So you don't know anything about her marriage," he said.

"Marriage?" Chet sounded genuinely astounded. "Hell, I didn't even know she'd been married. Well, I'll be darned. Is that a problem for you?"

"Of course not. I just get the feeling it is for her, but she won't talk about it."

"Well, I'll be darned," Chet said, still sounding stunned. "You know that friend of hers, Gillie Townsend?"

"Beth has spoken of her. We haven't met."

"Then I'd say a meeting is past due. She's usually down at Lou's after she drops her kids off at school. Fact is, I think one of her kids is about the same age as your daughter, so you'll surely be getting to know her. My guess is that she knows Beth as well as anyone around these parts."

"I'll keep that in mind," Ken said, trying to imagine himself going up to a total stranger and pumping her for information about a woman with whom he'd already been intimate. He doubted he could pull it off.

If the two women were as close as Chet had surmised, Gillie might know about his relationship with Beth and tell him to ask Beth directly, if there was something he wanted to know. If she didn't know about him, he would feel thoroughly underhanded. More important, Beth would probably string him up if she ever found out about it. And there wasn't a doubt in his mind that she would discover he'd been asking questions. Her best friend wouldn't keep that information a secret.

"Listen, Ken," Chet said, breaking into his thoughts. "Corinne's been busting my chops ever since I got on the phone to invite you to dinner tomorrow night. You free?"

"I'd love to come."

"You want to ask Beth?"

"To tell you the truth, Chet, I'm not at all sure she'd agree to come with me."

"Mind if we ask her, then?"

Ken couldn't help chuckling at how pitiful he'd become, allowing someone else to arrange his dates for him. It was a darn good thing Claude didn't know about this. Ken would never hear the end of it.

"Ask her," he said. "Maybe I'll call her later and offer to give her a lift. Surely she wouldn't refuse a neighborly gesture like that."

"Surely," Chet agreed heartily. "Seven o'clock?"

"Sounds good. Tell Corinne I'm looking forward to seeing all the things she brought back from the trip."

"Lordy, son, don't say that. We'll never get dinner on the table. Now if you want to take a look at my pictures—"

"On second thought…"

"Traitor," he accused, laughing. "See you tomorrow, son. We'll be looking forward to it."

Ken knew Chet would waste no time tracking Beth down. Nor did he doubt for a minute that the older man could talk her into coming to a dinner party. It remained to be seen, though, whether his own powers of persuasion would be equally successful. He waited until that evening to call.

"Beth, it's Ken."

"Oh, hello," she said, sounding cautious. "Is something wrong?"

He decided to ignore her assumption that he wouldn't call unless there was a problem. He also decided not to give her a chance to refuse his offer to pick her up for the dinner party. Didn't women tend to respond to confidence in a man? Or had that changed in the years since he'd been out of the dating scene?

"I just wanted to let you know I'd be by about six-thirty tomorrow to pick you up," he said matter-of-factly.

"Six-thirty? Tomorrow?"

"That's right. You are going to Chet's, aren't you?"

"Well, yes, but—"

"I told him I'd pick you up."

"You...told...him," she began, enunciating every word very carefully.

Ken grinned. She was royally ticked, all right. Hallelujah! He'd rather have her screaming at him than sinking into that quiet sadness he'd witnessed all too often. "Sure. I don't mind. You're not a bit out of my way."

"You don't mind," she said, her voice climbing.

"Is there a problem?" he inquired, injecting a note of innocence into his voice.

"Yes, there's a problem. First, I had no idea you'd even been invited. Second, I certainly had no idea you would dare to assume you would be my date. Third..."

She seemed at a loss to come up with anything else. Ken bit back a chuckle. "Third?" he prompted.

"Third, you are making me crazy."

He could no longer hold back the laughter.

"What's so damn funny?" she snapped irritably.

"You. You're fighting the inevitable, sweetheart."

"There's nothing inevitable about any of this and I am not your sweetheart. I am not your anything!"

"I suppose that's a matter of perspective," he conceded thoughtfully. "It's how I think of you, but perhaps you haven't quite gotten to that stage yet."

Beth heaved a sigh. "Why are you doing this?"

"Doing what?"

"Chasing after something that just can't be. Anyway, I thought you were furious with me."

"I was. It didn't last. The truth is, Ms. Callahan, I find you perplexing, frustrating, irritating and incredibly attractive."

"Most of those weren't even good traits," she noted pointedly.

"I know. Just shows you how perverse I can be. So, do we have a date or not?"

"We absolutely, positively do *not* have a date," she said very distinctly.

"Oh," he said, defeated.

"But you may pick me up at six-thirty."

He sucked in a deep breath and tried not to shout for joy. "See you then," he said, and hurriedly hung up before he lost even a sliver of the tiny bit of ground he'd gained.

This dinner party was a mistake, Beth thought as she pulled on a simple red wool dress, added diamond stud earrings and slipped into a pair of heels. Actually, the dinner wasn't the problem. She adored Chet and Corinne. It was the drive to and from that promised to be exasperating and dangerous.

She still didn't understand why Ken was so persistent in the face of her obvious reluctance to get more deeply involved with him. Perhaps it had something to do with the fact that she'd already slept with him, she thought wryly. Maybe he figured that suggested they were already pretty seriously involved. Maybe he figured that had meant something to her.

And maybe he was right, she conceded wearily. It had meant something. But that didn't mean she couldn't forget about it, if she tried hard enough. She just had to keep her distance, which was absolutely not possible in a cozy car on a starlit night unless she rode in the back seat. She doubted he'd go for that, not without an explanation. And telling him she was scared to death to be near him would create more problems than it would solve.

She paced through the house tidying up things that didn't need to be tidied. When the doorbell finally rang, promptly at six-thirty, she jumped as if it had been a gunshot. After one last glance in the hallway mirror, she opened the door. She took one look at Ken and her jaw went slack.

Oh, dear Heaven. It was the first time she had ever seen him all dressed up in a suit and tie. Obviously he knew how Corinne felt about dressing up for dinner. He was wearing a wool overcoat that looked as if it had cost twice the commission she was likely to make on the restoration of his house. Though it was obvious he'd carefully blown his hair dry in a neat style, it was already sexily tousled by the wind.

"You look…" she began.

"You look…" he said at the same time.

"Fantastic," they said in a murmured chorus.

He grinned. "I guess it's unanimous. We're going to knock 'em dead."

Beth flushed with pleasure and tried valiantly to ignore the way the gleam in his eyes made her feel. It was amazing that with one glance he could boost her self-confidence as a woman to new heights. If only it were as easy to restore her self-esteem as a mother.

The rest of the evening passed in a blur. Chet was a lavish, thoughtful host, as always. Corinne's dinner was superb. But it was Ken's quiet attentiveness that kept Beth glowing with an undeniable inner heat and a sense of expectation. Alone, with just the two of them, she dared to think that anything was possible. At least for this one night.

Being with Ken, feeling his body harden in response to her touch, breathing in the clean, masculine scent of him, giving herself to him until they were both crying out with the sheer exhilaration of their passion...

Those were the things she wanted, she finally admitted to herself. Those were the things she imagined on the quiet drive home. The images were so vivid that her pulse raced and her blood sizzled in anticipation.

In the soft glow of an old-fashioned streetlamp, Ken cut the engine and turned to her. His gaze locked with hers until she was trembling, wishing with every fiber that he would close the distance between them. He reached across and gently trailed a finger across her lips and left them quivering. The sensation ricocheted all the way through her.

"I want you," he said softly.

Beth swallowed hard. "I want you," she confessed.

"Then why is this so damn complicated?"

"It's not," she protested, even though she knew far more than he exactly how complicated it was. An admission, though, she knew with absolute certainty, would cost her dearly. She would lose not just the future, but tonight. This breathless moment.

"When I hold you or touch you, it's not," he agreed. "But all the other times..." His gaze studied her sorrowfully. "All the other times, you keep such distance between us."

"I didn't put it there."

"Then who did?"

Your daughter, she wanted to scream. *Your little girl.*

But she kept silent, because to say it would invite questions for which she had no answers.

Ken's eyes filled with something that might have been dismay. "There it is again," he said wearily. "The sadness. I can't know what to do about it, if you won't tell me what's causing it."

Tears of quiet despair pooled in her eyes, then spilled down her cheeks. "You couldn't fix it, if you knew," she said bleakly, opening the car door and stepping into the frigid night air that instantly froze the tears on her cheeks. She simply couldn't bear to tell him what a failure she had been as a mother. Right now he might be confused about why she had withdrawn from him, but at least he saw her as a complete woman. She had his respect. If he knew everything, nothing would change…except the way he looked at her. She wasn't sure she could bear that.

Even though she knew that parting now was best, all the way to the house she prayed he would follow. She listened for the car door, but heard nothing until, at last, the engine turned over and he slowly pulled away, the tires crunching on the ice.

Chelsea stood in the middle of her bedroom on Monday morning and pitched a tantrum that had Delores near tears and Ken ready to pack everything and head back to Washington.

"I won't go! I won't," she screamed, taking off school clothes as fast as Delores could dress her in them.

Ken's patience finally snapped, but somehow by the grace of God he managed to remain calm. "Delores, I'll handle this," he said finally. He figured this was one crisis he couldn't hand off to anyone else.

She regarded him worriedly. "Ken, maybe it would be better if—"

"No, it's okay. You go downstairs and put breakfast on the table. I want Chelsea to have a nice hot meal before she goes off to her first day of school here."

Delores nodded and left. Chelsea watched him warily, tears pooling in her eyes and streaking down her flushed cheeks.

"I won't go," she whispered, chin wobbling.

"Okay, let's talk about this." He held out his arms, but his daughter stood stiffly right where she was. Obviously she'd gotten her stubborn streak from him. "Why don't you want to go to school?"

"Because…"

"Not good enough. Because why?"

Huge eyes that could break a father's heart stared back at him. "Because I don't know…anybody…here." The words were punctuated by renewed sobs.

Ken sighed. "Shortstuff, the only way you'll make new friends here is by going to school. Remember when you went to school for the very first time? You didn't know anybody then either. First thing you knew you had lots of friends."

"That was different."

"Different how?"

Tiny shoulders heaved. "Mmm… Mmm… Mommy went with me."

His own tears clogging his throat, Ken reached for Chelsea and this time she didn't resist. She clung to him with all of her seven-year-old strength. "Sweetie, I'm going to go with you today. And I won't leave you there alone until you tell me it's okay. I promise."

She sniffed and regarded him distrustfully. "Really?"

"Absolutely."

"And if I want to come back home?"

He shook his head at that. "Sorry. That's not an option. So, how about it? Do we have a deal?"

"You won't go until I say so?" she said one more time.

"No. I promise."

She considered that thoughtfully, then finally nodded. "I guess that would be okay."

Two hours later, just as Ken had anticipated, Chelsea was caught up in the second grade class's activities and paying absolutely no attention to him. When it was time for a juice break and recess, she ran over and said with an air of grown-up nonchalance. "You can go now."

He grinned at her. "Having fun?"

"It's not like my old school, but it's okay, I guess."

He gave her a quick hug. "I'm glad. I'll see you this afternoon."

Not until he was walking back to his car did he finally allow himself a moment to savor a major parenting victory. If only he could solve the dilemma he was facing with Beth as easily.

The next week was hell. Just as Beth came to accept that Ken would rarely stay in the house while she was there, Beth slowly grew used to finding Chelsea peering at her from the doorway to Ken's office the minute she came in the door from school. As painful as it was, she came to expect the child to shadow her as she put the finishing touches on each room. Chelsea rarely said a word and neither did Beth. But Chelsea's apparent loneliness since her grandmother had returned to Washington spoke volumes. If she was making new friends at school, there was no sign of them at home. Ken had hired a housekeeper, but Chelsea seemed to distrust her even more than she did Beth.

Beth's heart ached every time she looked into Chelsea's sad, expectant eyes, but she steeled herself against the reaction. She would not lower her defenses. She would not love this child, who wielded such power over her father's life. She didn't dare.

The tantrums helped. They were frequent enough and disturbing enough to strengthen Beth's resolve. Those tantrums were just more demonstrative expressions of the same hateful behavior she'd experienced with Josh and Stephanie. She was sure if Chelsea could have run away from home, she would have. If she had been old enough to think of being sneakily spiteful, Beth was sure she would have done that, too.

Instead Chelsea's sabotage was less sophisticated and more open. She stole into the room whenever she sensed that Beth and Ken were sharing an all-too-rare quiet moment that excluded her. Not content that her presence alone was interruption enough, she usually managed to break something or spill something or demand attention in some other way that required an immediate response or punishment. Beth recognized that Ken was at his wit's end, but so was she. She'd bitten her tongue so often this past week, she was surprised the tip was still attached. It was ironic, too. Chelsea was trying to spoil a relationship that was already dead.

"Can I help?" Chelsea asked in a small voice after

watching Beth put the hooks into the drapes for the living room.

"Sure," Beth said, reluctant to include her, but just as uneasy with saying no. She couldn't bring herself to be mean to this child, no matter the cost to herself. Every time she looked into Chelsea's face, she saw the man she loved.

To her dismay, Chelsea settled right beside her, her little body snuggled close as she tried to mimic Beth's actions. Beth breathed in the little girl scent of her, the mix of shampoo and lotion and freshly ironed clothes. Her fingers suddenly became all thumbs as she fought to resist the urge to hug the child who so desperately needed to be reassured.

"Is this right?" Chelsea asked, her gray eyes fastened on Beth's face as her fingers fumbled with the hook.

"Exactly right," she answered.

"I got an *A* in school today," Chelsea confided. "My teacher said I'm the very best speller she's ever seen."

"That's wonderful! Your father will be really proud."

"Maybe he'll take me for pizza tonight."

"Maybe," Beth agreed.

"You could come, too," she said shyly. "If you want."

Beth's heart slammed against her ribs at the first tiny gesture of friendship Chelsea had ever offered. "We'll see," she said, her voice choked.

"Don't you like pizza?" Chelsea asked, studying her intently.

"It's not that."

Before she could explain, though, Chelsea's eyes filled with tears as she jumped up. "It's me, isn't it?

You just don't want to be with me. You're just like my mommy. She couldn't wait to leave me."

She moved so fast, Beth couldn't catch her. Her heart aching, she searched the house room by room, trying not to alarm the housekeeper in the process. Finally, downstairs again, she noticed that the back door was ajar.

At that point, sheer panic and instinct took over. Running outside, she followed the tiny footprints through the snow until she came to the pond. Chelsea was standing at the edge, her expression forlorn, tears still tracking down her cheeks. Without a coat, she was shivering violently.

Beth took her own jacket and wrapped it around her, then knelt down in front of her. "I'm sorry," she said softly. "I never, ever meant to make you think I didn't like you."

"But you don't, do you? You never want to be with me."

"Darling, it's far more complicated than that. And it doesn't have anything to do with you. It has to do with something that happened a long time ago."

Chelsea watched her with solemn eyes. "With another little girl?"

Beth nodded. "And a boy."

"Did you go away and leave them?"

The painful question cut right through her. "I did, but not because I didn't love them."

"Why did you go away, then?"

"Because they didn't love me," she finally admitted with a sigh. Before she could reveal any more to a child far too young to understand the details of what had happened, she added briskly, "Now, quick, let's get you back inside before you catch cold."

Chelsea tucked a hand in Beth's as they walked back to the house. "Beth?"

"What is it, sweetheart?"

"I really miss my mommy."

Tears stung Beth's eyes. "I know you do, but I'm sure you'll get to see her really, really soon. In the meantime, I know she misses you just as much as you miss her."

"I don't think so," Chelsea said with a resigned sigh. "She almost never, ever calls me." She turned a hopeful look on Beth. "Do you think maybe she's lost the phone number?"

"I'll bet that's it," Beth said. "Maybe your daddy can call her tonight and remind her. Would you like me to ask him to do that?"

"Would you?"

"I promise," she said.

Back inside, she made hot chocolate for the two of them and put some of the cookies Delores had baked on a plate. By then Chelsea's color was better and she had stopped shivering, but a familiar silence had fallen between the two of them. This time, though, Beth felt certain there was less tension in it.

That was the way they were when Ken came in.

"Hi, Daddy," Chelsea said as nonchalantly as if this was the scene he found every day when he came in. "Beth made hot chocolate. Want some?"

His gaze pinned on Beth's face, he nodded. "Hot chocolate sounds terrific. It's cold outside."

"I know. I ran out without my coat, but Beth came after me and she gave me hers."

Beth winced at the innocent revelation. "It's a long story."

"I'll bet." He looked at Chelsea. "Why don't you take your snack up to your room and watch TV for a little while before dinner."

When Chelsea had gone, he sat down across from Beth, his hands clenched, his expression grim.

"I think we'd better talk about it," he said.

"She was upset. She ran out without her coat. I found her right afterward. She couldn't have been out there more than five minutes."

"I don't care about that. Obviously, she's fine." His gaze captured hers and held. "I hate the distance between us. I hate the distance between you and Chelsea. Do you realize that this is the first time I have ever seen the two of you together?"

"We're here in the house almost every afternoon."

"But you're not talking. She tiptoes around you and you ignore her."

"I wasn't aware that I'd been hired as a baby-sitter," she said, her voice tight.

Ken sighed. "That's not the point and you know it. There is something about being around Chelsea that you find upsetting. Please tell me what it is." His gaze was unrelenting. "Please."

His voice was quiet, downright gentle in fact, but there was no mistaking his determination. Beth tried to evade that gaze, but he touched her chin and forced her to face him.

"What is this all about, Beth? Whatever it is, it can't be so terrible that you can't share it with me."

Maybe it was because her nerves were ragged from the days of tension. Maybe it was because she wanted so desperately for everything to be all right. Maybe it was because she genuinely believed what he was saying, that he would understand.

And so, she told him. About her marriage to Peter. About his two handsome children. And about her terrible failure to make it all work.

"They didn't just dislike me," she said, her eyes dry. She was sure there were no tears left to shed over the tragedy of it. "They hated me. They wanted their mother, not a poor substitute. No matter what I did, it was never good enough. I failed Peter and I failed them."

She faced him and injected a note of pure bravado into her voice. "So, as you can see, obviously I'm not anyone's idea of the perfect mother." She said it with a cavalier shrug, but Ken didn't seem to be buying her act.

"Oh, baby," he whispered, and pulled her close as a fresh batch of tears spilled down her cheeks and soaked his shirt. "Don't you see, that's nonsense. You're warm and generous and caring. Any child would be lucky to have you for a mother. Just look at what happened here this afternoon."

She sniffed. "Right. I upset Chelsea so badly she went tearing outside, where she could have caught pneumonia."

"She didn't look traumatized when I came home. How do you suppose that happened?"

"Hot chocolate can smooth over a lot."

"If that were all it took, wouldn't you have used that on your stepchildren?" he said dryly.

"I suppose so."

"Look, I'm sure Chelsea's behavior since her arrival

has done absolutely nothing to reassure you, but she's scared, too. She's afraid to reach out to someone who'll turn around and abandon her the way her mother did. I've probably been more tolerant than I should have been, but I assure you it won't be that way forever. I'm feeling my way as a single parent. It would make things a lot easier if I had you by my side, telling me if I'm making the right choices."

"I'm the last person to be giving anyone advice about parenting."

"It's not advice I want, so much as moral support."

"But Chelsea and I..." She held her hands up in a helpless gesture.

"I don't expect you and Chelsea to get along perfectly. Haven't you noticed that there are plenty of times when she and I don't get along worth a damn?"

"But you're her father."

"That doesn't come with guarantees or instructions." He tilted her chin up. "Try. Please. I know it's a risk. I know how fragile your self-confidence must be. But wouldn't the payoff be worth it?"

"Payoff," she repeated slowly.

"We might turn out to be a real family. That's what I want," he insisted. "More than anything."

A family, Beth repeated to herself. If she searched her heart, wasn't that what she really desperately wanted, as well?

Chapter 14

Delores had nailed it, Ken thought later that night. Once again his ex-mother-in-law had seen a situation with far clearer vision than his own. She had picked up on Beth's uneasiness around Chelsea immediately and labeled it anxiety rather than distaste. He'd been skeptical that a woman as strong as Beth could be controlled by fear of anything, especially a little girl. If only he'd listened to Delores, he might have solved this problem much sooner.

Still, now that he recognized that Beth's behavior was the result of something from her past, not dislike of Chelsea or children in general, he could do something about it. He could begin to reassure her that loving him and Chelsea would not be a repeat of the past.

Suddenly he felt free to allow his own growing feelings for her to flourish again, after days of trying to talk them out of existence. He had hated the sense of powerlessness her behavior had instilled in him. Now, at last, he was back in control.

Unfortunately, he doubted that Beth was going to be easily persuaded that her fears were groundless. Others had done that, had convinced her to ignore her instincts, and look what had happened to her first marriage. Now she would be a much tougher sell, much slower to believe that time could correct today's problems between Chelsea and any woman who wasn't her mother.

At the same time, he recognized that Chelsea could hardly be won over by a woman who wouldn't dare any overture that might be rebuffed. Given the nature of their fears, they might very well have faced a stalemate.

Fortunately, though, Ken had had a lot of experience at faking out defensive backs on some of the best teams in the NFL. Surely he could pull off a few sneaky maneuvers to allow one terrified lady and one pint-size hellion to discover what he already knew—they desperately needed each other.

And he needed them both, more and more with each passing day. The two of them had made his transition from star quarterback to private citizen an easy one. He had found all sorts of quiet satisfaction in raising his daughter, even when she was at her worst. He had found another sort of contentment entirely with Beth. Those discoveries made him more determined than ever to work things out. He was falling in love with her and he knew that what they had was based on a solid foundation, the kind of foundation that could last a lifetime.

The truth of it was, if he hadn't believed in his own

future with Beth with all his heart, he wouldn't have dared to set her and his daughter up for the eventual pain of another separation. His love, which had taken no one more by surprise than him, was growing stronger—strong enough to battle whatever lay ahead.

Over the next couple of weeks, Ken's campaign strategy was worthy of Super Bowl play. He had discovered on that fateful afternoon when Beth had finally revealed her painful past to him that she and Chelsea were far more likely to reach out to each other, if they weren't under his watchful eye.

He changed the housekeeper's hours, giving her most afternoons off. He suddenly found a dozen excuses to go into town every day about three o'clock, leaving Beth to welcome Chelsea home from school. After the first day or two, Beth no longer protested. The wariness began to fade.

Two or three times a week he suggested dinner, a movie, a shopping excursion. He made the suggestions to Chelsea, then casually extended the invitation to Beth, as well. She could hardly refuse with Chelsea's solemn gray eyes pinned on her. Ken sensed that with every passing day, Beth was less inclined to turn them down, that in fact she was beginning to look forward to sharing these times with them.

The weekdays, as a result of his careful timing and nonthreatening suggestions, were easy. It was weekend outings that required incredibly deft planning, especially as the holiday season approached and Christmas festivities began in earnest in Berry Ridge. Beth, it seemed, was involved in everything, quite possibly, he guessed, to keep the loneliness at bay.

At any rate, if he wanted to take the two of them out to a movie in a neighboring town, he had to be clever and quick about it. He discovered if he found an antique store in between and assured Beth that he really needed her input on some piece of furniture he'd spotted for the house, she was always more ready to accept. As a result, he spent hours during the week hunting down such stores and furniture and found, to his amazement, that it was fun. There was no way Beth could mistake his enthusiasm for guile.

Then, once they'd settled on whether to buy the chair or table or cabinet, it was easy enough to suggest that they go on to lunch and then a movie or perhaps Christmas shopping or a visit to Santa.

Pretty soon Beth was suggesting outings that Chelsea might enjoy—a visit to a woman who made quilts, an excursion to see apple cider pressed, a drive into Woodstock where there were four churchbells made by Paul Revere, a Christmas bazaar, an old-fashioned community potpie dinner in a neighboring town, a night of caroling.

He saw Beth slowly healing before his very eyes. She seemed to have an endless supply of patience for Chelsea's inquisitiveness. She no longer looked stung by an innocently sharp remark or a sullen expression. And he found in her courage yet another reason for his growing feelings for her.

As Beth's anxiety lessened, the bond between her and his daughter grew stronger each day. Giving them the space to find their own way, he rejoiced when Chelsea automatically slipped her mittened hand into Beth's. He took tremendous satisfaction when Beth instinctively knelt down and tucked Chelsea's scarf around her neck and buttoned her coat more tightly against the ever-more frigid air. Beth was, as he had always guessed, a nurturing woman, and now that side of her had a chance to flourish, surrounding his daughter in much-needed feminine warmth.

As the icy reserve began to thaw between the two females in his life, Ken might have felt left out of their laughter, jealous of their silly banter, envious of the quiet times they shared over hot chocolate and one of Chelsea's favorite books or puzzles.

Instead, he discovered that even when he was excluded, he was a sucker for their tender, warm rapport. He basked in their genuine enjoyment of the time they spent together. And as he closely observed this sexy, radiant, sensitive woman, his own hormones blazed hotter than the wood stove he'd installed in his kitchen.

Unfortunately, it was incredibly difficult to seduce a woman with a seven-year-old chaperon constantly along. He weighed the importance of the bond between Chelsea and Beth against his own needs and told himself he'd just have to keep sight of his goal, and take a lot of very cold showers.

He also had a plan that, with any luck, would bring an end to this self-enforced abstinence. He stood in the doorway of his den one night and watched Beth as she went over the last of the invoices. The house was essentially finished, the wood floors polished to a gleam, the molding repaired and painted, the drapes hung. He almost regretted that the happy chaos was over. He wondered if she felt the same way or if her sense of pride in her accomplishment made up for any regrets that she was through with her renovations of her beloved Grady place.

Ken smiled. She still called it that, correcting herself in midphrase with a rueful grin. To her, it would always be the Grady place, even if he could someday persuade her to call it home.

He looked up and caught her watching him.

"What are you smiling about?" she asked.

"You."

She sat back and regarded him warily. "I see. And what about me has you smiling?"

He shrugged. "I have no idea. I just like looking at you, I suppose." He gestured toward the invoices. "Just about done?"

"Yep. The last of the bills are paid. I told you you'd be settled before Christmas."

"The job's not quite over," he informed her.

"Oh?"

"We have holiday decorating to do and entertaining. I'm at a loss."

She shook her head. "Ken Hutchinson, you've never been at a loss in your life. Who are you trying to kid?"

"You don't believe me?" he said, injecting a wounded note into his voice.

"I don't believe you."

"Okay, take a Christmas tree, for instance. Where do I get one?"

"There's a small lot by town hall or you can go into the woods and cut one down."

"What do you do?"

"I dig one up, then replant it in my yard after the holiday."

"Ecology-minded. I like that. Where do we go?"

"We?"

"Sure. You don't expect me to do this on my own,

do you? We'll go on Saturday. Chelsea can come, too. She'll love it." He saw temptation written all over her face and knew that he had won yet another battle. "Eight o'clock?"

"Eight?" she said doubtfully.

"You know perfectly well you're up by dawn. We'll have breakfast first at Lou's," he said decisively. "Pancakes and warm maple syrup."

She laughed. "How do you manage to make food sound so seductive?"

"It's your wild imagination," he retorted. "First thing you know, you're picturing the two of us sharing those pancakes in bed."

"Now that is a thought," she admitted. Her voice was surprisingly and deliberately provocative and sent his pulse racing.

"Saturday," he repeated in a suddenly choked voice, then ducked out of the room before he was tempted to make love to her right there in the middle of his big, solid desk.

Beth had figured out what Ken was up to the first time he'd managed to lure her into accompanying him and Chelsea on some outing. She had clung to her resistance to his charms and his daughter's increasingly warm reception for days, but slowly she had given up fighting the longing she had to spend time with the two of them.

Each time, though, she swore would be the last. Though the number of successful, stress-free outings had mounted, there was always a nagging worry in the back of her mind that the next one would be a disaster. Chelsea might be accepting her as a friend, but that might be more by default than any real affection. What would happen if she feared that Beth was trying to take her mother's place? Beth was certain she knew the answer to that and it lurked on the fringes of her mind, spoiling any genuine joy she might have taken in the time she shared with Ken's precious daughter.

She found she was dreading the approaching holidays. No other time of year was more meant to be shared by families. Ken's determination to act as if that was what they were was as frightening as it was tempting.

This Christmas tree outing, for instance. It was just one more link in the emotional chain binding her to them. What would happen to her when the chain broke? It would be so much worse than last time, because over the past few weeks she had had a real taste of the promised sweetness of motherhood and the blessing of being loved—by father and child. It was more fulfilling than anything she had ever experienced or imagined.

There was no way to get out of the tree excursion, though. Every one of Ken's invitations was issued almost as a dare. He was asking her to take a risk. On him. On Chelsea. On the three of them. If he was willing to take such a dangerous chance, how could she do any less?

On Saturday morning, she walked to Lou's, wanting the quiet solitude to steel herself against the tender torment of the day ahead. Fresh snow had fallen overnight, blanketing the ground with a fluffy layer of white that caught the sun and glistened like a scattering of diamonds across soft, white velvet. Every shop window twinkled with Christmas lights and tempted with holiday decorations. Soft carols, piped over a loudspeaker system, broke the morning's silence. She stopped for a moment just to listen.

Oh, how she loved this town with its sense of community, its centuries' old traditions, its untainted beauty. Her growing feelings for Ken and for his daughter, only brought it all into sharper focus. This was a good place to raise a family, a good place to love, a good place to fulfill cherished dreams, a good place to grow old. Would all of that happen for her? Or would it slip away?

She looked up then and saw Ken waiting for her in front of Lou's bakery. He was leaning against the side of his car, his long legs crossed at the ankles, his arms folded across his middle as he watched her. Smiling, her heart suddenly light, she picked up her pace.

As she drew closer, she sniffed the air and, even from half a block away, she could smell the scent of fresh-baked cinnamon rolls, sizzling bacon and fresh-brewed coffee. As a lure, it was almost as powerful as the man waiting for her.

"A bit chilly for a leisurely stroll, don't you think?" he teased her.

"It's all in knowing how many layers to put on."

He grinned and reached for the top button of her jacket, drawing her close. "Too bad we're not someplace I can strip them off and count them."

She gave him her sassiest smile. "It is too bad, isn't it?"

He laughed as she swept past him and went inside. She spotted Chelsea seated in a back booth, already telling Lou what she wanted for breakfast. She scowled up at the two of them.

"I didn't think you were ever going to get here,"

she said, bouncing in her impatience to get the day under way.

Lou chuckled. "You two want coffee?"

"And food," Ken said. "We need lots of energy for the day we have planned."

"I hear you're going to find a Christmas tree."

"Two trees," Beth corrected. "One for me."

"And a really, really big one for me," Chelsea chimed in.

"I can't wait to see them."

"You'll have to come by on Christmas day," Ken said, surprising Beth. "We're going to have an open house from four to six."

Lou accepted readily, then went off to fill their order.

"An open house?" Beth said when she'd gone. "Sounds like a lot of work."

He grinned. "That's why I'll need your help."

"How will it look if you and I throw this party together?"

"As if we're a couple," he said readily. "Which we are."

"Oh?"

"Sure. Everyone in town knows that."

Unfortunately, Beth knew that was true. Gillie had been the first to pronounce them that when Beth had finally seen her elusive friend again. Invitations issued to the two of them had been arriving in her mailbox for the last week. It seemed a little late to start protesting the obvious. Surely she could get through the holidays before sitting down and explaining to Ken one more time why there was no future for them. He'd been lulled into a false sense of complacency by this détente between her and Chelsea. It wouldn't last, though. She knew that with everything in her.

But she did have today and tomorrow and the next ten days or so beyond that, days she could cram with memories. She smiled as she gazed into Chelsea's excited face and listened to her description of the tree they were going to find and where it was going to sit and how it should be decorated.

An hour later as they were trudging through the snow with Chelsea atop her father's shoulders, Beth realized that her resolve wasn't worth spit. Her defenses were toppling more rapidly than a house of cards in a stiff breeze. She wanted what she had found with Ken and Chelsea, wanted it with a desperation that she had fought and fought, all to no apparent avail.

Ken began the caroling as they ventured up and down the rows in an area that had been specifically forested for Christmas trees. Soon they were all singing, their voices wildly off-key, the words made up half the time when none of them could recall the right verses. They went from *Jingle Bells* to *Silent Night,* from *Rudolph, the Red-Nosed Reindeer* to *Joy to the World,* an eclectic mix of holiday songs that captured the season's true spirit. Beth thought she might very well burst from sheer happiness.

After begging to be allowed down in the snow, Chelsea ran up and down the rows, picking first one tree and then another, while Beth and Ken followed at a more leisurely pace. Beth spotted the perfect tree first, a dream Christmas tree with wide, sweeping branches that would hold an array of glittering ornaments and blinking colored lights. It was too big for her house by far, but in Ken's...

She stopped in front of it, just as Chelsea ran up, wide-eyed, and halted beside her. When a tiny mittened hand slipped into her own, Beth thought her heart might very well burst from all of the unexpected emotions crowding in.

"It's beautiful," Chelsea said, clearly awestruck.

"The prettiest tree I've ever seen," Beth agreed.

"It'll take up the whole living room," Ken grumbled, one hand resting on Chelsea's shoulder, the other on Beth's. "We'll have to take a foot off the top and take down the door, just to get it into the house."

"Daddy, please," Chelsea said.

Beth just looked at him imploringly. She was as determined as Chelsea and apparently Ken could see it. And he was clearly in a benevolent sort of mood, ready to grant wishes.

"Oh, for goodness' sake, I'll go tell the man this is the one we want," he grumbled, but Beth noticed he was grinning as he walked away.

They put the huge fir tree on top of Ken's SUV, then found Beth's smaller tree and put it in the back. They stopped by her house long enough to leave her tree propped up beside the back door.

"Do you have enough decorations?" she asked them. "I might have extras."

"We have plenty of lights," Ken said. "And I think I put one big box of ornaments in the attic."

"And the angel for the top," Chelsea said. "I saw it after we moved."

"It's a big tree," Beth warned.

"Which is why I bought popcorn and bags of cranberries," Ken informed her. "While I get this monster put up, you and Chelsea can start stringing them."

"I've never done that, Daddy."

"Neither have I," Beth said.

Ken glanced at her, amazement written all over his face. "But it's tradition."

"Whose?" she grumbled. "In California, the decorator did the tree and I guarantee you there were no strings of popcorn or cranberries involved."

There were so many things she'd missed in a household that had seemed to have everything. Some part of her, though, had always known what Christmas should be like, what families were supposed to share. Her parents, while giving her everything material, had offered her nothing of themselves. She knew that was why motherhood had mattered so much to her, why she had so desperately wanted to get it right. And why she had been so devastated when she hadn't.

"Then making these decorations will be a new experience for all of us," Ken said cheerfully. "An old-fashioned, New England Christmas."

Two hours later Beth had jabbed her fingers with a needle more times than she cared to recall. She had bitten back a stream of curses. But she couldn't help getting a warm feeling deep inside whenever she glanced at the frown of concentration on Chelsea's face as she labored over the lengthening strand of deep red cranberries or the pleasure in Ken's eyes as he watched the two of them.

They stopped at midafternoon for soup and sandwiches, then got back to work. At five they realized the box of elegant, expensive decorations they'd brought from Washington, even with the incongruous addition of several strands of cranberry and popcorn, was woefully inadequate.

"There's still time to get to town before the stores close," Ken said. "Let's go. We can have dinner afterward at the inn, then finish up here."

At the craft store, Chelsea found charming handmade wooden ornaments that were a startling contrast to the fragile glass balls they had brought to Vermont with them. In her delight over each one, it was obvious she didn't care that the tree would be a mismatched hodgepodge. Nor did Ken seem to care that he was spending a fortune on his daughter's whimsical choices.

"You haven't chosen any," he said to Beth after Chelsea had been at it for a while.

"It's your tree, yours and Chelsea's. You should have what you want."

He frowned at the deliberate distancing. "It's *our* tree," he insisted.

Beth shrugged. It wasn't worth arguing over and spoiling an otherwise perfect day.

He grabbed her hand and led her to the display of ornaments. "Pick something out," he insisted, his jaw set.

"Ken," she began, but the protest died on her lips as she read his expression. She had seen one just as stubborn on Chelsea's face often enough. "Okay," she finally agreed.

She fingered the wooden, hand-painted drummer boys, the miniature white doves, the colorful musical instruments, all carved by local craftsmen. She admired them all.

But it was a handblown glass angel that she loved. The glass was as fragile as a snowflake and just as cool to the touch. Pale traces of color had been blown into the piece, making it shimmer like a rainbow. It was meant for the top of the tree and she knew that Ken and Chelsea already had their angel, so she put it back, trying to hide her longing to own the lovely keepsake ornament.

She reached for a charming wooden nutcracker instead. "This one."

Ken shook his head. "I don't think so."

"You told me to choose."

"I know. And you did," he said, picking up the angel and handing it to the clerk. "We'll take this one, too." His gaze caught Beth's and held. "It will always remind us of our first Christmas together."

When she would have said something to counter the sentimental thought, he touched a finger to her lips to silence her. "Always," he insisted.

Chapter 15

With the promise of *always* ringing in her ears, Beth sat through their dinner at the inn in a daze. She didn't want to believe in the future. She didn't dare.

And yet Ken seemed so certain. Perhaps he believed enough for both of them.

But as hard as she tried to have faith, she couldn't help remembering how strong Peter's conviction had been, how certain he'd been that Stephanie and Josh would be just fine once they were married, and how terribly, terribly wrong he had turned out to be. How could she ignore her own experience? What would it take to make a believer of her? More than Ken's love, that was clear enough. This time she needed the love of the child, as well. She needed Chelsea's love.

None of them savored the delicious meal. Chelsea was too anxious to finish decorating the tree. She hadn't stopped chattering about the new ornaments since they'd sat down. Ken's attention was focused too completely on Beth. And Beth was lost in her own tumultuous thoughts. They all said no to dessert and were on the way home by seven-thirty.

The phone was ringing as they stepped through the door. "I'll get it," Chelsea said, racing for it.

A moment later a smile of pure delight broke across her face. "Mommy!"

Beth stopped in her tracks, her heart thudding dully in her chest. She tried to tell herself that the child's exuberance was only natural. She reminded herself that she had never intended to replace Pam Hutchinson in Chelsea's heart. She had known all along the folly of trying to fight a child's natural loyalty to a beloved parent. But there was no preventing the unexpected pain that knifed through her.

She glanced at Ken and saw that her dismay was mirrored in his eyes. No doubt he was worried, as she was, about the disruption the call was bound to cause in the insular world they had managed to create for the three of them during these past weeks when Pam had been silent.

"Guess what, Mommy, we're decorating our tree," Chelsea was saying. "Are you going to come to see it? I asked Santa to bring you home. I told him that was the present I wanted more than anything."

Beth swallowed hard against the bitter knot that suddenly seemed to be choking her. There was so much hope in Chelsea's voice, so much love still for the woman who had abandoned her. And that was as it should be, she told herself, as long as Pam didn't dash those hopes so that the healing process had to begin all over again. At seven, Chelsea didn't have the resilience to take another disappointment in stride. In years to come, she might, but not yet. And Chelsea's anguish would ultimately hurt all of them.

But even as Beth watched, Chelsea's face crumpled and her shoulders sagged. "But, Mommy, it's Christmas!" she protested, sounding pitiful. "You have to come. I've made you a present and everything."

Ken sucked in a deep breath and crossed the room, practically snatching the phone from Chelsea's hand. Beth saw the tears gathering in Chelsea's eyes. She knelt down and held out her arms, but Chelsea turned away, leaving her feeling totally bereft and furious with this thoughtless woman whose daughter's needs didn't seem to matter at all.

Not that she had wanted Pam to come to Vermont, she was forced to admit honestly. But for Chelsea's sake, she would have tried to find a way to make it work. Now, putting her own feelings aside, she said, "Chelsea, what did your mommy say?"

"She's not coming."

The reply wasn't unexpected, but Beth felt her heart wrench at Chelsea's obvious distress. What kind of mother would turn her back on her own child at Christmas? she wondered. While she ached to share the joy of waking up on Christmas morning to watch Chelsea's excitement, the woman who had the right to be there refused to come.

"I'm so sorry," she said softly as Ken concluded his hushed exchange with his ex-wife and hung up. "But we'll have a good time. Your daddy's here. Your grandmother's coming and your Uncle Claude and Aunt Harriet. I'll be here."

Chelsea faced her angrily. "I don't want them. I don't want you. I want my mommy," she shouted, and ran upstairs, her feet pounding on the steps as if to emphasize each bitter, hurtful word she'd screamed.

Beth took one step after her, only to have a grim-faced Ken stop her. "I'd better talk to her," he said. He reached out and touched her cheek. "She didn't mean it, you know. She's angry about Pam and taking it out on the rest of us."

"I know," Beth said wearily. She had been through it all before.

Taking off her coat, because she didn't know what else to do, she went into the living room and began unwrapping the new ornaments. She had them all spread out on the carpet when Ken and Chelsea finally came back downstairs. Chelsea's pinched little face was heartbreakingly streaked with tears.

Without even looking at Beth, she methodically picked up the ornaments and put them on the branches. Beth glanced toward Ken, but his thunderous expression didn't invite conversation. She sank back against the pillows on the sofa and felt the wonderful spirit they'd shared earlier in the day slowly evaporate until she had to wonder if it had been real at all. This, she decided bleakly, was reality for a stepfamily.

At last it was time to put the angel on the top of the tree. Chelsea stood in the middle of the floor, the two ornaments side by side in front of her—the traditional one and the brand-new one Ken had bought for Beth to mark their first Christmas together. Beth wondered which Chelsea would choose, as if that choice carried a significance that went far beyond the mere selection of an adornment for the treetop. She realized she was holding her breath as Chelsea's hand hovered above the two angels. When she reached at last for the glass angel, Beth's breath eased out.

Chelsea picked up the fragile ornament, held it for no longer than a heartbeat, then dropped it with obvious deliberation, not on the carpet, but on the wood floor, where it shattered into hundreds of tiny shards of glass.

"Oh, no," Beth cried, then fell silent as tears stung her eyes.

"Chelsea!" Ken shouted furiously. "Go to your room."

Stunned, Beth stared through her tears at the bits of glass and felt as if they represented the shattered remains of her broken heart. Finally she knelt and began to pick them up. She couldn't bring herself to look at the little girl who hadn't budged despite her father's angry order.

"Chelsea, you heard me," Ken insisted. "Go to your room this instant."

"No. I won't," she said, grabbing the other angel and clutching it tightly. Tears tracked down her forlorn face.

"Why would you do something like this?" he said, sounding more perplexed than furious.

Beth could have told him the answer. Chelsea was holding on to the past in the only way she knew how. She was rejecting a future that included Beth and not her mother.

As if to confirm it, Chelsea said, "I want this one on the tree. This one is ours. Mommy bought it."

So, Beth thought with a sigh of regret, that was that. Pam would always be there among them. She had known it from the outset, but as recently as a few hours ago she had almost dared to believe they could make it work. The shattered angel proved otherwise.

Holding back her own tears, she stood. "I think I'd better go."

"You don't have your car," Ken protested. "Wait a minute, until we settle this, and I'll take you."

"No," she said sharply. "I'll call Gillie. She'll come."

"Beth, please."

She shook her head. "I'll be fine. Chelsea needs you."

She made the call to Gillie, pulled on her coat and went outside to wait, quietly but ever-so-firmly shutting the door on her dreams.

Ken bit off a curse as he heard the quiet click of the front door. Suddenly he saw all of his plans for marriage going up in smoke. Chelsea was standing in front of him, her whole body shuddering with pent-up sobs. She turned frightened eyes on him.

"I'm sorry, Daddy," she whispered on a broken sob. "I'm sorry. I didn't mean to make Beth go away."

He held out his arms and gathered her close. "I'm sorry, too, baby. I'm sorry, too."

Eventually the storm of tears ended and Chelsea gazed at him sorrowfully. "Is Beth mad at me?"

"What do you think?"

"I'm sorry I broke her angel."

"Why did you?"

"Because I was mad."

"At Beth?"

"No," she said in a small voice. "At Mommy."

"Maybe tomorrow you can call Beth and tell her that."

Chelsea's expression brightened a little. "I have my allowance saved. I could buy her another angel."

He grinned. He knew her piggy bank didn't hold nearly enough to pay for the angel. He also knew that it was incredibly important that she was willing to make the gesture. "I think that might make her very happy."

"Maybe I'll give it to her on Christmas morning."

"Good idea," Ken agreed. He was reassured that Chelsea truly was learning to accept Beth and that this was simply a minor setback. But he wondered how the devil he would ever talk Beth into coming back into their house again. Just this once, he had a feeling his fate might very well be in his daughter's hands.

First thing in the morning, Chelsea brought the portable phone to him and asked him to dial Beth's number. Unfortunately, it rang for quite some time without an answer. Even her answering machine didn't pick up. She had retreated from the world, from them.

"You can try again later," he reassured Chelsea, whose disappointment was no greater than his own.

They spent the morning putting up garlands of evergreen, then went into town to buy another angel, which Chelsea awkwardly wrapped herself and put under the tree. Every hour or so they tried Beth again, all to no avail. Ken had a hunch she had the phone unplugged and the answering machine turned off deliberately.

It was late afternoon when the brainstorm hit him. He made a couple of calls, made a thermos of hot chocolate, tucked the engagement ring he'd bought a few days earlier into his pocket and bundled up Chelsea. He'd been thinking for weeks that Christmas would be the perfect time to propose, but somehow tonight seemed right.

"Where are we going, Daddy?"

"You'll see."

By the time they reached Roger Killington's, the bank president had hitched a team of horses to the restored sleigh that Ken had asked to store in his barn.

"Perfect night for a sleigh ride," Roger said. "You going to pick up Beth?"

"I'm going to try," Ken said.

Roger laughed at his grim tone. "Good luck."

"Believe me, I'll need it."

Chelsea was so excited about riding in the sleigh, it was all he could do to keep her seated beside him. They glided across the snow, following a stream of moonlight. The bells on the reins jingled a merry tune that had him grinning with anticipation. This had to charm the socks right off her. What woman could resist a romantic sleigh ride that was capped off with a proposal?

Apparently Beth had heard the bells—or else Roger had called to warn her—because she was waiting on her front porch when they pulled up outside.

"Go tell her you're sorry," Ken whispered to Chelsea. "She won't come with us unless you do."

Chelsea shot him a frightened look, but with an incredible display of pint-size bravado she slid down and scampered off across the snow. Ken couldn't hear what she said, but Beth knelt down and pulled her into a tight hug. He considered that a good sign. The best, in fact.

He walked over to join them. "Care to go for a sleigh ride with us? You promised, remember?"

Beth's gaze shifted from Chelsea to him, then moved on to the sleigh. "Is that the one you bought at the auction?" she inquired, amazement written all over her face.

"That's the one. Isn't it a beauty?"

Taking Chelsea's hand, she crossed over to the sleigh. The man Beth had hired to do the restoration had done it exactly as he'd envisioned. The runners glistened. The sleigh was shiny with new paint and gold trim. The seats had been upholstered with soft black leather. A bright red wool blanket was draped across the wide seat.

"I never would have believed it," Beth said. "It's like something from a Christmas card."

"A Currier and Ives print," he agreed.

"And Mr. Killington loaned us the horses," Chelsea chimed in. "They're gray. He says I can come over and he'll teach me to ride sometime. You know what else? He has cows. He showed them to me. And he says he has a granddaughter who's just my age. She's going to come for Christmas."

"That's right," Beth said. "Her name is Melanie. I think you'll really like her."

Chelsea's expression sobered. "Do you think she'd be my friend? I don't have any friends here yet, not like at home. My friends there came over to play. Here it's too far."

"I think she would love to be your friend. And my friend Gillie has a little girl who's in your class at school. Her name is Jessie."

Chelsea's expression brightened. "I know Jessie. She's really fun. You know her?"

"Very well. Maybe you could have a tea party for them on Christmas day when your daddy has his open house."

Chelsea's eyes widened as she looked up at him hopefully. "Can I, Daddy?"

"If Beth will help you. I'm afraid I don't know much about tea parties."

"Will you, Beth? Will you? We could have little sandwiches and cookies and ice cream and candy."

Ken gave an exaggerated groan, but his gaze was locked on Beth. Chelsea's request seemed to have gotten around her defenses again. Trying to keep the mood light, he said, "Dear Heaven, and I don't even know the dentist in town yet."

Beth grinned at him. "You will. In the meantime, Chelsea and I will try to come up with a slightly less sugary menu."

"Does that mean you'll help?" Chelsea demanded.

There was an instant's hesitation that had Ken holding his breath, then she nodded. "I would love to help," she agreed.

"Good, then that's settled," Ken said in a rush to conclude the deal before she could change her mind. "Now button up that coat and climb aboard. I can't wait to try this thing out and see if it's as romantic as I figured it would be."

He pinned his gaze on Beth as he said it and watched the color rise in her cheeks. He held out his hand to help her into the sleigh. Chelsea had already managed to climb in and was settled in the middle of the seat. He frowned at her. "Over, little one."

"But I want to sit next to you and Beth."

He caught Beth's grin and realized that his scheme had just gone up in smoke. So much for romance. Chelsea probably held the key to his capturing Beth's heart and holding it, anyway.

When his two ladies were settled, he took the reins in hand and guided the horses toward the open field behind Beth's house. For the next two hours they glided across the moonlit landscape, drinking hot chocolate and once again fracturing a long list of carols with their off-key voices and improvised words.

"If we don't get inside soon, our frostbite will be decidedly unromantic," Beth finally warned, her cheeks rosy and her eyes sparkling.

She looked, Ken thought, radiant. More, she appeared to be contented. If nothing else, this outing had washed away the shadows caused by Chelsea's behavior the day before.

"Come with me to drop the sleigh off and I'll drive you home afterward, okay?" he suggested, thinking of the diamond ring that was practically burning a hole in his pocket.

She nodded.

Ken slid his arm across his sleepy daughter and captured Beth's gloved hand in his own. "Thank you for coming tonight."

"I wouldn't have missed it."

A few minutes later as they returned to Roger's, he came out in the yard to greet them. At the sight of Beth, the older man grinned. "I see he talked you into going out. The man might make a New Englander yet. Doesn't seem to care that the temperature's heading for zero and more snow's expected any minute now."

Ken plucked a couple of foot warmers from the floor of the sleigh, along with the now-empty thermos. "The key is preparation."

Roger laughed. "I'd say the warmers and the hot chocolate didn't have much to do with it. I'd say there's more heat in the way you two look at each other."

Ken watched Beth's face flame and laughed along

with Roger. "There's some truth to that," he said, starting to lead the horses back to the barn.

"I'll take them," Roger offered. "You run along. Your girl there looks as if she's asleep on her feet and I think you and Beth have better things to do than stabling my horses."

Again, Ken's thoughts went to the ring in his pocket. "Just this once," he agreed.

"Merry Christmas," Roger called after them as they made their way to the car.

"Merry Christmas!" Ken called back. "We'll see you on Christmas afternoon. Chelsea's anxious to meet your granddaughter, so be sure to bring her along."

"Right, son. You drive carefully."

Turning onto the road a few minutes later, Ken headed toward his house. Beth glanced over at him. "I thought you were taking me home first."

"Chelsea needs to get to bed."

"But once she's there, you can't leave to take me home."

He kept his gaze level. "I know," he said quietly. "Stay tonight."

"Ken…" she began, but the protest never went any further.

"If you really insist, I'll turn around," he offered.

"I suppose… I suppose it will be okay," she said. Suddenly she grinned. "After all, there are plenty of bedrooms there. I should know. I decorated every one of them."

"You won't be staying in a guest room," he countered.

She settled back against the seat of the car, a half

smile on her lips. "We'll see," she said. "A man should never get too sure of himself."

The deliberate taunt stirred his blood. "You should never challenge a desperate man."

She faced him, her expression all innocence. "Why is that?"

"It just makes us all the more determined to get our way."

"How fascinating," she said. "I can hardly wait to see you try."

If Chelsea hadn't been in the car, Ken would have started trying right then and there. He knew for a fact how quickly he could make Beth's pulse race, how easily he could set off a trembling that scrambled through her entire body. The more she resisted, the more fun it was to sneak past her defenses.

He sent her a look that he hoped spoke volumes about his intentions. Her response was a sassy grin that made his entire body tighten with need. Right now, he figured it was a toss-up which one of them was better at the game he'd foolishly initiated.

He carried Chelsea inside and headed up the stairs with her. At the top, she woke up. "Are we home?"

"Yep. Change into your nightgown and hop into bed."

"But I haven't had my bath," she protested sleepily.

"You don't need one tonight."

"But I always take a bath before I go to bed."

Ken thought of the woman waiting downstairs for him. "Just this once, your bath can wait until morning," he assured Chelsea. "Come on. Into your nightgown and into bed."

"Is Beth here?"

"She's downstairs."

"I want her to read me a story."

Ken barely contained a groan. "Sweetie, you'll be asleep before she reads the first paragraph."

"I always have a bedtime story, Daddy. You know that," she insisted stubbornly.

Sighing deeply, he finally relented, mainly because he knew Beth would be pleased by the request. "I'll get her, but you'd better be all tucked in when I get back."

"Okay."

He called to Beth from the top of the stairs. When she appeared in the foyer below, he said, "Chelsea wants you to read her a bedtime story."

A smile of absolute pleasure spread across her face. She looked so delighted, Ken was glad he'd broken down and asked. She practically took the steps two at a time, though it was clear she was trying to contain her enthusiasm.

"What book does she want me to read? Does she have a favorite?" She looked up at him worriedly. "What if I'm no good at this?"

"Didn't you ever read to your stepchildren?"

"They were too old."

"Well, take it from me, the technique is less important than just showing up. Chelsea loves this ritual. I couldn't talk her out of it."

"I'm glad you didn't," Beth admitted.

Inside Chelsea's room, he stood back and watched as Beth and his daughter chose a book from the dozens on Chelsea's shelves.

"Little Women," Beth said, rubbing her hand over the embossed binding. "Oh, how I loved this when I was a little girl."

"You've read it?" Chelsea asked, her astonishment plain.

"Over and over," Beth admitted.

"Will you read it to me? All of it?"

"It's a big book and you're very sleepy."

"We don't have to finish tonight. You could read it to me every night," Chelsea said, yawning as she scrambled under the covers.

Beth pulled them up under her chin, then settled into the chair beside the bed and began to read. As Ken had anticipated, her voice quickly lulled Chelsea to sleep, but still she read on as if just being there brought her joy. He couldn't bring himself to cut her off.

Finally, when the chapter ended, she closed the book and glanced his way. Putting the book aside, she leaned down and kissed Chelsea's cheek and smoothed her hair away from her face. "Sleep well," she whispered, then joined Ken in the hallway.

"I told you you'd do fine," he said. "You made her very happy."

"Not nearly as happy as she made me. If only…" Her voice trailed off.

"Stop that," he told her, silencing her with a kiss. "*If only* is a very sad phrase. There are only certainties in our future."

She smiled, but there was no mistaking the regret in her eyes. "If only…" she began, mocking him. "If only that were true."

"We can make it true," he told her, leading her into the living room where the lights twinkling on the tree provided the only illumination. When she was curled up at the end of the sofa, he settled himself beside her and drew in a deep breath. Her suddenly wary expression wasn't helping matters.

"Beth, you know how I feel about you," he began.

"Ken, don't," she whispered, touching a finger to his lips. "It won't work and you know it."

"No," he insisted, taking her hand, brushing a kiss across the knuckles, then holding it tightly. "Listen to me, please. If I haven't told you in words how much I love you, then I hope you've seen it in the way I am when I'm with you. I'm at peace with myself and, believe me, contentment is something I never expected to find when I moved here. You make me want to look ahead, not back."

He looked into her dismayed eyes and nearly stopped. Instead he hurried on. "You would make me extremely happy if you would agree to become my wife." He pulled the velvet box from his pocket, flipped it open to reveal a stunning diamond and held it out.

She didn't take it. She barely even looked at it. Suddenly his heart seemed to still and then outright panic set in. She was going to turn him down, he realized as his heart thudded dully in his chest.

Finally she glanced at the ring, then at the precariously tilting angel on the top of the Christmas tree. Pam's angel. Her expression filled with dismay and Ken cursed his decision to propose to her in the very room where Chelsea had so recently rejected her.

He studied her face and wished he had done things differently. Gazing at last directly into her troubled eyes, he thought he saw longing. Longing and dread.

In that moment he realized that the dread would win. All of her doubts hadn't been erased. Even a blind man should have been able to tell that. Even a fool would have had sense enough to wait. He also saw now that no matter how much she loved him, no matter how much she loved Chelsea, she would never agree to marry him until his daughter gave them her wholehearted blessing, as well.

That fragile glass angel, too recently shattered, stood between them as staunchly as a wall made of stone.

Chapter 16

Ken was at a loss. How was he going to convince Beth that Chelsea would be happy about their marriage? She would never just take his word for it. She might not even take Chelsea's word. It might require more solid proof, more bedtime stories, more spontaneous, similarly trusting gestures on his daughter's part. In time those would add up, but Ken was impatient. He desperately wanted to find a way to prod things along.

He sat downstairs long after Beth had gone up to sleep in one of the guest rooms, alone, refusing to even consider his company beneath the pile of down comforters. He considered a dozen schemes to charm or seduce her, then dismissed them. It was past time for schemes, charm or seduction. Only honesty and straightforward actions would accomplish the results he wanted.

Ken thought he knew how Chelsea had come to feel

about Beth, but it was clear that Beth didn't trust her own assessment of the child's feelings. An image of that shattered angel came back to haunt him.

And then he was struck by the realization that a replacement, bought with nickels and dimes and a little parental monetary assistance, and wrapped with loving if inept hands, was sitting right under the tree. Would it be enough? Would that send a message to Beth as nothing else had?

Finally, a plan beginning to form in his mind, he climbed the stairs. Hesitating outside the door to the guest room, he sighed and moved on to the beautifully decorated but incredibly lonely master suite. Despite what she thought when she chose the room down the hall, he knew that Beth would be in that king-size bed with him tonight. He would feel her presence, ache for her, as if she were physically right beside him.

Sure enough, no sooner had his head hit the pillow than his imagination went wild. He pictured her pale skin touched by moonlight, the tips of her breasts hardening beneath his touch, her legs wrapping around him as her hips rose to meet his. His body throbbed under the vivid spell she had cast over his senses.

"Damn," he muttered, cursing her for a passionate witch.

He could see her laughing at the curse, taunting him to come closer, closer, and then holding him at bay. He moaned and buried his head under a pillow, as if that would keep out the images.

It didn't. He was still tossing and turning, tormented by a restless, unfulfilled longing when dawn broke on what he knew was going to be the most important day of his entire life.

* * *

Beth slipped downstairs on the morning following Ken's proposal and made yet another desperate call to Gillie.

"This is getting to be a habit," her friend said fifteen minutes later when she had pulled up in front of the house and Beth was in the car. "I wonder if I should charge taxi rates."

"You owe me," Beth reminded her curtly. "I would never have gotten involved with the man in the first place, if you hadn't neglected to tell me that Ken had a daughter."

"I know. I thought once the two of you got to know each other it really wouldn't matter. I figured the kind of disaster you'd been through with Peter couldn't possibly happen a second time." Gillie regarded her with obvious regret. "I'm sorry. How many times do I have to tell you that?"

"I'll let you know when you can stop," Beth said dryly.

Gillie glanced away, but not before Beth caught her smile.

"Are we going for coffee?" Gillie asked.

"Might as well, unless you have to get home to take the kids to school."

"Daniel said he'd get them there this morning." She glanced at Beth. "Would it be considered extremely indelicate of me to point out that a woman sneaking out of a man's house at dawn does not seem like a woman who's protesting too much over the state of their affair?"

"There is no affair," Beth said bleakly. "Not anymore, anyway."

"But you stayed there last night."

"In a guest room."

Gillie shook her head as if to clear it. "Maybe this better wait until I have coffee."

Beth scowled at her. "I can almost guarantee it won't make any more sense then."

"Let's just see about that," Gillie said, pulling into a space in front of Lou's bakery. "Not another word until I have caffeine pumping through my veins."

Beth would have let the conversation lag a whole lot longer than that, but the instant her friend had her coffee and a heavily frosted cinnamon bun, Gillie said, "Okay, what's going on?"

Beth gave her the short version, which included only the call from Pam, the deliberately shattered angel, and Ken's proposal.

"I see," Gillie said slowly. She shook her head. "No, I don't see, at all. He loves you. He proposed to you. Chelsea apologized. What do you want? If you're waiting for a guarantee carved in stone that nothing like this will ever happen again, forget it. It will. Kids fling hateful words at their birth parents, too, whenever things don't suit them."

Beth regarded her with skepticism. "Jessie and Daniel Jr. have never said they hated you."

"Jessie told me just last week she hated me and would never speak to me again," Gillie countered.

"Why?" Beth asked, shocked.

"Because I wouldn't let her wear her shorts and a T-shirt to school. She didn't want to hear that it was below freezing outside."

Beth waved it off. "But that's just plain silly. Of course she didn't mean it."

"At the time she meant it. And when she said it, it hurt," Gillie admitted. "But over the course of a lifetime, it was an insignificant, meaningless bit of rebellion. I suspect I'll hear it again and again, especially when she wants to date, wear makeup and take the car."

"What about Daniel Jr.?" Beth asked. The preschooler was the most placid child she'd ever seen. She couldn't imagine him getting riled up enough to hate anything. He'd never even splattered his baby food in protest over the abominable taste.

"We exchanged several heated words during potty training," Gillie said, grinning at her.

Beth sighed. "You think I'm making too much out of all this."

"No. Given your past, I'd say you are being sensibly cautious." Her gaze turned serious. "Do you love him?"

"Yes."

"Do you love Chelsea?"

Beth grinned ruefully. "Most of the time."

"Will giving them up now hurt any less than giving them up if it doesn't work out?"

"Probably not," she admitted.

"Nothing of value in this life comes without risks," Gillie observed. "You could wait around for some bachelor who's never been married, who doesn't have kids, and then discover that he's still tied to Mama's apron strings. It's hard to find anyone our age who doesn't come without some sort of emotional baggage. You included, I might point out. Ken knows what you've been through. Isn't he making a real effort to prove that it won't be the same this time? Isn't he disciplining Chelsea? Hasn't he done everything in his power to build the bond between the two of you?"

Beth thought of all the engineered meetings, of all the space he'd given to her and Chelsea, putting his own desires on a back burner for the sake of a long-term relationship. "He's been wonderful," she admitted.

"Not like Peter?"

"Nothing at all like Peter," she agreed, and suddenly she could feel hope blossoming again. Ken was infinitely wiser than Peter. He had the patience to mediate, the strength to discipline, the determination to find answers rather than to place blame. She smiled as relief and a sudden buoyant optimism sighed through her. "Thank you."

"Does that mean I should start dieting so I can fit into a dress suitable for a fancy wedding?"

Beth shook her head. "Start looking for one you can wear as matron of honor."

Right up until Christmas Eve, Ken worked on his plan. He'd been dismayed when he'd realized that Beth had slipped out of the house the morning after his proposal, but then he'd decided it was for the best. It would give him time to do it right the next time. He wanted the time, the setting, everything working in his favor. What could be better than Christmas morning?

He waited until he and Chelsea were exiting Christmas Eve services to approach Beth. The smile she turned on him was just a little uncertain and yet there was an unmistakable air of serenity about her. He wondered what that was all about. He could only pray that it would prove beneficial for achieving his goal.

"Merry Christmas," he said quietly.

"Merry Christmas."

"Guess what?" Chelsea chimed in. "Santa Claus is

coming tonight." A worried frown suddenly puckered her brow. "He wouldn't come while we're not there, would he, Daddy?"

"Nope. He makes his rounds in the middle of the night, when good little boys and girls are sound asleep."

Chelsea reached for his hand and tugged. "Then let's hurry. I want to go to sleep, so Santa can come."

"In just a minute. I need to ask Beth something." He turned back to her. "Will you join us in the morning? We would really like you there when we open presents."

"Please come," Chelsea chimed in.

Ken was grateful for the spontaneous accord. He knew the invitation would be more likely to be successful if it clearly came from both of them.

Beth's eyes sparkled. "I would love to. What time?"

"The earlier the better. I'm not sure how long after dawn I can contain Chelsea."

"Then I'll be there at dawn," she agreed.

As she walked away, Ken uttered a sigh of relief. So far, so good. He wasn't about to kid himself, though. The hardest part was yet to come.

On Christmas morning Ken had coffee perking by 6:00 a.m. This was one year when his impatience outpaced Chelsea's. He'd already showered and dressed. He'd turned on the tree lights, built a fire, and played some music on low, filling the downstairs with carols.

Every five minutes he paced to the bottom of the stairs to listen for Chelsea, then walked back to the window to peer out into the darkness, hoping to see Beth's car. He wanted Chelsea downstairs first, all dressed and ready for their guest. In another five minutes, he'd go up and wake her, he decided.

Fortunately, excitement and the softly playing music did the trick. Chelsea appeared at the top of the stairs. "Daddy, did Santa come?" she asked sleepily.

Ken met her halfway up the stairs. "He certainly did. Why don't you put on some clothes, so you'll look really pretty when Beth gets here? Then we can see what Santa left."

Within minutes, Chelsea was racing down the stairs in a new dress and her best patent leather shoes. Just as they reached the living room, where piles of presents waited beneath the tree, he heard Beth's car drive up, then the sound of her footsteps crunching through the snow. He knew that at any second she would walk through the front door.

Silently mouthing a heartfelt prayer that he could pull this off, he placed the engagement ring on the coffee table in front of Chelsea. His daughter regarded it with a frown creasing her brow.

"What's that?"

"An engagement ring."

"For Beth?"

He heard Beth's footsteps come to a halt just inside the front door, which he'd left ajar for her. "Actually Beth turned it down," he said loudly enough to be heard by anyone who happened to be eavesdropping.

Chelsea's eyes widened. A satisfying expression of disbelief spread across her face. "She doesn't want to marry you? Why not?"

"I think she's worried about how you'll feel about having her as a stepmother," he said bluntly. It was a calculated risk. He'd learned the hard way that Chelsea could be unpredictable. But he also believed with all his heart that she adored Beth as much as he did. And an uncensored response was the only kind Beth would ever trust. He waited, his breath caught in his throat.

To his astonishment, Chelsea climbed down from the sofa and walked into the foyer. Ken followed and saw her facing down the woman in question, hands on tiny hips. Her whole body was practically quivering with indignation.

"Is it true?" she demanded.

"Is what true?" Beth asked with amazing aplomb for a woman being cross-examined by a pint-size interrogator who could hold the key to her future.

"That you don't want to marry my daddy?"

Beth's gaze came up and met his. "That's not what I said."

"Will you or won't you?" Chelsea demanded impatiently. "He's a great daddy."

"Thanks for the vote of confidence, Shortstuff," Ken said, his gaze locked with Beth's. "So, what's it going to be?"

Beth looked from him to Chelsea and back again. Then she hunkered down in front of the child. "Are you proposing to me on your father's behalf, or is this what you want, too?"

Chelsea considered the question thoughtfully, while Ken held his breath. His daughter's answer was going to make all the difference in how this unorthodox proposal turned out.

"You don't yell at me much," Chelsea conceded. "And you picked out a great Christmas tree." Her gaze narrowed. "Will you ever punish me?"

"Only if you're bad."

"Oh," Chelsea said, then seemed to accept the honest answer. "Can you bake chocolate-chip cookies?"

"They're my favorite," Beth admitted, rising to stand beside Ken.

Chelsea nodded. "Then I guess you'd make an okay stepmom."

"Is that a yes?" Ken inquired hopefully, looking from one to the other.

"Yes," his daughter said, and held out the ring to Beth. "Want it?"

So much for flowery words, Ken thought ruefully. Beth's reply was so long in coming and so softly spoken that at first he wasn't sure he'd heard her.

"Was that a yes?" he asked.

She knelt down and took Chelsea's hands in her own. "Are you sure?"

Chelsea nodded and Beth's gaze rose to meet his. "Then the answer is definitely yes. Yes, I will marry you."

"All right!" Chelsea whooped. "Can we bake cookies right after we open Christmas presents?"

"We can bake them every day for the next month," Ken said as he drew Beth and then his daughter into his arms. "First, though, don't you have a present you'd like to give Beth?"

"Oh, yeah," Chelsea said, running ahead of them into the living room and plucking the awkwardly wrapped gift from the pile under the tree. "This is for you from me."

There was a glow in Beth's eyes that Ken could have sworn he'd never seen before.

"I wonder what this could be?" Beth said, shaking the box gently as Chelsea watched worriedly.

"Open it."

Beth undid the ribbon with slow deliberation, almost as if she couldn't quite bear to have this special moment end. She was just as cautious as she slipped off the paper.

Chelsea rested her hands on Beth's knees and watched her intently. "Hurry," she urged.

When Beth finally lifted the lid from the box and saw the angel cushioned in its nest of tissue paper, tears welled up in her eyes and spilled down her cheeks.

Chelsea regarded her with dismay. "Don't you like it? It's just like the one I broke."

Shaking her head, Beth gathered the child into her arms. "No, it's not," she said gently. "This one is truly special."

"Why?" Chelsea asked.

"Because it came from you." She tilted her head until her gaze met Ken's. "I love you. Both of you."

Ken swallowed hard against the emotion clogging his throat. Before he could find the words to express how it felt to share Christmas morning with the woman he loved and the daughter he adored, Chelsea broke free of Beth's embrace and raced back to the tree. She stood there staring indecisively at all the presents, then turned back to Beth.

"I think you're the very best present I'm going to get this year."

"Oh, baby," Beth whispered. "You are definitely the very best present I'm getting." She glanced up at Ken and smiled. "And you, of course."

He sighed. Upstaged by his daughter again. "Of course," he said, then leaned down to kiss his bride-to-be. This, however, was one area where he definitely had the edge.

* * * * *

Also by Allison Leigh

Return to the Double C

A Weaver Christmas Gift
A Weaver Beginning
A Weaver Vow
A Weaver Proposal
Courtney's Baby Plan

Men of the Double C

A Weaver Holiday Homecoming
A Weaver Baby
A Weaver Wedding
Wed in Wyoming
Sarah and the Sheriff

Don't miss Allison Leigh's

One Night in Weaver...

Visit the Author Profile page
at Harlequin.com for more titles.

ONCE UPON A PROPOSAL

Allison Leigh

For my fellow hunters, Christine Flynn,
Lois Faye Dyer and Patricia Kay.
It's always a pleasure!

Prologue

"Corny, I promise you that I'm not meddling in the boys' affairs anymore." Harrison Hunt sat at his desk talking on the phone in an office high atop the Hunt-Com complex in Seattle. He no longer ran the computer juggernaut that had been a brainchild of his and his best friend, George Fairchild, a lifetime ago. Harry's eldest son, Grayson, ran the corporation now. But Harry still maintained this office at their headquarters.

He still kept his finger in a lot of pies—mostly because it pleased him to ruffle Gray's feathers. To keep the boy from becoming too much like his old man.

He didn't want his sons making the same mistakes he had. And while he hadn't been too popular with them a few years earlier when he'd forced their hands—into donning wedding rings—everything *had* turned out well all around. Even they managed to admit that.

Now.

"Don't lie to me, Harry," Cornelia Fairchild was saying. She was George's widow. More importantly to Harry, she was his oldest friend. "I had lunch with Amelia this afternoon."

Amelia. Gray's wife and, if truth be told, not at all the pushover that her sweet name and demeanor would suggest. Harry picked up one of the framed photographs on his desk of Gray and Amelia and their brood—larger than Harry had ever dared hope, considering his son and daughter-in-law were also raising Amelia's niece and nephews. "All I did was suggest that Gray wasn't getting any younger. If they want another baby, they ought to get cracking. That's true enough, isn't it?" He replaced the photograph among the others in his collection.

And there *was* a collection where, for much of his lifetime, there had been none at all.

"Coming from anyone but you, that might be a good enough assurance," Cornelia said warily. "Let your sons be, Harry. They've chosen their wives well. They're *happy.*"

"Yes, they are," Harry agreed. Evidenced by their rapidly expanding families. He'd wanted grandchildren. And he'd gotten them.

At last he was happy. Wasn't he?

He decided to change tack, not wanting the conversation to end when it was the first time he'd heard her voice in nearly a week. "How are the girls?"

"Fine," Cornelia said immediately. "Georgie's enjoying working with Alex and all the traveling it includes. Frankie is busier than ever at the university. Tommi's working nonstop at that little bistro of hers."

"And Bobbie? She doesn't seem to be moping any-more about that idiot who broke up with her." He picked up the tall, insulated cup sitting on his desk pad. It was currently empty, but would be filled soon enough with a rich, caffeinated brew. Bobbie was Corny and George's youngest daughter. And *he* knew that he prob-ably saw her more often than Corny did, since Bob-bie personally delivered the high-octane drink to him twice a week.

"Thankfully. She's busy raising those dogs that she can barely afford to feed."

"Say the word, Corny, and none of your girls would have to work another day in their lives." It was an old argument. One he'd given up on ever winning.

Once George was gone and the financial plight he'd been hiding had come to light, Corny had insisted on cleaning up the mess all on her own. She'd flatly re-fused Harry's assistance in every single way. By any-one's standards, she'd managed to do well by her girls despite her diminished circumstances. Harry was as proud of each of them as he was of his own sons. But the most *he'd* ever been allowed to do for George's daughters was make an occasional gift to them. He'd still managed to spike Corny's guns a little, though. He'd given each of the girls a substantial monetary gift when they'd graduated from high school, as well as honorary seats on HuntCom's board. Seats they would have had eventually if their father hadn't secretly gam-bled away nearly every asset he'd possessed. Even in Harry's socially backward way, he'd wanted them to have options.

The girls, each of them, had been beyond thrilled. Corny? Less so.

She hadn't spoken to him for a solid month.

"Don't even bring up the subject of money with me, Harrison Hunt," Corny said, sounding testy. "Anyway, the girls are all fine. Alone, of course, but I guess I shouldn't complain when that's generally of their own choosing."

"Living up to their mother's example," Harry pointed out, not for the first time. Cornelia had never remarried after George. She'd never been seriously involved with anyone again. As if she'd been determined to prove—after having had a marriage that turned out less perfect than it had seemed on the surface—that she needed only her daughters to be happy.

Even he could see the irony that it had taken him nearly two decades to recognize that particular point. But he'd been the one who could make a computer sing. It was George who'd had the gift of dealing with people, Cornelia in particular.

"I want my daughters to have fulfilling lives of *their* choosing," Cornelia returned pointedly. Harry's method where his fully grown sons had been concerned had been much more hands-on, considering he'd threatened to take away everything that mattered to them if they didn't get married and start families within the twelve months he'd allotted them. But he'd had good reason at the time, and even now he couldn't entirely regret the course he'd taken.

"You telling me you don't wish you could hold your own grandbabies in your arms before you die?"

Corny gave a short, muffled laugh. "Trust you, Harry, to remind me just how *old* I am."

He grinned, looking at the framed photograph from Gray and Amelia's wedding that sat in the center of all the rest. But it wasn't his son and new bride in the picture. It was Cornelia. Clothed in soft gold, slender and fair-haired and looking every bit as lovely as she had when she, George and Harry had been youngsters chasing around together. "What are friends for?"

She laughed again and his smile widened. It was there, even after they'd hung up. And a few minutes later, a familiar brunette with corkscrew hair peeked her head around his office door. She was holding a familiar-looking coffee cup.

How many times had he wanted to make Corny's dreams come true? Too many to count.

He waved his dearest friend's youngest daughter into his office, his mind suddenly ticking. He'd gotten his boys onto the road of marital bliss, hadn't he?

Why not his dear Corny's girls?

His smile widened as Bobbie crossed the office toward him.

After all, what were friends for?

Chapter 1

"Kiss me."

Gabriel Gannon stared at the petite bundle of curly-haired brunette energy standing in the doorway of his grandmother's carriage house. "Excuse—"

He didn't even get the rest of it out, as the girl—after a harried glance around him—grabbed his shoulders and yanked him down with an urgency that surprised him so much, he couldn't help but go with it.

Her mouth pressed against his. *"Kiss me,"* she muttered again, her lips moving against his as she twined her arms around his neck. "And for pity's sake, make it look good."

Look good? His brain was faintly aware of some insult there, but his hands were too busy being filled by the shapely body practically climbing up his. He had a vague recollection of the last time he'd kissed a woman. Some leggy blond architect he'd met in Colorado. Maybe he'd even taken her to bed.

Hell. Who could remember a minor detail like that when he had the taste of this little body-climber in his mouth, making him feel like the top of his head was about to blow right off?

His fingers flexed against her waist. Spread against her back, feeling the supple stretch of her spine through the soft fabric of her cherry-red shirt.

He'd seen her before, of course. She was his grandmother's new tenant, living in the old carriage house at the rear of Fiona Gannon's stately Seattle property.

But he damn sure had never figured on *this*.

His fingers flexed again and it took every speck of self-control he had not to run them down to her hips, to her rear, and drag her even tighter against him. Not to press her back against the opened front door—which he fleetingly remembered that he was there to fix—and really make it look good...

She made a soft sound, her mouth opening, her fingers sliding through his hair and her tongue dancing against his. Even through their shirts he could feel the soft push of her breasts; could feel, too, the way her heartbeat raced.

Or maybe that was his.

All he could think about was where in the hell was the nearest bed. Or couch. Or floor.

He took a step. Then another. Over the threshold of the doorway.

"Bobbie?" The deep voice came from behind them and an oath raced through Gabe's thoughts, but not past his lips, which were still fused to hers. "What's going on here?"

Gabe tore his mouth away, hauling in a deep gasp. His hands slowly—way too slowly—let go of his kissing bandit as he lowered her feet back to the floor. He caught a glimpse of startled gray eyes before her thick lashes fell and she looked around him at the man who'd interrupted them.

"Tim," she greeted, sounding as breathless as Gabe felt. "What are you doing here?"

Gabe couldn't even move away. For one thing, she had her arms wrapped around him in a maddening way that kept him trapped against her luscious curves. For another, he was none too anxious to face a strange guy while he felt strangled by jeans that had gone too tight.

He might as well be seventeen again, instead of the forty-one he really was, for the amount of self-control he seemed to have just then.

"I brought you these," the other guy—*Tim*—was saying, as he passed a bunch of sickly-sweet smelling roses between Gabe's shoulder and the doorjamb.

"Oh." Bobbie finally had to let go of Gabe's arm to take the flowers and he used the moment to take a step away. But her free hand frantically grasped his, holding him close with a strength that was surprising. "That's very sweet of you."

The fingernails digging into Gabe's palm didn't feel all that sweet. He looked down at the top of her head. It barely reached his shoulder. And behind the veil of the flowers that she was sniffing, the glance she flashed up at him looked decidedly panicked. Gabe's nerves tightened and this time it had nothing to do with wanting a woman for the first time in longer than he cared to admit.

He turned to face the intruder, casually sliding his

arm around Bobbie's shoulders, tucking her neatly against his side.

Tim—who'd evidently been the reason why Gabe had needed to make anything look good on this particular October morning—didn't appear particularly threatening. Medium brown hair. Medium brown eyes. Creased khaki pants and a navy-blue crew-neck sweater. If anything, he looked like he belonged in one of those yuppie-courting store catalogs that Gabe's daughter, Lisette, had suddenly begun showing an interest in.

But there was still no mistaking Bobbie's anxiety. So he curled his palm around the point of her shoulder in a possessive move that the other guy couldn't fail to notice. "Who is this, honey?"

"Tim." The other guy introduced himself before Bobbie could utter a word. "Tim Boering." He stuck his hand out, obviously not as put off by Gabe's arm around Bobbie as Gabe had hoped. "And *you?*"

"This is...is Gabriel Gannon," Bobbie finally spoke. She was probably trying to sound cheerful, but her musical voice mostly just sounded high-pitched and half-strangled. "Gabriel, Tim is a, um, a friend of Uncle Harry."

Gabe nodded, as if he had a single clue who in the hell her uncle was.

"Not just Mr. Hunt's friend, I hope." Tim shot Gabe a tight look before smiling winsomely at Bobbie. "You and I *did* spend a very memorable day together last weekend."

"Sightseeing," Bobbie put in quickly. "Uncle Harry asked me to show Tim around the city. He's just moved here from…" She trailed off, looking back at Tim with a question in her eyes.

"Minneapolis," Tim provided after the faintest of hesitations. He smiled a little deprecatingly, and Gabe supposed that if a woman liked that pretty-boy kind of guy, she'd probably lap it up. But in Gabe's estimation, Bobbie didn't seem the least bit thirsty. And the look Tim directed at Gabe was entirely competitive. "Are you an old friend of Bobbie's?"

Gabe smiled faintly, amused at the other guy's attempt to point out that he was plainly older than Tim. And Bobbie. He looked down at her. She was giving him another gray-eyed look of pleading. "Something like that," he murmured, his voice low. Intimate.

Her eyes widened slightly and that cool, panicky gray turned soft and warm. Then she blinked suddenly, looking away. She moistened her bow-shaped lips and color suffused her cheeks.

"I see," Tim said slowly. He tugged at his ear. "Bobbie, maybe I could call you later?"

Clearly, a lack of persistence wasn't one of Tim's faults.

Bobbie's mouth was opening and closing, as if she didn't know what to say. "I, well, I—"

Tim's gaze went from Bobbie to Gabe and back again. "I wasn't trying to poach. I just got the impression from Mr. Hunt that you weren't involved with anyone." He gave that toothy smile again. "I got that impression last weekend, too," he said to Bobbie.

If Gabe had to guess, he'd bet that Bobbie was wishing she could disappear into thin air as she hemmed around for something to say.

Gabe thought of the door he still had to fix for his

grandmother before he could get out of there and pick up his kids for the day. At this rate, with Bobbie not getting rid of the guy she clearly wanted to get rid of, it was going to take more time than Gabe had.

"Blame that on me," he said smoothly. He nudged a finger beneath Bobbie's slightly pointed chin, and nudged it upward. "A misunderstanding, I'm afraid."

He lowered his head and pressed a kiss to the softly surprised O of her lips.

When he lifted his head, those gray eyes had a distinct silvery cast. He'd never seen anyone with eyes so expressively changeable. Fascinating. For a man with the time to explore it.

Which did *not* describe him.

He didn't even want to recognize the regret he felt as he brushed his thumb over the lips he'd just kissed, keeping up the act for young Tim. "But that's all worked out now, isn't it, sweetheart?"

She nodded hurriedly. "Mmm-hmm. For, um, for better or worse." Her cheeks were pinker than ever when she smiled brightly at Tim again.

"I see." Tim's expression tightened. "Well. Congratulations, then." He gave Gabe a terse nod and turned on his heel, striding back down the three porch steps to the stone walkway that led beyond the large main house and out to the hillside street.

Gabe leaned down again toward the riotous brown spirals covering her head. "I'm guessing you don't want to run and stop him?"

She let out a breathless sound and tilted her head to look up at him. "I...no." Her lips closed, softly pursed. They were pink and rosy. Lushly curved.

And now he knew they tasted sweeter than a summer strawberry.

It was all he could do not to take them again. He pressed his hand against the doorjamb above her head, realizing belatedly that he was still holding his hammer.

He didn't know whether to laugh at himself or curse. So he did neither. He straightened away from her and nodded toward the bouquet she was clutching. "Remind me never to give you roses. Lord knows what other innocent person you might attack."

She flushed and looked at the bouquet as if she'd forgotten all about it. "It's not the roses," she assured, running her hand over the perfectly pink blooms. "I love any sort of flower. And, I *am* sorry about, well, about all that."

He couldn't say that he was. "Getting kissed by a pretty girl isn't the worst thing that's ever happened to me."

Her lashes flew up and again he couldn't help but think that she really did have the most distinctive eyes. And right now, they were as soft a gray as a mourning dove.

"Thank you." A dimple came and went in her smooth cheek. "I think."

"Just for future reference, though, if it wasn't the roses, what was so objectionable about the guy?"

"Boering wasn't just his last name." She gave a little huff, shaking her head and causing silky brown curls to dance around her shoulders. "And honestly, I never encouraged him. We spent a few hours visiting Pike Place and the Space Needle and I've been dodging his phone calls since."

"Ever think about just telling the guy you weren't interested?"

Her smooth forehead crinkled. "I tried!" She huffed a little at the look he gave her. "Honestly, I did. It's just not as easy as you make it sound. And I really didn't want to offend him. He's a friend of Uncle—"

"—Harry's," Gabe finished.

"Right."

"Well, I hope your Uncle Harry doesn't have too many friends like Boering that he sets you up with or you're—"

"No, no, no." Her curls danced some more. "Uncle Harry didn't set us up. He just happened to introduce us when I delivered some coffee to his office. He's not supposed to be drinking it, you see, but when he called me—" Her shoulders lifted.

"You couldn't say no to him, either." Gabe grinned a little.

Her lips curved, and that dimple flirted into view again. "I was just doing a favor. Really."

"Well." He tapped the doorjamb with the butt of his hammer. "Someday you can thank your Uncle Harry for me. Whoever he is."

This time her cheeks went even rosier than the velvety flowers. Her eyes sparkled. "You're pretty gracious, considering everything."

"My grandmother would expect nothing less," he assured wryly.

"Right. And though Fiona has talked about you, we haven't ever been properly introduced." She tucked the roses under her arm and stuck out her hand. "I'm Bobbie Fairchild."

He took her palm in his. His hand practically swallowed her smaller one. "Gabe Gannon. It's nice to kiss you, Bobbie Fairchild."

She laughed. "I suppose I deserve the teasing."

If he teased long enough, maybe he could forget the taste of her. Which would be the smartest thing all around. For one thing, he had seriously more pressing issues going on than his dearth of a love life. For another, he figured Bobbie was one of the causes that his grandmother had taken under her wing. What other reason would Fiona have for suddenly renting out the carriage house the way she had?

It wasn't as if his grandmother needed the money. And it wasn't as if the carriage house was in such great shape. Structurally sound, maybe. But nobody had lived in the place for longer than Gabe could remember.

Which reminded him all over again about the door.

He lifted the hammer between them. "Fiona asked me to fix the door. It's been sticking?"

"If it's not sticking, then it's not locking properly." Bobbie was grateful to focus on something other than the way she'd virtually attacked the poor man. It seemed like hours since she'd yanked open the door at his knock, but she knew it really had only been a matter of minutes.

Only when she'd seen Tim Boering bearing down the walkway with determination in his step and roses in his hand, she'd simply panicked. No amount of hinting had been able to convince the man that she wasn't interested. And since there'd been six-plus feet of very manly man already standing on her porch, she'd impetuously decided to *show* Tim that she wasn't interested.

She just hadn't expected to find herself wrapped around a ticking bomb of sex appeal.

Her heart was still dancing around inside her chest.

And she realized that Gabriel Gannon, her sweet Fiona's oft talked-about grandson, was clearly waiting for her to say something.

The door. Right.

Her face felt hotter than ever as she backed up until she was out of the way of the opened door. "It stuck so badly the other day that I couldn't make it budge. I had to climb out the back window to get to work on time."

He had the decency not to laugh at that, though he didn't stifle his grin all that quickly. "Can only imagine. This old door's been warped since I was a kid." He was running his very long-fingered hand down the edge of the door but his gaze—impossibly blue—was on her. "You work with my grandmother, don't you?"

"At Golden Ability?" Fiona was the founder and long-time director of the small nonprofit canine assistance agency. "I'm just a volunteer for them. I actually work at Between the Bean. It's a coffee place downtown." Just the latest job in a long string of them, but she wasn't about to tell this man that. "Lots of, um, business people stop in there," she added even though she knew she was rambling. She just couldn't quite seem to help herself. Her brains still felt scrambled.

"What sort of volunteering do you do?" He straightened again from studying the door and moved around to the inside, giving her another whiff of the intoxicating scent that she'd noticed when she was kissing him.

"I'm a puppy raiser." She dumped the roses on the narrow entry table that was a general collecting ground for her mail and keys and puppy toys, effectively moving far enough away from him so that she wouldn't be in danger of accidentally drooling on him. He'd pulled a hefty screwdriver out of his back pocket and used it, along with the hammer, to tap out the hinges on the door. "Have been for about ten years." It was the longest she'd ever stuck with anything.

But then how could you not stick with raising golden retrievers that could—someday—become invaluable assistance dogs?

"For some reason, I had the impression that you were in the office with her." The hinges freed. He stuck the handles of his tools in the back pocket of his well-washed jeans, then wrapped his long, bare fingers around both sides of the weighty wooden door, lifting it right out of the door frame.

"Well, I've helped out now and then when she's short-staffed or something special's going on." She realized she was staring at the play of muscles beneath the short-sleeved white T-shirt he wore and quickly backed out of the way when he turned the door sideways to carry it out to the porch and down the steps where he leaned it against the iron railing. "What do you do with the door now?"

He dusted his hands together as he straightened. "I'll plane the edges. Shave off the warped parts," he translated when she gave him a blank look. "I've got the tools in my truck." He glanced at the sturdy watch that circled his wrist. "Won't take me long, and then your door will be back in business."

"Good grief." She darted down the steps, grabbing his wrist to look at his watch. "I forgot all about the time. I've got a class to get to." She raced back into the house, straight to the kitchen where she kept the puppies' kennel cages. Even when she was home, they preferred sleeping there, but when they heard her, the two fourteen-month-old dogs jumped to their feet and dashed out of the opened doors to race in circles around her. She snatched their leashes off the hook on the wall as well as the puppy jackets they wore when she took them out in public, and quickly clipped the leads onto their collars.

It took only a matter of seconds, yet the exuberant pups nearly pulled her after them, their paws scrambling as they ran across the hardwood floor to the front door. She had them back under control by the time they made it outside, though, and they waited obediently until she allowed them to go sniffing around the bushes that clustered against the foundation of the carriage house.

"Handsome dogs," Gabriel commented.

"They are." Glad for a reason to keep her eyes off of Gabriel's—well, *everything*—she crouched down and fondly scrubbed her fingers through Zeus's golden ruff. His eyes nearly rolled back in his head with pleasure. Archimedes wasn't so quick to finish his business before seeking out her attention, but that didn't surprise Bobbie. She'd gotten the pups just after they'd been weaned and even then, their personalities had been developing. "Zeus here is a little lover, plain and simple." She patted him on the back and nodded toward the other dog. "Archimedes there is the explorer."

And the explorer had moved from sniffing his way around the azaleas to the wooden door that was definitely not where he was used to it being.

He whined a little and trotted back to Bobbie, obviously ready for his share of petting when he sat his too-big-for-his-body paws right on her thigh, nearly knocking her over. She laughed and righted herself even as Gabriel's hand shot out to catch her arm.

"You okay?"

"Fine." Except that her arm was tingling all over again from his touch. "After all these years with puppies like these two, I'm pretty used to it. Have a collection of bruises most days," she added blithely as she moved away from him so she could breathe normally again and clipped on the leashes once more.

"Maybe you should try smaller dogs," he suggested dryly. "Ones that aren't half your size before they're even full-grown."

"Why?" She crouched down with the pups again, getting her face slathered with sloppy tongues while she deftly fastened their guide-puppy-in-training jackets on their backs. "What's a bruise or two when you get love like this?"

"There are bruises and then there are bruises."

She straightened again, unreasonably curious about the suddenly grim set of his lips, but he was already striding across the lawn toward the big dark blue pickup truck that was parked in the narrow drive in front of her cottage. A sign on the truck's door said *Gannon-Morris Ltd.*

"Come on, guys," she told the dogs as she followed him. "You'll be all right if I leave you?"

He reached into the bed of his truck and hefted out a large, red toolbox. "I think I can manage," he assured her solemnly.

She smiled. "Right." Of the two of them, there was no question that he would be the one in the "good at managing" column, whereas she was usually so *not*.

The corner of his lips twitched as he watched her just stand there. "Thought you had a class to get to."

"Criminy." Her face heated again. "I do." She lifted the dogs' leashes. "Obedience class, actually. It's held in the park at the end of the block, rain or shine." She glanced up at the partially cloudy sky. "So far, looks like we'll have a little shine. Thanks for fixing the door. And, thanks also for...you know—"

"Making it look good?" His gaze slid her way, and this time, the heat slowly oozed from her face and down her body into all manner of interesting places.

Zeus and Archimedes were tugging at their leashes. They knew they had a walk in store.

"Yes," she managed around her dry throat as her feet slowly followed their pull toward the street. "Making it look good." And then, before she could admit the painfully obvious—that he'd made it *feel* pretty darn good, too—she turned and followed the exuberant dogs.

At least trying to keep up with them gave her a safe excuse on which to blame her racing heart.

Chapter 2

"Fiona!" A few hours later, the door repairs nearly completed, Gabe entered the rear of his grandmother's house, going through the laundry room that—as far as he knew—had never once been used personally by his feisty, diminutive grandmother. That was something she'd always left for the "help"—individuals who, in Gabe's mother's opinion, were more in need of that particular quality than they were competent in providing it to Fiona.

"Fiona," he called again, gesturing for his son and daughter to go inside before he followed them with his heavy toolbox.

"I don't see why we can't stay home." Lisette continued her argument that had begun the moment she'd climbed in the passenger seat of his truck when he'd picked her up after her ballet lesson. "Twelve is old enough to babysit Todd."

"I don't need no babysitter," Todd returned acidly. He was two years younger than his sister, who never failed to remind him of her superior age. He headed straight to Fiona's oversize refrigerator and pulled open the door, sticking his rumpled blond head inside. "I'm hungry."

"You're always hungry," Lisette observed with a sniff that would have done her mother proud.

Gabe closed his hand around the back of her slender neck beneath the tight little knot she'd made of her pale-blond hair. "You should eat something, too," he told her, managing to contain the rest of his thought— that she was too thin.

"I'm not hungry." The response was predictable. Unfortunately, the way she shimmied out from his touch was predictable, too.

He stifled a sigh and set his toolbox on the floor in the kitchen. "Then help your brother. And if you wouldn't mind, fix a sandwich for me, too. I'm going to find your great-grandmother." Without waiting for an argument, he headed through a narrow hallway that led from the kitchen to his grandmother's office. But she wasn't behind the massive desk that had once belonged to Gabe's grandfather. Nor was she in the sunroom, fussing over her orchids and begonias. Where he did find his nearly 85-year-old grandmother was up stairs, standing on a six-foot ladder with a long-handled duster in her hand, trying to reach the lower arms of the enormous antique chandelier that hung suspended over the two-story foyer.

"Fiona," he said calmly from the foot of the stairs, because the last thing he wanted to do was startle her, even though he had to clench his hand over the carved newel top to keep from bolting up the stairs, "You told me you hired someone to clean the chandelier."

"Oh, I did." Leaning precariously over the handrail, she swiped the duster toward the chandelier. It groaned a little as it swayed slightly. "But Rosalie's poor husband was arrested."

"Ah." He began climbing the stairs. "The husband was the one you hired?"

"No, no." Fiona shook her head, and looked down, waving her duster at him as if he ought to know better. "Rosalie was the one I hired. But she obviously couldn't be *here* when she needed to be at her husband's side." She turned her attention back to the lofty chandelier.

"When was he arrested?" *And for what?*

"Oh, a week ago. I told Rosalie not to worry about a thing, financially or otherwise."

Gabe let out a slow sigh. Between his kids, who gave every impression of wanting him to disappear from their lives—again—and his grandmother, who was a soft-hearted target for every soul needing some sort of break, he had definitely been learning the fine art of keeping his patience.

He reached the top of the stairs and turned along the landing. "Grandma," he said mildly, "why not hire someone else?" He knew from long habit that there was no point in trying to convince Fiona that she didn't need to save everyone she met. "Or wait for me to get here and save your money altogether? You knew I'd be here today." He made it to the ladder and reached up, closing his hands around her waist and lifting her right off the ladder.

"Gabriel—" she swatted at him with the duster, giving him a face full of dust "—put me down this instant."

"That's what I'm—" he let out a huge sneeze "—doing." He set her well away from the ladder. And kept himself between her and it. He sneezed again, and swiped his hand down his face. "How much dust was *up* there?"

"A lot," Fiona said tartly. "Which is why it needed to be done." She propped her narrow hands on her skinny hips and eyed him with no small amount of relish when he sneezed a third time. "That's what you get for interrupting me."

He snatched the wooden handle out of her hand before she could brandish the feathery thing in his face again. "I'll finish it."

"Don't be ridiculous." She grabbed the handle right back, proof that age hadn't slowed her much at all. "I thought you had Lisette and Todd this afternoon?"

"I do. And they're downstairs raiding your kitchen as we speak."

Fiona's eyes lit up. "They're here, then? That's wonderful. For how long?"

"Not long enough." He grimaced. "I tried to get Stephanie to let me keep them overnight, but—" He shook his head.

Fiona's gave a frowning sniff. "As usual, she wants to make things as difficult for you as she possibly can."

Gabe could have denied it, but what would have been the point? His grandmother knew as well as anyone in the family just how little love was lost between him and his former wife. Fiona was about the only one, though, who didn't blame him for it.

Now, she patted him on the arm and waved at the

ladder. "It really needs to be cleaned up before that dreadful birthday party your mother is insisting on next weekend."

"Would that be dreadful because it is *your* birthday? Or because Astrid is throwing it?" Not only did his mother like to control everything, but she was far from a devoted daughter-in-law. Any party his mom threw would be about appearances—hers. Sweet and loving, she was not.

Fiona gave him a look. "Take your pick. Were you able to fix Bobbie's door for her earlier?"

She didn't wait around for an answer, but tugged at the sleeves of her sweater as she wandered along the long landing, straightening the frames of the portraits hanging there. Three generations of Gannons and not a blue-collar guy like Gabe among them.

"Yeah." He climbed the ladder and began finishing the job his grandmother had begun. "I'm going to replace the lock set, though, before I leave today. She said she's been having problems with that, too."

"So you saw her, then."

"I saw her." An understatement if there ever was one.

"What did you think of her?" Fiona stopped in front of the portrait of her husband, cocking her white head as she nudged one corner of the frame. "A dear girl."

That "girl" had felt like she was all woman when she'd been filling his arms. "Seemed friendly enough," he offered. Another understatement. He realized he was grinning like some damn fool at the crystal prisms above his head. "She was taking her dogs out to some class."

"She teaches it, actually. When it comes to the dogs,

she'll do most anything." Evidently satisfied with the portraits, Fiona moved to the top of the stairs. "That's good enough, darling. If your mother wants to get up on a ladder to inspect the thing, she's welcome to do so." She shook her head. "As if I need some darn party to remind me just how old I am." She started down the steps with an ease that belied her age. "Will that lock thing take you long enough that I can purloin your children for an hour or so?"

He eyed her from his perch atop the ladder. "What are you planning?"

She waved her hand at him. "Nothing for you to worry yourself about."

He made a face. "The last time you told me that, I ended up with two hamsters that had to live with me," he reminded her. And those two hamsters had quickly multiplied...fertile devils that they were. It had taken him nearly three months to find homes that had been satisfactory to his kids.

"We won't come back with anything that breathes," she assured, disappearing down the hallway where he could hear her cheerfully greeting his kids.

He shook his head and climbed off the ladder. Just because whatever it was didn't breathe didn't necessarily mean it would be welcome. But he wasn't going to complain.

Neither Todd nor Lisette was chomping at the bit to spend time with their old man, but they *did* enjoy their great-grandmother and for that, Gabe could be grateful. He folded up the ladder and carried it and the duster downstairs, stowing them both in the cluttered utility closet. Fiona and the kids were still in the kitchen when he got there. Not surprisingly, there was no sandwich waiting for him and the way their chattering clammed up the second they spotted him wasn't exactly comforting. "No new pets," he warned again, giving each of them—including Fiona—a stern look before he picked up his toolbox and headed for the door. "I'll be done in an hour and maybe, *maybe,* I'll take you to the movies afterward. Okay?"

One thing Gabe knew was that Stephanie and Ethan rarely let the kids go to a movie theater. And maybe he shouldn't be proud of offering them this particular treat, but sometimes a man had to pick his battles. He'd had an ongoing one with Stephanie when it came to the children since they'd split up eight years earlier, but now the stakes had escalated.

And sometimes he simply needed to see a smile on his kids' faces. One that was directed at him.

Right now, both Lisette and Todd were looking surprised and pleased. "Check the newspaper for the movie times," he added. "And nothing rated R."

"Dad." Lisette rolled her dark blue eyes—the only feature she'd inherited from him. "Don't be lame."

"Would you rather I said to find something rated G?"

She rolled her eyes again, but shook her head. "I'm not going to the theater in my leotard, though. Somebody might see me."

"You'll have time to change," he promised, smiling faintly.

"Nobody cares what you look like anyway," Todd added, ever the supportive little brother. "'Specially not *Jeffrey* Russell," he goaded.

"Shut up." Lisette rounded on him, lifting her fist. "Or you'll—"

"Make me change my mind about the movie altogether," Gabe warned.

Lisette's hand slowly dropped, though she gave Todd a killing glare. One that he returned, complete with crossed eyes.

Fiona quickly nudged Gabe out the door. "Go on. Finish Bobbie's door. Everything's fine here."

He wouldn't go so far as to say *fine,* but they were pretty much standard. The only thing Lisette and Todd could unequivocally agree on was their mutual annoyance with each another.

That at least was something that Gabe understood. He'd grown up with two older brothers, and a day hadn't passed when they hadn't been squabbling about something. But as he crossed the expanse of lawn leading toward the carriage house, he hoped to hell that he could keep Lisette and Todd from growing up to be as distant from one another as he was now from Liam and Paul.

When he reached the carriage house, he could hear dogs barking inside. Evidently the obedience class was over.

He knocked and a moment later Bobbie pulled open the door, a phone tucked between her ear and her shoulder and her other hand latched onto Zeus's collar. Her dark brown hair hung in dozens of long spirals around her shoulders. "Hey," she mouthed. "Door works great." She swung it back and forth.

He held up the new lock set. "It'll just take a few minutes."

Her mother was chattering in her ear, but Bobbie didn't really hear her. "You're replacing the lock, too?"

Gabe's deep blue eyes crinkled at the corners.

"Neighborhood like this, a pretty woman should be able to lock her door securely."

She couldn't help but laugh at that. Fiona Gannon's neighborhood wasn't exactly one prone to petty crime and break-ins. It was far too well-bred.

"Bobbie?" Her mother's voice had sharpened in her ear. "Are you listening at *all?*"

"Sorry, Mom. Can you hold on for just a second?" She didn't wait for an answer, but tucked the receiver under her arm and focused on her landlady's handsome grandson again. Not exactly a hardship. The man was eye candy in a serious way. And he'd taken note when she'd mentioned the troublesome lock. "You didn't need to replace it," she told him now. "I figured it just needed a squirt of oil or something."

"It needs replacing," he assured. "The tumblers are worn down to nothing."

"Well." She moistened her lips, very aware of the fact that she was practically staring at him. "That's really nice of you. Thanks."

"We at Gannon-Morris are all about full service."

Warmth zipped through her. "I'll bet."

"Bobbie? RobertaNicoleFairchild—"

She realized the faint voice was coming from the forgotten telephone tucked beneath her arm and felt a new flush—this one entirely from embarrassment— flood her cheeks. "Excuse me," she told Gabe and quickly turned away, pulling Zeus with her into the kitchen. She pointed, and he trotted into the kennel cage alongside Archimedes, turned a few circles and plopped down with a noisy breath. "Sorry, Mom. I wasn't ignoring you." She stuck the phone back to her ear, keeping her voice low. "I just had someone at my door."

She heard her mother give a faint sigh. "And you still haven't answered me. Why did I have to learn from Harry, of all people, that my own daughter is engaged again? You can imagine what he thought when it was clear I had no idea what he was talking about." Cornelia Fairchild's voice rose slightly, a true indicator that she was genuinely perturbed.

If there was one person in the family to perturb the normally unflappable, elegant woman, Bobbie knew it was she, Cornelia's youngest daughter. The one who was entirely flappable. And decidedly *in*elegant.

A pain was beginning to form between her eyebrows. "I'm not—" she broke off, lowering her voice again. "I'm not engaged," she said in a half-whisper.

"Then why is Harry so certain that you are?"

There could be only one reason, Bobbie knew, though she really couldn't fathom why Tim Boering would have immediately trotted out the story for her honorary uncle. Only a few hours had passed since then, for heaven's sake. "It's just a misunderstanding," she assured. She lifted the roses out of the plastic pitcher that she'd stuck them in, and dumped them in the trash.

"Harry sounded perfectly clear to me, Bobbie. He said you and this Gabriel person were engaged!"

"Honestly, Mom—" her voice rose despite herself "—do you *really* think I would be seriously involved with someone and not tell you?"

Cornelia's silence was telling and Bobbie pressed a finger to that pain over her nose. Yes, over the years, there had been a few things she hadn't told her mother.

Mostly because she knew it would just make Cornelia worry. And Bobbie had already caused her mother enough worry to last a lifetime.

"I promise you," she said more quietly, "I am *not* engaged." Particularly not to the eminently kissable man who was working on her door not twenty feet away from her, probably overhearing every word, even though she was nearly whispering.

"It's not the idea of you being engaged that alarms me, Bobbie," Cornelia countered smoothly. "It was the fact that I thought you hadn't *told* me first. I would be delighted to think that one of my daughters is finally settling down."

The pain went from a dull ache to a sharp throb. "You mean that *I* was finally settling down." Sticking with something. Anything.

"Don't put words in my mouth, darling. That's not what I meant at all."

Bobbie paced the confines of the small kitchen. She was twenty-seven years old and kept telling herself that she should be past the need for her mother's approval.

But saying it and feeling it were two very different things.

"I'm not even dating anyone, Mom. I haven't since—" She broke off. There was no need to finish. Her mother knew what she was referring to, and Bobbie had no desire for Gabe to overhear that her love life had as much altitude as Death Valley. A state of reality since the beginning of the year, ever since the man she'd been in love with—Lawrence McKay—had thrown her over for an entirely more suitable woman to stand at his side while he took the political scene by storm. A woman whose hair didn't look like she'd stuck her finger in an electric socket and who didn't need to stand on a stool just to reach the shelves in her own kitchen cabinets. A woman who was cool and elegant and who always had the right words for any situation.

A woman just like Bobbie's mother. Or her sisters, for that matter.

She pinched the bridge of her nose. Zeus started whining. She heard her mother sigh again. Faintly.

"All right. I'll just have to call Harry and correct his misinformation."

"I'll call him if you want me to," Bobbie offered. Her honorary uncle was an eccentric one, but she had a soft spot for the man anyway. After Bobbie's father died when she was little, Harrison Hunt had been one of the few males left in her life. Whether it was the fact that he'd been childhood friends with George and Cornelia, or the fact that George had later married Cornelia, or even that George had been in business with Harry, once Bobbie's father had gone, Harry had tried—in his oft-awkward way—to do his best by the Fairchild family. The man was insanely brilliant but had—according to some—a computer chip like those that had made him rich for a heart. And given the way he'd treated his own sons for most of their lives, it wasn't an entirely inaccurate accusation. But to Bobbie, he was just her rather odd-duck Uncle Harry. And being an odd duck herself, maybe that's why she felt a kinship to him.

"I know he enjoys hearing from you," Cornelia was saying. "Particularly since you sneak him those coffees he loves—and don't bother denying it, darling. I've been onto this collusion between the two of you since you went back to work at that little coffee house after you and Lawrence ended things. But I'm having lunch with Harry tomorrow, anyway, so I'll set him straight. Now. Do you need grocery money? What about gas for the car?"

Bobbie couldn't prevent a groaning laugh. "No, Mom. I don't need grocery money or gas! I do have a job, remember? I can afford to take care of myself."

"Yes, I know you have a job. And I also can guess just how much of your income you're spending on those dogs of yours. If I came over there right this moment and looked in your pantry, would I actually see food for *you* and not just enormous bags of dog food?"

"Yes, you would." She childishly crossed her fingers as she envisioned the virtual void behind the pantry door.

Cornelia made a soft sound that Bobbie translated as disbelief. But her mother didn't pursue the matter. Maybe because she herself was the most independent woman that Bobbie knew. And she'd raised her daughters to be the same.

"Besides," Bobbie added, "I'm helping Tommi out this week at the bistro." She smiled, thinking of her older sister's penchant for feeding the world through her charming Corner Bistro in downtown Seattle. "So you know I'll be eating well there, at least." As far as Bobbie was concerned, Tommi was the best chef in town. What her sister could do in the kitchen was simply magical.

"That's something, I suppose," Cornelia allowed. "All right, then. You're *certain* there isn't anything going on in your life that I should know about?"

The sound of a hammer filled the small cottage, a needless reminder of the man on the other side of the very thin kitchen wall. "Positive." She had no intention of informing her mother that she'd practically accosted Gabriel Gannon in order to avoid her uncle's young friend. "Tell Uncle Harry hello for me when you see him tomorrow. Love you."

She barely waited to hear her mother return the sentiment before she hung up the phone.

Alongside his sleeping companion, Zeus cocked his golden head, watching her as if he knew exactly how many times she'd skirted the facts with her mother. She rubbed her hand over his silky head and tossed him the hard rubber bone he liked to chew. Then she ran her hands over her hair in a vain attempt to smooth it down, straightened the hem of her long-sleeved T-shirt around her hips, and went back out into the living room.

Gabriel was crouched down next to the open door, working on the latch and the lock, his muscular thighs bulging against his worn jeans. She sucked in a careful breath and managed a smile when his vivid gaze turned toward her. "Your mother, I take it?"

Feeling more like a schoolgirl than a grown woman, she nodded and willed herself not to blush.

"Sounds like news traveled fast."

Forget staving off the blush. She felt heat plow up her neck into her face. "Yeah." She rubbed her palms down her thighs. "Guess you heard."

"I tried not to." He looked amused as he focused again on the new lock he was installing. "But it's kind of a small space."

And feeling smaller by the second. "I'm sorry."

"For what?"

She lifted her shoulders. "Getting your name involved in all this."

"Like you said, it's just a misunderstanding. No sweat." He finished tightening a screw, twisted the door latch a few times and pushed to his feet. "And I know how mothers can be." He shut the door and turned the lock. It latched with a soft, decisive click. He looked down at her. "Ought to keep you snug as a bug in here now."

She was feeling quite snug, with the door shutting out the world and shutting *him* in. "I, um, should pay you for the lock."

"Not necessary." He shook his head and smoothly unlocked and opened the door again, letting in a rush of cool, damp air. "Fiona has a long list of things she wants fixed or replaced over here. One lock set isn't going to make a difference." He leaned over to fit his tools back into the tool box and his shirt stretched tightly across his back.

She quickly looked past the tantalizing play of muscles beneath white cotton, through the open door, grateful for the waft of fresh air. "I told Fiona she didn't have to fix anything. Except for the door sticking, everything is fine over here." And the rent was ridiculously low.

"Don't say that," he drawled. "Business down the way it is, I need all the work I can get."

Horrified, she opened her mouth, not certain what to say.

But he was giving her that crooked grin again. The one that sent strange little squiggles of excitement through her belly. "I'm kidding. Playing Mr. Fix-it for my grandmother isn't exactly a hardship and after all the hours I'm spending in the office these days, it helps keep me from forgetting where I started." He lifted the toolbox. "If it stays dry enough tomorrow, I'll get new shingles up on your roof. Otherwise it'll be the floor in your bathroom."

She was almost afraid that he'd ask to see it, and considering the lingerie that was hanging over the shower rod to dry, she really wanted to avoid that. "When Fiona said she'd send someone to fix the door, I didn't expect it to be you." In fact, her elderly friend had implied it would be someone *employed* by her grandson's construction firm. Not her grandson himself. From what she'd heard over the years from Fiona about her wealthy family, very few of them were the hands-on type. Doctors and lawyers. Administrators.

Only her grandson had bucked the old money and professional tradition and gone into construction. And now he had branches in Colorado and Texas as well as Washington State. All details courtesy of Fiona, of course. The woman didn't try to hide how proud she was of him.

"Afraid you're stuck with me," he said. "I've got everyone on my payroll working at the moment."

"That's good, though, right?" She knew how construction had taken a terrible hit in this economy. "A sign of better things?"

He looked out the door. "I'm hoping so."

Something in his voice caught at her, but she didn't have time to examine it, because footsteps pounded on the walkway outside and a moment later, two kids—a boy and a girl—practically skidded to a stop on her porch.

"We picked the movie," the tousle-haired boy said. "But it starts in twenty minutes."

"And I still have to change," the girl said. She was

wearing a black leotard with a short, filmy skirt over pale-pink tights, her hair fastened in a classic knot at the back of her blond head.

"Right." Gabriel looked back at Bobbie. "But first say hello to Ms. Fairchild. This is my daughter, Lisette. And my son, Todd."

Of course. He had children. Fiona had mentioned them. As well as the fact that their father was doing his best to regain partial custody of them. "It's nice to meet you," she greeted. "But call me Bobbie. Please."

Both of the youngsters had their father's brilliant blue eyes, but that was all. His hair was as dark a brown as theirs was pale blond. Even their features were different, not as sharply drawn, though she supposed that could just be the difference between youth and maturity.

"Hi." Todd was the first to speak. "You have the curliest hair I ever seen."

"Todd," Lisette groaned, rolling her eyes.

"Well she *does*," he defended innocently.

Bobbie laughed. "It is pretty curly," she admitted. "I always wanted smooth, blond hair, just like your sister's."

Lisette's hand flew up to her bun, looking away shyly. "Mother won't let me cut it," she said.

"All right," Gabe inserted. "Enough talk of hair. Go get in the truck. I'll be there in a sec." He gave Bobbie that smile again. "A movie awaits."

"Enjoy." She reached for the door. "Wait. Is there a new key for the lock?"

He shook his head. "It's already keyed to match the old one."

She realized she was staring at his lips again. "Thanks.

Yet again." She smiled, feeling strangely awkward. As if he could read her mind.

And maybe he could, because his smile widened slightly. "The pleasure was all mine."

Then he turned and went after his kids.

And for the second time that day, Gabriel Gannon left Bobbie with a racing heart.

Chapter 3

"*I'll have a medium iced mocha with extra cream and a large iced tea.*"

Bobbie's head whipped up from the inventory sheet she was completing when she recognized the voice on the other side of the counter. She left the paperwork on the tiny desk in the minuscule office and peered around the doorway.

Yes. It *was* Gabriel, looking much more polished and no less devastating in a white button-down shirt and black trousers than when he'd been wearing worn jeans and a T-shirt while muscling her front door out of its frame. Before he could spot her, she pulled her head back into the office like some nervous turtle retreating into its shell.

What was he doing here?

She saw herself in the little mirror that Holly, the

manager of Between the Bean, kept hanging on the wall in her office. At least her hair was contained in a ponytail. More or less. And she'd put on some makeup that morning before leaving the house.

Then she rolled her eyes at herself. It wasn't as if he'd come to the coffee shop to see *her*. All he'd done was order a drink for himself and his son.

Chewing the inside of her lip, she tilted her head again, sliding centimeters forward until she could see once more around the doorway.

"Bobbie?"

She straightened like a shot when his gaze fastened on her across the array of pastries and oversized cookies displayed above the counter. "Gabriel." She stepped out of the office, moving to the counter beside Doreen, who was preparing his order. "What a surprise." She smiled at the boy standing at his side who was avidly eyeing an enormous chocolate-chip cookie. "Hello, Todd." The boy was dressed in tan pants and a navy-blue polo shirt—clearly a school uniform.

The boy grunted a greeting in return. "Can I have a cookie?" he asked his father.

"Your mother will have enough of a fit when she finds out we stopped and got you a mocha." Gabe handed the boy the change that Doreen had given him and pointed at the arrangement of chairs around a vintage video game in one corner of the small coffee shop. "You can play that game over there, though."

Evidently it was a satisfactory substitution, because Todd scooped up the coins and ambled over to the empty corner. Within seconds, the electronic beeps and chimes of the game began accompanying the funky music that was already playing through the sound system. Bobbie watched Doreen squirt a generous help-ing of whipped cream on top of the iced mocha drink. "For the boy?" Doreen asked and when Gabe nodded, she slid his tall glass of tea toward him then carried the mocha around the counter to deliver it to Todd.

Bobbie's curiosity couldn't be contained, no matter how it made her look. And she couldn't imagine what had brought him to this area of downtown. "What are you doing here?"

Doctoring his tea with sugar—the real stuff—he slanted a glance at her through lashes that were ridic-ulously thick. "Getting a drink?"

"Obviously." She toyed with the narrow tie of her dark-brown apron. Since the day that he'd worked on her door, she hadn't seen him again, though she'd come home last night after working a late shift for Tommi at the bistro to find that the cracked linoleum in her mi-nuscule bathroom had been replaced by silky-smooth travertine. He'd left a note tucked against the mirror that he'd be back soon to finish it up. "I've just never seen you in here before." She would have definitely re-membered him, even *before* the kissing attack.

"I had to pick up Todd from school. He attends Brandlebury Academy."

It was a prestigious private school. She drove by its ivy-covered walls every day on her way to the coffee shop. And *it* most certainly was in the area.

Which meant that Gabe hadn't been seeking her out, after all.

She didn't like acknowledging the disappointment that swept through her, so she smiled more brightly than ever. "Some of Uncle Harry's older grandchildren attend Brandlebury," she said. "I hear it's an excellent school."

Gabe's dark brows pulled together for a moment. "For the cost, it ought to be. Wouldn't those grandchildren be your cousins?"

"Yes, I guess they would be. But Harry's not really my uncle. He's a family friend."

Doreen snorted softly as she returned to the counter and picked up the rag she'd been using to polish the glass counters. "And wouldn't we all like to have Harrison Hunt as a family friend?"

Gabe gave Bobbie a startled look. "Harrison *Hunt* is your Uncle Harry?"

Bobbie gave Doreen an annoyed glare that didn't faze her coworker in the least, though she fortunately moved out from behind the counter and over to the windows that overlooked the sidewalk and began polishing them. Doreen knew about Harry only because of the coffee that Bobbie delivered to him several times a week. She also knew that the relationship wasn't one that Bobbie necessarily wanted to advertise.

People expected things from you—things you couldn't provide—when they learned you were all but family to one of the wealthiest men in the country. Even people you thought you could trust.

She blocked off the thought and focused on Gabe, who was still staring at her with surprise. "Yes," she admitted shortly. "Harrison Hunt is my Uncle Harry."

"Fiona never mentioned that," Gabe murmured.

"Why would she? It's not as if Uncle Harry—or HuntCom—has anything to do with Fiona's agency."

Gabe still looked a little bemused. "Considering

how often Fiona *does* talk about you, I'm surprised it didn't come up even just in passing."

"Fiona talks to you about me?" Now it was her turn to be surprised.

"You're one of her favorite people," Gabe said. "Yeah, she talks about you quite a bit." He didn't use a straw to drink his tea, but lifted the cup to his lips instead. "It's good."

They sold gallons of the brew every day, so she'd assumed it was passably drinkable. "Fiona is one of my favorite people, too," she said truthfully.

He looked at her over the cup, his eyes crinkling at the corners. "Then we have something in common."

She suddenly felt a little breathless and she quickly began reorganizing the collection of stirrers and coffee cup lids sitting on the counter. "Do you always pick up your son from school?"

The smile lines around his eyes disappeared so instantly that she almost wondered if she'd imagined them in the first place. "No."

That was all. Just *no*. Which left her feeling like she'd awkwardly put her foot in her mouth, without even knowing why. Nothing new there. Saying the wrong thing was her specialty. Always had been.

She moistened her lips and pulled a fresh sleeve of small coffee lids from beneath the counter. "Thanks for the work you did in the bathroom. The tile looks great."

"I still need to grout it. I'll come by Saturday morning if that works for you."

"Sure."

"Dad." Todd had left the video game and stopped next to Gabe. "Can I get more whipped cream?" He held up his cup.

"One helping was enough."

The boy's brows drew together, and Bobbie realized that Gabe's son did share more than just the color of his father's eyes. He had the same expressions. "It's, um, no big deal," Bobbie offered softly. She pulled the can from its refrigerated slot behind her and held it up.

Gabe's gaze went from Bobbie to his son and back again. "Okay." He took Todd's cup and handed it over to Bobbie. "But just this once."

Todd's expression went straight to shock, giving Bobbie the sense that Gabe didn't often give in once he'd made a decision. She added the extra helping of cream and slid the drink back to Gabe, wishing that her interest in the man wasn't increasing with every encounter they had. She had no desire to change the zero status of her love life. Not when she still felt the bruises from Lawrence's defection.

"What do you say?" Gabe prompted his son and the boy gave Bobbie a brilliant, grinning "thanks," before carrying his drink with him back to the video game.

Doreen had disappeared into the back storeroom and the rest of the shop was still unoccupied. Yet there was no earthly reason for Bobbie to feel as if she and Gabe were suddenly the last two people on earth. Alone, together.

She couldn't help but smile a little at her own non-sensical thought.

"What?"

She shook her head. "Nothing." She pushed the sleeve of lids back beneath the counter—the holders were already full. She pushed her hands into the patch pockets of her apron to keep from fidgeting. He had his iced tea. His son had his mocha with extra, *extra* cream. So why wasn't he going on his way? "Is there anything else I can get for you?"

It wasn't often that Gabe found himself struggling for words. Unfortunately, that day, it had happened twice. The first time had been when he'd heard his attorney's thoroughly crazy and unwelcome advice that he find himself a wife—and fast. And the second time—now—when he was faced with the young woman he realized could possibly help him get around the attorney.

He glanced over his shoulder. Todd was completely occupied with the game in the corner. He looked back at Bobbie, who was watching him with those changeable gray eyes of hers. "Would you like to have dinner tonight?"

Her lips parted softly. "I...can't. I'm sorry." Her silky lashes swept down for a moment. "I'm helping to cover a shift at my sister's bistro this week." She looked up at him again and a hint of pink crept into her cheeks. "Maybe another time?"

He couldn't afford to wait a week. "What time are you finished at the bistro?"

"Between ten and eleven, usually."

"Where's it located? I could give you a lift home."

Her eyes narrowed a little. Her voice cooled—entering the same territory it had been in when she was dealing with her wannabe suitor, Tim. "I have a car."

"This is coming out wrong," he admitted, exhaling. "I'm not trying to sound like a stalker."

She shifted and placed her palms flat on the gleaming glass countertop. Her fingers were long and slender, the nails cut short and unvarnished. The only jewelry she wore was a narrow watch with an equally narrow leather band. "Why don't you tell me what *this* is, then?"

"There's something I'd like to talk to you about. Somewhere a little more private."

"Is Fiona all right?"

"Yeah," he assured quickly. "Fine as always. This doesn't concern her at all." He lowered his voice. "It's about my children, actually."

The wariness didn't entirely leave her face. She looked over at Todd. "What about them? I suppose Fiona told you that I had a job as a nanny a few years ago, but—"

"No, actually, she hasn't. But child care's not the kind of help I'm looking for."

"Then what—"

"I'll tell you everything, just not here. Not now."

Her gaze dropped to the counter, to his hand, which had covered hers. Then she looked up again, her shoulder moving in a faint shrug beneath the gleaming brown ringlets spilling over it. "All right." She slipped her hands from beneath his and tucked them back in her apron pockets. "If it can't wait until you come to work on the floor this weekend, you can meet me at Tommi's place. The Corner Bistro." She told him where it was located. "If you want the best meal you've ever had, then come early before she shuts down the kitchen."

He wasn't worried about finding a good meal. He was worried about losing his children for good. "Thanks. I'll see you tonight."

Then, before he could second-guess what he was even contemplating, he peeled Todd away from the game, and quickly left.

* * *

"You wanted a private place to talk." Bobbie untied the red apron from her hips and neatly folded it before sitting down across from Gabe. "You've got it."

All of the other tables in her sister's small bistro had been emptied. The other servers had finished their duties and departed for the evening. Even Tommi—after sending ping-ponging looks of concern between Bobbie and the lone man occupying a table near the wine bar—had finished her tasks in the kitchen and gone to her apartment upstairs, leaving Bobbie the responsibility of locking the back door after herself when she left.

"Want a glass?" He held up the wine bottle that was sitting in the center of the table.

Drinking one of her sister's very excellent wines was one thing. Drinking that wine while alone with the man she couldn't seem to stop thinking about was another. She shook her head. "No, thank you."

He refilled his own glass. His dishes had been cleared away—by Bobbie herself, who'd prayed all evening that she wouldn't do something stupid, like spill his entree in his lap. It was one prayer that she'd been granted, at least. "Only thing better than a good wine is a cold beer. And you're right about the food," he offered now. "Your sister is a remarkable chef."

"I'll tell her you said so." She was immensely proud of her sister's accomplishment where the Bistro was concerned. But she didn't want to talk about Tommi. "So, what is it, exactly, that you wanted to talk to me about?"

He took a sip of his wine. He'd abandoned the fine slacks and shirt of that afternoon and replaced them with black jeans and a thickly woven black sweater with the sleeves shoved up his forearms. The sturdy watch circling his sinewy wrist gleamed in the soft light coming from the wine bar as he set the glass down again, and she had to swallow a little. He was *so* incredibly masculine.

"My ex-wife's husband is a corporate lawyer," he said, managing to jerk her from the entranced haze she was in danger of slipping into. "He's been offered a prestigious contract in Europe that will run for at least the next five years."

Since he'd left the coffee shop that afternoon, Bobbie had mentally run through at least a dozen scenarios about what Gabe wanted to discuss. His ex-wife's husband had *not* been one of them. "Um…congratulations to him?"

Gabe's lips twisted. "I know. This makes no sense to you. What has Fiona told you about me?"

"Besides you being successful and very, *very* eligible?" His hooded blue gaze sharpened on her face and she managed a wry smile that hopefully hid the shivers dancing down her spine. "We're usually busy talking about what's going on at Golden Ability. It doesn't seem to leave a lot of time to chatter about her family. Or mine." She reasoned that the white lie was better than admitting how much his grandmother praised his qualities.

His dark head tipped a few centimeters. "My wife and I divorced nearly eight years ago." He slowly turned the wineglass on top of the white linen table covering. "It wasn't what you'd call amicable."

"I'm sorry."

"I share plenty of the responsibility in that," he admitted. "But that's beside the point. What is the point, are my kids. Steph was awarded custody of them when we split. The ink was barely dry on our divorce decree when she became Mrs. Ethan Walker, and then within a year they'd moved to Switzerland. It had been hard enough to keep her to the terms of my visitation before she moved, but after—" He shook his head. "A few years ago, though, her husband's job brought them back here to Seattle. Supposedly to stay, so I decided to move here, too. It was the only sure way I had of reminding my kids that I was their father—not just some guy who came to visit for a few days once a year."

Bobbie's heart squeezed at the pain on his face.

"Anyway, my business partner remained in Colorado, and I started up another branch here. We're making it when a lot of companies aren't, but it hasn't been easy."

The shivers that had been dancing down Bobbie's spine suddenly felt like jagged little spears instead, as realization dawned. "Harrison Hunt might be a family friend, but I have no influence when it comes to HuntCom."

Gabe's brows yanked together. "What are you talking about?"

She sat up straighter in her chair. "It's not like I don't understand. Or…or sympathize. Even in this economy, HuntCom still has building projects going on all over the world." If they weren't building a new manufacturing facility for themselves, they were building something else. She knew, because she had to make an appearance at least once a year at the board of directors' meeting, at which time she always gave her proxy to Gray, who'd been running the privately-held company since Harry's health had forced him into retirement. "But the best I can do is get you a name." She'd have to call Harry and find out who the chief architect was now. Since J.T.—one of Gray's younger brothers—had vacated the position to hang out his own shingle in Portland, she couldn't even hazard a guess who was responsible for the property development arm of the enormous company.

"I'm not looking to do business with HuntCom," Gabe said slowly. "Is that what you expected?"

"It's what most people expect once they realize I have a connection there." Her chin lifted. "You're hardly the first." Lawrence had simply been the most recent.

Gabe was silent for a moment, his gaze measuring. "As it happens," he finally said evenly, "I don't give a flip about HuntCom. The only thing I'm trying to do is keep my ex-wife from moving my kids to another damn country again."

She blinked.

He shoved to his feet and paced along the narrow aisle between the empty tables. "If the judge doesn't approve my petition for joint custody, there's not one thing I'll be able to do to stop her." He grimaced. "Short of kidnapping them."

Bobbie reached for the wineglass he'd abandoned and took a long drink.

"I'm kidding." His voice was dark. "The last thing I need is more trouble with the law."

More trouble?

She took another sip of wine and then carefully set the glass down. "I'm sorry about your children, but what does that have to do with me?"

"I need a wife."

Her hand twitched violently. She knocked the glass right over, sending deep-red liquid pouring across the perfect white linen tablecloth. She hastily flipped up the side of the cloth to keep it from running onto the floor. "I beg your pardon?"

"Not a real wife." He shoved one hand through his hair. "The last thing I want is to get married again. Once was enough to last a lifetime." He visibly shuddered. "But I need to make the impression that I'll have a wife, soon. Ray—my attorney—wants me to have a real one, of course, though he swears he'll deny it if the truth ever gets out."

"I'm not even sure what the truth *is*." She watched him cautiously. "You want me to pretend to be married to you?"

"I want everyone to think we're *getting* married." He pulled the chair out from behind the table to straddle it directly in front of her. "It won't have to be for long. My custody hearing is scheduled for right after Thanksgiving. As long as the judge believes that I can provide Todd and Lissi with what Steph and Ethan provide—a stable family life—there's no reason why he would deny my petition for joint custody."

"And that's going to prevent your ex-wife from moving again to Europe?"

He grimaced. "Nothing prevents Steph from doing what she wants. But she won't be able to keep the kids with her for the entire time. Instead of the sixteen hours a week I'm allowed now—assuming it doesn't inconvenience her—she'll have to agree to new terms. *Joint* terms. Ray says that there's a possibility that I could have them for the entire school year, even. That they'd only go to Europe for vacation and holiday breaks." He grabbed her hands. "The only good things to come out of my marriage were Lisette and Todd. And for too long, they barely even knew I was their father. I'm not going to lose them again."

"But we'd be lying. You have no intention of marrying me."

"Being married shouldn't matter. Technically, it's not even supposed to," Gabe said. "I should have been awarded joint custody in the first place."

"Why weren't you?"

"Because I made the mistake of loving my wife." His voice went flat. "And when I caught her in bed—*our* bed—with Ethan, I lost my temper." His hands curled. "I decked him and got charged with assault as a result. Then I stupidly followed that up by crawling into a whiskey bottle for a while. The assault charge was dropped eventually, but the damage was done. The bastard ended up with my wife *and* my kids." His lips twisted. "Proof that the lawyers in his family are better than the lawyers in mine."

She let out a long breath. "No wonder you wanted some privacy to talk." Buying time—and not exactly sure why—she gathered up the wet tablecloth and took it into the back, where she ran water and left it to soak. Then she returned to the front, where she found him pacing between the tables. But he stopped when he spotted her.

She had to remind herself that the intensity in his gaze had everything to do with his children and nothing to do with her personally. But she still had to concentrate on keeping her knees steady, though she pressed her back against the hard edge of the wine bar for extra support. "I can understand your position," she began carefully, "but I don't think I'm the right person for the job."

"Why? You have some secret scandal in your past that's worse than me being charged with assault?"

"No. No scandals." Humiliation wasn't scandal, was it? She tugged nervously at the silky red scarf that was holding her hair back in a low ponytail. "It's just, well, I like you."

He waited. "So?"

She should have just made up a scandal. It would have been simpler. And much less mortifying. "I mean, I—" She swallowed, feeling foolish. "I *like* you."

"Ah." Add a faint curve of his mobile lips to that laser-like gaze and she felt even more out of her depth. "Why would that be a problem?"

She grimaced. "Do I have to spell it out?"

"Apparently."

"It's one-sided," she said baldly. "And nobody would believe you could be seriously engaged to me, anyway."

He eyed her. "Because I'm old enough to be your father?"

She let out a half laugh. "You're forty-one. Hardly old enough to be my father." And the feelings he roused in her weren't the least bit daughterly.

"How'd you know how old I was?"

"Fiona," she admitted, realizing she'd given herself away much too easily.

"Thought you didn't talk about your families much."

Her face was getting hot. "All right. I asked. Is that a crime?"

"Not at all. And you're twenty-seven." That little smile was back. "I asked."

She didn't know what to say to that, so for once in her life, she kept her mouth shut.

He walked up to her, not stopping until the toes of his shoes were practically bumping hers. He rested his hands on the wine bar to either side of her.

She swallowed, more aware than ever just how alone they were. And just how tall he was. And how broad his shoulders were. And…how incredible he smelled.

"For the record—" his head dropped and his whisper tickled at her ear, not helping her case one whit "—it's not one-sided. I *like* you, too. Maybe you didn't notice that when you were telling me to make it look good. It's one of the reasons why I think a sudden engagement between us would be…convincing." He shifted slightly until he was looking her right in the eyes. "So let's get that cleared up right now." He closed his mouth over hers.

The taste of him went straight to her head. Her joints went soft. And instead of pushing against him, her palms slowly slid up his chest, over his shoulders. Colors splashed in her mind and her head fell back when the low sound he made filled her mouth as his kiss deepened. Lengthened.

And then he was tearing away, pulling in a whistling breath.

She was shaking. She realized his hand was in her hair, cradling her neck. Beyond that, she couldn't seem to gather a functioning thought.

"Think about it." His voice was a low caress, stirring a curl of hair at her temple. "I'll give you whatever you want in return."

Her addled brain might as well have been an old engine, coughing and stuttering, before it finally fired and she began to understand what he was saying. He meant think about pretending to be his fiancée. Her bones felt liquefied and her muscles felt shaky, but she still managed to shake her head. "I don't want anything. It's not a good idea. One-sided or two-sided. It's still not a good idea." She couldn't stand to find herself, once again, a hindrance to someone she cared about. "You should find someone else."

"There is no one else."

"Someone you've dated—"

"I don't date." He grimaced. "Not anymore. Look. Just give yourself a day or two to think about it," he advised. "Think about Fiona. As young at heart as she is, she is not a young woman. How many chances will she have to enjoy her only great-grandchildren if they're out of the country again for the better part of what's left of their childhood?"

He couldn't have found a more vulnerable button to push. Fiona was extremely dear to Bobbie.

"All right," she agreed reluctantly. "I'll *think* about it. But you—" she lifted her finger and jabbed it into the center of his hard chest "—would be wise to spend the next day or two thinking of someone more suitable to make your pretend fiancée."

"Believe me, Bobbie. You're very suitable."

She managed a smile, but there was no humor in it. "You'll change your mind," she promised.

People always did.

Chapter 4

By Saturday afternoon, Bobbie felt certain that Gabe had done just what she'd expected. Changed his mind.

He hadn't shown up that morning to finish the grout work on her newly tiled bathroom floor. Nor had he called to explain his absence. His silence didn't seem to fit with the man she thought she was coming to know, but it definitely served as a reminder that just because he was Fiona's grandson, it didn't mean that she really knew him at all.

So they'd shared a few kisses and a few confidences. What did that mean in the scheme of things? She'd shared a lot more than that with her ex-fiancé, thinking they would be spending a lifetime together.

Only now, Lawrence had a sleekly elegant blond woman with a stellar pedigree wearing his wedding ring on her finger. She'd been the one standing next to

him at the podium after his reelection, smiling her perfectly aligned smile, waving her perfectly manicured
hands and charming the press with her perfectly timed,
perfectly worded comments. She'd been the one he'd
loved all along, even when he'd been sweeping Bobbie off her feet.

"Ah, Bobbie, dear." Fiona's voice interrupted the
gathering steam of her memories. "Ujjayi breathing
is meant to be relaxing and energizing. Aim for the
soothing sound of an ocean. Not the menacing sound
of a freight train heading for derailment."

Bobbie opened her eyes and looked across at Fiona's
wry expression.

They were sitting cross-legged on yoga mats on the
floor in the middle of Fiona's spacious sunroom. The
lengthening sunlight gilded the plants surrounding the
room and water dripped soothingly over the small rock
fountain in the midst of them. It was a perfect place to
practice yoga, and they'd done so at least once a week
for months—well before Bobbie had moved into the
carriage house.

"Sorry." She rolled her head around her shoulders
and drew in a long breath. Usually, practicing yoga
was one of the few times that she could count on to
get out of her own head. To let go of whatever nonsense plagued her thoughts during the day, to thoroughly de-stress.

Why hadn't Gabe at least called?

"You know," Fiona said, unwinding her legs and
pushing to her bare feet, "there are times that call for
yoga, and there are times that call for cocktails." She
grinned. "I'm thinking...cocktail."

Bobbie laughed and straightened her legs. "A true yogi wouldn't even consider consuming alcohol."

"Fortunately, I have no aspirations in that direction," Fiona assured dryly. "And what does that song say? It's five o'clock somewhere?" She gestured. "Come with me."

Bobbie pushed to her feet and followed her friend out of the sunroom. She tightened the band holding her hair on the top of her head and tried not to look out the windows for some sign of Gabe's truck as they walked through the house. When she did sneak a peek, all she saw was the gardening crew working on the lush landscape and the catering truck, there to set up the outdoor tent that would house the dance floor for the party tomorrow night that Fiona didn't even want.

When they reached Fiona's office, which overlooked the half-acre sweep of lawn leading to the carriage house, Fiona waved at the massive leather wing chairs angled in front of the fireplace. "Sit." She moved to the ornate cabinet standing against the wall.

Bobbie sat, watching her elderly friend pull open the cabinet to reveal an extremely well-stocked bar. Fiona had once told her that she hadn't changed a single thing in the office after her husband had died. It was the only room she had left untouched in the entire house, because it felt like he was still with her whenever she worked in there.

"I meant to thank you again for helping out at the office yesterday. It took months to get an appointment with the community affairs rep from Cragmin, and I'd have hated to reschedule."

Bobbie shrugged, though she still was a little surprised that Fiona had managed to double-book her schedule the way she had. She'd been across town making another funding request when the manufacturing company's community affairs manager had shown up at Golden's office and Fiona had called Bobbie in a rush to fill in for her. "I'm always willing. You know that, though I'm a poor substitute for you."

Fiona waved the cocktail shaker as she pulled it off the shelf. "You did wonderfully well, as I knew you would. I got an email last night from the CEO that we were on the short list for the grant." She added ice from a small, cleverly hidden freezer to the shaker. "But enough of that. How are your mother and sisters?"

"All fine. I've been helping Tommi at the bistro this past week. One of her servers has been on vacation."

Fiona was nodding as she added a shot of this and a dash of that. "I wish my daughter-in-law would have thought to ask your sister to cater this thing tomorrow." She capped the shaker and shook it so vigorously that Bobbie wondered if she was mentally wringing Astrid Gannon's neck. "Then at least the food would have been wonderful."

"I'm sure the food will be fine," Bobbie soothed. "And I think Tommi has enough on her plate with the bistro being as busy as it is." She'd thought her sister had seemed particularly stressed the past week, but of course, Tommi had simply dismissed the very idea when Bobbie had tried to broach the subject. And since Bobbie hadn't wanted to answer Tommi's questions about Gabe's presence at the bistro the other night either, she'd kept most of her thoughts to herself. "You've said before that your daughter-in-law hosts some magnificent parties."

"Trust you to remember that," Fiona muttered

darkly. She poured the pale yellow contents of the shaker into two martini glasses and handed one to Bobbie. "Cheers."

Bobbie lifted her glass in salute and sipped gingerly, well used to Fiona's less-than-delicate hand when it came to mixing a cocktail. Predictably, the drink was light on lemon and heavy on vodka. "I think it's nice that your family wants to celebrate your birthday with you."

Fiona waved her hand. "It would be nice if it were just family and a few friends." She sank down into a corner of the opposite chair. "Instead, I believe Astrid has invited half of the world. She never even asked who I would like to invite. I suppose she was afraid I'd invite someone *unsuitable.*" She made a face. "Like my own employees and volunteers."

"Well, it'll be over soon enough."

"I'm not sure I appreciate a phrase like that at my age," Fiona replied dryly.

Bobbie couldn't help but laugh, even though she was immediately reminded of Gabe's words about his grandmother. "You're one of the youngest people I know. And it has nothing to do with the calendar."

Fiona leaned forward and patted Bobbie's knee. "You're a dear. Now tell me what you think of Gabriel."

Bobbie nearly choked on her cocktail. She swallowed, trying not to gasp a little at the strong alcohol. "He's very…handy." She lifted her shoulder and hoped Fiona would blame the color in her cheeks on the drink. "The work he's doing around the carriage house has been great."

Fiona's eyes sparkled. "Yes. But what do you think of *him?*"

For a moment, Bobbie wondered if Gabe had told his grandmother about their unconventional meeting. Or about what had happened since.

But then she dismissed it as unlikely.

"I think he's—" *sexy, handsome, unreasonably attractive* "—nice," she managed weakly. "He certainly loves his children."

Fiona nodded. Her eyes narrowed slightly as she sipped her cocktail. "He'd do anything for them."

"Mmm." Bobbie took another too-hasty drink that burned all the way down her throat. Already her head was beginning to swim a little and she quickly set the glass on the small table next to the chair while she could still set it safely without spilling it. "I imagine they'll all be here for your party tomorrow evening?"

"I'd certainly prefer Todd and Lisette over their mother's presence, but Astrid hasn't included the children."

Bobbie blinked. "Gabe's…ex-wife is coming?" Given their strained relationship, she hadn't expected that. Had he exaggerated the situation?

"Yes. I know it sounds odd. But Astrid and Stephanie's mother are dear friends and for some reason, Astrid still believes that Stephanie and Gabe will reconcile. Doesn't seem to matter that Stephanie betrayed Gabe in the worst possible way, or that she's doing her level best to keep Gabe's children from him as much as she can. She picked Stephanie for Gabe years ago, and can't bring herself to realize that her choice stunk." Fiona let out an exasperated sigh. "The woman doesn't even know her own son. And *my* son doesn't seem any better. Even though I myself haven't seen Stephanie in years, I'm not holding out hope that she'd have the good taste to decline the invitation." Fiona drained her glass and with no seeming regard for the fine crystal, set it on the side table with a clunk. "I think *you* should come to the party. I don't know why I didn't think of it before."

Bobbie straightened her spine. "What?"

Fiona lifted her eyebrows. "It's *my* birthday party. I should be able to invite at least one person that I want to be there, shouldn't I?"

"Well, of course, but—"

"Then it's done." She pushed to her feet. "Sadly, it's black tie." She rolled her eyes. "Astrid's doing, of course. You have something suitable? Maybe a dress left over from that drip of a fiancé you had?"

"I have a gown or two." Shoved in the back of her closet because she didn't have the good sense to get rid of clothing that she never wore—or never planned to wear again. Until her involvement with Lawrence, the only times she'd had to dress formally were for the annual Christmas parties that her Uncle Harry always threw. "But honestly, Fiona, I'll feel like I'm gatecrashing." She knew Astrid Gannon had sent out the engraved invitations weeks ago, because Fiona had been bemoaning the upcoming party ever since.

"Frankly, I feel like *I* am gatecrashing," Fiona countered. "Mark my words. It will be stuffy and boring. But I beg you. Just come for a few minutes. Long enough to give me *someone* besides Gabriel I can honestly say how nice it is to see."

"One of these days I'm going to learn how to say no to you, and mean it." Bobbie stood up also. Her head felt light from just those few sips of her cocktail. She needed to eat.

Fiona smiled victoriously and tucked her arm through Bobbie's as they strolled through the house toward the kitchen. "You'll be the belle of the ball."

"Now I *know* your cocktail has gone to your head," Bobbie accused wryly. "Since you know as well as I do how unlikely that will be. If you want a belle, you'd need Frankie or Georgie." Both of her older sisters could sweep into any setting and have the masses charmed with barely a flick of their fingers. It was a talent they'd come by naturally from their mother. Even Tommi possessed it—when she could be dragged out from the kitchen, where she usually ended up even when she wasn't the chef.

"Give yourself a little more credit." Fiona pulled open the back door for Bobbie. "You might surprise yourself."

"I doubt it." Bobbie hugged Fiona. "But I'll be there, for you."

"Be where?"

Bobbie straightened like a shot, spinning around so fast that she nearly tipped over.

Gabe's hand shot out, catching her shoulder. "Steady there."

She didn't know which was worse. The dizzying effect of Fiona's lethal cocktail, the sudden thrill of Gabe's touch, or the fact that both were probably as plain as the nose on her face to Fiona, Gabe *and* his daughter and son, who were standing on the porch beside him.

"At the party tomorrow," Fiona answered, which was good because Bobbie didn't seem able to make her mouth work in concert with her brain. "Bobbie's coming, too. Isn't that lovely?"

"Sure." Gabe's gaze rested on her face and she couldn't tell what he was thinking to save her life.

What she was thinking about was what he'd asked her to do. And that she knew she should refuse. Again. Which wasn't something that she could very well tell him right then and there. Not with his grandmother and kids witnessing her non-conversation with him. "I, um, I need to get home," she finally managed to say to the air in general. She glanced at Fiona. "See you tomorrow." She moved past Gabe without looking at him directly, and managed to smile at his kids as she quickly ran down the porch steps.

"I'll come with you." His deep voice followed her, putting an abrupt end to her hasty departure. "Still need to finish that tile job."

She looked back, not meeting his eyes or Fiona's, and nodded jerkily. "Okay."

"Lissi, Todd, you go inside with Grandma and finish your homework."

Bobbie realized belatedly that both of his children were sporting extremely fat, heavy-looking backpacks.

"We'll go out for dinner when I've finished at Ms. Fairchild's," he added.

They both nodded without argument and went inside the main house with Fiona.

"Ready?" Gabe prompted when Bobbie didn't start moving again toward the carriage house.

She stopped staring after the children and started walking instead. Even without letting her gaze sidle toward him, she was excruciatingly aware of him. "Your kids seemed rather subdued."

"I guess that's one way of putting it."

She couldn't help herself. She looked right at him,

taking in his unshaven jaw and bloodshot eyes. "And you look like you haven't slept in days. What's wrong?"

"Nothing that another ten hours in every day wouldn't cure." He took her elbow, helping her along the uneven stone pathway that led to her door, even though he had to know that she'd walked over it hundreds of times before. "One of my construction managers had a car accident a few days ago and I've had to fill in on the job site for him." They stopped at the door of the cottage and he waited for her to unlock it.

"Is he going to be all right?"

He gave her an odd look. "Yeah. Broke a few bones, but he'll probably be nagging me to get him back at the site before the doctor even says it's okay." He followed her inside. "You're the only one who has asked that."

Her little carriage house felt cozy at the best of times. With him standing in the center of her living room between the leather chair that she'd purloined from her mother's basement and the outdated floral-patterned but immensely comfortable couch she'd bought at a consignment store, the space felt even smaller. More intimate. "I'm sorry? I'm sure his co-workers wanted to know how—"

He waved his hand. "Yeah. Of course folks on the crew and at the office asked." He ran his hand tiredly down his face, then around to the back of his neck. "Don't mind me." He turned toward the short, narrow hall that would lead him to the bathroom, only to do an about-face a second later.

She nearly bumped into him and he caught her shoulders in his hands again. "Sorry." He stepped around her. "Tools are in my truck."

She chewed the inside of her lip, watching him leave.

He hadn't brought up the business about her posing as his fiancée. Maybe he wouldn't. Maybe he'd changed his mind so thoroughly that he didn't even want to bring it up.

As if she'd have forgotten it if he didn't.

She exhaled roughly and headed into the kitchen to let the dogs out of their kennels. The light on her answering machine was blinking, and she poked the button before opening the cage.

"Bobbie, this is Quentin Rich."

She glanced at the machine as she snapped on Archimedes's leash. "Who?"

"We met at the Hunt Christmas party last year. I heard you were available and I thought it would be nice to get together again. Maybe dinner? Call me." The caller reeled off his number.

Bobbie looked down at Archimedes. "Do you remember him?"

The dog's tongue lolled out of his mouth. He gave her a goofy look.

"Me either. And that party was ten months ago." She erased the message and called Zeus, who'd been patiently waiting. With their leashes on, they both bolted out the front door, pulling her along with them. They veered away from their original target—the bushes—when they spotted Gabe and raced toward him instead.

A grin stretched across his face, erasing years of tiredness, as he set down his bucket filled with tiling tools and crouched down to greet them. "How you doing, Zeus?" He rubbed one dog down, then the other. "Archie? You staying away from eating Bobbie's couch cushions?"

"I'm surprised." Bobbie slowly walked closer, giving the leashes more play. "Not even Fiona can tell them apart."

Gabe figured it was safer all around for him to focus on the oversized puppies slathering slobber over his hands and arms than on Bobbie.

Or he'd be the one likely to start slobbering over himself.

He was used to being around beautiful women. Hell, he'd been married to one, even if she'd turned out to be carved from ice. So what was it about *this* woman that turned his guts inside out? He knew he should look at her and think "too young," but her age was truthfully the last thing he had on his mind when she was around.

Maybe that explained midlife crises...

"They've got their differences," he pointed out a little doggedly. "Archie here has a quirk in the way he holds his ears. And Zeus just looks at you like he wants to lie on your feet and sleep for a week. Which is a thought I've had myself lately."

Bobbie laughed softly, and he couldn't help himself. He looked up at her.

She wore stretchy black pants that clung to every inch of her shapely legs from knee to hip. And even though she had some gauzy white shirt on, it didn't do diddly to disguise the lush curves adoringly displayed by a sleeveless black top beneath it that ended well above her waist. What the thin fabric did succeed at was taunting him mercilessly with the filmy silhouette of those inches of bare skin exposed between the top and the pants. Bare skin that nipped in over a tiny waist that made everything else seem even more...curved.

He stifled on oath, dragging his gaze away.

Archimedes slapped his gold, feathered tail on the

ground, still grinning sloppily as if he read Gabe's mind all too easily.

And maybe the dogs did, because Zeus trotted back over to his mistress, leaning his healthy, growing body protectively against Bobbie's legs. Her hand dropped to her side, her slender fingers sliding over his well-shaped head. The dog looked as if he wanted to purr. "They're both good boys," she said. "Once they go to their trainer, I'm sure they'll end up being excellent assistance dogs."

Gabe distracted Archimedes from sniffing the bag of grout sitting inside the bucket. "How many puppies have you raised for Fiona's group?"

"Counting these two?" She didn't hesitate. "Seventeen."

"That's a lot of dogs. You have them for nearly two years, don't you?"

"They usually go into training around eighteen months. I generally get them when they're about eight weeks old, but sometimes it's later because they've been moved from another raiser for some reason. These guys were littermates, so I got them at the same time. Usually, I have a mixture of ages. One time I had four dogs at once." She grinned wryly. "Needless to say, my mother and sisters thought I'd lost a few screws. And it was a little...crazy. Compared to that, just having these two now is pretty quiet, actually. I have photo albums of all of my puppies on the shelf in the hall."

The shelf he'd nearly knocked over the day he'd brought the tile in for her bathroom floor. "But in the end, you give them all up."

She looked down at the dog beside her. "That's the

point. I'm just the puppy raiser. Not one of Fiona's dog trainers."

"Why not?"

"Because this is something I'm actually good at. All of the puppies I've raised have been successfully part-nered with someone. Guide dogs for the blind, a few hearing dogs, a few service dogs. One even became a search and rescue dog out in Montana." She lifted her shoulder and the filmy shirt shimmied around her hips. "It's my one part in helping someone else's life be a lit-tle easier." Her cheeks colored and her eyes looked like fog clouding Rainier. "I know that probably sounds—"

"—like Fiona talking."

She shook her head, her lips curving slightly. "That wasn't what I was going to say."

"But it's the truth." For several generations, the Gan-non family had had nearly every advantage in life. But instead of simply donating her money to some cause she believed in, his grandmother had spent most of Gabe's life personally involved in one. She'd founded her small agency that trained and placed assistance dogs around the country, and even though the rest of Gabe's family thought she was more than a little ec-centric for working so hard for so long when she didn't have to, he'd admired her for it.

In her way, Fiona Gannon was as much the oddball in the family as he was.

"You're doing a good thing," he told Bobbie now. Truthfully. He pushed tiredly to his feet. "And for the record, I'm certain that you're good at a lot more than raising puppies. But I still think it's gotta be damn hard to give them up when it's time."

Her lashes swept down for a moment. "It's always

hard to say goodbye. But I get to meet the person they're partnered with when they finish their training, and the dogs always remember me." She looked up then with a crooked grin. "And I receive a ton of Christmas cards with the dogs' pictures in them."

"Well, you're still a better person than I am." He picked up the heavy bucket, lifting it away from Archimedes's inquisitive snout. "I probably wouldn't want to let them go."

"You really don't have to finish the floor today, you know. It's not going anywhere. Take a break."

Her gaze danced over him, then away again, and he wished to hell he knew what he could do to ease her obvious nervousness. But he wasn't ready to hear her tell him again that he was on his own when it came to the fake fiancée business, so they were both stuck. Unfortunately, every day that ticked past was a day that took him closer to the judge's courtroom.

"It's not like you haven't been working hard enough already, covering for your injured guy," she continued.

Unlike his ex-wife, who'd quite vocally considered Gabe's injured worker to be a personal inconvenience to her. "It won't take me long to grout the floor." Not when her bathroom was barely large enough to turn around in.

"And then you'll go and have dinner with your children?"

"I'll take them to dinner," he clarified. "They're none too happy right now to begin with, since their mother decided to go to D.C. with Ethan a few days ago for some meetings. The last thing to help that situation would be my cooking."

She worried her soft lower lip with the pearly edge

of her teeth for a moment. "Lisette and Todd have been staying with you, then? When is their mother coming back?"

"Tomorrow, and it was surprising that Steph was willing to leave them with me." Particularly when she'd learned he was putting in even more hours on the job than usual, until she'd realized the advantage the situation might afford her. "But then she realized that I might do such a rotten job of caring for them full-time for a few days that she'll have extra ammunition against me when we go to court again."

Bobbie's soft lips tightened. "No wonder you're tired. Extra work on that job site on top of your usual load, plus having the kids and getting them to and from school?" Shaking her head, she walked over to him and wrapped her free hand around the bucket handle, unsuccessfully trying to dislodge his hand in the process. "Give me that. My floor can definitely wait." The curls coiled on top of her head tickled his chin, smelling faintly of lemon.

He still didn't let go of the bucket. "I'll let the floor wait if you'll come to dinner with me and the kids."

He had to steel his nerves against the soft gaze she turned toward him. "I think that's bribery or something."

Bribery and a good dose of self-torture. "Is it working?"

"You're as bad as your grandmother," she accused. But there was a faint smile on her soft, soft lips.

"That's probably one of the nicer things I've been accused of," he admitted wryly. "Is that a yes?"

"Yes. To dinner," she added quickly.

But he didn't mind the qualification.

After a little time with his kids, maybe she'd see that one more "yes" would be just another way of making someone else's life a little easier for a while.

Namely, his.

And if she did, the trick then would be for all of them to get through it unscathed when their arrangement was no longer necessary.

Chapter 5

The next evening, Bobbie tilted her head sideways and studied her reflection in the full-length mirror attached to the front of her closet door. The hem of the pewter-colored gown was pooling on the carpet around her bare feet, but that would be solved well enough when she put on her high heels. Squinting at herself, she gathered up two fists of ringlets and piled her hair on top of her head.

"I don't know, Zeus. What do you think? Does it look like I'm trying to play dress-up? What do you think Gabe will think?" She looked at the dog's reflection in the mirror. He was watching her with patient eyes from where he lay on the floor at the foot of her bed that was strewn with a half-dozen gowns, already tried and rejected.

The only gown left was the one she was wearing.

She'd bought it on a shopping spree with Frankie—with her fashionable sister's mild approval—shortly before Lawrence had dumped her. She'd never actually worn it out. She would have returned it to the store, in fact, except it had been a clearance dress and it had been less embarrassing just to shove it in the back of her closet than go back to the store and admit she hadn't needed the dress after all.

Not when her fiancé had decided *she* didn't need to accompany him to any more fund-raisers. Or to anything else, for that matter. He particularly didn't want her working on his reelection campaign. What was the point, since she didn't have a pipeline into the treasures of the HuntCom empire after all?

She let go of her hair and it fell down past her shoulders, settling into its usual disarray. Her hand swept down the folds of gleaming fabric that fell in a column from the empire waist. The gown had tiny cap sleeves that were little more than wide straps hugging the points of her shoulders. The front of the bodice was cut low and straight across her breasts, leaving more of her cleavage on view than Bobbie was accustomed to. But Frankie hadn't vetoed the dress, so Bobbie could only cross her fingers in the hope that it suited her as much as anything could.

Her phone jangled, startling her from her critical study of herself, and she picked up the extension on the nightstand. "Hello?"

"Bobbie?" The deep voice was unfamiliar. "This is Quentin. Quentin Rich. I've been hoping to reach you."

She wrinkled her nose. The guy who'd left the phone message. Tucking the phone against her shoulder, she stepped over Archimedes, who was sleeping in the doorway, and went into the bathroom to rummage through the drawer for some hairpins. Where were the sparkly ones that Georgie had given her for Christmas? "Right. Quentin." Whom she still couldn't remember. "How are you?"

"Great. Just great. Listen, I was wondering if you'd like to meet up again. There's a new restaurant that's been getting rave reviews I've been dying to take you to."

She lifted her eyebrows, a little taken aback by his enthusiasm. "Really. Dying, huh?"

"I know you'd love the place," he continued confidently. "You actually dine in the dark. So you don't even see what's on your plate. It's all very…tactile."

"Messy, you mean." She couldn't help but laugh, as it finally came to her when they'd met. "Which seemed fitting, since you saw me spill a plate of hors d'oeuvres on myself at last year's Christmas party."

"It was hardly your fault," he assured quickly. "And that wasn't it at all."

She rolled her eyes and slammed the drawer shut. Maybe the hair clips were in her jewelry box. "As I recall, you were pitching some sort of software to Hunt-Com. How'd that go?" She hitched up her dress again, stepping over the dogs on her way to her dresser.

"Great. Just great. Mr. Hunt's taken quite a personal interest lately, too."

A stray thought had her hesitating. "Which Mr. Hunt?" As far as she knew, Gray was way too occupied with helming the worldwide company while keeping up with his wife and their kids to get personally involved with a software project that even she remembered had been relatively small and unexciting.

"Harrison," Quentin provided smoothly. "I'll admit it's pretty flattering to have such a pioneer taking an interest in my work—"

The man prattled on, but Bobbie barely heard.

Harry.

First it had been Tim Boering. And now it was this guy. She hadn't had so much as a date since Lawrence dumped her, but now, in a matter of weeks, she'd had two men claiming interest. And both were connected to Harry?

Suspicion niggled at her, but she dismissed it. Admittedly, Harry was one of the most manipulative—if oddly charming—men that Bobbie knew. But he knew what a blow the whole Lawrence episode had been; she couldn't imagine why he'd nudge guys her way now. He never had before.

If anything, he was probably looking for some innocuous person to keep Quentin and his latest software project safely entertained.

Satisfied with her reasoning, she snatched up the sparkling hair clips shaped like daisies where they were buried beneath a jumble of inexpensive earrings and necklaces that would have given the orderly Georgie fits. "Listen, Quentin, I'm sorry, but I'm just on my way out." Nearly.

"Ah. Then why don't I call you tomorrow?"

"No!" She winced a little at her own vehemence. "I mean, I appreciate you thinking of me, but I'm—"

"—seeing someone again already, I suppose."

She opened her mouth to deny it, but the words didn't come. A vision of Gabe and his children crowding around her coffee table the night before to wolf down the best pizza Seattle had to offer swam inside her head much too readily.

"Well…" She forced a little laugh, hoping he'd draw his own conclusions without her actually having to tell an outright lie. She'd never claimed that she wasn't a coward. And she didn't want to hurt his feelings any more than she'd wanted to hurt Boering's. They were associates of her Uncle Harry's, after all.

"Message understood," Quentin was saying. "But seriously, if you change your mind, you have my number."

"Right." Actually, she didn't, since she'd erased his earlier message with no thought or regret whatsoever. "I'll keep that in mind. I've really got to run now."

"Sure. Good night, Bobbie."

"'Bye, Quentin." She quickly disconnected and tossed the phone on her jumbled bed. "Zeus, remind me to tell Uncle Harry I'm not the welcoming committee lady the next time I see him, will you?"

Zeus yawned hugely, then lowered his head down onto his outstretched paws.

"Thanks for the support," Bobbie muttered. She stepped over him again to reach the mirror and pinned back several curls of hair with Georgie's fancy little clips. Then she pushed her feet into the shimmery silver shoes with the deadly spiked heels that Frankie had insisted were made to go with the gown and grabbed the long, black cashmere coat that had been a birthday present from her mother two years earlier.

There was no need for her purse since she was just going across to the main house. She swung the coat around her shoulders and snatched up the box containing the scrapbook she'd made as a gift for Fiona, then headed outside.

The enormous tent that had been erected on the graceful lawn was surrounded by little white lights that sparkled wetly in the damp night air. She could hear the band playing some old, sedate melody that sounded more in keeping with a museum opening than a birthday celebration and as she neared the tent, she could see that only a few couples were moving about on the dance floor. The floor was surrounded by linen and crystal-covered round tables, most of them occupied, and the nervousness that Bobbie had been more or less successfully holding at bay since she'd woken up that morning came barreling down the chute.

A uniformed young man carrying a gilded tray of filled champagne flutes crossed her path. "Wait." The heels of her fancy shoes sunk into the grass a little as she took a step after him. "Can I—"

"Certainly." He waited for her to take one of the flutes, which she did carefully lest she knock the other glasses over.

"Thanks." She took a quick drink as her gaze skimmed over the crowd. "You wouldn't happen to know where the birthday girl is, would you?"

"Inside, I believe." The young man continued on his way toward the guests.

Bobbie looked up at the deep terrace that led into the house. There were tables and guests there, too. She took another sip of champagne, chiding herself inwardly for feeling so nervous.

She'd spent several thoroughly enjoyable hours with Gabe and his children the evening before and he hadn't uttered one single syllable about his suggestion that she pretend to be his fiancée for the benefit of his child custody case. If anything, he'd treated her more like a sister. Certainly not like someone he'd twisted inside out with his very kiss.

And it wasn't as if he hadn't had an opportunity to talk to her privately, because after they'd ravenously consumed the pizza that she'd talked him into letting her order while he'd been wedged into her bathroom working on the floor, Todd and Lisette had been totally occupied playing with the dogs in the yard outside.

For all she knew, he'd come to his senses and realized the potholes in his thinking, so there would be no need for her to get into all the reasons why going along with his scheme was a bad idea.

Tightening her arm around the large gift-wrapped box, she went up the shallow steps to the terrace. On the way, she recognized Kanya, the community affairs manager from the company that Fiona was hoping to get that substantial grant from, and stopped long enough to exchange pleasantries. Hers was the only familiar face that Bobbie saw.

But when she spotted Gabe standing just inside the open French doors of the living room, she forgot how to speak altogether.

Over the years, Bobbie figured she'd seen countless men in countless tuxedos. But not once had she ever been dumbstruck by the very sight. He looked... magnificent.

It wasn't just the formal wear, though the midnight-blue jacket and trousers were miles away from his usual jeans and T-shirt. He'd slicked back his dark hair from his face and when he shifted, looking out over the terrace, even from several yards away she was struck by the sharp angles of his handsome face, by the startling clarity of his blue, blue eyes.

And then those eyes turned her way.

His lips turned up at the corners and even though she knew it was fanciful of her, when his hand left his pocket to lift in her direction, it all seemed to happen in an achingly slow motion, accompanied by a swell of music from the band.

Her stomach dipped and swayed woozily, and she had the ridiculous sense that her life, in that moment, had just changed forever.

"So we're hoping to get an answer for Fiona on the grant," she heard Kanya saying, though it might as well have been gibberish.

Bobbie dragged in a shaking breath and swallowed hard, mumbling something—hopefully coherent—to Kanya before she headed toward Gabe and his extended palm.

Only when she neared the open doors did she notice the other people he was with. Two men easily as tall as he was, though not quite as broad in the shoulders, but with hair equally as dark as Gabe's. She guessed that they were his older brothers, Liam and Paul. And the women with them were undoubtedly their wives—who looked like cookie-cutter socialites with their upswept hair, diamonds circling their long throats and strapless black gowns showing their svelte figures to their best advantage.

They were so picture-perfect that Bobbie felt even more like a schoolgirl playing at dress-up.

Then Gabe stepped out onto the terrace, closing the distance between them. "I was beginning to think I was going to have to come and find you," he greeted.

His gaze ran over her. "But the wait was worth every second. Let me take that." He plucked the box out from beneath her arm. "Heavy," he commented.

She was still shaking, and she ordered herself to get a grip. "I made a scrapbook showing everything that's gone on at the agency since Fiona started it. You wouldn't believe some of the dusty old boxes I hunted through," she added nervously. "I had everyone working there helping me keep it a secret. There ended up being a, um, a lot of stuff."

His lips tilted. "I'll bet. And she'll love it." Then he leaned toward her. "You take my breath away." His low voice whispered over her ear as his lips brushed her cheek.

She actually felt faint for a moment and stared up at him as he straightened. "How can you tell?" She cleared her throat and tugged her collar. "I'm wearing a coat."

He brushed his thumb over her chin. "Believe me. I can tell. Everything all right?"

Except that she knew she was being dazzled by him? "Fine." She took another sip of her champagne, willing her heart to move back down into her chest where it belonged. "I didn't mean to be this late. I was held up this afternoon having lunch with my mother. Where's Fiona?"

"Being held captive by *my* mother and some guests she's introducing." Gabe took her hand, setting off yet another bout of weak knees as he tucked it around his arm and turned her toward the house. He added her gift to the collection already gathered on a long table and his head lowered again so she could hear his soft voice.

"Astrid doesn't seem to recognize the irony in having to introduce someone to Fiona at Fiona's own party."

"Maybe we should mount a rescue," Bobbie suggested just as softly.

Gabe's eyes crinkled. "I knew you were a kindred spirit."

Her smile felt shaky. The man was much too appealing. It was an effort to remind herself that he was still a man with an agenda—even as justified as his cause was.

She had no desire to get burned again, and every speck of self-preservation that she possessed was shrieking at her that she would be in even more deeply over her head where Gabriel Gannon was concerned than she had ever been with Lawrence. And even though she was finally realizing that she hadn't wanted to die of a broken heart when *that* had ended, the experience had still been a humiliating disaster.

Unfortunately, there was also a small voice inside her head that was screaming at her that it was already too late.

Her fingertips pressed against the hard biceps she could feel through the very fine fabric of his exquisitely cut dinner jacket. She tipped the champagne glass to her lips again, swallowing down the last sip of the sparkling wine before depositing the glass on an elegantly draped high-top table near the doorway. "Then what are we waiting for?"

Gabe's smile grew slowly. He covered her hand on his arm with his and squeezed as he escorted her into the house.

Several sets of eyes immediately turned toward them, but Bobbie didn't have a chance to shy away because his hand tightened even more on hers. "Every-body, this—" he looked down at her in a way that had her heart jumping back into her throat all over again "—is Bobbie. She's—"

"—the one renting Fiona's carriage house," one of the cookie-cutter wives put in with a tone that had Bobbie's smile stiffening.

"—a close friend of mine," Gabe continued as if he hadn't been interrupted at all.

"And one of my all-time favorite people." Fiona's voice was as bright as her yellow gown as she swept into the room, giving Bobbie barely enough time to notice the way Gabe's brothers had glanced at each other after his words.

"Bobbie, dear, you've never looked lovelier." Fiona brushed her cheek against Bobbie's before straightening and smiling at her and Gabe. "Give me your coat and let me see your gown. We won't let you freeze. There are heaters going outside."

Bobbie obediently slipped out of her coat and Fiona handed it off to a server she flagged down. "Now," she said with satisfaction, "you two are surely the most striking couple here."

Couple? Bobbie hoped to heaven she didn't look as jarred as she felt hearing the term, particularly hearing it from Gabe's own grandmother.

And the way that Gabe tucked her hand around his arm again didn't help any.

"Grandmother, you're going to hurt our feelings." The same woman who'd set Bobbie's teeth on edge pouted prettily as she snuggled up next to her husband.

Fiona waved her hand dismissively. "Renée, don't

worry. We all know you and Diana both have a closet full of beauty pageant crowns."

Renée smiled, evidently mollified.

"Has Gabriel introduced you to everyone?" Fiona tucked her arm through Bobbie's other one, making her feel surrounded by support.

"He was working on it."

"Ah." Fiona gestured to Renée and her husband, a tall man with a sprinkling of gray in his brown hair. "This is Liam and Renée." Liam, Bobbie knew was Gabe's oldest brother. "And Paul and Diana." She gestured to the other couple. "Liam and Paul, of course, are the Gannon part of the Gannon Law Group, along with their—oh, there he is. Colin." Fiona waited for the tall, silver-haired man to join them. "My son, Colin. Dear, this is Bobbie Fairchild. I've told you about her."

"Of course." Bobbie found herself face to face with Gabe's father and knew she was seeing what the future Gabe would probably look like: silver-haired and incredibly handsome. And his smile was much more natural than either Liam's or Paul's. More like Gabe's, in fact. "I'm glad to finally meet you, Bobbie. I've met your mother, actually. She served on a committee with Astrid several years ago. She's a lovely woman."

"Thank you." Bobbie managed a smile. She still felt rather like a specimen on a pin. "It's nice to meet all of you." She took in the others with her smile.

"And now that the niceties have been observed," Fiona said brightly, "you all go on and have a dance." She waved toward the French doors and the tent outside. "I'm going to see if I can get that band to play something from this century." She headed out.

"I'd better make sure she doesn't cross swords with

Astrid again," Colin murmured with a wry smile that reminded Bobbie even more strongly of his youngest son before he strode out the doors. His daughters-in-law were hard on his heels as they prodded Liam and Paul out into the evening.

Which left Bobbie standing there alone with Gabe and she was suddenly very aware that her breast was pressed closely against the arm she was clutching.

She moistened her lips and carefully loosened her grip, stepping a few inches away. "Your family seems nice."

He cocked an eyebrow. "They're judgmental and pretentious and my sisters-in-law care more about how many diamonds they're wearing and how long they can stave off their wrinkles than anything else."

"Gabe!"

His lips tilted. "Don't worry. It's nothing I haven't told them to their faces. And they, in turn, find me as alien as I find them. But we all do care about one thing."

"Fiona?"

"Exactly." He turned her toward him, his hands cupping her shoulders. His thumbs brushed over the sleeves of her gown and her breathing went all scrambled again. "I did tell you how incredible you look, right?"

She nodded. "You—" the word came out sounding like a croak and she winced. "You clean up pretty well yourself. I like the bow tie," she added unwisely. Unwise because what she was thinking wasn't how urbane he looked in his dressy clothing, but how much she wanted to tug that tie apart. To slowly unfasten the mother-of-pearl studs down the front of his white shirt and peel it back—

She blinked and looked out the doors beside them, desperately trying to focus on the reality of the tent, the sparkling lights, the guests...

Anything but her increasingly uncontrolled attraction to him.

"You all right?" His thumbs brushed over her collarbones again. "You're looking flushed."

She was flushed.

From head to toe and every point in between.

Not even Lawrence had had such an effect on her, and she'd actually planned to marry him!

She swallowed and looked up at him. "You haven't given up on the idea of passing me off as your fiancée at all, have you," she accused bluntly.

His gaze didn't waver from her face. "I never claimed that I had."

"You haven't brought it up since the evening at my sister's bistro."

"If I had, you would have said no again. And I wanted to give you some time to really consider it. Because once you're in, I need you to stay in until the end."

"The end being a satisfactory custody ruling." She didn't wait for a verbal confirmation of what was plain on his face. "I'm not unsympathetic, Gabe. I've seen for myself how much you love your kids." It had been as much an ingredient during their shared dinner the night before as the pizza and lemonades. "And I really do hope you get what you want. For all of your sakes. But surely I'm not the only woman you can ask."

"I told you already. I don't date."

Her hands flopped. "Which I find just as hard to believe now as I did when you said it." She realized her voice had risen, and, flushing, looked guiltily around them. But they were the only ones in the spacious living room with its collection of comfortably feminine sofas and chairs and priceless artwork, probably because outside, the band had actually begun playing something from a recent decade. More people had joined Gabe's brothers and their wives on the dance floor. Nobody was paying Bobbie and Gabe any attention at all.

She lowered her voice anyway. "Maybe you're not dating anyone right this minute—" goodness knew she wasn't either "—but someone you *used* to—" She went silent when he pressed his finger over her mouth.

"If I tell you that I haven't dated anyone since I came to Seattle, will that convince you?"

"But that was a few years ago," she exclaimed, even though he hadn't moved his finger at all.

Which only succeeded in making her lips tingle even more.

"I know that was years ago. Look, I'll admit that there were women—" he grimaced a little "—a lot of women, for a while after Steph and I split. But none of them mattered. And since I've come to Seattle, I've had more important things on my plate." He moved his hand back to her shoulder. His lips twisted wryly. "If that gets me a sympathy vote, I'm not above using it to my advantage, either."

Sympathy wasn't what was curling through her.

"I don't want to mess anything up for you."

His hands tightened. "You won't."

"That's what my fiancé told me," she countered, "and he learned how wrong he was, too."

"You were engaged?"

"*Were* being the operative word."

"When?"

"Nearly a year ago."

"What happened?"

She exhaled. Maybe if he knew, he'd understand. "I was engaged to Lawrence McKay."

His brows pulled together. "He has something to do with the city, doesn't he?"

"He's on the city council, though he has much grander aspirations." At least he had when they were dating.

She stepped away from Gabe's hands, hoping that her mind would function more clearly if he wasn't touching her. But when she stepped backward, her sharp heel caught in her gown and she heard an ominous rip as she tottered backward.

"Whoa." He caught her before she could fall flat on her rear.

"See?" She craned her head around, lifting the back of her gleaming gown to see the torn hem. "This is the kind of stuff that always happens!"

"You catch your heel?"

"Or I spill cherry pie down the front of a white blouse at a fund-raising luncheon, or I laugh too loud, or I don't get a joke when everyone else does. Or I tell the largest supporter of my fiancé's congressional aspirations that he's a hypocrite for publicly criticizing a waterfront project that he's privately investing in!"

"Sounds like he was a hypocrite."

"Which wasn't the point. Lawrence needed a woman

by his side who was a credit to him, not someone who hadn't stuck with one job for more than a year at a time and that he was constantly having to find excuses for, or—"

"He sounds like a drip," Gabe said flatly.

Bobbie stared. "That's what Fiona calls him."

"And she's generally right when it comes to summing up people. So what happened after you called the hypocrite a hypocrite?"

She made a face. "Lawrence learned that I wasn't sitting on the trust fund he assumed I'd have."

"Why would he think you had a trust fund?"

"Because my father was Harrison Hunt's partner when he started HuntCom and I'd already donated a... small amount to his campaign." If nearly every dime she'd had left in her savings could be considered small. She rubbed the side of her nose, looking away.

Uncle Harry had given her and her sisters each a hundred thousand dollars when they'd graduated from high school. Bobbie, of course, was the only one who had managed to fritter away the money without accomplishing something brilliant first. Like opening her own restaurant or traveling the world or getting a fancy degree.

"He made the same assumption that a lot of people have, who know about my connection with the Hunts. But my father died when I was little and with expenses and, um, stuff, there wasn't as much left over for us as there might have been. HuntCom didn't really take off until after that."

"And McKay?"

"Broke off the engagement, of course."

"He's an idiot."

"In front of five hundred people attending the fund-raising dinner," she added.

He grimaced. "A drip with no class. Politics is probably the perfect place for him."

An unexpected laugh bubbled out of her lips. "Don't make me laugh. This is serious."

"I can't take anyone seriously who is stupid enough to hurt the person he's supposed to love. But it's my luck that you're free of him now."

She felt unsteady all over again, and it didn't take stepping through the hem of her dress to do it.

All it took was Gabe.

She sternly reminded herself that he wasn't talking about love and forever with *her*.

He was talking about a pretend engagement for the next several weeks for the express purpose of salvaging his right to his own children.

Could she do that?

Help him, while remembering that helping was the *only* thing she was supposed to be doing?

She stared up at him, at his blue eyes, which seemed to hold nothing but sincerity.

"I—"

"Gabriel." The cool, feminine voice cut across Bobbie's words, making her start. "If you're done flirting with the help, I'd like a moment."

Chapter 6

Gabe barely managed to hold back an oath at the sound of his ex-wife's voice.

Bobbie had been about to agree.

It had been as plain as the straight, slightly short nose on her pretty face.

And now, the gaze that had been locked on his face had turned from that soft, warm gray to a panicky silver.

He gave her a smile that he hoped to hell was calmer than he felt, and slid his arm around her shoulder as he turned to face his ex-wife, who'd entered the living room from within the house. Calling Steph on her rudeness would have been as futile as pointing out the same failure in his sisters-in-law.

They just didn't get it.

"What is it, Stephanie? I'm fresh out of flies for you to pull the wings off of."

Her lips thinned as she strolled into the room as if she owned it. Her figure-hugging, sparkling gown was as icy blue as the eyes studying his arm around Bobbie's shoulders. "This is a private matter. Regarding your children."

He felt Bobbie starting to inch away. "I'll leave you alone—"

"No need." He held her close, still watching his ex-wife. "Whatever you have to say, you can say in front of Bobbie."

Stephanie lifted an imperious eyebrow. She didn't even spare Bobbie so much as a glance, and Gabe's jaw tightened until his back teeth felt on edge.

She tossed her white fur wrap carelessly over the arm of a couch. "*This* is the Bobbie person that Toddy mentioned? I thought *he* was a friend of yours."

"As you can see, *she* is. More than a friend."

If anything, his ex-wife's thin lips went even thinner. She walked toward the French doors, looking out for a moment before turning on him. "In that case, I don't appreciate you parading your girlfriends in front of my children when you are *supposed* to be taking care of them."

"We had dinner with Bobbie, Steph. It's not like we got caught romping around in your bed," he added pointedly.

"Gabe," Bobbie murmured beside him. "Really, I should go."

"Yes," Stephanie agreed immediately. "You should. Gabriel needs to be considering *his* children, not making a fool of himself *over* a child."

"You're sinking to depths that are low, even for you, Steph."

"Excuse me." Bobbie moved out from beneath his arm. Her voice was determined. "I'll leave you both alone to discuss whatever it is you need to discuss."

She stopped next to Stephanie, who stood at least six inches taller than her, and Gabe nearly laughed when it looked to him as if she still managed to look down her nose at his ex-wife. "It's been...interesting to meet you, Mrs. Walker. But let me just say that in my experience, Gabe has never done anything where he *didn't* have the best welfare of his children in mind."

Then she looked back at him, and there were flags of color in her cheeks. "Which is one of the reasons why I think he's going to be a wonderful husband." She smiled at him before turning on her heel and sweeping past Stephanie through the French doors.

He watched her sail across the terrace. She looked so purposeful that it was hardly even noticeable that she was holding up the side of her dress in her hand to keep the torn hem from dragging behind her.

He didn't know if he was more stunned by Bobbie's in-your-face announcement of their intentions, or in awe.

"Don't tell me you're planning to actually marry that girl." Stephanie recovered more quickly than he, and her tone was more acidic than ever. "She's not even in *your* class...such as it is."

Gabe rounded on her. "What is your problem, Steph? I'm used to you flinging everything I do around in the mud, but you usually keep that nastiness reserved just for me. I wonder how your husband would feel knowing you insulted a woman that Harrison Hunt considers almost family?"

"What are you talking about?"

"Bobbie Fairchild." He knew that Stephanie wouldn't give a fig that Bobbie was very dear to Fiona, because Stephanie didn't care in the least about Fiona. But he knew what Stephanie did care about.

The same thing she'd always cared about.

Her husband and his high-paying career as one of HuntCom's legal eagles.

"She knows Harrison Hunt *very* well," he finished.

His ex-wife paled and he knew the dart had finally hit home.

She glanced outside, probably spotting Bobbie's distinct head of curls among the guests as easily as he did. "That...girl...knows Mr. Hunt?"

Gabe smiled coldly. "More than knows him. Family friends. She even calls him Uncle Harry."

"Ethan doesn't answer to Mr. Hunt. He works for *Grayson* Hunt." Her chin had lifted, but there was still a wariness in her voice that—if he were a forgiving sort—would have made him feel some regret over having put there.

Only he wasn't the forgiving sort.

"But they're all one big happy family, aren't they? Isn't that one of the things Ethan's talked about? How the Hunts keep the power to themselves? An international company the size of HuntCom...and it's all privately held by Harrison Hunt and his family."

"Fine," she snapped. "I'll...apologize to her."

"I thought you might. Nothing can ever get in the way of dear Ethan's career. Where is he, by the way?"

"Still in D.C. and he's worked hard to get where he is."

That, actually, was something that Gabe didn't dispute. Didn't make him love the guy any, but there was

no denying the man's success. Or that he'd been generous with the results when it came to Lisette and Todd.
They had the best of everything.

But that, too, made Gabe's fight that much steeper.

"I still don't believe you really intend to marry her."
Evidently, Steph couldn't leave well enough alone.
"You don't even believe in marriage. You swore you'd
never make that mistake again."

"You know what they say about the wonders of the
right woman."

Her glare would have done Medusa proud. "So when
is the happy day?"

"We wanted to wait until after Fiona's party and tell
the kids before announcing it officially." The lies came
so easily he wondered if he was all that different than
his brothers after all. Neither one of them took a truthful track if they could accomplish more with a lie. "We
haven't set a date yet. Bobbie's never been married, and
I want her to have the wedding of her dreams."

At that, his ex-wife finally looked away, and the
compunction that Gabe hadn't been able to feel earlier
crept in anyway. She and Gabe had eloped. And Gabe
knew her wedding with Ethan had been even more
hurried. He'd been surprised that she hadn't turned up
pregnant shortly after, since that was the only reason
she'd been willing to forgo a traditional, all-the-trim-
mings wedding with Gabe. She hadn't wanted her un-
planned pregnancy to show while walking down the
aisle in a fancy wedding gown.

"How nice for her," she said stiffly. "If you'll excuse
me, I haven't managed to give my birthday wishes to
Fiona yet." She grabbed up her wrap.

He exhaled tiredly. Even before their divorce, they'd

traded more jabs than anything else, and after years of sniping, he was heartily sick of the habit. The only good things that had resulted from their union had been Lisette and Todd. It would be nice if they could stop battling over them, too, though he couldn't see that ever happening when Stephanie considered his effort to gain joint custody tantamount to stealing them completely. "What was it about the kids you wanted to discuss?"

She slid the fur around her shoulders. "Todd's school counselor wants to have another meeting with us on Wednesday to discuss moving him to a different math class."

"You mean *you* want to have another meeting." They'd been arguing the subject for a month.

"I don't want Toddy feeling like a failure if I let them move him to an easier math class," Stephanie said.

Gabe shook his head. "He won't. And neither should you." Which was the real crux of the problem, he was certain.

"As if," she sniffed. "Just because you always choose the easy way out doesn't mean I want my son learning to do so."

He almost laughed. The easy way in the Gannon family meant following the same pattern. Which he hadn't done, in spades.

But Stephanie knew that he agreed with the counselor, who not only insisted that both of Todd's parents be included in their sessions, but believed that moving the boy to a class more suited to his skills would help him gain the confidence he needed in order to excel. Unfortunately, what Gabe thought didn't "officially" matter, since Stephanie had the legal right to make such decisions.

Which had left them at an impasse for too long. And Todd was the one suffering for it.

"Let me know what time the meeting is, and I'll be there."

She didn't look particularly mollified, but then he hadn't expected her to. "And Lisette has a dance recital Thursday evening. She insisted that I remind you, even though I warned her you would be too busy for that, too."

"I'm not too busy for either Todd or Lisette."

"Only for your wife," she countered. "Perhaps having a friendly chat with Bobbie won't be so difficult after all. I should probably warn her what she's getting herself into. Woman to woman, and all."

"Stay away from Bobbie."

"I thought I was supposed to apologize to her."

"I've changed my mind. Your apologies are too similar to poisonous apples."

Stephanie laughed coolly. "You always did have such a charming way with words." Assured of having the last say, she moved out onto the terrace and he heard her voice above the music. "Renée, honey. How long has it been? A year? Two! You look fabulous."

He let out a breath as her voice faded. God, he was glad that she was gone.

"Hey." Bobbie appeared in the same doorway that Stephanie had come from to interrupt them. "Is the coast clear?"

He wondered how much she'd overheard, then decided it really didn't matter. Before all was said and done, she would probably hear plenty of verbal sword fighting between him and Stephanie, and be glad to wash her hands of all of them. "It's clear."

"Good. I've been hiding out in the kitchen for the last ten minutes." She lifted her hands and he realized she was holding two bottles of beer. "Want one?"

Almost more than his next breath. He took the cold bottle from her. "Where'd you find these?"

"Fiona's fridge." She grinned, though her expression wasn't entirely easy. "The bar that your mother arranged has everything under the sun from pinot grigio to limoncello and all things in between, but no beer."

"Not surprising. Astrid considers any beer—" he glanced at the label on the bottle "—even local brews like this, an inferior breed." He eyed her. "I'm sorry."

"For what?"

"Need you ask? The charming delight that is my former wife."

"She's hardly the first person to think I am an inferior breed." She lifted her shoulder and took a sip of her beer. A tiny jeweled flower sparkled amongst her rioting spirals of hair. "Besides. You're not responsible for what she says."

He rolled the cold beer against his palm, cooling the itch to touch those shining curls. "Unfortunately, that's not necessarily true."

She looked up at him and for a blinding second, he nearly forgot what he intended to say. But then her smooth eyebrows quirked together a little over her nose, and he dragged himself out of the warmth of her gaze.

"I'm the one who brings out the worst in her," he finally admitted. "I made her miserable during the few years we were married, and she's never forgotten it. And *you* are anything but inferior. I don't know how I'm going to be able to thank you."

"You don't have to." She held his gaze for a moment, then her lashes swept down as she took another sip of her beer.

He cleared his throat and focused on his own beer bottle. It was safer. "I told her that we wanted to wait until after the party was over to announce it, but word's probably going to get around pretty quickly anyway," he said after a moment. "Discretion has never been one of Stephanie's strong suits."

She nodded. Another little sparkle in her hair flashed in the light. "Fiona's not going to be fooled. And what about your children? What are you going to tell them?"

"I'm not worried about my grandmother. She's always on my side." He knew it unequivocally. She was the only one in his family who never wavered in that regard. "As for my kids, I'll tell them only as much as I need to."

She frowned. "We'll be lying to them, too."

He'd already realized that. "It can't be helped. It's not as if I can give them the real scoop." And fortunately he knew his ex-wife wouldn't be in any hurry to tell them, either. She'd figure that announcing an engagement would be his problem.

"I suppose it's also probably too much to hope for that word won't get back to *my* family somehow. The city sometimes feels ridiculously small. You never know who knows who. I'm not going to lie to my mother, though. Or my sisters. They are discreet. So don't worry about that."

"I'm not worried about your family. But there's something I need to tell you before it comes back and bites me on the butt. Something that I probably should have told you before."

She gave him a sideways glance. "That sounds ominous."

"It's not important to me. But it just goes to prove that you're right. The city is small." And he hadn't told her yet that she wasn't the only one in this mess who had a connection to Harrison Hunt, though his was a whole lot less important.

He glanced outside. Now that the music was more lively, none of the partygoers were looking their direction, much less approaching the house. "Ethan—the guy trying to raise my kids like they're his own—works for HuntCom."

As she absorbed that, her eyes visibly cooled. "I... see."

Her expression, combined with the itch at the back of his neck, assured him that she undoubtedly didn't. At least not from his point of view. "He's in their legal department."

"What do you want me to do about that?" She set her beer carefully on an antique side table. "Dial up Uncle Harry and ask him to fire Ethan so there's no European job at all? Seems to me that would have been a better plan on your part than trying to pull one over on the judge in your custody battle."

Coming on the heels of the unpleasantness with Stephanie, her assessment bit like sharp, pointed teeth. "I would never put you in that position," he said slowly. Truthfully.

He set down his own beer, taking the time to let that quick shard of anger inside him dull. "But that's the second time you've jumped to the conclusion that

I wanted something from you specifically because of your association with Hunt. I'll tell you the same thing I told you before. I'm not interested in HuntCom or trying to use your connection there to my advantage." He didn't count using it to stop his ex-wife from bad-mouthing Bobbie behind her back. "Just because that's what people have wanted from you in the past doesn't mean that's what I want. The only reason I'm even bringing it up now is because I didn't want you hearing it from someone else and starting to think exactly what you're thinking."

"So you could have told me before. When you first learned about Uncle Harry."

"I was wrong, all right? You deserved full disclosure right from the start, but frankly, I was more interested in convincing you to help me follow my attorney's advice!" At least as much of the advice as Gabe could stand to follow. "It wouldn't matter to me if you'd never *heard* of Harrison Hunt."

He exhaled and found another store of patience from some place that he didn't even know existed.

She was standing there so stiffly in her pretty, torn gown, as if she were braced for the inevitable worst, and just then he wanted to string up everyone from their thumbs who'd ever put such doubt in her.

"Bobbie," he began again, more calmly. "I'm a simple man. I build things. I don't go around manipulating people and situations. I'm just trying to hold onto my kids. Despite your suspicions that nobody could possibly want something from you simply because you are *you,* I'm telling you the truth. I just need you to help me level the playing field when I get to court."

She chewed her lower lip. "I work in a coffee shop,

Gabe. I can barely pay my own bills. How on earth is that going to provide any sort of leveling?"

"Not everything is about money." He could almost hear the Gannon family collectively gasping. "And I'm not exactly standing in the welfare lines. A lot of what I have is tied up in the company, but that doesn't mean I can't provide just as well for my children as Stephanie does, courtesy of her husband's billable hours." It would just take a helluva lot larger chunk of his income, but he'd deal with it.

"If you're going to change your mind about all this, then let me know now," he added, "because the closer we get to the hearing, the worse it'll be if you do. I'm trying to prove my stability and now that Steph thinks we're engaged, if we turn out suddenly not to be right before we go to court, she'll try using that to her advantage."

Bobbie pushed her fingers through her hair, holding the mass of long curls away from her heart-shaped face. She closed her gray eyes and shook her head a little. Her dark hair slid in curling ribbons against her pale skin. "I'm not going to change my mind." She opened her eyes again, dropping her hands. A smile that struck him as oddly sad played around her soft lips. "In it until the end, and all that, right?"

He didn't even realize how much he'd been afraid she would reconsider until the relief hit him after her words. "Right." His throat felt unaccountably tight.

"Do me a favor? While we're pretending for everyone else, don't pretend with me. Custody of your children is so much more important than me ruining some stupid fund-raising dinner for a jerk. If you think I'm becoming a hindrance, you have to tell me, so—"

He caught her face in his hands and her eyes went wide as her voice trailed off. "Have a little faith in yourself, Bobbie. I do."

She blinked, looking startled, and moistened her lips. "I'll…try."

"Good." He realized he was staring at her glistening lower lip and made himself drop his hands. "Good," he said again and picked up his beer to wash down the gruffness in his throat. "Now that we've got that straightened out, maybe we should go join the party. Do you want to dance?" She was young and beautiful. Of course she'd want to dance. And he wasn't hypocritical enough to deny that putting his arms around her for the few measures of a song was an appealing notion.

"I'm not much good at it." She lifted her skirt a few inches, smiling wryly. "My coordination only seems to come together when I'm playing sports."

"What about yoga?"

"Well." She tilted her hand back and forth, suddenly looking discomfited. "I guess I do passably well. Sometimes."

He knew only too well that she'd looked more than passably sexy in her yoga getup. He took another pull of cold beer, willing his body back into order. "That leaves a lot of other sports still. Tiddlywinks. Boxing."

The dimple in her cheek appeared. "Neither, I'm afraid." She shrugged, looking more at ease. "I like golf and softball. Volleyball. Basketball was a no-go for obvious reasons." She waved her hand at herself. "I did run track in school, though. High jump. Hurdles. Relay."

All of which required plenty of coordination. "Discus," he offered.

"Ah." Her smile broadened suddenly, mischievously. "Discobolos. The Discus Thrower." Her gaze ran down his body as if she were comparing him to Myron's famous Greek sculpture. "I can imagine that."

The heat running up his spine might have been embarrassment. It was more likely knowing she was comparing him to a naked statue and, judging by her expression, he wasn't faring too badly.

He let out a laugh aimed more at himself than anything and drank down the rest of the beer. This is what he got for spending months—years—focused on things more important than his sex life. Now it was an effort to think about anything else.

"Outside," he suggested. The chilly night air would have to suffice since a cold shower wasn't available as long as he was at Fiona's.

She nodded and headed for the doorway. Her chin ducked for a moment, but not quickly enough to hide her flushed cheeks from him. "Maybe Fiona will open her gifts soon and we can go home." She didn't wait for him, but hurried outside, still holding her torn skirt off to the side.

He let out a long, long breath and started to follow. But a sparkle on the carpet caught his attention and he bent down to pick it up.

A tiny, faceted daisy winked up at him.

Smiling slightly, he slipped the hairpin into his pocket and followed Bobbie into the night.

Fiona, they soon found, was not even remotely close to opening her gifts. Even though his grandmother had complained loudly about the party, she was the one in the center of the dance floor cutting a rug with Gabe's father.

Gabe stood behind Bobbie, where she'd stopped to watch from the edge of the crowded dance floor. It was even more crowded around the wooden square, though, which was his only excuse for standing so close to her that he could smell that hint of lemony freshness in her hair. And when a couple brushed against them as they sidled through to the dance floor, it was only natural for Gabe to slide his arm around Bobbie's waist to keep her from being knocked sideways.

She looked up at him and her eyes seemed darker, more like the smoky color of her dress in the soft light from the twinkling strands circling the tent above their heads. "Thanks."

He managed a nod. He could feel the natural curve of her waist beneath the smooth, silky fabric of her gown.

"Fiona and your father are putting everyone else to shame."

He nodded again, making himself look away from her face. On the opposite side of the dance floor, he could see his mother standing arm-in-arm with Stephanie. Fortunately, both of them seemed more interested in whatever they were talking about—most likely the spectacle Fiona was making of herself as she swung around with abandon to a song he was pretty sure Lisette listened to on her MP3 player—than in paying him any heed.

Barely a few minutes had passed when the pounding song ended, though, giving way to a slower beat. He could hear his grandmother's breathless laughter amid the small exodus from the dance floor.

He leaned down so Bobbie would hear. "This is

more my speed. You game?" His arm was still wrapped around her waist and he felt her quick inhale.

"I suppose I can't do more damage to my dress than I've already done." She gave a little turn right out from beneath his arm, then caught his hand in hers as she stepped off the grass onto the dance floor.

Fiona passed by them, smiling benevolently. "That's what I've been waiting to see." She patted their arms before stepping off the dance floor. "Where's that boy with the cocktails?" he heard her asking.

"I hope I'm as fabulous as she is when I'm her age." Bobbie stepped into his arms, though her gaze seemed carefully fixed on Fiona's movements.

"You're pretty fabulous now." God knew she felt fabulous. He'd have to be dead not to know it. And lately, since he'd met her, he was feeling more alive than he had in years.

Her lips curving, she looked up at him through the dark fringe of her eyelashes. "You're just saying that because I've fallen in with your plans."

They were barely shuffling around on the crowded dance floor. He tucked his knuckle beneath her softly pointed chin and nudged it upward.

Her playful smile slowly died as he looked into her wide eyes. "I'm saying it because it's true."

"Gabe—" Her soft voice broke off.

He'd never before thought his thumb had a mind of its own, but evidently it did, brushing across the fullness of her lower lip.

Her gaze flickered. "Let's not forget what we're really doing here."

His left hand seemed damnably independent, too, sliding more firmly around her back, drawing her silk-draped curves even closer against him. "What I'm really doing," he murmured in her ear, "is trying not to kiss you right now."

Her head went back a little further. Her long, spiraling curls tickled his fingers pressing against her spine. "Really?"

"Don't be surprised," he reminded. "You started it." His lips closed over hers.

That quick inhale. That faint little *mmming* sound of delight. It burned through him as suddenly as the flare of a match. Only this flame wasn't going to burn itself out quickly...or easily. Just then, as unwise as he knew it was, he didn't care. His fingertips pressed into the smooth arch of her back and he felt her hands sliding up his chest, over his shoulders—

"Oh. I'm so sorry!"

Gabe barely heard the exclamation, but Bobbie yanked back from him. "It's not your fault," he heard her breathless assurance.

Feeling half-witted, he realized the woman dancing behind them had stepped on Bobbie's dress that she'd forgotten to hold up, making the tear ten times worse, and ten times more noticeable.

Her face was flushed and she didn't meet his eyes when she turned back toward him. "I have to go."

"It's just a tear—"

"I know." She was already backing away from him. Physically and mentally. "But I, um, I should do something about it." Her lips stretched. "Fortunately, I don't have to go far."

"I'll come with you."

"No!" She shook her head. "Stay. Fiona will miss you. I'll just...later. We'll...later."

Nonsensical, but perfectly meaningful.

She looked panicked.

So he shoved his hands in his pockets to keep them from getting any more ideas, and let her go. "All right."

She barely hesitated before hurrying from beneath the warmth and light of the tent. He watched her as she practically ran in her high heels and flapping hem across the lawn and down the slight hill toward her carriage house.

She might as well have been Cinderella on the run.

Inside his pocket, he rolled her tiny, sharp-edged hair clip between his fingers.

Unfortunately, in this fairy tale, he knew he was no prince.

Not when he'd long ago stopped believing in happily-ever-afters.

Chapter 7

"So, how was the birthday party last night?" Bobbie's sister Tommi, looking flushed from the heat of the kitchen, flicked open the top few buttons of her white chef's jacket and sat down on one of the barstools next to where Bobbie was sitting, filling salt shakers. It was the only "payment" Tommi would accept for the delicious crab bisque and baguettes that Bobbie had scarfed down for lunch.

The afternoon shift was over, the waitstaff and last of the customers departed, and this being Monday, Tommi wouldn't be reopening in a few hours again for dinner like on the other days of the week. "It was okay. I didn't stay all that long, actually." Bobbie focused hard on not letting the plastic funnel overflow. "Aside from Fiona, I didn't really know anyone."

"Wasn't her Mr. Handyman grandson there?"

Bobbie nodded casually. "Gabe? Sure. Of course. Most of Fiona's family were there."

Tommi's fingertips slowly drummed the bar's surface. "So…?"

There was never any fooling the Fairchild women. Not their mother, Cornelia, nor Cornelia's daughters.

But Bobbie could still try. She'd warned Gabe that she wouldn't lie to her family. And even though she knew it would be better to tell them herself than chance them hearing about their "engagement" through gossip, she still couldn't summon any enthusiasm for admitting to them what she'd agreed to. No matter what the reason, none of them would approve of her participation in something deceitful.

"So…nothing." Bobbie tucked her tongue between her teeth, moving the salt shaker to the trio of filled ones before sliding another in its place. She glanced at her sister's tired face. "I wish you'd hire another sous chef," she said. The guy who'd held the position had been gone for over a month now. "This place has gotten way too busy for you to handle everything alone."

Tommi just shrugged. "We'll see. Finding the right person isn't all that easy. Is there something going on between you and Gabe?"

Bobbie scattered salt across the bar before quickly redirecting the funnel. "Why would you think that?"

Tommi smoothly scooped the salt off the black granite and into the tall, empty coffee cup from Between the Bean that Bobbie had left sitting beside her. "Maybe the fact that you can't say the man's name without looking flushed."

"What can I say? I'm still not exactly proud of the way I attacked his lips the day we met." Tommi knew about that episode but Bobbie hadn't admitted that any more lip-locking had occurred—instigated by either one of them.

"Fair enough. Except you've also now filled four salt shakers with sugar. Which is pretty odd even for you, so I'm thinking there's still something on your mind."

Bobbie blinked. She looked down at the plastic container she'd grabbed from Tommi's shelves and groaned. The label on it did say *sugar*.

She dumped the funnel's contents back into the container. "Some help I am, huh?" She slid off the black barstool, heading toward the narrow swinging doors that led to the kitchen. "I'll fix it."

But Tommi caught her by the cowl neck of her orange sweater, halting her escape. "The salt can wait. What's really going on? You've never been this preoccupied, not even when you were in the throes of infatuation for Larry-the-political-dweeb."

Bobbie tugged her collar free. "It's complicated."

"Why? Because he's too old for you?"

"He is not!"

Tommi gave her a serenely patient smile. "I *knew* you were interested in him," she said with the superiority of a year-older sister.

Bobbie exhaled. "Fat lot of good it will do me," she muttered. She picked up the sugar container. "He's not exactly long-term material," she said before pushing through the swinging doors. She slid the heavy container back into its spot on the orderly dry goods shelves and retrieved the one marked *salt* instead. She also grabbed four empty salt shakers from storage and when she carried everything back out to the wine bar,

Tommi was tipping the incorrect contents into the empty coffee cup.

"I'm going to take it as a sign that you've realized Lawrence was all wrong for you, considering the words *long* and *term* have even reentered your vocabulary."

Bobbie slid onto the barstool again. "Maybe," she allowed. "Doesn't make it any less humiliating the way he dumped me."

"He has no class."

"Gabe said that, too."

Tommi's dark eyes sparkled. "Ah. I'm liking him more and more."

Bobbie couldn't help but smile. "You would like him," she said after a moment. "He's a good man. Works hard." She looked down at the large plastic container, but in her mind all she could see was his handsome face. "And there's nothing he won't do for his kids."

Tommi fit the caps back on the salt shakers and pushed them to one side before reaching for the fresh ones Bobbie had brought out from the kitchen. "There are two, right?"

"Mmm-hmm." She propped her elbows on the bar, resting her chin on her hands. "Lisette and Todd. She's twelve and I'm not sure which she's more passionate about—ballet or rap music. Which isn't exactly the music Gabe wants her listening to, but he definitely knows he has to pick his battles where she's concerned. And Todd's ten and so much smarter than he realizes. Honestly, the boy's a whiz when it comes to computers." She smiled to herself. "He ought to be in Hunt-Com's research and development department."

Tommi reached over and pulled the lid off the salt

container when Bobbie didn't make any move to. She scooped out a portion to fill the funnel. "Gabe doesn't have them full-time?"

"No, but not for lack of trying. Last week he had them for several days, though. Their mother was out of town." Her lips twisted when she thought of Gabe's former wife. The woman had stood at least five inches taller than Bobbie and she'd worn her self-confidence as easily as she had the numbingly sophisticated gown that had shown off her impeccable figure to its best advantage. "She was at the party, too."

Tommi's smooth motions as she filled the shakers came to a brief pause. "His ex-wife was at Fiona's birthday party? How…well-adjusted."

Bobbie let out a soft snort. "Not exactly." She filled her sister in on Gabe's mother's connection to Stephanie. "His ex and her husband are planning to move outside the country again and take the kids, naturally. Gabe's trying to get their custody arrangement changed so he'll be able to spend more time with the kids, keep them with him for at least part of the year."

"That sounds fairly admirable of him. Seems like there are a lot of men around these days who would happily leave the responsibility to someone else." With the spare efficiency that came with long practice, Tommi capped the shakers and gathered them all up in her hands to take around to the tables that had already been draped with fresh, white linens for the next day. "But you think Gabe's not long-term material."

Bobbie twisted around on her stool, watching Tommi. "He says he's not," she corrected. "Can't get much plainer than that."

"Not unless he packs up and leaves, I suppose,"

Tommi agreed. Finished with her task, she moved to the large front window that was stenciled in gold with *The Corner Bistro* and looked out on the rain-drenched street. "Hard to believe it's going to be Christmas in a couple of months," she murmured. "Your Gabe sounds like a man who comes with a closetful of baggage."

Bobbie bristled. "Which means what, exactly?"

Tommi glanced over her shoulder. "Meaning just that, sis. You said yourself it was complicated. You don't have to get defensive."

Bobbie exhaled and deliberately relaxed her shoulders. "Well, the complications get even more twisted."

From across the cozy bistro, she saw her sister's smooth brown eyebrows lift warily. "How…twisted?"

Bobbie wrapped her fingers around the sides of the seat beneath her. "Some people at the party might think I'm engaged to marry him," she admitted slowly.

Tommi's hands lifted. "Why would they think that?"

"Because-I-told-his-ex-wife-we-were."

There. She'd admitted it.

Which still didn't make her own behavior feel any more real.

Her sister put a hand to her head, released the clip holding her smooth, dark hair up in the back and thrust her fingers through the strands as if she'd developed a sudden headache. She pulled out the nearest chair and sat down.

Bobbie picked at a tiny jag in her thumbnail. "And Gabe figures she's not likely to keep the news to herself," she added more slowly.

"Bobbie."

Her shoulders hunched again, even though she tried to stop them. "I told you it was complicated."

"Why don't you start at the beginning and uncomplicate it for me, then."

So Bobbie did. Skirting a few of the more intimate details—like how she'd been dissolving from the inside out when she'd danced with Gabe beneath the tent's twinkling lights or how she'd known that if he'd disregarded her words and followed her anyway when she'd left, she would have invited him in for a whole lot more than coffee and a good-night kiss—she told her sister everything.

And when she was finished, she didn't know if she felt more exhausted or relieved. "I promised him that all of you would have our backs."

Tommi gave a half a laugh, though she didn't sound amused. "Who would I know to tell otherwise?"

"Ethan—that's Stephanie's current husband—works for HuntCom," Bobbie reminded her. "Not that I think Uncle Harry would care about any of this, but I guess I wouldn't want to chance it. He's not exactly predictable."

"And if you want to look at the money and the board seats he gave us in this particular light, you could say he's been known to be protective of us."

"Right." Bobbie brushed her hands down the thighs of her blue jeans and pushed off the barstool. "I do want to help Gabe—he *really* loves those kids, Tom—but I would hate for someone's career to be jeopardized. Even if he is married to the first cousin of the Wicked Witch."

"There's no earthly reason why Uncle Harry would ever learn about any of this from me." Tommi's voice turned brisk. "I haven't talked to him in weeks. I'm certainly not going to tell him."

"What if Mom does?"

"She wouldn't for the same reasons. Are you clear on the reasons why *you're* doing this?"

"I'm just helping Fiona's grandson," Bobbie insisted. "I know it's not going to lead anywhere…permanent." But she also couldn't stop from wishing otherwise.

"I know Fiona means a lot to you." Her sister grimaced wryly. "But I can also see a look in your eyes when you talk about Gabe that doesn't have anything to do with his grandmother. So just…watch yourself, okay?"

"I'm not under any illusions," she assured. Having her sister's support went a long way toward settling the nerves inside her. "Now, since I didn't even fill any salt shakers, I owe you for the therapy session *and* the lunch."

Tommi smiled again, this time for real. "And when have you ever paid for lunch before?"

Bobbie laughed. They both knew that Tommi would have refused to take her money even if she'd offered it. "Well is there something else I can do around here to help you out?"

Tommi shook her head. "I'm going to catch up on the books a little and then call it a day myself."

"Good." Bobbie retrieved her hooded jacket from where she'd dumped it at the end of the wine bar and slid her arms into it. "You look like you need a long bath and a tall glass of one of those Italian wines you like." She leaned over and hugged her sister, who was still sitting near the front door. "And hire another sous chef, already, so you don't have to work so hard."

Tommi hugged her back. "You work on straightening out your own life and leave me to worry about

the bistro," she advised lightly. "What are you dressing up as for Halloween at the Bean tomorrow?" The
coffee shop's employees always dressed in costumes
for the holiday.

Bobbie lifted her shoulders. "I haven't thought about
it much." She'd been more than a little preoccupied of
late, though the kids had brought up the issue when
they'd been at her house. Their mother considered
trick-or-treating too déclassé, but they were planning
to dress up for school, though neither child had been
particularly enthusiastic about their store-bought costumes.

Tommi looked surprised. And Bobbie couldn't
blame her. Since she'd been a girl, she'd always enjoyed putting thought and effort into her Halloween
costumes. Even when she had nothing else to do on
the day but answer the door and hand out sweets to the
children who came knocking. "Aren't you working?"

"Yeah. I've got the morning shift all this week."
Even though she usually came and went through the
restaurant's back door, she flipped open the lock on
the brass-trimmed front glass door. It was pouring,
and she had managed to find a coveted street parking
spot down the block, which meant leaving through the
front door was quicker. "I'll figure out something."

"Go as a bride," Tommi suggested.

"Ha ha." But she managed to laugh, too, as she left
her sister to lock up behind her.

When she got home, she let the dogs outside. They
loved to play in the rain, so she put them on their chains
and left them to it while she went to her closet to find
some inspiration for a Halloween costume.

When her phone rang a little while later, she very

nearly ignored it, since the only one to call her lately had been Quentin Rich. But it kept ringing and ringing, so she pushed herself off the floor of her closet and went to the phone.

"Bobbie? This is Cheryl. I've been trying to reach you for hours."

Cheryl was Fiona's secretary at the agency. "What's wrong?"

"Fiona. She collapsed in the middle of a meeting over at Cragmin's a few hours ago."

Bobbie's knees went out and she sank onto the corner of her bed. "Is she all right? Where's she now? Does her family know?" *Does Gabe?*

"I reached Mr. Gannon at the law office." Cheryl named the hospital that Fiona had been taken to. "But I don't know what to do about the agency. Everyone here is asking what to do. We have a class of dogs that are supposed to graduate this weekend, and I know she also hasn't finished payroll. Nobody knows what to do!"

Bobbie exhaled. "Keep doing what you normally do," she said simply. "Aaron's the head trainer. He knows what to do for the graduation. The match list of the recipients for the dogs is already done; I saw it on Fiona's credenza when I was there the other day." They would all be present at the training graduation, when the dogs were handed over to their new partners.

"Should I call in someone to do the payroll, or what?" Cheryl sounded only slightly less frantic. "I hate to even bring it up, but none of us can afford to miss a check. And I obviously can't go asking Mr. Gannon about it now."

"I'll think of something, Cheryl." Though she didn't

know what. The office would be closing in little more than an hour. "Don't worry. Just tell everyone to keep doing their jobs. I'll get back to you before the end of the day. Okay?"

"Okay." The other woman hung up, sounding somewhat less frantic. Bobbie, on the other hand, felt like her stomach had been tied into a knot. She called the dogs in and re-crated them with fresh food and water. "Your wet coats are going to have to wait this time," she told them as she added fresh towels to the floor of their cage for them to lie on. As soon as they were settled, she was out the door again, heading to the hospital.

She'd barely gotten off the freeway when her cell phone rang. Not even glancing at where it sat on her console, she thumbed the speaker button and braked behind the long line of cars at a stop light. "Hello?"

"It's Gabe." His deep voice came through loud and clear on the little phone.

"Gabe!" She tightened her hands around the steering wheel. "I'm on my way to the hospital. How is she? How are *you?*"

"She's going to be fine," he said quickly. "I guess I don't have to ask if you heard."

Thank you, thank you, thank you.

"Fiona's secretary called me." She inched forward in traffic while one portion of her mind considered alternate routes. "What happened?"

"She had a mild heart attack."

Bobbie sank her teeth into her tongue to keep them from chattering. She still remembered Harry's heart attack from a few years ago. And her father had died of one.

She'd just seen Fiona the evening before, dancing the night away in her yellow gown.

"Bobbie? Did you hear me?"

She nodded. Foolish. He couldn't see her. "I heard." She swallowed past the knot in her throat again. "How mild?"

"If everything goes well, she should be out of the hospital by the end of the week."

"That's good." She took advantage of a break in traffic to change lanes, turning down a side street. She'd make faster time going through the neighborhoods than on the main streets that were clogged with construction and rush-hour traffic. "Is everyone there?"

"Yeah. Fiona wants to see you."

She had to slow down for a school zone. "I'd have been there by now if not for this damn traffic."

"You're fine," he assured. "She's having some tests run right now, anyway."

"You're sure she's all right?"

"Talked to the doctor myself. Obviously there are some things he wants her to watch, but she got immediate medical attention when it happened and the damage to her heart was minimal." She heard a rustling and then his voice was less clear. "She thinks we're *really* engaged."

Bobbie glanced down at the phone as if she could see Gabe's face. "What?"

"Stephanie told Renée, who told Astrid, who naturally told Fiona."

Her fingers flexed around the steering wheel again. "That wouldn't have caused her—"

"No," he cut her off. "That I can promise you. I left the party shortly after you did, but Fiona evidently knew last night. She told me just a little while ago that she had no intentions of going anywhere before she had the pleasure of seeing us walking down the aisle."

"I *knew* this would blow up in our faces! Didn't I tell you it was a bad idea?"

"Don't panic. Everything will be fine. I just wanted you to know what she was thinking before you see her."

"She should know better than anyone that we haven't been involved."

"Yeah, well, I guess we were wrong in thinking that. From what she's said to me, she takes full credit for putting us together in the first place. I'll tell her the truth when I have to, but not until she's stronger and well again."

"Of course." The last thing Bobbie wanted was to upset Fiona in any way. She turned down another block and could see the tall lines of the hospital building in the distance. "Have you told Lisette and Todd about Fiona?"

"Stephanie did. She brought them to the hospital about a half hour ago."

"Is she still there?" The thought of encountering Gabe's ex-wife again so soon wasn't palatable, but it also wasn't enough to keep her from going to see Fiona.

"She has to leave soon to get ready for some business dinner Ethan's got. She had a sitter lined up for them, but the kids don't want to leave."

"Can you blame them?"

"I don't," he assured mildly. "Getting their mother to agree is another matter, and Fiona doesn't need to hear us arguing about it now."

"Of course not." She turned another corner and nosed her way back onto the main street. The entrance to the hospital was fifty yards away. "I'll be there in a minute. Are you all in the emergency room?"

"She's already been moved to a private room." He told her the number. "It's a little crowded up here, though, so I'll just meet you downstairs by the main entrance." He didn't wait for an answer before he hung up.

Bobbie thumbed the end button on her phone and turned in to the parking lot. There were a half-dozen signs directing people to various areas and she found herself heading up the emergency ramp instead of entering the visitor's parking lot. Cursing under her breath, she turned around at the first opportunity and managed to get herself back where she belonged.

The parking lot was crowded there, too, and she had to park some distance from the entrance, which meant that several minutes had passed before she finally made her way through the automatically sliding doors.

She spotted Gabe right away. He was the tall, broad man in blue jeans and a gray flannel shirt swooping down on her, pulling her into a fierce hug despite the water clinging to her raincoat.

Her heart jumped into her throat as she wrapped her arms around his shoulders. When she stood on her toes, her nose found a spot in the warm crook of his neck. "You told me she's going to be fine," she reminded him huskily.

He nodded and she felt a deep breath work through his chest. Then he was pulling back a little. Enough to press a hard, fast kiss to her lips. "I'm glad you came."

Quick or not, she still felt absurdly rocked by the kiss. "Of course I came."

"For Fiona?" His voice was low.

She pressed her tingling lips together for a moment.

"Yes." Telling him she'd been concerned for him, too, would be as good as admitting how quickly she was getting in over her head with him. But she still couldn't prevent her hands from rubbing over his bunched shoulders. He could reassure her that his grandmother was going to be fine, but he was clearly still stressed. "How long have you been here?"

"A few hours. Dad called as soon as he heard. I was on my way out to a job site in Ballard and just turned around to come here. I called your house, but didn't want to leave the news on your answering machine. Would have called your cell sooner, but I didn't know your number until I got hold of Fiona's phone."

She grimaced. What believable couple wouldn't know the phone numbers of their beloved? "How many more things like that should we have thought of?"

"It doesn't matter. I have it now. And you have mine." He tucked her head beneath his chin.

She closed her eyes, breathing in the warmth and comfort of him. "How long do you think it'll be before I can see her?"

"Shouldn't be long." His chest expanded beneath her cheek. "We can go up to her room if you're ready."

She wasn't sure she was, but she nodded anyway. He waited while she slid out of her raincoat, then took her hand and walked to one of the elevator banks. They rode up several floors and all too quickly he was leading her down one hallway after another, until they finally stopped at the end of one.

She could see into the rectangular room just how crowded it was with every Gannon *but* Fiona, and the low heels of her leather boots suddenly wanted to drag on the tile floor. But Gabe drew her through the opened doorway anyway. Her self-consciousness solidified when all conversation dropped as everyone turned to look at them.

It was Colin, Gabe's father, who broke the awkward lull. He stepped forward and took her hands before dropping a light kiss on her cheek as if it were perfectly natural for him to do so. "It's good of you to come. I know Fiona will be pleased to see you."

"Thank you." Gabe's hand on the small of her back was the only thing keeping her grounded. "I'll be glad when I can see her, too."

Colin moved slightly to one side, looking at his wife, who was sitting on the foot of the single hospital bed, a magazine open on her lap. "Astrid?"

The woman tossed aside her magazine and looked at Bobbie. "Hello, Bobbie," she greeted, though her eyes were anything but welcoming. "That's short for Roberta, I presume?"

Bobbie kept her smile from dying through sheer grit. "Yes." If she really *were* engaged to Gabe, she'd have been terrified of having the intimidating woman as her mother-in-law.

"Hmm. I suppose Bobbie suits you better." Her tone was smooth, but Bobbie still had the distinct impression that Astrid hadn't meant it as a compliment.

"I think it does," Gabe agreed, and his tone made it clear that it *was*. He picked up Bobbie's cold hand and pressed a kiss to the back of it.

Astrid's lips twisted in a mockery of a smile before she picked up her magazine again.

Bobbie was just relieved not to be under the cool stare of the woman. She nodded a murmured greeting at Gabe's brothers and their wives, who were perched on the only chair the room offered and the wide windowsill. "Where are Todd and Lisette?"

"Stephanie took them down to the cafeteria for a drink," Renée supplied. She gave her a look. "She'll be back."

It was more of a threatened promise than a friendly warning.

Bobbie glanced around the crowded room. Renée was still filing her long fingernails. Diana was busily texting on her BlackBerry. Paul and Liam were leaning against the wall in the corner, talking quietly as if they were anywhere other than a hospital room. Only Colin looked truly concerned for his mother. His suit coat was abandoned, his red tie was loosened and he'd folded his shirtsleeves up his arms.

She decided that she could maybe like Gabe's father after all.

She slid her arm through Gabe's, and looked up at him with a smile. "Why don't we go find them," she suggested.

He looked surprised but then nodded. Before leaving, Bobbie looked back into the room. "Can we get something for anyone?"

Colin just shook his head and did another three-pace circuit. Bobbie figured nobody else would respond— as if it were a crime against the one they figured Gabe *should* be with—and bit back a faint sigh.

"I'd love a coffee," Diana announced before they stepped out the door.

Bobbie looked back, surprised. The other woman had slid her BlackBerry into her case and was watching Bobbie with a vaguely puzzled look. As if she couldn't figure out why Bobbie had made the offer.

"Sugar or cream?" The woman looked as if she hadn't partaken of either pleasure in a decade.

"Artificial sweetener," Diana said. Then she smiled a little. "Thank you."

"Sure." Bobbie glanced around, but Diana's words hadn't managed to break through any significant dam with the others. She and Gabe left the room and she slid her hand into his, feeling his warm fingers weave with hers.

Considering there was nothing permanent—nothing long-term—about her engagement to Gabe, she knew she had no business feeling a spurt of victory at even the smallest sign of acceptance from his family.

No business at all.

Chapter 8

Despite the doctor's assurance, it was hours before Fiona finally returned to her room. By then, Gabe's brothers and sisters-in-law had departed, as had his mother. Colin remained, though, and Bobbie knew better than to suggest Gabe go home and get some rest.

He had managed to convince Stephanie to leave the children at the hospital with him, however, while she went off to her husband's business dinner.

Bobbie had fully expected another dose of Stephanie's vitriolic attitude, and had been surprised when none had been forthcoming at all. Maybe it was because the children were there, listening, or maybe it was because they were in a hospital. Whatever the reason, she'd been relieved when the other woman had suddenly capitulated and left the kids in Gabe's care.

Unfortunately, that meant that Lisette and Todd had been forced to sit around for hours, too.

And even if they'd badly wanted to see their great-grandmother, the long wait had definitely been taking its toll on their patience.

When Fiona was delivered in a wheelchair back to her hospital room, only the fact that the children were there kept Bobbie's tears at bay. Her dear friend had never looked so worn. And for the first time, it was almost easy to believe that Fiona had just turned eighty-five.

Once the nurse had gotten Fiona situated with the various wires and tubes tethering her and departed, Fiona let Todd use the buttons to raise the bed more until she was sitting up to her liking.

"Can we do it again?" he asked hopefully, holding the controller.

"It's not a video game, dummy," Lisette scoffed.

Fiona grinned, though her eyes were tired. "I'd rather be playing video games right now," she assured him. "You can play with this darn bed all you want tomorrow if you get to come and see me." She eyed Colin. "Go home and get some rest. You look like *you're* the one ready to have a heart attack."

"Don't joke," he chided, bending over to kiss her cheek. "You gave us a scare. I've been telling you for several years now that it was time you cut back. Those dogs don't need you working yourself to death."

"Don't exaggerate. And it's not the dogs I do it for, as you well know." She patted his cheek and looked at Bobbie and Gabe. Despite her health crisis, there was still a glint in her eyes. "Soooo. Some mischief has been afoot? I suspected there was more going on than repairs over at the carriage house and once I saw you together last night, I knew I was right."

Bobbie felt her cheeks go hot. "Fiona—"

"We can get into all that later," Gabe assured, giving his children a pointed glance.

Fiona rolled her eyes, but she dropped the subject easily enough. "Payroll isn't done. Bobbie, you have a key to the office. Could—"

"Mother—" Colin started, but she just waved his protest aside.

"—you go to the office and bring me the checkbook? It's locked in my desk, but you know where the key is. I'll sign the checks. All you have to do is fill in the same amounts for everyone as the last pay period and get them back to the office for Cheryl to hand out before the end of the day tomorrow."

Bobbie stared. She'd pinch-hit any number of tasks at the agency over the years, but never had anything to do with the nine paid employees' compensation.

"Mother," Colin said again, this time with enough steel in his voice that Bobbie had a sudden impression of him in a courtroom. "You do *not* need to be signing those godforsaken paychecks," he said flatly.

But Fiona eyed Colin with just as much steel, proving where he'd come by the trait. "I'm the only signer on the account," she pointed out. "And when I want your opinion, I'll ask for it."

He gave an irritated sigh and turned away from the bedside. "Talk to your grandmother," he told Gabe, who was standing at the foot of the bed. "She listens to *you.*"

"Bobbie can sign your name for you," Gabe told her without hesitation. "At least this once. Nobody's going to come charging after anyone for fraud, after all. And

I'll get new signature cards from the bank tomorrow so you can get someone else added on to the account."

Fiona crossed her thin arms over the pale-blue hospital gown that she was nearly swimming in. "Fine. Bobbie?"

She lifted her shoulder in a shrug, feeling distinctly uncomfortable. "I'll do whatever you need, Fiona, you know that."

Fiona suddenly smiled benevolently. "Yes, I do know that, my dear." Then she looked at Todd. "You can push the button to lower the bed now. After all the poking and prodding I've had, I want some sleep, assuming I don't get caught in the web of wires they've got going here." Her gaze went back to the adults as the motorized bed started to lower. "Now, go on and get out of here. I'm told I probably won't kick the bucket tonight, so you can come back and see me tomorrow."

"Mother," Colin chided in a tone that told Bobbie he knew he was fighting for a lost cause, but he leaned over and kissed his mother's cheek again. There was no doubt of his affection for his mother, even if she did exasperate him. He gave Bobbie a smile and clapped his hand over Gabe's shoulder as he left.

"All right. You, too," Fiona looked from Bobbie to Gabe and back again. "The last place Todd and Lisette want to be is hanging out in some musty old hospital."

It was a poor description of the comfortably modern, high-tech institution. "You're not gonna die, are you?" Todd wrinkled his nose. He was still holding the remote control for the bed, his fingers stroking the sides of it.

"Heavens, no. Not today," Fiona assured him. She

reached out her arms. "Give this old lady a hug. You, too, Lissi."

Both kids easily bent over their great-grandmother, hugging her as enthusiastically as she hugged them.

Bobbie blinked hard and looked down at the floor. A moment later, Gabe's hand closed around hers.

Startled, she looked up at him. But he wasn't looking at her. He was watching his children hug their great-grandmother with a stark expression on his face.

She knew in that moment that it no longer mattered what her reservations in the beginning had been regarding the wisdom of their little deception. She couldn't stand by and not do something to help him.

Her hand squeezed his and his gaze slowly came around to her. "It's going to be okay." Her words were nearly inaudible. But she knew he heard.

And when he lifted their linked hands and brushed his lips across her knuckles, she also knew that no matter what their brief future together held, she was never going to be the same.

When she managed to drag her gaze away from him, it was only to find Fiona's attention focused squarely on them. She looked decidedly satisfied and Bobbie felt warmth begin to creep up her throat. She vainly willed it to stop.

The children finally moved aside and Gabe let go of Bobbie's hand then, to get his own hug in. Then it was Bobbie's turn, and she kissed Fiona's gently lined cheek. "Don't scare us like this," she whispered.

Fiona patted her hand. "Don't you waste time fretting about me when you've got much more interesting things to concern yourself with." She glanced past Bobbie and her smile widened. "Like all of *them*."

"I...right." The flush sped up unstoppably and she quickly changed subjects. "Don't worry about the agency, either."

Fiona leaned her white head back against the pillows. "I'm not. Now off with you." She flapped her hands as if she were shooing flies. But there was still a faint smile on her lips, even as she closed her eyes.

Bobbie gathered up her purse and long-dry raincoat and followed the children and Gabe out of the room.

"Can we go back to Bobbie's?" Lisette suggested when Gabe asked what they wanted to do about dinner.

Todd, who'd run ahead of them to punch the elevator's call button, started nodding, too. "We could have pizza and play with the dogs again!"

Bobbie bit back a smile and tried to pretend she wasn't ridiculously touched. "I think Zeus and Archimedes are the real draw." They all stepped into the empty elevator when the doors slid open.

"Bobbie might have other plans for the evening," Gabe said mildly and she suddenly found herself the focus of two sets of very anxious eyes.

"No." She smiled a little shakily. "No other plans at all."

Todd gave his father a "duh" sort of look that amused Bobbie so much she forgot all about that tender shakiness. "What?" She tugged lightly on Todd's ear. "You think there's no way on earth I might have something else to do?"

Todd's cheeks went crimson. Bobbie laughed out loud and caught the boy's face in her hands, giving him a smacking kiss on the forehead. "I'm just teasing you," she assured. "I would like nothing better than for you all to come over. And I'm sure that Zeus and

Archimedes will be very happy to see you, too. But maybe we can come up with something a little more nutritious than pizza."

He went from red-cheeked to looking suspicious in a heartbeat. "I don't like spinach," he warned hurriedly. "Or anything else green."

"Todd," Gabe inserted, "you'll eat what's put in front of you. Even green vegetables."

Bobbie bit back another grin as the boy's expression went from suspicious to purely horrified. "What about carrots?" she asked.

Todd gave the matter some consideration. "I guess they're okay."

"Then I think maybe we can manage something." She didn't know what, considering the yawning caverns that masqueraded as her kitchen cupboards, but fortunately, she could call Tommi on the way home for some advice, and nobody would be the wiser. "What about you, Lisette? Anything you don't like?"

The elevator arrived at the ground level and they stepped off. Lisette tucked her pale hair behind her ear and handed Bobbie her backpack while she put on her jacket. "I don't care what we eat as long as we get to sit on the floor. Mother *never* lets us sit on the floor."

Compared to the former Mrs. Gannon—witchy attitude aside—Bobbie figured she'd more often than not come up short. "Well, if I *had* a kitchen table at all, I can assure you that we'd be sitting at it." She returned the backpack.

"Then I'm glad you don't have one." Todd was matter-of-fact. He trotted ahead of them toward the automatic door and his backpack—camouflage-green in comparison to Lisette's pale-blue—bounced between his shoulders. "It's more fun."

Only because it was a novelty to them, she figured, as they followed Todd outside where it was still raining.

"I'm parked in the north forty," Gabe said. "Wait here while I get the truck. Then I'll drive you to yours." Not waiting for an argument, he set off at an easy jog, his long legs eating up the distance.

She couldn't remember the last time someone worried that she might get wet walking to her car. Had someone—other than her mother—ever worried about that?

She dragged her thoughts together and looked back at the children. "What do you usually do for meals at your dad's house?"

"We go to restaurants mostly, 'cause the only things he can cook are tuna sandwiches or steak on the grill."

Bobbie grinned. "I don't want to alarm you, but my repertoire doesn't include much more than that."

Todd rocked back and forth on his shoes. "Can you make macaroni and cheese?"

She nodded.

"Out of a box?" Lisette gave her an intrigued look.

"Well. Yes. I can make it in the oven, too, though." Tommi had given her a recipe for it that used about four kinds of cheese and took hours to prepare. She'd made it once and promptly decided that if she ever wanted it again, she'd go to her sister's bistro and order it.

"The box kind is what I want," Lisette said with certainty. "I had it once when I was at a sleepover with my friend Ellie Roman." She leaned closer. "We made it ourselves." She whispered it as if it might have been a crime.

"Was it a long time ago?"

She shook her head and tucked her hair behind her ear again. "Before Christmas. But then their cook found out and he got mad and told Ellie's mom he was going to quit if she didn't keep the nuisances out of the kitchen. That's what he calls Ellie and her little sister. The nuisances." She let out a breath. "I never cooked anything before. It was fun. Until we all got in trouble. Louisa—that's *our* housekeeper—says the Romans' cook is a—" more whispering "—lunatic."

Bobbie wasn't certain that she didn't agree. It was also inconceivable to her how the things she considered everyday were not part of Lisette's and Todd's world at all.

She tucked her arm through the girl's. Even at twelve, Gabe's daughter was nearly as tall as she was. "My sister Tommi was cooking in the kitchen before she was Todd's age. Now she owns her own restaurant."

Lisette's eyes rounded. "Cool."

"I've always thought so. Maybe we'll all go there sometime."

"Tonight?" Todd asked just as Gabe pulled his truck up to the curb and pushed open the passenger door from the inside.

"Not tonight. She's closed." Bobbie nudged them forward and they darted across the sidewalk, scrambling up into the back seat of the big truck. She brought up the rear, and once inside, pointed out the location of her car to Gabe.

"Why don't we leave it for now," he suggested. "I'll bring you by later to get it after we go by the agency to do the checks for Fiona. No point in having us both driving when we'll have to backtrack this way, any-way."

Bobbie was fully aware that it was feeling too much like a cozy family inside his truck, with his long-fingered hand casually resting on the console just a few inches from her arm and his kids squabbling over the video game that Todd had in his backpack. No matter what she'd agreed to help him with, she knew it would be smarter to find some distance. To go to her own car, even if it did mean a little extra driving in the rain.

Which just proved how little she cared about smarts, when she blindly reached for the safety belt to fasten it around her. "Okay, but we'll have to stop at the grocery store to pick up a few things on the way."

"You should have said so. We'll just go out," he said immediately.

"No, Dad!" Lisette poked her head between the seats. "Bobbie's gonna make us macaroni and cheese. Out of a box!"

Gabe looked from his daughter's unusually ani-mated face to Bobbie and felt a dangerous warmth in-side him. "Little did I know that cheap mac and cheese could get such a positive reaction."

"Does that mean we don't gotta have carrots?" Todd asked from the rear.

"We'll have carrots, too," Bobbie said, giving Gabe a smile that seemed a little shaky around the edges. "And maybe orange slices. We'll just have a whole orange-colored theme going on in honor of Hallow-een tomorrow."

Lisette giggled and sat back in her seat. Gabe looked at Bobbie. "You don't have to do all this, you know." The more time they spent together, the more his children accepted her as part of his world, the easier it would be to tell them about the "engagement." And the better it would be in court for him if any questions arose about his and Bobbie's supposedly altar-bound relationship. He knew it. But it was getting damn hard to remember that was his only motivation.

"I know I don't have to." She lifted her finger and he realized that the traffic light had turned green.

He dragged his head out of the gray mist of her eyes and drove out of the parking lot. Rush-hour traffic had abated and it didn't take long to get to Fiona's neighborhood and the grocery store that Bobbie directed him to.

When his kids scrambled out of the truck and raced to the row of shopping baskets lined up outside the entrance, arguing over who would get to push it, Gabe shook his head again. "You'd think they'd never been in a grocery store."

Bobbie looked up at him. "Have they?"

He started to answer, only to realize he didn't know. And wasn't that a helluva note? Something so ordinary, yet something he'd never done with his own children. And he couldn't be certain, but he doubted that it was something their mother had done with them, since Stephanie had grown up in a house full of servants, and even when she'd married him had expected to keep on a full-time housekeeper. The fact that such a luxury was not in his budget since nearly every dime he'd been making had gone back into expanding Gannon-Morris had been one of the more minor bones of contention between them.

"Relax. It's only a store." Bobbie patted his hand before sliding out of the truck. She flipped the hood of her raincoat over her head and darted after the children.

But Gabe knew it was more than that.

It was one more reminder of the kind of life his children led with their mother and stepfather.

He didn't *want* his kids growing up insulated from such simple, normal things. He'd grown up that way. And if it hadn't been for Fiona's encouragement, he'd have never found his way out of the privileged life that had felt like it was strangling him even before he was out of his private high school.

Bobbie had reached the wet row of shopping carts stacked up outside the store. She pulled one out, propped her foot on the bottom rack, and pushed off, sailing across the empty sidewalk toward the store. Her hood fell off her head and the tails of her jacket swung out behind her as she rode the careening cart.

He heard his kids laugh. Both of them. And beneath that, he could hear the musical sound of Bobbie laughing with them.

He even could feel the corners of his own lips start to turn upward. Addictive, that laugh was.

He let out a low breath, shoved his balled hands in the pockets of his leather jacket. In the right one, his fingertips felt the sharp edges of a flower-shaped hair clip.

He took it out and looked at it. The little jewels on it sparkled beneath the parking lot lights.

He didn't know why he still hadn't given it back to her. Or why he kept carrying it around with him.

He pushed the tiny thing back in his pocket, pushing aside, too, the speculation that wasn't leading him anywhere he ought to be going, and followed them into the store.

In the end, what should have taken only a few minutes to gather up what they needed for dinner took considerably longer. And when they left the store, they were all carrying bags. But when they arrived at Bobbie's place, both Lisette and Todd quickly lost their avid interest in the groceries they'd chosen in favor of Bobbie's dogs. Once Zeus and Archie were out of their kennel and free to play, all four of the youngsters— human and canine—were rolling around on the floor in the living room.

Gabe pulled the last box of macaroni and cheese out of the reusable fabric bags that Lisette had insisted they purchase instead of using plastic and handed the box to Bobbie where she was loading things into what had been a nearly empty cupboard. "I can't remember the last time I heard Lissi giggle like that."

Bobbie glanced up at him. "Kids and puppies. They're a pretty surefire combination."

"You're the surefire combination," he countered.

Her eyes widened a little and then she blinked, briskly shutting the cupboard door and bending over to the lower one to noisily pull out a large pot that she handed him. "Mind filling that with water? I've gotta find the lid."

He took the pot, and figured there was a hot spot in hell waiting for him, considering the way he couldn't pull his gaze away from the view she made bending over to root through her cupboard. And when she reached an arm in even farther, the back of her short orange sweater rode up a few inches, baring the creamy skin at the small of her back. A sheer stretch of narrow purple with a tiny bow at the center peeked above her blue jeans and even though his kids were giggling from the other room and his grandmother was in the freaking hospital, the only thing he wanted to do right then was to let his fingers do the walking over that bow and beyond.

"Hey, Dad?"

He swallowed an oath, jerking around like he was thirteen and had been caught looking at pictures of naked ladies. "What is it, Lissi?"

His daughter gave him a shy smile. "I'm glad we came here."

Bobbie made a faint sound and straightened, too.

"I'm glad, too, honey," he agreed quietly.

Then Lisette smiled again, a little less shyly, and she pirouetted out of the kitchen. A second later, they could hear her and Todd whispering, followed by peals of laughter.

He swallowed and shoved the pot under the ancient faucet. A moment later, Bobbie set the pot lid on the counter.

"Thanks." Her hands slid over his as she took the filled pot from him to set on the stove. She didn't look at him. "You don't have to stay in here and help, you know." She turned on the burner and plopped the lid on the pot. "It's not like there's much room left in here, anyway." She waved at the dog kennels taking up half the floor area.

In answer, he reached for the bag of carrots. "Got a peeler?"

She looked like she wanted to say something more, but just pressed her soft lips together and pulled open the drawer next to the stove. She rooted through the contents for a moment, then pulled out a vegetable peeler and handed it to him.

But he caught her hand, along with the peeler. "Thanks."

"It's just a vegetable peeler."

His thumb rubbed over her knuckles. "You know that's not what I mean."

Her lashes swept down. "I know." Her voice was low. "But you—we—don't need things to get any more complicated than they already are. Right?" She looked up at him then, giving him a blast of her soft gray eyes.

Eyes that were practically pleading for him not to bring any more hurt into her life.

Yeah, he'd wanted her the day they'd met. When she'd latched her lips onto his and blown every thought of every single thing in his life right out of his mind. And with every day since, that want was becoming even more sharply hewn.

But after that, what did he have to offer a young woman like her? A woman who deserved the whole deal. White roses and rings and picket fences and babies.

Things he'd tried once and had failed at so miserably that he—and those he'd hurt along the way—were still paying the price.

So he made himself nod. Made himself agree. "Right," he said gruffly, and slipped the peeler out of her hand. Then he pulled out a carrot and began peeling the damn thing.

But the only thing he was seeing was the expression on Bobbie's face.

The one that told him she was no more convinced of her words than he was.

Chapter 9

"I feel like I'm committing some sort of crime," Bobbie murmured later that evening.

Gabe had dropped off the children at their mother's house after their orange-themed dinner, then driven Bobbie to Golden Ability. Now she was sitting behind Fiona's desk, an oversized checkbook flipped open on top of it. Beside her was the salary spreadsheet that she'd somehow managed to find in Fiona's crowded filing cabinets. She consulted it as she carefully wrote out the staff's paychecks.

"You're doing everyone a favor," Gabe reminded her. He was leaning against the doorjamb between Fiona's office and the rest of the administrative space at Golden Ability. "Just sign and stop thinking so much."

She'd be better off if she could stop thinking so much about a lot of things. She clicked the ballpoint pen again and quickly penned Fiona's name.

Only when the first check was completed did she realize she'd been holding her breath.

She let it out and carefully tore out the check, making certain she'd recorded all of the information in the register. "Fiona needs to have all this computerized," she said, moving on to the second paycheck. "It would be a lot easier."

"Tell her that."

"I have." She added the signature, tore it out and enveloped it. Concentrating on this task for Fiona was the only thing keeping her from dwelling on Gabe. "She keeps every other thing around here on the computer. I don't know why she doesn't handle her accounts payable and payroll that way, too, but she just says that she'll leave that task for the next person to run Golden Ability." She shook her head. "As if anyone else could fill her shoes. This place would cease to exist if it weren't for her."

"That would be a shame."

"No kidding." She wrote out a few more checks. "Fiona serves more than a hundred people a year. No fees for them to participate, no charges to be partnered with a service dog. Golden bears the cost for all of it and for an agency this small, that's amazing."

"She ever tell you why she started the agency in the first place?"

Bobbie shook her head and quickly turned her attention back to the checkbook when Gabe suddenly straightened away from his slouch against the jamb and entered the small, crowded office. "I assume what everyone does—that she must have had a heart for it. It's not like she's earned the money that would buy that huge house of hers from the profits."

"She had my grandfather to thank for that." He flipped a narrow, straight-backed chair away from the wall on the other side of the desk and sat down on it, crossing his arms over the top of the back.

"You must have been pretty young when he died."

"About five."

"Do you remember him?"

"Some things. Does Fiona talk about him?"

"Not much." She pressed the end of the pen against her chin for a moment. Her gaze settled on the sinewy lines of Gabe's tanned forearms where he'd rolled up his shirtsleeves, and her fingers tightened around the pen. It was a miserable substitute for the feel of his warm skin.

She looked back down at the checkbook. The cozy office already felt cramped with him there; now she realized it also felt too warm. "I, um, I know she changed everything in her house except his study after he was gone, and never married again. I figured that even after all those years, some losses still remain too deep to talk about."

"He had macular degeneration. He was going blind."

She looked up, and realized she wasn't terribly surprised at the detail. "Which explains why Fiona gained an interest in all this, obviously." She waved her hand around in a loose gesture, then clicked the pen and began tending to business once more. "How did he die?"

"The official story is that he had a heart attack. I learned when I was a teenager, though, that he'd killed himself."

Aghast, she looked up at him. "What?"

"He chose death over a life of blindness."

She pressed her hand to the sudden ache in her chest. "Fiona must have been devastated. And your father, too."

"She never wanted anyone to feel as desperate as my grandfather did about their loss of sight. But the rest of the family just wanted to pretend he'd died of natural causes. To this day, they still maintain that story. And none of the family, including my father, supported Fiona's decision when she started up the agency."

Her lips twisted a little. "Except for you, none of her family seems to support her decision even now, some thirty-odd years later."

"She didn't do what was expected of her. She was supposed to have ladies' teas and sit on the boards of charities. Not run one. She couldn't even count on financial support from the Gannon Law Group. A woman with less resolve would probably have caved to the pressure."

"Is that why you admire her so much? She didn't cave to family demands?"

"She didn't cave, and she backed me when I refused to go to law school."

The more Bobbie knew about him, the more fascinated she became.

And there was danger in that. A danger she wanted to run headlong into.

She realized she was staring at him again and forced herself to look away.

She signed the last of the paychecks and set down the pen again. "You're a successful businessman, though," she managed to say, with a credible degree of calm, considering the way her nerves were dancing around. "I'm sure Colin is proud of you now."

"He might have been if I'd at least become an architect. Instead, I'm a contractor."

"Which is nothing to be sneezed at," she defended.

"It's blue-collar."

"So? Honest work is honest work." Bobbie locked the checkbook back inside the desk drawer and gathered up the sealed envelopes, tapping them neatly into a pile. "And it must suit you. Why else would you spend your entire adulthood making your company a success?"

"Success is relative."

She squared the pile of envelopes on the center of Fiona's ink blotter. It was the only place in the office that was immaculately tidy. The rest of the place was cluttered with books and reports and the odd frippery that Fiona had collected over the last several decades. "I suppose it is."

She pushed back from the desk and scooted out between it and the filing cabinets that lined the wall. She dropped Fiona's desk key back in the ceramic turtle, a handmade gift from the first client that Golden had served all those years ago, and went to the door. "I've never been particularly successful at anything, so I'm hardly qualified to say."

He looked over his shoulder at her, his eyebrow cocked. "You're pretty damn successful, in my opinion."

She tried to squelch the bolt of pleasure his words caused and failed miserably. "All right, I can raise puppies pretty well," she allowed. "But that's certainly not going to get me into the Fairchild hall of fame."

He swung his legs around until he was sitting properly in the chair, facing her. "And what would that take?"

She glanced at the large-faced round clock hanging on the wall. "Don't you want to get going? It's nearly ten o'clock." He was still bearing a heavier load than usual at work because of his injured construction manager, and she couldn't stop thinking how... alone...they were.

He sat forward, forearms on his thighs, his hands loosely linked together. His blue eyes didn't waver from her face. "Turnabout is fair play. You know all the secrets of the Gannon family," he pointed out. "And I'm not feeling particularly hurried."

Which didn't do a thing to calm the butterflies that had been flitting around inside her midsection ever since they'd gone to the grocery store together.

As if they'd been playing house together. Just a quick trip around the grocery with the kids, honey, then back home for dinner and a little homework, consisting solely of creative Halloween costume-planning. For Lisette, they'd come up with a fitting Odette costume made out of a fuzzy white sweater that Bobbie had unintentionally shrunk in the laundry and feathers from a white boa from costumes past. Todd would be a thoroughly hilarious video game character, complete with a French beret that would have probably shocked Georgie—who'd given it to Bobbie as a gift from one of her travels—and a set of fake glasses and mustache.

It didn't matter how good her intentions were to keep things "safe" between her and Gabe: she kept backsliding into the overwhelming allure of him.

And right now, that allure had her wanting to move

over to him, to put her hands on those wide shoulders and sink into his lap and…

She dragged her thoughts, kicking and screaming, out of fantasyland. Hadn't they already agreed not to complicate things?

She cleared her throat.

"My mother, Cornelia, raised all of us pretty much on her own once my father died. Frankly, she's the most accomplished, independent, elegant woman on the planet."

"You love her."

"Of course."

The corners of his lips kicked up. "And the other Fairchilds?"

Butterflies danced even more frantically in response to that sexy half smile.

She swallowed and fixed her gaze somewhere over his left ear. But even that seemed fraught with setbacks, because he had exceptionally nice ears.

She honestly couldn't remember ever noticing a man's ears before.

"Well?"

She hoped he couldn't see the flush riding up her neck when he had to prompt her out of her silence. "My eldest sister, Georgie, has a master's in counseling, but works for the Hunt Foundation, basically vetting out worthwhile charities for them to support. She's based here in Seattle but travels all around the world. She's been in Haiti and I think the Sudan is up next, as a matter of fact."

"Hunt Foundation as in your Uncle Harry."

"It's a philanthropic foundation that came out of HuntCom, yes. Alex—that's Harry's third son—runs it."

"I've seen him in the news," he murmured.

"Right. Well, anyway, what can I say about Georgie? She's this tall." Bobbie straightened her arm above her head, waving at an imaginary height. "Long blond hair. Curves in all the right places. *Loves* to tell people what to do." Her lips twisted wryly. "She's always right, too, which is maddening. She's got more brains than I do curls *and* can play the piano and men's hearts with equal ease. There's nothing Georgie can't do."

"Sounds scary."

Bobbie smiled a little. "Intimidating, maybe, but she still has a heart of gold. Then there's Frankie."

Hand still in the air, she bent her elbow a little. "She comes to about here. More blond hair. More curves. She's next in line—we're stair-steps—she's a librarian at the University of Washington and probably the sole reason why most of the male students there like to frequent the place as much as they do. *Not* your stereotypical librarian. But she's still probably memorized every textbook there by now—and understands them."

Her hand dropped a little more, but still hovered above her head. "You've already met Tommi. She put herself through culinary school and even worked in Europe for a while. Opened her own bistro here and I don't have to tell you her wonderful reviews are well-earned, since you've tasted her food for yourself. But if Tommi could, I think she'd feed every hungry person in Seattle. Love through a full tummy. That's Tommi."

She dropped her hand altogether. "Then there's me. The one who usually has dog hair on her clothes, who barely managed to graduate from community college at all. We all got money when we graduated from high school, from Uncle Harry. My sisters used it for their educations and smart things." She shook her head. "Not me."

"Okay, I'll bite."

Her gaze got caught in his.

An entirely different meaning to the words shivered through her.

"I, um—" She blinked and marshaled her too-easily scattered thoughts. "I spent the last of it on Lawrence's campaign, actually." If nothing else could, surely *that* foolishly naive act would take the warmth out of Gabe's eyes.

"You believed in him."

"And he believed I had access to *real* money. Hunt money, remember? All things being relative, my last ten thousand dollars was a pittance compared to that." She plucked her raincoat off the coat tree jammed into the corner of the office.

"That doesn't mean what you did was stupid."

Her fingers crumpled the coat. "It sure felt that way when he dumped me."

"Are you still in love with him?"

If anyone had asked her that even just two weeks earlier, she wasn't sure what she'd have said.

But that was before she'd kissed—then met— Gabriel Gannon.

She moistened her lips and slowly turned to face him. "No."

He studied her for a moment, as if weighing her answer. "Good for you."

She wanted badly to turn the question on him.

Was *he* still in love with his ex-wife? No matter how badly things had ended between them, he'd cared about her enough at one time to marry her. To have children with her.

She'd cheated on him, but that didn't necessarily mean the end of his feelings, even if it had meant the end of the marriage. And Bobbie had seen for herself the tension between Gabe and his ex-wife at Fiona's birthday party. Who was Bobbie to say what emotions were at the base of it?

But the question stayed jammed high in her chest.

Maybe because she was afraid of what his answer would be.

So she stood there, twisting her coat between her hands and after a moment, Gabe pushed to his feet. "It's late. Let's get you back to your car."

She wasn't sure if she felt relieved…or let down.

But she managed a jerky nod and they left the administrative building, stopping only long enough for her to lock up.

The rest of the grounds—classrooms, dining hall and the partially-covered outdoor training areas—were silent with only the safety lights flicking on then off when they walked past. They passed through the front gate, which Bobbie locked behind them. Gabe's truck gleamed wetly where it was parked in the roomy parking lot beneath one of the light poles. She headed toward it, trying not to think anything of his light touch at the small of her back as they crossed the lot.

He'd touched her the same way when they'd danced at Fiona's birthday party, too. Probably just a habit of his. A gentleman and all that.

They reached the truck, and he unlocked the passenger door and helped her up onto the high seat. She gathered her coat around her but he didn't move away and close the door. She looked at him. His eyes were shadowed and mysterious in the light as he looked back.

Her heart suddenly beat a little faster. Her breath suddenly felt a little shorter and then he leaned closer... and reached across her. She heard the safety belt snap into place and realized all he'd done was fasten her in. Like a child.

She swallowed that unpalatable thought as he finally closed the door and walked around the truck to his side and got in.

They drove back to the hospital and her waiting car with only the low sound of music from the radio and the occasional swipe of his windshield wiper blades against the lingering drizzle to break the silence. Finally, by the time the hospital was in sight, that silence felt like corkscrews tightening around her nerves. "I hope your ex-wife won't be upset about the costumes we came up with for Todd and Lisette for school tomorrow."

His thumb slowly tapped the steering wheel. "I don't care if she is or not. At least the kids are happy with what they'll be wearing. They definitely weren't thrilled with the store-bought getups that Steph got them." She felt the glance he slid her way. "Don't worry about it."

"I just don't want to be the cause of any problems."

"I'll worry about Steph. I'm happy the kids have been content to be with *me*. Something else I have to thank you for."

"That's not true."

He gave a rueful laugh. "Yeah, it is. Believe me. So...you didn't say what you'll be dressing up as tomorrow, but I heard Lisette laughing about it when you and she were in your room while Todd and I cleaned up the kitchen."

"Oh, right." She looked out the side window. Did he think it was immature to dress up? "Pippi Longstocking." He was so silent that she finally looked over at him. "Silly, I know, but I've got a few things that'll work for the clothes without much effort, and the only thing I'll have to worry about are getting the braids to stick out from the sides of my head."

"Considering your curly hair, I almost expected a Little Orphan Annie."

"I've already done that one once."

"You dress up every year?"

"Pretty much. Either there's a party to go to, or where I'm working requires it." She gave him a quick look. "Like this year."

"Do you mind? Get tired of it?"

She thought about denying it. But what would be the point. "Not usually. When's the last time you dressed up for Halloween?"

He slowed to turn into the hospital parking lot. "A long time ago."

She plucked at the folds of her coat. "Not since you were a kid, I suppose."

He exhaled. "Steph dragged me to a party when we were dating. I dressed up then. Does that count?"

Suddenly wishing that she hadn't brought up the matter at all, she pulled her purse onto her lap to root through it for her car keys. "Sure. It counts. Um… what—"

"Zorro. And yes, I felt like a damn idiot wearing the mask."

She managed a smile for him. "I'm sure you were

very dashing." And his date had probably looked like some svelte bombshell in whatever costume she'd worn. Bobbie knew well enough not to voice *that* question. And fortunately, he'd pulled up behind her parked car, anyway.

Her keys jingled when she pulled them out of her purse before pushing open the door. She waved him back. "Don't get out. I'm fine."

He subsided in his seat. "Thanks again for everything."

"You don't have to thank me." She looked up at the tall hospital building. "It's probably too late to go in and see her again."

His hand slid up her spine, not stopping until he reached the nape of her neck. He squeezed gently. "Probably. Come and see her tomorrow. She'd get a kick out of Pippi."

She didn't know why she suddenly felt tears burning deep behind her eyes, but she did.

Which meant that she needed to get out of his vehicle and into hers before she completely lost her composure. "I'll probably do that. Maybe after my shift at the Bean." She cleared her throat. "Don't forget to take Fiona the signature card from the bank so she can get another signer on her checking account."

"I won't." He could have sounded amused that she'd reminded him of something that he, himself, had suggested in the first place, but he didn't. He just pressed his fingers gently against the back of her neck again, and then his hand moved away. "Do you want me to follow you home?"

"No!" She swallowed and slipped out of the vehicle. "No," she said more normally. "I am a big girl, you know. I can make the drive on my own." And if he followed her back to her place, what were the odds that she'd be able to keep herself from inviting him in?

Not good. Not good at all.

And then he would probably be uncomfortable, and try to let her down without hurting her too-young feelings.

"Drive carefully, then."

She nodded and closed the truck door and went to her own car. She'd just fit the key in the ignition when she realized he'd gotten out of his truck anyway, and was looking down at her through her window.

She rolled it down. "Did I forget something?"

He hunkered beside the car, folding his arms on top of the opened window. "Just for the record, *no*. I'm not still in love with my ex-wife."

Her jaw went loose and her insides suddenly went soft. "I didn't—"

"—ask. I know you didn't." His gaze roved over her face. "Strangely enough, I still wanted you to be clear on that point."

She felt breathless. "Okay."

He nodded once. "Okay." Then he nodded again, straightened enough to lean inside the car, and pressed an achingly slow kiss to her lips. A kiss that said all too clearly that he knew she was definitely not a child. And when he finally pulled away, she could only sit here, dazed and silent. "I'll call you tomorrow."

He thumped his hand on the roof of her car and was moving back to his truck before she could shake herself out of her trance.

Then his truck slowly moved further away in the parking lot and when she saw his brake lights go on and stay on, she realized that he wasn't going anywhere until he was certain that she was safely on her way home.

Fresh warmth spread through her. The kind of warmth that came not just from passion, but from something else entirely.

Something even more dangerous.

Her hand shook as she started up the car and backed out of the parking space. His truck was still sitting there, so she inched past him. Only when she was driving in front of him did he begin driving again, too.

He stayed behind her until their routes home took them in opposite directions. When she heard the staccato toot of his horn as he turned off, she rolled her window down enough to stick her hand out in a little wave.

And then he was gone, his taillights disappearing into the night.

But that warmth stayed inside her all the way home.

Chapter 10

It took hours for Bobbie to get to sleep that night. And then when she did sleep, it was only to wake up tangled in her sheets and sweating from dreams about Gabe.

Intimate dreams.

The kind of dreams that had you jerking out of your sleep from sheer pleasure, only to realize that it was *just* a dream.

She was due into work at seven-thirty in the morning. And even though she'd set her alarm for the usual ninety minutes earlier, she dragged herself out of bed with an extra hour to spare on top of it.

Staying in bed, trying to sleep, thinking about the man she was engaged-in-name-only to, was just too torturous.

So she took the dogs out for a chilly, dark walk around the block, fixed herself a yogurt and fruit smoothie, and set about transforming herself into some recognizable form of Pippi Longstocking. Once she was finished, she decided she hadn't done too badly.

The yellow dress that she'd sewn red patches all over was really a long T-shirt, but as long as she was careful not to bend over, the hem of it managed to cover the tops of the red and green thigh-high knit stockings that she'd found from a few Christmases ago. And once she'd wrapped enough wiry pipe cleaners around a red headband, she was able to work her two braids onto the wires so they were sticking out oddly from the sides of her head. A dozen freckles painted onto her cheeks with an eyeliner pencil and she was good to go, even if she did earn a few whines from the dogs when she gave them a last pat before leaving the house.

She started to head to the coffee shop, but since she was running early for once, she decided halfway there to face the music with her mother. So she drove to the house that Cornelia had moved them to not long after Bobbie's father had died.

Bobbie had only hazy memories of that first house. It had been much larger and grander. But the place where Cornelia now lived was the place Bobbie had called home and she let herself in without even knocking.

Despite the early hour, her mother was exactly where Bobbie had expected her to be: sitting at the breakfast table with a pot of tea and the morning paper.

She glanced up when Bobbie entered. "Bobbie, dear! What a surprise." She got up to take the jacket that Bobbie was shrugging out of. "Look at you. You've outdone yourself this year. Is everything all right?"

Bobbie let out a breath. "One day I'm going to pop

in on you and you're not going to automatically think something is wrong."

Cornelia frowned as she draped the jacket over the back of a chair. "I don't always think that."

"Don't you?" Bobbie bit her lip. "I'm sorry. It's just been a bit of a day." Or two or three.

"It's not even seven o'clock in the morning," Cornelia chided gently. "And not that I'm averse to seeing you at any time, but this *is* a bit of a surprise." She tugged gently on the end of one of Bobbie's gravity-defying braids. "So…what's wrong?"

Bobbie let out a breath and sat down. "Fiona had a heart attack yesterday."

"Good heavens." Cornelia touched the gold pendant hanging around her neck and sat back down in her chair. She reached across the table to cover Bobbie's fidgeting fingers with her own. "I'm so sorry to hear that. Is she all right?"

"She will be. But that's only part of what I need to tell you." Maybe it was the scare with Fiona or having already gone through a version of this conversation with Tommi, but Bobbie managed to condense matters more than usual when she was faced with telling her always collected mother about her marriage-bound pretense with Gabe.

When she was finished, Cornelia rose again from the breakfast table and moved across the kitchen to look out the window above the sink.

Even at this early hour, her pale-blond hair was pulled back in its usual chignon and she was dressed impeccably in a soft salmon-colored sweater set that perfectly matched her narrow slacks. "Tell me the truth,

Bobbie. *Were* you already engaged to this man when Harry told me you were before?"

"No!" Bobbie pushed off her chair and went to stand next to her mother. She could see faint reflections of themselves in the window pane. Cornelia, tall and slender and fair and more beautiful than most women half her age. And Bobbie. Short and rounder in places than she liked, with her dark hair currently confined in ridiculous, wired braids. "If I'd intended to lie to you about any of this, I wouldn't be here now."

Her mother sighed a little and slid her arm around the shoulders of Bobbie's red-and-yellow patchwork dress. "Are you in love with this man?"

"No!"

Cornelia lifted a brow. "Are you certain?"

Bobbie swallowed. "Yes. No. I don't know. I only met him a few weeks ago."

"And look where you are," her mother countered quietly. "You jumped into an engagement with Lawrence after only a month," she reminded. "I don't want to see you hurt again."

"I'll be fine. And *someone* has to help him, Mom. You'd be appalled at his ex-wife's attitude."

"Stephanie Walker. I've met her and her husband, actually, at a HuntCom function last year."

"I told Gabe this was a small city," she muttered.

Cornelia patted her shoulder. "She was perfectly lovely, actually, though maybe a tad uptight about her husband's career. I find it hard to believe that she wouldn't see reason when it comes to the custody of her children."

"She called me *the help* the first time we met."

"Mmm. Unfortunate, of course. And I'm well aware

how communications between former spouses can deteriorate beyond all measure. I'm sure you were just too close to the blast range."

Bobbie wasn't sure of any such thing, but she wasn't going to argue the point with her mother. For one thing, she hadn't been shocked right out of her gourd and insisted Bobbie get herself immediately uninvolved—which had been her first reaction when Bobbie had told her she'd planned to marry Lawrence.

"Colin—that's Gabe's father—said he knew you, too."

"Colin Gannon. Of course." Cornelia nodded. She smiled faintly. "Handsome devil. His wife is an interesting woman, as I remember. She didn't strike me as particularly maternal."

"That's one way of putting it. So you're not, um, going to disown me or anything?"

Cornelia tsked. "Where do you get these silly ideas?" She pressed a kiss to Bobbie's forehead. "I love you, darling. I just want to see you happy."

If it weren't for knowing that her involvement with Gabe was one of necessity rather than emotion, she would have been able to say that she was perfectly happy.

So she just smiled and hoped her mother would take that as answer enough.

Knowing that the morning traffic would be thickening, Bobbie left soon after, and the rest of the day flew by quickly. The shop was busy, and when she wasn't making coffees, she was fielding calls from Cheryl at the agency.

By the time Bobbie got off shift at four, she was feeling exhausted. But the sky was clear for once, so she walked the few doors down to a local floral shop and bought a pot of yellow daisies. They were cheerful-looking enough to give her a fresh shot of energy that carried her back to her car and across town to see Fiona.

Gabe had left a message on her cell phone while she'd been working that he had to run out to Ballard to finish the consultation he hadn't made it to at all the previous day. He'd also visited the bank for his grandmother and the paperwork was still with Fiona. He'd ended the no-nonsense call with "See you later, Pippi."

There was nothing romantic about the message.

No undercurrents in his voice that told her anything other than what his words conveyed.

She'd still listened to it five times in the office at Between the Bean during her lunch break. Doreen, dressed all in pink organza as Glinda the Good Witch, had finally stuck her head around the office door. She'd jabbed her wand—a silver-painted dowel with a foil-wrapped star stuck on the end of it—toward Bobbie. "Just call the man back already if you want to hear his voice so darn bad."

Bobbie had flushed and turned off the phone before finishing her peanut butter sandwich. She hadn't called Gabe, knowing he would be busy enough without having to answer a call from her. What would have been the point of her interrupting him, other than to tell him she couldn't get him out of her head?

But she hadn't erased the message.

And as she drove to the hospital, she couldn't help but wonder if she'd run into him there. She also couldn't help but worry how she would keep up the pretense of their relationship in front of Fiona. The last thing Bobbie wanted to do was cause the woman any sort of stress. If she actually believed that romance had bloomed so quickly between Bobbie and her grandson, telling her that it was all for show was bound to be troubling.

As it happened, though, Bobbie needn't have worried about that.

Gabe wasn't in Fiona's room.

His ex-wife and his children, however, were, and while both Todd and Lisette—dressed in the costumes that they'd come up with at Bobbie's the evening before—seemed genuinely pleased to see Bobbie, their mother most definitely wasn't.

She gave Bobbie a glacial look, but moved aside so that Bobbie could place the large, cheery plant on the windowsill, which was a little crowded, thanks to a big crystal vase overflowing with an amazing orchid bouquet. Bobbie then went to Fiona's side to kiss her cheek. Her dear friend was sitting upright in the bed. "You're getting quite a garden in here," she told her.

Fiona smiled and patted her cheek. "The daisies are lovely, dear. So bright and cheerful. Thank you."

"We brought the orchids," Lisette piped in. She'd completed her swan costume with a white tutu from home and looked quite the young ballerina as she struck poses around the confining room, despite her mother's quiet words to be still.

Bobbie glanced at the impressive floral display sitting next to her very ordinary daisy plant. She glanced at Gabe's ex-wife and tried to remember that her own mother had claimed the woman was perfectly nice. "They're beautiful."

Stephanie smiled back, but the effort could have

frozen water. She brushed a languid hand down her perfectly cut, deep-red sheath dress. "The children insisted on visiting their grandmother before getting out of their costumes."

"And I appreciate you bringing them," Fiona put in, giving Todd a wink.

Stephanie looked marginally warmer. "Yes. Well, now they need to be getting home. Ethan will be home this evening and I'm planning a special dinner."

Todd grimaced. "I'd rather be trick-or-treating."

"You're too old for those things," Stephanie told him. "And it's hardly a safe activity, anyway."

Bobbie sank her teeth into her tongue to keep from protesting that. Todd was only ten. Lisette, twelve. And if they had adult supervision while visiting a few of the neighborhood houses, what was the harm?

Todd's shoulders drooped a little.

Even though Bobbie had worried that she would upset the former Mrs. Gannon by helping the children find costumes more to their liking than the plastic ghost-sheet and cowboy vest that their mother had purchased, she was glad now that she had.

At least the kids had been able to enjoy their costumes at school.

She returned their hugs when they offered them, and tried to ignore the frost that returned ten-fold to their mother's expression as she did so. Bobbie was almost giddy with relief when the other woman departed without adding any words to the animosity in her eyes.

When they were alone, Bobbie pulled a bag out of her oversized purse and handed it to Fiona before scooting one of the side chairs closer to the bed.

"What is this?"

"A few toiletries."

Fiona peered inside, pulling out the comb and the new tube of toothpaste and toothbrush. "Bless you." She took the comb and dragged it through her short hair.

Bobbie smiled, glad that she'd thought to pick up the few simple items. "There's lotion in there, too, and a few magazines. So, how are you feeling today?"

Fiona grimaced at the wires still coming out from beneath her hospital gown, leading to the machines beside the bed. "Like I'm ready to get out of here." She pointed with the comb toward a manila folder sitting on the rolling tray that hovered over the foot of the bed. "Hand me that, will you? It's all of the banking information that Gabriel brought me this morning."

Bobbie handed her the folder, then sat back in the chair again. "Cheryl's called me a half-dozen times today. Everything's going fine at the agency. The graduation for Saturday morning is on course. There's a new crop of pups being turned over from their puppy raisers to the trainers the following Saturday." That particular event was always held in conjunction with a festive picnic. It was one way of honoring and thanking the raisers for being an important part of the process. "I told her to confirm the times and dates with the caterer for the picnic, and to stop worrying so much."

Fiona smiled faintly. She set aside her comb, flipped open the folder and pulled out a sheet of paper that she handed to Bobbie. "Sign by the red X there at the bottom."

Bobbie automatically took the sheet. "For what?"

"To be a signer on the agency's bank accounts."

Bobbie went still. Alarm inflated inside her belly. "Fiona—"

Fiona held up her hand. "Don't bother arguing with me."

"But your son should—"

"—nothing. Colin would sooner close the agency's doors than get involved there."

"Or Gabe—"

"He has enough on his plate." Fiona waved her hand toward the paper. "You're the one I want. So sign."

"But Fiona, I don't even *work* for you. Not that way."

"And I think it's about time we changed that, don't you?"

"And just what would you hire me as? The official check signer? You have no open staff positions. You haven't for two solid years. And why would you? Everyone who comes to work for you at Golden never wants to work for anyone or anywhere else."

"There is a position open. Director."

Bobbie could only stare.

"It's something I've been thinking about for a while," Fiona continued. She flicked a finger against the monitor wires keeping her tethered. "I'm told this was just a warning that I'm supposed to slow down. And frankly, I'd rather do it while I have some control over what happens to my life's work than wait till I'm six feet under and my family gets to sweep everything I've worked for under the rug."

Bobbie leaned forward and closed her hand over Fiona's. "They wouldn't do that."

Without her customary cosmetics, the eyebrows that Fiona raised were pale and faint. "I'm quite certain that they would."

Knowing what she did now about the way Fiona's husband had died, Bobbie couldn't even offer an argument. "They love you, Fiona. If nothing else was apparent at your birthday party, that most certainly was."

Fiona made a face. "Gannons aren't like the Fairchilds, dear. Love in this family doesn't necessarily mean unquestionable support. I knew it when I married Sean and his mother wore black to our wedding."

"Ouch."

"Indeed. Black might be a fashion choice these days, but back then, it simply wasn't done. It was quite the scandal. She didn't appreciate at all the fact that Sean and I married only a month after we'd met—and she'd had another match already picked out for him. Then I gave Mrs. Gannon—that was my mother-in-law, of course—only one grandchild. Another faux pas, though it was no different than what she had done in her marriage. The only blessing was that she didn't live long enough to see her son die before his time. She would have blamed me for that, too."

"Fiona."

"Don't fret, Bobbie. Gabe told me this morning he let you in on the big family secret."

"I'm so sorry."

"Sean and I had a good life together. It was just too short, and even though I knew he loved me, I also understood the pressure he felt to live up to his family's expectations. When his eyesight was going, he tried to hide it from them all and there was nothing I could do to ease his fears." She shook her head, her faraway expression focusing in again on Bobbie's face. "I like to think Sean's passing wasn't for nothing. It gave me the drive to begin Golden Ability. And now who better to take on the reins than you? You remind me so much of myself when I was young, Bobbie."

"I find that hard to believe. You're always so…focused."

"I found my focus," Fiona countered gently. "Because of circumstances. But you've always been focused when it comes to the agency."

"Sure. Raising puppies!"

"And ensuring that we have other wonderful puppy raisers, too. And filling in whenever and wherever I needed you. My dear, don't you realize that no matter what else you were doing in your life, you've always stayed committed to your part at Golden Ability? You know the staff. You know what we do and why. Cheryl has worked for me for nearly seven years. She still calls you when I'm unavailable and she has a question about something. I have no doubts that you can do this. And I'm still going to be around to show you the ropes until you're as confident about your own abilities as I am."

A litany of arguments against every point that Fiona was making raced through Bobbie's mind, but she didn't even manage to voice one when Fiona continued.

"And now you're going to marry my grandson." Fiona crossed her arms, looking as satisfied as a cat who'd caught the canary.

Bobbie barely managed not to wince. The litany in her head simply lay down and died. "That's what this is really about. Because I-I'm suddenly engaged to marry Gabe?"

Fiona's head cocked slightly. Her eyes—Bobbie had never noticed before just how similar they were to Gabe's—narrowed slightly. "Actually, one thing has little to do with the other."

Bobbie narrowed her own eyes, trying to read Fiona's. "Are you certain?"

"Have I ever lied to you?"

"No," Bobbie allowed slowly. But there was still a craftiness in Fiona's expression that worried her.

"So sign. At least do that so I don't have to worry about the a/p for a while." She rolled her gaze over to the machines keeping her company. "And so I know if something else does happen, the agency can at least function for a while before Colin gets his hooks in."

"Nothing else is going to happen to you. And I don't want to hear another word from you that it might." She slid the pen off the front of the folder where it was hooked and scratched her signature on the paper. "This does *not* mean anything, Fiona, except that I won't have to forge your name on a few checks. All right?"

Fiona's smile turned angelic. "For now." She pushed a button and the head of her bed lowered a little until she wasn't sitting quite so upright. "Now, tell me how Gabriel proposed. And have you set a date?"

Bobbie nearly choked. They hadn't thought to come up with details like this to support their story. And how could she lie right to Fiona's face? "We, um, we haven't set a date yet."

"I know how everyone loves a June bride, but winter weddings are wonderful, too. And I mean *this* winter," Fiona added. "Not another twelve-plus months down the road."

"What's another twelve-plus months down the road?"

Bobbie looked past Fiona's bed to see Gabe standing in the doorway. Despite the wholly unrestful night she'd had thanks to her dreams about him, relief had her shooting shakily to her feet, and the document she'd just signed slid onto the floor. "Nothing," she said hurriedly before going down onto her knees to fish it out from beneath the metal workings of Fiona's bed.

"Your wedding date," she heard Fiona tell Gabe and when she straightened again, it was to find him standing beside her at the bed, a faint smile on his face as he looked at her.

"Quite an outfit, Pippi," he drawled. His gaze traveled down her torso.

She remembered what she looked like and felt a flush that was surely as bright as the patches sewn roughly onto her T-shirt. She hurriedly dragged the hem back down from where it had ridden dangerously high up her thighs and tucked the paper safely inside the manila folder again. "It's the braids," she said overbrightly. "They make the costume."

His gaze drifted over her thighs once more. "Right." Then he caught her chin with his knuckle and dropped a kiss onto her lips. "The freckles, too."

Bobbie had to forcibly remind herself that the kiss probably was for Fiona's benefit. "I, um, I didn't want to take time to go home and change before I came to see Fiona."

"She brought me the daisies," Fiona inserted.

Gabe glanced at the plant. "Nice." He picked up the folder. "This ready to go back to the bank?"

Fiona nodded and Bobbie skewered Gabe with a look. "I suppose she told you what she wanted."

"Yup." He tapped the folder's edge against the rolling table. "And it makes perfect sense to me."

"I also told her I want her to replace me as director at the agency," Fiona added, "but she's being stubborn. Soften her up for me. I'm sure your persuasive methods are far more enjoyable than my playing on her sympathy."

Bobbie's face felt even hotter. "I'm standing right here, Fiona," she muttered.

Fiona just laughed. "Go on, now. Newly engaged couples shouldn't waste time in boring hospital rooms when there's a date to be set and a wedding to be planned."

"There's nothing boring about *your* hospital room," Bobbie assured feelingly. But she figured exiting as quickly as possible was probably a good idea under the circumstances. She leaned over to give Fiona a careful hug that wouldn't have her T-shirt riding up too high and then followed Gabe out into the hall.

"You might have warned me," she murmured once they'd reached the safe distance of the elevator and were riding down to the main floor.

"About this?" He lifted the folder. "That's Fiona's deal with you. I'm just playing the courier."

"Well, just because my signature is on those papers doesn't mean I'm going to go along with the rest of her idea." She plucked at a loose thread on one of her patches. "I'd be a disaster." Even contemplating taking Fiona up on her offer had her feeling panicky inside.

"Why?"

"Because!"

He lifted his brows slightly. "Again…why?"

She exhaled noisily. Their acquaintance may have been short, but Gabe should understand her shortcomings by now as well as anyone. "Forget it. Are you taking that thing back to the bank now?"

He glanced at the sturdy black watch around his

wrist. "If I can make it before they close." The elevator doors slid open and he settled his hand at the small of her back as she stepped out first.

She pulled in a silent, careful breath and was glad he couldn't see her face. All he'd done was touch her back and she wanted to dissolve.

They turned in the direction of the front entrance and his hand fell away. "Are you heading home now?"

"I don't know if there will be any trick-or-treaters who make it around to the carriage house, but I want to be there just in case." She ruthlessly bit back the suggestion that he join her. "And, um, you?"

"I'm in an apartment. Never had any kids come by before."

"Not even Todd and Lisette, I suppose." She tried to focus on buttoning her jacket rather than the brush of his arm against hers as they neared the doorway, and failed miserably. "Your ex-wife brought them by to see Fiona. They were still there when I got here. They both looked adorable."

The sliding doors opened. "I'm glad at least one of us got to see them."

She looked up at him, then. "Maybe they're still dressed up. You should go by and see."

"Can't. I've got a meeting back at the office at six with a new commercial developer, plus my attorney's been playing phone tag with me all afternoon. I need to find out what he wants. Where are you parked?"

She automatically gestured toward the right, but her mind wasn't on her vehicle. Gabe wouldn't have been able to come by her place even if she'd asked, and the disappointment that swept through her was intense and all the more disturbing as a result. "Well, good luck then, with all of that." She started to step off the curb, but he caught her arm, holding her back from walking in front of an SUV.

She felt the solidness of him standing behind her and after a shaky moment, made herself straighten away from him. "Thanks."

He squeezed her shoulder. "You just need to watch where you're going." Then he tugged lightly on the end of her braid and headed off the curb toward his own truck that she could see parked to the left of the entrance.

She watched his long legs eat up the distance.

He was right.

She did need to watch where she was going. Most particularly where he was concerned, or she was going to end up with her heart hurting in ways that it had never hurt before.

Chapter 11

Bobbie waved her hand at the two adults standing behind the trio of children dressed like a band of pirates who'd just scored a handful of candy from her bowl of wrapped sweets. Then she closed the door, leaning back against it for a moment. Zeus and Archimedes were lying on the floor next to her couch. They both had bands over their heads with devil horns sticking up from them, but the lazy thumps of their tails were hardly devilish.

They'd behaved beautifully all evening, not once getting upset or agitated over the surprisingly frequent buzzing of her ancient doorbell or the unfamiliar children who greeted the opening of her door with varying decibels of "Trick or treat!" She tossed them each a small, crunchy dog treat before carrying her empty candy bowl into the kitchen to refill it. The dogs were so well behaved already, she knew that she could turn them over even now to an assistance trainer and they'd do well, even if it was several months earlier than scheduled.

Her doorbell rang again, and she turned back around to answer. Even before she pulled the door open, though, the dogs scrambled to her feet, woofing softly, as they crowded around her.

"Guys," she chided and pointed. "Sit."

They sat, but Archie still whined under his breath.

"Maybe not so ready, after all," she told them, and scratched her fingers over his nose while she pulled open the door, a smile already on her face.

But it wasn't another costumed child, holding up a plastic pumpkin for a treat.

It was Gabe.

And after that first, quick leap of excitement inside her, she realized he looked more harried than she'd ever seen him. His hair looked like he'd been combing it with a garden rake and there were lines around his eyes that hadn't been there when she'd seen him just a few hours earlier.

Her pleasure abruptly turned to worry. "Is Fiona all right?"

His frown was quick. "Yeah."

She let out a relieved breath and pulled the door open more widely. "Come on in. I wasn't expecting to see you."

He stepped into her living room, his hands dropping to the dogs' heads. "Even they get the Halloween treatment, huh?"

She lifted her shoulders, suddenly feeling foolish. "The kids who came by seemed to like it."

"Had some takers after all, then, did you?"

She held up the empty bowl. "Enough to go through the first batch." She headed back to the kitchen again and carried the full bowl back out to the living room. "How'd your meeting go?" She held the bowl out to him in offering.

But he shook his head and she set the bowl on the table by the door.

"I ended up having to reschedule," he said. He paced across the small confines of the living room. Zeus and Archimedes trotted after him. "The custody hearing has been moved up."

"Why?" Alarmed, she sank down onto the arm of the couch. No wonder he looked stressed.

"Because of Ethan's schedule. HuntCom's now sending him to Europe in a few weeks, instead of a few months."

"And just like that—" she snapped her fingers together "—the hearing is rescheduled?"

"Ethan works for HuntCom. What they want has a lot of sway in this area," he reminded her a little grimly.

Bobbie's nerves started to knot, but he said nothing more about her connection to the company. "That doesn't seem very fair," she said after a moment.

Gabe shoved his hand through his hair, and looked at Bobbie's face. The freckles she'd drawn on stood out even more noticeably against her pale cheeks. "*Fair* hasn't exactly been part of the equation so far," he pointed out. Not from his perspective, anyway. "So why would now be any different?"

"What can I do?"

His jaw felt tight. He pulled a jeweler's box out of his jacket pocket and held it out to her. "Wear this."

The fake freckles stood out even more. Her gray gaze finally looked away from his and to the box. She slowly took it from him and thumbed it open. She lowered the box to her lap, the tender nape of her neck exposed below her crazy braids as she looked at the ring.

"My attorney wants you to go to court with me."

She shot him a startled look. "That wasn't part of our agreement."

"I know."

Her throat worked. She slid off her perch on the arm of the couch and onto the cushion properly. An inch of smooth thigh was visible above the edge of her high, striped stockings. "I don't have a good feeling about this, Gabe."

"You won't have to say a word when you're there." He'd grilled his attorney on that point.

"Are you sure?" She looked up at him. "I can't lie outright to a judge."

"I know." She couldn't carry off a lie if it was stuck inside a bucket. It was a wonder that Fiona hadn't already seen through their pretense, despite her health crisis. "I wouldn't ask you to." Short of convincing Bobbie to marry him for real before the court date— something he'd actually found himself considering while he'd been blindly driving around the city after his attorney had delivered the news—he didn't know what else he could do.

A real marriage was not an option. Not even if it meant winning his case.

She rubbed the pad of her thumb over the emerald-cut solitaire diamond. "Is this a real diamond?"

It was the last question he expected. "Yeah." He cleared his throat. "Band is platinum." And picking it out should have been a no-brainer, yet he'd stood in that infernal jewelry store studying one ring after another, trying to imagine which one would please her best.

"It would have been better to get a fake stone," she said after a moment. Her voice was low. "Since everything else about this charade is fake."

"There's nothing fake about how much I need you."

If he weren't so serious, he could have laughed at himself over that one. He'd "needed" her on a visceral level that was probably illegal in some states since she'd jumped into his arms and ordered him to make it look good. If anything, that need had only intensified since then.

She closed her eyes. "You need me because of the children."

He was dying. He needed all his focus on Todd and Lisette. Not on falling for a woman who deserved a lot more than he could offer. He took the jeweler's box out of her unresistant fingers and opened it again. He pulled out the ring.

"Will you wear this?" Everything inside him felt tight, waiting.

She looked up at him, a solemn Pippi Longstocking. Her throat worked in a swallow. And then she slowly lifted her left hand.

He slid the ring into place and her fingers curled. She lowered her hand to her lap and looked at the ring. "It's beautiful," she said huskily. "You, um, you'll tell the kids now?"

"Yes." And they'd be thrilled, which was just another reason to hate himself. "I'll tell them tomorrow."

She nodded and plucked at the hem of her dress

then, seeming to realize how much thigh she was revealing. "So when is it? The court date."

"Friday."

"*This* Friday?" She looked alarmed all over again. "Good grief. They really don't give a person much warning, do they?" The doorbell buzzed and she jerked a little. She pushed to her feet and answered the door.

Gabe had to give her credit. His announcement had definitely thrown her for a loop, but she was cheerful and kind when she greeted the two little kids—a boy in a cowboy hat and a girl in fairy wings—and doled out more candy.

But when she shut the door and leaned back against it, her smile disappeared. She looked at him for a long moment, then turned around and opened the door even though the bell hadn't rung, and set the still full container of candy on the step. Then she closed the door, locked it and yanked down the old-fashioned rolling shade that covered the only window facing the front of the carriage house.

His nerves ratcheted up another notch. "You know you've just guaranteed some enterprising kid a full haul when he takes the entire bowl for himself."

She just shook her head, and reached for one of the red ribbons tied around the end of a braid. "Have a little faith." Blindly working at the ribbon, she straightened away from the door and kicked off her high-heeled shiny black shoes.

Gabe actually felt his mouth run dry. But all she did was move past him on her way into the kitchen. Zeus and Archimedes trailed after her.

"I suppose you didn't take time to eat dinner, did you?"

Eating had been the last thing on his mind. "No." Feeling some sympathy for the blindly faithful dogs, he followed her, too. "What'd you have in mind?"

"Frozen pizza." She dropped the ribbon on the counter before yanking open her freezer door to pull out a large, flat box that she dumped on the counter, followed by a bottle of wine from her refrigerator that was treated only marginally more gently. "Don't tell Todd or Lisette about the pizza and lack of veggies. They'll never let me forget it." She turned on the oven and yanked open a drawer, rummaging for a moment before unearthing a corkscrew from the jumble. "Here." She handed it to him. "Sorry, but it's just a cheap chardonnay. Otherwise there's still the rest of the orange juice we had with dinner last night."

Only Bobbie could have come up with that color-themed meal and gotten away with it.

His kids had been wholly won over by her.

He cleared his throat. "Wine's fine." Then he picked up the bottle and began peeling away the foil around the cork while watching her jerky motions around the kitchen. She pulled off the dogs' horns and gave them fresh water before starting on putting away the dishes from the night before. "Would you rather I left?"

She looked at him over her shoulder. "I don't know." Then she shook her head. Her braids stuck out at lopsided right angles from the sides of her head, one with a ribbon, one without. "No."

She didn't sound particularly sure about it, but he decided to take her answer at face value, rather than probe more. Leaving was the last thing he wanted to do.

He twisted the corkscrew into the cork and slowly pulled it out of the wine bottle. "Glasses?"

She opened a cupboard and pulled out two crystal stems. She held them while he poured, and then handed him one. He lifted the glass into the light.

"I know. It's Waterford. Hardly goes with the plastic plates from last night's dinner. But these were a gift and even cheap wine tastes decent when it's in a beautiful glass." She took a drink of her wine and padded back into the living room. "The oven will take a while to heat." She sat down in the leather chair and crossed her legs.

He got another glimpse of smooth, toned thigh.

He threw back a mouthful of wine as if it were a tequila shooter. "How's the floor doing in the bathroom?" He went down the short hallway, feeling an abrupt need to escape.

He still felt her gaze following him. "Perfect. Did you expect it to be otherwise?"

He looked into the bathroom. But instead of surveying the tile job he'd done, his eyes landed on the three sheer bras hanging over the shower curtain rod and the equally sheer panties looped alongside them.

The palms of his hands suddenly itched and he prowled back to the living room. He paced off a triangle in the room, then repeated it. "The ceiling needs painting."

"So do the walls," she pointed out accurately enough. "But I'm perfectly capable of rolling a coat of paint on the walls myself." She sipped her wine, watching him over the delicate crystal.

He knew what was on his mind. *Her.*

But he wished to hell he knew what she was thinking.

"What's your place like? An apartment, you said?"

He was struck by a sense of strangeness. He could almost count on two hands the number of days they'd known one another, but it still felt as if he'd known her much longer. And that, somehow, the prosaic details of his existence had already been covered. "It's just a place to sleep, as far as I'm concerned. There are two extra bedrooms for Todd and Lisette, which have only been actually used once—when Steph left them with me last week." He studied a settling crack in her plaster wall. "I got it just because it was close to the kids. Even the furniture is rented. All my own stuff is still back in Colorado. I built a place there about six years ago."

"And what will you do if you get joint custody?"

"I don't want to uproot them again. I'll buy here. Or build again if I find a lot to my liking."

Her fingertip slowly tapped the rim of her glass, and the ring sparkled in the light. "And if you don't? Will you try again?"

He didn't have to ask her what she meant. "I could keep pulling Steph back into court every time I turned around, even with her out of the country. But what does that end up doing to Todd and Lissi?" He still didn't have a good answer for that. "I don't know. I'll probably go back to Colorado." Following his children to Switzerland wasn't an option. He had too much tied up in Gannon-Morris. If he couldn't keep his kids in the country, the company was the only thing he'd have left.

Her lashes lowered. She sipped a little more wine. "What about your company here?"

"My partner and I can hire a manager, the same as we have for the branch in Texas."

"Wouldn't you miss Fiona?"

"I'd miss a lot of things," he muttered. Not least of

which was Bobbie. There was a beep from the kitchen and she started to push out of her chair, but he waved her back. "I'll stick the pizza in."

She subsided and he went into the kitchen. He drank down the rest of his wine in two gulps, unwrapped the pizza and slid it onto the ancient oven rack. He found the directions on the box, studied the front of the oven for a minute and decided there was no timer on it. So he pressed a button on his watch and set the timer there. Then he refilled his glass and took the wine bottle with him back out to the living room.

Zeus and Archimedes had sprawled across the floor, leaving very little space left to pace. Bobbie held up her glass and he topped it off, then set the bottle on top of the crowded bookshelf beside her chair. Then, because he wanted to fill his hands with her, he plucked out one of the photo albums instead and flipped it open.

A younger Bobbie, her curls tumbling from where they were clipped on top of her head, with two full-grown golden retrievers. He flipped the page. More dogs of various ages. More people. A couple of striking blonds he assumed were her sisters that he hadn't yet met. "You should consider Fiona's offer." He closed the album and by some miracle, managed to fit it back into the too-narrow space on the shelf. "You'd be good at it."

She shook her head. "I'm fine where I'm at."

"Serving coffee?"

Her gray eyes narrowed. "Something wrong with that?"

"Not a thing if that was all you aspire to do. Is it?"

She looked away. "I'm not cut out for that sort of work. It's too much of a commitment." Her gaze flicked back to him at the word and he had the feeling they were treading over too-thin boards.

"Are you sure you're not just afraid of failing?"

Her lips twisted. "Well, of course there's that, too." She pushed out of the chair. "I'm going to make a salad to go with the pizza after all. Would you mind letting the dogs out for a few minutes?"

She wanted a little space. It worked for him. He wanted a little space, too.

Maybe then he could remember all the reasons why it was important to keep his hands off her and not complicate the hell out of their arrangement.

He opened the door and called the dogs. They immediately trotted out into the chilly evening, jumping right over the bowl of candy that was not as full as it had been when she'd put it out. But it wasn't empty, either.

She'd told him to have a little faith.

He followed the dogs outside and pulled the door nearly closed behind him before sitting down on the step to watch them. Across the expansive lawn, all signs of Fiona's birthday party had disappeared. Aside from a light that illuminated the back terrace, the house was dark.

He sighed and ran his hand around the back of his neck, then plucked a miniature candy bar out of the bowl and tore off the wrapper. Chocolates and wine and an uncommonly clear night and here he was, sitting on his damn butt while a wholly desirable woman was inside and as off-limits as she'd ever been.

"This is what makes men drink," he told the dogs, toasting them with his wineglass.

Zeus trotted back to him and sniffed at his boots, then moved off again to visit yet another bush. After a few minutes, both dogs returned to sit quietly at the base of the concrete steps. Their tails thumped a few times and he set his wineglass on the step beside him. "How does she let you guys go," he asked, rubbing his hands over their heads.

He heard a soft creak behind him and knew that Bobbie had pulled open the door he hadn't latched. "They're meant for greater things than just being my pets." She stepped out onto the porch and he picked up the wineglass so she had room to sit down beside him.

"Are you going to get cold without a sweater?" He knew plenty of ways to warm her. They marched through his mind with frustrating ease.

But she was shaking her head and wrapped her arms around her bent knees as she looked up at the night sky. "I was getting too warm inside, anyway."

She hadn't been the only one.

"And it's a pretty night," she added.

"Yeah." He looked at her. She'd undone her braids, and her hair—curlier than ever—hung over one shoulder, barely contained in a loop of red ribbon.

His fingers tightened around his wineglass. "You should consider what Fiona's offering you."

He heard her soft sigh. "There's safety in sticking with what I know."

"And there's a lot of life to be experienced when you step outside your comfort zone." He handed her the candy bowl. "You can have faith in complete strangers—kids, yet—not to take more than their share of candy. Have some faith in yourself."

"You've said that before," she murmured.

And he meant it even more now.

She set the bowl behind them. "I'll think about it," she said after a moment.

"Good girl."

"Hmm." She pressed her palms together then looked sideways at him. "Is that how you see me, Gabe? A girl?"

He was suddenly back on those too-thin boards, and they were creaking ominously under his weight. "You should know the answer to that by now."

"Sometimes I think I do." Despite the small porch light that glowed behind them and the stars that sparkled above, the shadows were still too deep for him to read her eyes. To know whether those gray irises were soft as a fog, or as silvered as liquid metal. She slowly ran her hand along the length of her hair. "Sometimes I don't."

He wanted *his* hand running through her hair.

He looked across to Fiona's house. Creaking boards had become cracking ones. "Bobbie, when I look at you, all I see is a woman." A woman he wanted and should know better than to take.

She drew in a soft breath, leaned back on her hands and stretched out her legs, which seemed impossibly long for someone so petite, until her toes were rubbing in Zeus's ruff. "Even when I'm dressed like this?"

He couldn't have stopped looking back at her if his life depended on it.

He ran his gaze over the goofy yellow dress that clung in all the right spots, down over the smooth skin on her thighs to the edge of her crazy, striped socks that reached well over her knees.

"Even now." He tossed back the rest of his wine. "Especially now."

She drew in a long breath that only succeeded in drawing his attention even more keenly to the taut curves of her breasts beneath the thin fabric. "Gabe—"

His watch suddenly began beeping and they both jerked.

He stifled an oath and shut off the noise. "Pizza should be done."

"Ah. Right." She nodded and gathered her feet beneath her again to stand. She stepped around him, her thigh brushing his shoulder, and went inside.

He exhaled roughly. He didn't need any freaking pizza.

He needed a cold shower. Extremely cold.

He wrapped his hand around the hard iron railing and pulled himself up and followed her inside. The dogs came after him and he closed the door, only to open it right back up again when he realized there was smoke billowing out of the kitchen. He strode into the kitchen and found Bobbie crouched in front of the opened oven, which was clearly the source of the smoke.

"I burned the pizza."

"I'm the one who set the timer."

She closed the oven door, but stayed crouched there, her back toward him. "I'm the one who set the temperature fifty degrees higher than it should have been." She raked her fingers through her hair, got caught on the ribbon tied around it, and yanked out the bright red length, pitching it onto the counter where it slithered off the edge onto the floor. Archimedes sniffed at it, cocked an ear toward Bobbie, who wasn't watching, and looked as if he were going to steal it, only to think better of it when he turned and looked at Zeus. Both dogs wandered back into the living room.

"I can't even bake a damn pizza," she was saying, "and *you* think I can run Fiona's agency?"

He set his wineglass on the counter and went up behind her, sliding his hands beneath her arm. He lifted her to her feet and turned her around to face him. "It's just a pizza."

"It's the story of my life," she countered thickly.

He tipped her face up. The freckles she'd drawn onto her cheeks were smearing beneath a track of tears and he slowly rubbed his thumbs over them. "Then write a new story."

Her shimmering eyes held something he couldn't decipher. "Will you be in it? Or come next week, when your custody hearing is finished, one way or the other, will I be a thing of the past, too?"

He could feel his jaw tightening again. Now that he knew her, could he imagine her absence from his life?

"You don't have to answer that," she said into the silence. She twisted her face away from him and scrubbed her hands down her cheeks. "Pizza is obviously toast. What kind of dressing do you want on your salad?"

He caught her shoulders again and pulled her around to him. "Forget the damn salad." Then he covered her mouth with his.

She made a soft sound that rippled through his blood and he pulled her even closer. Her hands slid around his neck, her mouth opening beneath his. She tasted headier than any wine and he'd never felt more parched with thirst.

He dragged his mouth from hers, hauling in a harsh

breath. He wanted her so badly it was a physical ache. "If I don't leave now, I'm not going to leave at all tonight."

She looked up at him, her lips red and swollen from his kiss, bright spots of color burning high in her cheeks. "Would that be so bad?"

He met her gaze. "You tell me."

She drew in a deep breath, the hard peaks of her breasts easily visible through the soft fabric of her dress.

And then she was suddenly reaching for the hem of that dress, drawing it over her head and he had the drowning feeling that he was never going to be the same again.

She held the dress out to the side and released it and it seemed to fall almost in slow motion to the floor, leaving her standing before him wearing nothing but brief black panties, a sheer black bra and those crazy red and green stockings that he was pretty sure were going to give him gray hair if he didn't peel them down her legs and soon.

"Is this enough of an answer for you?"

He couldn't have managed a word just then to save his own life. And he couldn't seem to make himself care, just then, that he'd told himself again and again why things would be better—safer—if they didn't head down this road.

So he nodded and reached for her, and was damned to realize his own hands were trembling while she seemed not to hesitate at all as she slid her palm against his, threaded her fingers through his, and turned to lead him out of the kitchen, down the short hall and into her bedroom, which was lit only by the whisper of moon-light shining through the window opposite her bed.

She let go of his hand then, and even in the dim light he could see the silvery gleam of her wide eyes as she slowly slid off her bra, her hands hesitating shyly over the high thrust of her bare breasts for a moment. Then she lowered her palms to the edge of the panties that skimmed the tight curve of her hips. She slowly drew them off and started to reach for the thigh-high socks.

He caught her wrists, though, and silently shook his head. Her lips parted a little. Her fingers curled softly and subsided at her sides.

He wanted to race his hands over every inch of her silky, pale skin, but he controlled the impulse to rush, to hurry, to plunder and take quickly before she realized what she was doing, before she changed her mind, before she turned him away.

So he grazed his fingers over the slender slope of her shoulder, and watched the way her eyes fluttered and the pulse at the base of her long throat visibly beat.

He traced the lines of her collarbone, skimmed along the outer curves of her breasts and watched the pale crests turn crimson and pearl even more tightly. He felt the narrowness of her waist, the inviting flare of her hips and the shadowy down at the juncture of her thighs that promised more heaven than he was sure he could survive.

He nudged her back a step, then two. Her legs met the bed and she slowly sat. He trailed his fingers down her legs, behind her knees and he heard her catch her breath a little, a hitching sound that snuck down in-side him and twisted his nerves into a fresh, torturous knot. Then he found the elastic edge of the high stocking and slowly rolled it down her smooth, shapely leg.

She drew in another shuddering breath and moistened her lips, leaving behind a distracting glisten. He tugged the knit stocking off her leg and dropped it on the floor. Before he could reach for the other, she silently leaned back on the mattress, her elbows supporting her, and lifted her leg, delicately placing her toes in the center of his chest. Her gaze met his. Challenging. Waiting. Inviting.

He wondered then just who was leading this dance, and decided it didn't matter. He slowly rolled down the second stocking and tossed it aside, then bent her knee as he leaned over her and took her lips.

He felt her murmur his name through his kiss, and her hands tugged at his shirt, then his belt. He raised up long enough to get rid of the annoying clothes separating them, and then he was covering her again and her arms were holding him, and before he could think another coherent thought, she was guiding him into her and she felt so tight, so wet, so *home,* that he could have cried like a baby.

He sucked in oxygen through his clenched teeth, pressed his forehead against hers and tried to remember that she was a petite woman and he was not a small man. He didn't want to crush her. But she was wrapping her strong legs around him, her hips urging his on and on and on. And then her mouth was burning over his shoulder, his neck, as he felt fine ripples start exploding at the ends of his nerves.

"Don't stop," she begged when she reached his ear. "Please, Gabe, don't ever stop."

And then she cried out and he felt her convulsing

around him and all he wanted to do, all he *could* do, was follow her again.

Right into the fire.

Chapter 12

Bobbie heard the buzzing of her doorbell and rolled over, feeling an unfamiliar, delicious ache in her muscles, and peeled her eyes open to peer at the clock.

It was just after seven in the morning.

She inhaled, and slowly ran her hand over the rumpled pillow beside her own, unable to stop a silly smile.

Gabe had stayed the entire night and she hadn't even had to ask him to.

Reality was *so* much better than dreams.

She let out a contented sigh, then held the pillow to her face, imagining the scent of him there. She could hear the rattling of her water pipes. Gabe was taking a shower.

The doorbell buzzed again like an angry bee, distracting her from her delight, and she sighed, tossing aside the pillow as she rolled out of bed. The morning air was cold and she shivered hard, grabbing up the blue crocheted afghan off the floor to wrap around herself as she headed out of the bedroom. Her footsteps hesitated as she passed the bathroom door. It was ajar and steam was rolling around the doorframe.

Shivers danced through her, the memories of Gabe's lovemaking exquisitely fresh.

Would he like it if she joined him in the shower?

The doorbell buzzed again and, sighing, she put aside the temptation. She went to the front door and yanked it open, not sure who she expected to be on the other side, but it certainly wasn't the woman standing there on the step.

Gabe's ex-wife.

Stephanie's hair was pinned back from her face and a trench coat that Bobbie recognized as seriously expensive was wrapped around her slender form. Even in the thin light from the early sun, the other woman's gaze ran over Bobbie, from her thoroughly mussed hair to her bare shoulders to her equally bare toes peeping out from beneath the blanket.

"I guess I can tell why it took you so long to answer the door." Stephanie's voice was as cold as the morning air.

It was all Bobbie could do not to cringe. It was bad enough that she could feel her skin flushing as if she'd been caught doing something terrible.

Gabe was a free man. She was a free woman.

And as far as his ex-wife was concerned, they were even engaged to be married.

Why shouldn't they spend the night together?

Wishing like fury that she'd bothered to put on something more substantial than a ridiculous afghan, she kept her shoulders straight with an effort. "What can I do for you, Stephanie? Are the children all right?"

The other woman's lips thinned. "They're fine, except that Todd left his book in Gabe's truck the other day and he needs it for his reading class this morning. Believe me, I have no desire to track his father down like this." Her gaze raked down Bobbie again, her distaste more than obvious. "When I couldn't reach him at his apartment or his office, I figured he'd be here with *you*."

Bobbie knew that, no matter how objectionable the other woman was, the polite thing would have been to invite her inside. But she just couldn't make herself do it. "I'll get his truck keys," she said and turned away from the door.

The shower was still running when she went back to the bedroom, and she found Gabe's keys in the pocket of his jeans, which were still lying in a heap on the floor.

She pushed her bare feet into fuzzy slippers and exchanged the afghan for an oversized Mariners sweatshirt that nearly reached her knees. Then she went outside.

Stephanie was waiting by Gabe's truck, her arms crossed and her toe tapping, as if Bobbie had deliberately taken her time. Ignoring her, Bobbie unlocked the truck and peered into the back where, sure enough, a thin reading book had slipped beneath the seat. She pulled it out and handed it to Stephanie. "I'm sorry we didn't notice it earlier."

Stephanie didn't acknowledge the words as she took the book and turned toward her own car—a sleek BMW that Bobbie figured was worth more than she'd earned in the last five years combined. "Tell Gabe not to forget our appointment with Toddy's counselor this afternoon."

Bobbie highly doubted that Gabe would have forgotten it, but she had no desire to antagonize the other woman. "I will."

Stephanie pulled open her car door and tossed the book inside. But instead of getting in, she looked back at Bobbie. "He'll break your heart, too, you know."

At first, Bobbie wasn't certain she'd even heard right. She stared at the other woman across the uneven pathway and it slowly dawned on her that Stephanie's rigid posture wasn't entirely formed by disapproval.

Bobbie also knew that she was afraid of that very thing—a broken heart—just as she knew it was already too late to prevent it.

It had been from the night she'd walked up Fiona's terrace for the birthday party and Gabe had held out his hand toward her.

But she took a few steps toward the other woman. "I think he's worth taking the chance."

"Hmm." The other woman looked over at Gabe's truck. "I suppose you're young enough that you can afford to think that way." She looked back at Bobbie. "I'm not anymore. All I have are my husband and my children. Ethan has given me everything that Gabriel wouldn't, and he wants me at his side when he goes to Switzerland, and I want to be with him. Gabe's intent on destroying that. You do realize that, don't you?"

Bobbie took another step closer. She could feel the hard edge of the stone paver beneath her soft slippers, and let the solidness of it ground her. "Gabe's not trying to destroy anything. He's just trying to hold onto his children."

"By taking them away from me."

"By *sharing* them with you!" She lifted her hands. "Stephanie, all he wants is to be their father, but how can he do that when they're halfway around the world?"

"How can I be their mother if they're halfway around the world from me?" Stephanie's voice rose. "He hates me. He'll turn them against me."

Bobbie shook her head. There'd been an edge of something painful and hurting in Stephanie's voice that made the other woman seem suddenly far more human than before. "He wouldn't do that," she said quietly.

"He's hauled us all back into court," Stephanie clipped.

"Because you've given him no other choice! That doesn't mean he's trying to turn your children against you."

Stephanie gave a cool smile that was nevertheless tinged with something sad. "I've known Gabe for more than twenty years. How long have *you* known him?"

Bobbie didn't answer that.

How could she?

Because the truth of the matter was, she had only known Gabe a matter of weeks. And even if every cell inside her said to trust him, what had her judgment in the past ever shown her other than that her judgment was all too fallible? "All I know is that the two of you managed to create two really wonderful children. Maybe the only thing you have in common anymore is your love for them, but that's still a lot of love that Todd and Lisette deserve to know. It just seems to me that there ought to be a way for you to work things out."

Stephanie just shook her head and tsked, the cool, superior tone right back in place as if it had never been displaced. "Young *and* naive. I wonder how much your connection to Harrison Hunt will shield you when those qualities wear off?" Then she slid into the car and closed the door with a soft, final click.

A moment later, she was backing out of the long drive, and then driving off.

Bobbie exhaled.

So Stephanie knew about Harry, too.

Was that why she'd kept her claws mostly sheathed? Did even she think Bobbie held some sway when it came to Harry and HuntCom?

She slowly turned and went back inside, taking the now-empty candy bowl that was still sitting on the step with her. She called the dogs out of their kennel where they'd been sleeping and let them outside for a few minutes. When they came back in, she had a pot of coffee brewed and the shower had finally stopped.

She filled a sturdy white mug with coffee and carried it to the bathroom door, knocking softly. "Coffee?"

The door opened and Gabe stood there in front of the mirror, one of her plain white towels wrapped around his hips. "Thanks." His smile was slow and easy as he took the mug from her and she felt her insides melting all over again. "You need a new showerhead."

Bobbie blocked out Stephanie's words that wanted to twine through her mind. There would be time enough to worry about Gabe's ex-wife. Right now, she knew her time with Gabe was slowly ticking down to the custody hearing and she was feeling very protective of that time. If it meant wringing every moment with him that she could out of it, then that's what she would do.

So she leaned her shoulder against the doorjamb and put a faint smile on her face. "Know any available handymen who might want to help me out?"

His eyes narrowed as he sipped the hot brew, then he set the mug on the little shelf near her sink. "I think I might." He looped his fingers into the collar of her sweatshirt and reeled her toward him. "Did the shower wake you up?" He nudged her head back to kiss her chin. Her nose.

Her breath shortened. "No." Her hands settled on his wide chest, her fingers pressing into his warm, damp skin. She would never get tired of the feel of him, even if she had fifty years to enjoy it. "We had a visitor," she murmured as his lips settled over hers.

He tasted like her minty toothpaste, only far, far more delicious.

"Hmm?" His hand cradled the back of her neck as he drew her even closer. His other hand dragged at the long sweatshirt until she felt his palm meet the skin of her thigh. Then her hip.

His fingers trailed teasingly around to the small of her back, drifting lower over her rear.

"Stephanie," she managed before she could forget how to speak altogether.

His hand paused.

"Todd forgot a book in your truck the other night." She wriggled a little, until her backside felt the delightful warmth of his palm again. "He needed it for today." She trailed her hands down his torso, loving the feel of his tight muscles bunching beneath her touch. He might be forty-one, but he had the tightest abs she'd ever seen. And since she'd once done a brief stint as a receptionist at a fitness center, she'd seen plenty.

She grazed her knuckles over the edge of the towel, very much aware of the hard length of him barely contained beneath it.

"She say anything else?"

Bobbie pressed her lips against his collarbone. Tasted the moisture still clinging there. "Nothing important."

His hands slid beneath her rear and he lifted her onto the chilly edge of the sink, then he stepped between her knees and she forgot all about the cool porcelain beneath her. "I don't want her upsetting you."

"She didn't." *Not exactly.* Bobbie ran the sole of her foot along the back of his leg. "What time do you have to be at the office?"

He smiled faintly. His damp hair was tumbling over his forehead and his blue eyes gleamed. His hands delved beneath the sweatshirt again, setting off ripples of delight as his fingers skimmed over her waist, walked along her ribs, and then slowly curved around her breasts. His thumbs brushed circles over her nipples until they felt positively frenzied. "I'm the boss, remember?"

"Thank goodness." Her voice had gone breathless. She tugged at the towel and it slid off his narrow hips. She leaned forward to nibble at his chin, then his lips. Her fingers grazed over the length of him, loving the feel of that velvet-covered steel. "I want you, Gabriel Gannon, like I've never wanted anyone."

His chest expanded against her. "Good. I'd have to kill the other guy if you did." His hands moved suddenly, and she had to let go of him when he pulled the sweatshirt over her head. He tugged it off her arms and pitched it aside, then filled his hands with her breasts. "Perfect," he murmured, and bent low enough to capture one peak between his lips.

Sensation streaked from her breast straight to her core and her head fell back until it hit the mirror behind her. She ran her hands over his shoulders, then slid them along his corded neck. She sank her fingers into his hair and tried not to cry out when his teeth gently grazed her, followed by the slick heat of his tongue.

"I know something else that's perfect," she managed. Her thighs slid along his, her ankles looping behind his back. Even hunched over her the way he was, she could feel the nudge of him against the very heart of her, demanding and very hard where all she felt was wet and wanting.

She lifted her hips toward him, flushing at her blatant invitation, but was too far gone to care. Besides, she had been pretty blatant the night before, and that hadn't exactly sent him running for the hills. "You inside of me," she finished throatily.

His lashes lifted and his gaze met hers above the achingly tight nipple he was tormenting with his tongue. The faint lines at the corners of his eyes crinkled a little and then his lips were burning along the valley between her breasts, then upward, ever upward until he'd straightened again and his mouth was hovering a hairsbreadth away from hers. "I wouldn't want to disappoint a lady," he murmured.

His hands curved around her hips, slid beneath her bottom and lifted her onto him.

She cried out, nearly convulsing right then and there

as he sank into her so deeply, so completely, that she felt consumed.

She hauled in a shaking breath. Then another. "No disappointment here," she finally managed and felt her heart fall open even more when he gave a short bark of a laugh.

"What am I going to do with you, Bobbie?"

Love me. The words rang insistently inside of her head. But she just smiled into his eyes. "Make love to me."

The corners of his lips kicked up in that faint smile that never failed to make her breathless. "That—" his hands cradled her rear "—I can definitely do."

Then she felt the pulse of him reach to the very center of her and her head fell forward, her forehead resting in the heated crook of his neck.

She could hear the charging beat of his heart, could feel the raggedness of his breathing and she twined her arms around his shoulders, clinging for dear life when he lifted her a few inches, then lowered her again. His name was in her breath. His body was in her very cells. And then he was moving again, and she shuddered, clinging ever tighter as he carried her out of the bathroom, down the hall and back to her bedroom.

A thin band of sunlight from the window was creeping across her tumbled mattress as he slowly lowered her to the bed, never parting from her. And when she drew his weight down over her, she cried out again.

His mouth found hers, his fingers twined with hers as he slowly, devastatingly thrust into her, until every molecule of her soul felt ready to explode. She gasped and he raised himself up on his hands, the cords in his arms and his shoulders standing out. The pleasure was almost more than she could bear.

And then, when his gaze finally lowered, hers followed and she realized the band of sunlight was slowly widening. It flowed across her breasts, her abdomen, and the heat inside her flamed even brighter as if Gabe directed the golden light himself, stoking it wider, brighter, until that ray of light was cutting over their bodies where they were joined as closely as two could ever be.

Her breath caught as she hung at the edge of an exquisite precipice, dangling there at his mercy, at his pleasure. And then he whispered her name, roughly, half broken, and just like that, she slid so smoothly, so perfectly, over the edge, her head falling back, her eyes closing as she tumbled into bliss, giving him everything that she was.

And she knew that in this moment, at least, he was giving her everything in return.

"This was the best start to a day that I've had... ever." Gabe's arm was wrapped around her waist, holding her on the running board of his truck. The sun was steadily climbing above the horizon. "Is it bad etiquette to say thanks?"

She grinned. "I'd be hurt if you didn't."

His eyes crinkled. "Then thank you." He punctuated it with a kiss. "Thank you." Another kiss. "And thank you." Another. Then he slapped her playfully on the rear. "Now go inside before I blow off the entire day."

"I have to go brew coffee for people, anyway."

"As long as you don't accompany it with the kind of service you treated me to."

"I have some standards, you know. I don't—" she waved her hand in the air "—you know, with just any customer."

"Glad to hear it," he drawled. "Or men across Seattle would be dropping like flies from heart attacks. It's a wonder *I* survived."

She rolled her eyes. "Being the ancient soul that you are and all that, I suppose. I guess for an old guy, you did fairly well." She hopped down onto the ground, her slippers barely cushioning her feet against the hard ground, and gave him a mischievous smile.

"I'll give you old," he warned, smiling slightly.

A shiver danced down her spine. "I do hope so."

He muttered an oath and shook his head. "Go inside, woman, before I forget we both have jobs to get to."

Smiling, she turned on her heel and sauntered back to the house, giving him one last look over her shoulder and nearly laughing with delight to find that he was still watching her.

After she went inside and closed the door, she heard his engine start, and then the crunch of his tires rolling over the drive.

Still smiling, she raced into the kitchen to feed the dogs. She picked up her Pippi costume, which was still lying in the center of the kitchen floor, and felt herself flush all over again at her own wholly unfamiliar boldness. She went into the bathroom and took a quick shower, raked some smoothing lotion through her wet curls before pulling them back in a ponytail, and put on clean clothes.

Only when she was ready to step outside her door did she suddenly slow down.

She held out her hand and the diamond ring on her finger winked up at her.

The narrow, nearly white band fit perfectly.

She curled her trembling fingers into a knot and the diamond caught the light again, sending prisms dancing across her living room. She exhaled shakily.

If only the intent behind the ring was as real as the diamond itself.

The day passed quickly once Bobbie reached the Bean, with plenty of customers to be served, while in between she and Doreen switched the Halloween decorations—ghosts and spiders—for cornucopias and stuffed turkeys wearing pilgrim hats. She tried not to keep checking her cell phone to see if Gabe called, but it was hard.

On her lunch hour, she raced over to Tommi's bistro for a panini. Her sister was too slammed with customers to do more than lift her head when Bobbie poked hers into the kitchen for a second, and maybe that was just as well, because she wasn't sure what she'd have said to Tommi about Gabe if she'd had enough time to talk. Knowing her sister, Tommi would probably have known right off that something major had occurred.

And Bobbie wasn't ready to have the fragile connection she had with Gabe picked apart. There'd be time enough for that after his custody hearing.

So she took her panini with her back to the Bean, and even by the time she finished her shift, her phone was still stubbornly silent. No calls from Gabe.

She drove to the hospital to visit Fiona, but she was dozing over a magazine, so Bobbie quietly sat down in the side chair and stared out the window, watching the clouds slowly drift in the sky, moving in, then out of the sunbeams.

She sighed. She'd never again be able to look at a shaft of sunlight and not think of Gabriel...

"That's a pretty heavy sounding sigh."

She looked over at Fiona. "I hope I didn't wake you."

Fiona waved her hand. "All I've been doing is sleeping," she dismissed. She yawned as she closed her magazine and set it aside. "So is that a Gabriel sigh or something else?"

"Fiona—"

"Oh, relax, dear. I'm not going to grill you about your engagement." She exhaled tiredly and leaned her head back against her pillow. "I know it's not real."

Bobbie blinked. "But...how? Did Gabe tell you?"

"Heavens, no. All I have to do is look at your face whenever the subject comes up."

Guilt swamped her. "We never intended to lie to you, Fiona."

"I figured that, too. And I suspect you never intended to fall in love with my grandson, either."

Bobbie stared. "I—"

"—can't even deny it," Fiona inserted gently. "Just because I'm an old woman doesn't mean I've forgotten what it feels like to be swept off my feet with love for a man when you least expect it."

"It's not going to get me anywhere," she said huskily.

"Hmm. Maybe. Maybe not. Gabe felt responsible for the breakup of his marriage, even if it was Stephanie who did the cheating. I'd dearly love to think he'd get over that self-blame and find the sort of future he deserves. I suppose this little pretense of yours is to aid his cause where Todd and Lisette are concerned?"

"Yes."

"Well. I'm certainly not going to judge you on that score. I don't want my great-grandchildren spending the next several years in another country, either. Gabe's been fighting this issue for longer than he should have had to."

"His children are what matters most to him."

"And what matters most to you, Bobbie?"

Bobbie's lips parted, but words felt elusive. "Not letting everyone around me down."

"What about letting yourself down?" Fiona leaned forward until she could catch Bobbie's hand in her own. "I've known you for more than ten years, Bobbie, and you have more enthusiasm and passion for life than anyone else I know. You're far harder on yourself than you need to be. So what if you've had a lot of different jobs. It's given you experience in a dozen different ways. And so what if you don't have a PhD or a graduate degree? With all of these dogs you've raised, you've touched the world in ways that most people can never imagine. I hate seeing fear of making a misstep hold you back. Life isn't always about the perfect decision at the perfect time in the perfect place. It's also about all the missteps we make in between."

Bobbie realized her cheeks were damp. She swiped her hand over them. "Golden Ability is too important."

"It's too important to be left to someone who doesn't care about it as much as you do." Fiona squeezed her hand. "I *know* you can do this, Bobbie."

Bobbie inhaled. Could she?

Everyone around her seemed to think she could.

If she wanted more out of life, didn't she have to take the step?

"Okay," she said on an exhale, and then had to sit there, still, while the world seemed to spin around her just a little.

"Good girl," Fiona said.

Another rush of tears burned suddenly behind her eyes, but she blinked them back. "I hope none of us end up regretting this," she muttered.

"Well, I know I won't," Fiona assured. "Now. Go find me some lime Jell-O, would you? It's the only thing around here that is remotely appetizing, since they won't let me have cheeseburgers and fries."

Bobbie laughed brokenly. She leaned over her friend and hugged her tightly. "I love you, Fiona."

Fiona's hand patted her back. "And I love you. Now stop worrying so much. Everything will work out. Even Gabe."

Bobbie straightened and slid her fingers beneath her eyelashes again. She badly wanted to believe Fiona, but not even she could guarantee her grandson's heart.

So Bobbie went and tracked down the lime gelatin—three little cups of it—and left them with Fiona, along with a promise to come back the next day to start working on the process of becoming the director of Golden Ability. Then she went home to Zeus and Archimedes, who'd been patiently waiting to be let out.

The light on her message machine was blinking and she jabbed it, fully expecting to hear Gabe's voice at last, but even there she was disappointed.

"Bobbie, this is Martin Paredes. We met at a Hunt-Com picnic this summer and it's taken me this long to track down a way to contact you." He laughed. "Anyway, I've got two tickets for the Seahawks this weekend, and I remember you had an interest in football, so I thought you might—"

Frustrated, Bobbie hit the *delete* button while he was still talking. It was the only message on the machine.

She exhaled and told herself there was no reason why she had to wait for Gabe to call *her,* but old habits died hard. And one thing Cornelia hadn't raised her daughters to do was chase down a man. Even if he had given her the most incredible night—and morning—of her life.

So she took the dogs for a walk that was long enough to work some of the pent-up energy out of them, fed and watered them, and heated herself a can of soup before sitting down in front of the oven to try to scrape up the mess left by the charcoal briquette that had once been a frozen pizza.

"In my next life, I'm going to have an oven that's self-cleaning," she told the dogs after she'd scraped blackened cheese off the bottom of the oven for so long that her wrist ached and her ears hurt from the screeching sound of metal against metal.

"Take the job that Fiona's offering you and you could afford to buy a decent oven in *this* life."

She dropped her metal spatula and spun around on the floor. The brilliance that suddenly filled her chest at the sight of Gabe standing there was almost scary. "Well, I guess we'll find out, since I told her this afternoon I'd take it."

"You did?" He smiled widely. "That's great!"

She lifted her shoulders, feeling strangely self-conscious. "I'm going to give it my best shot, anyway." It was all that she could do. "I, um, I didn't hear you come in."

"Obviously." He dropped a paper bag from a local fast-food joint on the counter and crouched down to rub the dogs, who looked like they were ready to go into delirious fits of pleasure as a result.

She knew how they felt.

"I knocked *and* rang the bell."

"Sorry." She folded her arms around her knees, afraid that if she didn't contain them, she'd crawl over to him to get his hand on *her* instead of the dogs. "How'd the meeting with Todd's counselor go?"

"Same as always." His smile died and his voice went short. "But since Steph figures she'll be taking them both out of Brandlebury within the next few weeks, that's even more reason not to move him to a different math class."

Forget her intentions. She let go of her knees and instead walked over to him. She ran her fingers through his hair, and settled her palm alongside his jaw. "That's not going to happen."

"Glad one of us thinks that." He took a deep breath and slid his arms around her waist until she was pressed closely against him. She could feel the weariness in him when his head lowered onto her shoulder. "I told the kids we were engaged. Lissi wanted to know if she can be a bridesmaid and Todd warned me that he wasn't going to wear any suit."

Her throat went tight and her eyes burned. If only it could all be true. She stroked her hand through the heavy silk of his dark hair and pressed her lips softly to his temple. "Everything's going to be okay, Gabriel."

But even as she said the words, she couldn't help wondering *how*.

Chapter 13

"Bobbie, this is my attorney, Ray Chilton."

Bobbie managed a nervous smile and shook Gabe's lawyer's hand. "Pleased to meet you."

They were standing outside the courtroom, waiting to go inside where Stephanie, her husband and the children were already seated. The middle-aged man peered so closely through his bifocals at Bobbie that she couldn't help worry that she'd worn the completely wrong thing to a child custody hearing.

"You're younger than I expected," he finally said.

Bobbie felt herself flush, but she managed a smile anyway. "Sorry." She might have been able to take Tommi's advice that her new slate-gray skirt suit was the epitome of conservative and responsible-looking, but she couldn't add on years that she didn't possess.

"Don't let her age fool you," Gabe inserted. "She's the new director of Golden Ability."

"Oh?" Ray cast another look at her as if he were mentally adding that fact to her qualifications as Gabe's fiancée and prospective stepmother to the children he was there to fight over. "Interesting."

Bobbie kept her smile in place. It wasn't easy, though. She still could barely believe that she'd accepted the position that Fiona had offered, not even after having spent most of the previous day with her at the hospital, taking a virtual crash course in running a non-profit.

For now, the plan was for her to begin at the administrative offices on Monday. Fiona was supposed to be released from the hospital by then, and she would spend an hour at the agency with Bobbie each afternoon.

The idea still took some getting used to, though Bobbie had to admit it wasn't as terrifying as she'd expected it to be. And her sisters and mother had been positively thrilled when she'd called to tell them the news. They'd each even claimed that they weren't surprised by the turn of events at all.

The court clerk stuck her head out into the hall, catching their attention. "We're ready," she chirped brightly.

Bobbie suddenly felt a wave of nausea. She brushed her hands down the front of her suit and reminded herself that she was there for appearances only. Gabe grabbed her hand, though, as they entered a courtroom that was hardly larger than her own living room.

She took a seat in the row of seats behind Gabe, and folded her hands in her lap, trying to smile naturally at Lisette and Todd, who were sitting pale-faced and fidgeting behind their mother alongside a tall, good-

looking man that Bobbie assumed was their stepfather, Ethan.

She knew the children had already spoken privately
with Judge Gainer in his chambers before the hearing
had begun, and could only imagine how hard that had
been for them.

Were children supposed to have to choose one parent over another?

She inhaled and looked forward again as the judge—
a short, gray-haired man—entered the courtroom and
took his seat behind a wide desk. Her fingers nervously
twisted the diamond ring on her finger while the court
clerk read off their purpose there, and then it was a
matter of sitting silently while Stephanie's lawyer re-
counted all the reasons why Stephanie and Ethan should
be allowed to retain full custody of the minor children,
Todd and Lisette.

After a while even the judge started to look bored,
or at least that was Bobbie's hopeful impression.

And then it was Gabe's turn, and she held her breath,
watching him approach the stand—which in this case,
was simply a hard-backed chair sitting next to the
judge's desk. Like Ethan, he was wearing a charcoal-
gray suit, and in that moment, he looked much more
like his name should be on the masthead of the Gannon Law Group rather than a man who usually wore a
hard-hat and work boots, with a roll of building plans
resting over his shoulder.

Across the courtroom, his gaze met Bobbie's for a
moment, and then he was looking back at his lawyer
as Ray started speaking.

She twisted her hands more tightly in her lap until

the diamond was cutting an impression into her palm and she forcibly relaxed them. She didn't know how Gabe could manage to look so calm and controlled when she knew beneath that smooth surface he was even more wound up than she was.

"Your honor, Mr. Gannon has proved his dedication to his children," Ray was saying. "He's relocated here to Seattle at some professional cost to his company, Gannon-Morris—"

"Excuse me," Stephanie's lawyer interrupted. "Gannon-Morris *expanded* by Mr. Gannon's relocation here. Their profits are higher than ever. We have copies of Gannon-Morris Limited's financials if—"

The judge waved impatiently. "No, thank you. Continue, Mr. Chilton."

Ray smoothed down his tie and continued pacing in front of the judge's desk. "My client has adjusted his entire life to allow for more time with his children. His standing in the community is well-known; his character references that you've already reviewed are impeccable. There's no reason to believe he's unfit for joint custody with Mrs. Walker."

Stephanie's lawyer rose again. "What about his fabricated engagement to marry Bobbie Fairchild for the sole purpose of making himself look less like the man-about-town and more like a more suitable parent?"

Bobbie went still, her eyes meeting Gabe's again. His expression didn't change one iota. "There's nothing fabricated about it," he said evenly.

The other lawyer leaned over while Stephanie whispered in his ear. Then he straightened again. "You met Ms. Fairchild only a few weeks ago, isn't that right?"

"Your Honor—" Ray started to protest, but the judge lifted his hand.

He was suddenly looking far more interested and he leaned on his arm, directing his attention toward Gabe where he sat beside the desk. "Mr. Gannon?"

"Yes, I met Bobbie a few weeks ago. She rents my grandmother's carriage house and I was doing some repairs there."

Bobbie couldn't help holding her breath, though she knew there was simply no way any of these people here besides Gabe and herself could know just exactly how that first meeting had gone.

"Must have been love at first sight, then," Stephanie's attorney drawled mockingly.

Other than a slightly lifted eyebrow, Gabe didn't respond to the goad.

"My client doesn't make a habit of casual relationships," Ray stated.

"Or serious ones," they all heard Stephanie mutter.

"Control your client, Mr. Hayward," the judge said calmly.

"Sorry, Your Honor," Stephanie's lawyer quickly apologized.

The gray-haired judge's lips twisted a little. He looked back at Gabe. "When do you plan to marry this woman?"

Bobbie held her breath again.

"We haven't set a date," Gabe said, which was true. "My grandmother recently had a heart attack and is still in the hospital. Naturally, that takes precedence at the moment over wedding planning."

"And your fiancée understands," Mr. Hayward said, again sounding mocking.

"Bobbie's the most understanding woman I know," Gabe returned. His gaze met hers across the courtroom.

The judge tapped his pen against his desk for a moment. Then he straightened in his chair again. "I see no reason why Mr. Gannon's engagement should adversely affect my decision here today. In fact, both Todd and Lisette had positive things to say about her."

"Notwithstanding the judgment of *children*," Mr. Hayward said, "since Ms. Fairchild is going to be the stepmother of my client's children—and therefore involved to some extent in their caretaking—perhaps we should hear from *her*."

"Your Honor, Ms. Fairchild's character isn't in question right now," Ray interjected.

"Perhaps it should be," Hayward suggested silkily.

Bobbie wanted to sink through the floor when the judge cast her a speculative look. "Presumably, you *are* the fiancée in question?"

She nodded.

He gestured her forward. "Come up here, then."

"Your Honor, this is highly irregular."

"And it's my courtroom, Ray," the judge reminded Gabe's lawyer testily, "so I'd like both you and Luke there to shut up and sit down and I'll ask the questions that I figure need answering, if that's all right with you?"

Both lawyers abruptly sat.

"Come up here, Miss… Fairchild, is it?" The judge glanced at his clerk, who nodded.

Certain that everyone would be able to see her knees knocking together below the modest hem of her skirt, Bobbie went forward. The clerk popped up from her chair, looking annoyingly cheerful and perky, and swore her in.

"Have a seat," the judge invited. "Mr. Gannon, you can step down."

Gabe rose and Bobbie met his gaze as she moved around him to take the chair he'd just vacated.

"It's okay," he murmured.

Which meant what, exactly?

That he knew she was going to blow everything for him?

She swallowed the knot in her throat and sat down, staring mutely at the judge.

"That's a nice ring," he offered.

Startled, she looked down at the diamond solitaire. "Thank you." Her fingers curled. "I—I think so, too." That, at least, was the God's honest truth.

He smiled a little. "Family court is a nerve-wracking place to be most times."

She shot Gabe a quick glance. He was sitting beside his lawyer, his blue gaze steady on her face. "I imagine so. I've never been in a courtroom before at all."

"Most people would consider that fortunate." The judge tapped his pen again. "Tell me about yourself."

"Um—"

"Your age, your profession. That sort of thing."

Her shoulders relaxed a little. "Twenty-seven. And I've just accepted the position of director at Golden Ability. It's a canine assistance agency here in Seattle."

He nodded. "I've heard of it."

And how glad she was to say that, rather than that she was a lowly clerk at Between the Bean. Not that she was ashamed of her time working at the coffee shop, but even she knew "clerk" didn't exactly smack of responsibility and capableness the way "director" did.

"I'm also a puppy raiser for the agency," she added. "Which essentially means that I foster pups that eventually go on to become assistance dogs of one type or another. I've done that for about ten years."

The judge was nodding. "Pretty steady work, sounds like. And you've lived in Seattle for a while, then?"

"Born and raised."

"Prior marriages or children?"

She shook her head. "No."

"Excuse me, Your Honor." Stephanie's lawyer rose again. "But our understanding is that Ms. Fairchild *was* previously engaged."

Bobbie realized if she could just keep her focus on Gabe's face, she didn't feel quite so nervous. "That's true," she allowed. She flicked a glance at the judge. "I was briefly engaged to Lawrence McKay."

"The councilmember? What happened?"

She felt a flush working up her throat. "We realized we weren't right for each other." She moistened her lips, waiting for some reminder at any second of the public nature of that particular event. But, thankfully, none came. "He's since married someone else and I'm sure they're much better suited," she added.

"I had a broken engagement myself, before I met my wife," the judge said, casting a censorious look toward Stephanie's table that had the lawyer subsiding in his seat once again. "A broken engagement usually has fewer consequences than a broken marriage. I ought to know," he added with obvious irony. Then he tapped his pen a few more times. "What do you think of your fiancé's children?"

Bobbie relaxed a little more. "They're wonderful, of course. Bright and imaginative and well-mannered."

"Would you be able to provide discipline if it were necessary if they weren't so well-mannered after all, or do you think a stepparent's position shouldn't extend into that area?"

"I'm afraid I don't know how to answer that." She twisted the ring on her finger. "Todd and Lisette have a mother who loves them. I certainly have no expectations of replacing her. But that doesn't mean I couldn't love Todd and Lisette as well." She knew that she already did. She swallowed again, searching carefully for a truthful answer. "If there was some situation where I had to assert my authority, I like to believe that I could."

"And as far as you're concerned, your engagement is not—as Mr. Hayward has implied—manufactured simply to help Mr. Gannon's case here today?"

Gabe's nerves tightened to a screaming pitch.

He looked across at Bobbie, whose gray eyes were so wide they dominated her pale, heart-shaped face.

He leaned toward his attorney. "Stop this now," he whispered harshly.

Ray shook his head. "I can't."

Gabe looked at Bobbie again and wished to hell and back again that he'd never dragged her into this.

She was in agony.

Everyone there could see it.

Then her gaze dropped to her lap. She moistened her lips, then looked to her side at the judge. "I'm wearing this diamond ring for only one reason," she said in a low voice that was nevertheless perfectly audible. Perfectly clear. "Because I'm in love with Gabriel Gannon."

The room was so silent he could hear his heart pounding in his ears.

She had always said she wouldn't lie for him in court.

And he knew, in that moment, that she hadn't.

A pain knotted inside his chest as he willed her to lift her head, to lift her gaze back to him.

But now, she wouldn't look at him at all.

"That's not exactly an answer to Your Honor's question." Stephanie's lawyer was the first one to speak into the hushed silence that followed Bobbie's husky admission.

Gabe saw Bobbie's lashes flutter as she looked back down at her hands.

He pushed to his feet. "It's answer enough," he said gruffly. "She's not here to be picked apart just because my ex-wife is still mad that I wasn't the kind of husband she wanted."

Bobbie's lashes flew up, her gray eyes startled.

"Counselors, it seems to me that neither one of you can control your clients very well," the judge commented. He leaned toward Bobbie. "You can step down now, Ms. Fairchild. I know what I need to know."

She nodded jerkily and rose from the chair and headed toward Gabe. "I'm sorry," she whispered thickly.

"I suppose you're going to make sure that Hunt-Com takes this out on Ethan, now," Stephanie accused curtly. "What a perfect little fiancée Gabe picked. If the court doesn't rule his way, he can have you ruin my husband's career. Either way, he wins."

The judge huffed, clearly irritated, and picked up his gavel. He slammed it once, hard, on his desk. "Enough!"

Bobbie just shook her head, looking at the other woman. "There's no winning here! And you don't know Gabe as well as you claim if you think he'd stoop to that level. Since you don't know me at all, I suppose I can't blame you for thinking I'd be a party to it." She looked at Ethan. "But *you* work for HuntCom. And *you* should know they don't operate that way either." Then her gaze skimmed over Gabe as she looked back at the judge. "I'm sorry for speaking out of turn."

He grimaced. "Everyone else has." Then he smacked his gavel again. "Everyone out except Mr. Gannon and Mrs. Walker and their legal representatives."

"Come on, kids." Ethan rose and began scooting Todd and Lisette out of the courtroom.

Gabe saw Bobbie's teeth sink into her lip, and then she, too, was heading toward the door, believing what she'd feared.

That she'd ruined things for him.

He couldn't let her go. Not like this.

He went to follow her.

"Where are you going?" Ray clamped his hand on his shoulder but Gabe shrugged him off.

"I have to talk to her."

"If you walk out now, you're just going to piss of Judge Gainer even more. Is that what you want?"

Gabe looked from his lawyer to the judge, and finally landed on his ex-wife. "You know this is wrong, Steph. I'm sorry I hurt you. That I wasn't the husband you needed. If you still need to punish me by taking my kids away yet again—even though you now have with Ethan everything you ever used to want—then I guess you've got to do what you have to." His throat felt tight. "But I won't ever stop fighting for them. They're the only things you and I did right together. And I wish to God that you could see that we could still do one more thing right together, by raising them jointly." He looked from Stephanie's stone-faced expression back to the judge. "Right now my future is walking out that door, and if I let her go, this time I'll have nobody to blame but myself."

Bobbie's heels rang on the tiled corridor outside the courtroom. All she could think of was escape.

"You're right about HuntCom."

She nearly skidded to a stop when Ethan suddenly spoke. He was the only one who'd maintained his silence inside the courtroom, and now he was looking more than a little pained as he stroked his hand over Lisette's head. "Everyone who works there does so on their own merit, and that's all that's ever mattered. I've tried to tell Steph that, but she just can't see reason when it comes to Gabe."

Bobbie lifted her hands, feeling futility in every breath she drew. "I'm sorry."

"Bobbie?" Lisette was giving her a worried look. "Is that judge really going to say we don't get to see Daddy anymore?"

"That's not what this is about, honey," Ethan assured her softly.

Bobbie pressed her lips together for a moment. "Ethan's right," she finally managed. She looked at Todd, too. "You'll always be able to see your dad. He'll make certain of it, even if you do move back to Switzerland." Which, thanks to her miserable performance for the judge, was surely a foregone conclusion.

She pressed a kiss to Lisette's forehead, then to Todd's, who ducked his chin shyly. "He loves you two more than anything, you see? And your dad won't let anything stand between him and the ones he loves." And then, because she didn't think she could hold back her tears a second longer, she straightened.

And found Gabe standing there.

She inhaled sharply. "You're supposed to be in the courtroom."

"The judge ordered a recess." His hands were balled in his pockets and his blue eyes were stark. "You didn't lie."

A tear burned its way from the corner of her eye. "I… I told you I wouldn't.

"You couldn't. Even if you wanted to."

Bobbie was vaguely aware of Ethan silently moving Lisette and Todd further down the empty corridor. "I wanted to," she whispered.

"To keep me from knowing that you loved me?"

A fresh ache crept through her. "No." She twisted her arms around her waist, trying to still her quaking. She jerked her chin toward the courtroom door. "To make them believe we were real."

"They believe it," he said quietly.

"But I didn't tell them that."

"You didn't have to." He pulled his hands out of his pockets and slowly closed the distance between them. And when he lifted his hands to stroke his fingers down her face, she realized they were trembling just as badly as she was. "All you needed to do was be you." His jaw cocked to one side for a moment, then centered again. "I knew all along that you were some-one remarkable. I just didn't let myself face how much you meant to me until you were walking out of the courtroom and I was suddenly afraid that you would keep on walking. God knows I've given you reason."

Bobbie's vision blurred. Her heart leapt into her throat. She tried to speak, but the only thing that came out was a garbled, "Gabe."

His thumbs slowly trailed along her jaw. "I'm sorry you ever had to answer the judge like that, that I put you in a position where you had to justify anything about yourself."

"You didn't know," she managed thickly.

"I should have. But whatever happens in that court-room, I can deal with it, as long as I know I haven't lost you." His eyes stared fiercely into hers as if he were trying to see all the way to her soul. "Have I? Lost you?"

She covered his hands with her own. Drew them away from her face to slowly press a kiss to his palms. And then she looked up at him again, and this time it was she who was seeing through to his soul.

It was right there, open and bare and just as uncer-tain of being loved as she'd ever felt herself.

Her shaking calmed.

Her heart steadied.

She stepped closer until their hands were caught be-tween them. Caught between her heart and his. "You haven't lost me."

"Are you sure? You deserve more than a guy like me, Bobbie. You deserve everything."

His uncertainty melted her. "Then I deserve *you*." She went on her toes, pressing her lips to his. "And I'm more certain of that than I've ever been of anything in my life," she whispered.

His hands slipped away from hers, but only to draw her against him in a fierce embrace. "I love you, Bobbie Fairchild." His voice was low and thick. "And I didn't think I'd ever love anyone again."

She twined her arms around his neck, her heart so full it could have burst out of her chest. "I love you, too." And then she drew in a shaking breath. Let it out in an even shakier sough. "When I told you to make it look good, I never expected this."

He laughed then, and slowly set her back onto her feet. "Once upon a time, there was a kiss," he murmured.

His gaze roved over her face, full and warmer than any burst of sunlight could ever be. He reached into the inside pocket of his lapel. "And the lucky guy caught a princess." He held out his hand, and a tiny, jeweled hair clip sat on his palm.

Bobbie's chest tightened. "I was wearing them the night of Fiona's birthday party."

"It almost feels like a lifetime ago." He slowly lifted one of her curls and pinned it back with the clip.

Fresh tears fell, but Bobbie didn't care. She stared up into his face. "The lifetime is ahead of us," she whispered.

"A brand-new story?" He lifted her hand, kissing the finger that wore his ring. "One with a white dress and a wedding ring to match this?"

She caught her breath. Then nodded. "Yes. And we'll be together in every chapter."

And when he smiled, so slow and so easy, and drew

her into his arms once more, she knew deep in her heart that this time, they'd write their happy ending.

They'd write it together.

Epilogue

"You've got someone here to see you, Bobbie."

Bobbie glanced up from the budget she was studying to see Fiona's—no, *her*—secretary standing there. "Who is it?"

But Cheryl just lifted her shoulders and disappeared from the doorway of Bobbie's office.

Bobbie glanced at her watch, then her appointment book. She didn't think she had anything scheduled, but then she'd only been running Golden Ability for two weeks, and she was still nervous about missing something important. But her calendar was clear and Fiona had already put in her daily allotment of time with Bobbie. Less than an hour, actually, because she'd insisted that Bobbie was doing fine, and she had a new yoga instructor she was working with…a fine young man named Juan.

Fiona was clearly throwing herself into her retirement with as much enthusiasm as she did everything else.

Bobbie left the budget on her desk. She'd already managed to find several thousand extra dollars by transferring it from one cost area to another, but she was perfectly happy not to look at numbers for a few minutes.

She worked her way out of the office that had grown even more crowded since Fiona's abrupt retirement, smoothing her hands down the sides of her deep-red sweater dress, and walked out into the administrative area.

The sight of Gabe still made her heart skitter crazily around in her chest, and she grinned, quickly crossing to him. "This is a nice surprise." She caught his hands in hers and reached up for his kiss. "I wasn't expecting you. Aren't you supposed to be working?"

"Boss's perks, remember?" His eyes crinkled. "I brought you something." He held up a slender box and she laughed and took the box from him.

"You're spoiling me."

"That's a fiancé's prerogative, isn't it?"

She just shook her head again, and flipped open the box. Inside, was a delicate silver bracelet with three shining daisies dangling from it. "Another one?"

"For some reason, I feel a need to fill your life with flowers." He took the bracelet from her and fastened it around her wrist. "Besides. It matches the necklace."

She couldn't seem to stop smiling. She touched her finger to the diamond pendant that hung around her neck. It, too, was in the shape of a daisy. "And the earrings." She shook her head a little and she felt the dangling earrings dancing in her ears. She looked at the bracelet. "It's beautiful. Thank you." Then she laughed a little. "Little did Georgie know what she was starting when she gave me those hair clips."

Gabe was still grinning. "I have something else for you."

She huffed a little. "Gabe! I have a necklace, a bracelet and earrings. What else is there left?"

"This." He reached into the pocket of his battered suede overcoat, and pulled out a thick sheaf of folded papers. He handed it to her.

"What is it?"

"Read."

Her hands were suddenly shaking. She unfolded the papers. The top was a handwritten letter on fine parchment paper. Bobbie skimmed through the sloping writing. "It's from Stephanie."

"She's agreed to send the kids back before Thanksgiving." His voice went gruff. "And to let them stay until the summer. The rest of the stuff there is a modified visitation agreement, giving me physical custody of Todd and Lissi for the rest of the school year."

Bobbie gasped, pressing her hand to her mouth. She set the papers aside before she dropped them. "I... I can't believe it. When Judge Gainer postponed his ruling and she and Ethan took the children to Switzerland, I was afraid she'd never let them come back here again." It had been the only thing to mar the perfection of the last two weeks. The parting had been agonizing. But she and Gabe had spoken to—and seen, thanks to the wondrous invention of the webcam—both kids every single day since. It wasn't the same as being with them, but it made the situation a little more bearable. "Why'd she change her mind?"

"I told Ray to withdraw my petition."

Shocked, Bobbie sank down onto the edge of an empty desk. "*When?* Why didn't you tell me?"

"Last week. And I didn't tell you because I didn't want you thinking that I'd given up."

Bobbie made a soft sound. It never failed to undo her to realize that for all of his secure confidence, Gabe had his fears, too. "I'd never think that." She touched his hand. "You wouldn't."

His hand turned over, his fingers closing around hers. "I told Ray to let Stephanie know that I wasn't going to keep yanking the kids into our battle. I love them enough to leave them with her, if that was the best thing for them."

Bobbie lifted her eyebrows. "But you've never thought that was the best thing for them."

He grimaced. "Maybe not. But even I had to start facing the fact that, for all her faults, Stephanie does love them." He tugged at the ends of her hair, which she'd tied into a ponytail. "A very smart woman opened my eyes to that fact."

Bobbie smiled faintly. "I'm still surprised." She picked up the letter again, then let out another laugh. "Stunned, really."

"I guess once I stopped pushing, she could afford to start giving a little."

"So it would appear. Personally, I think Ethan might have softened her up."

"Ethan?"

"Well, he's not a stupid man, or he wouldn't be working for Uncle Harry's company, would he?"

His eyes suddenly narrowed. "You didn't—"

She shook her head. "Of course not. But I can't help it if he's wanted to know everything about the man I intend to marry. Harry's very protective sometimes."

"And what'd you tell him?"

"That he can judge you for himself when we see him over Christmas."

"That's all?"

"That's all," she assured softly. "But I'll warn you that he's taking credit for our getting together. Seems to think that if he'd never asked me to show Tim Boering around Seattle, you and I would never have met."

"Fiona would have made sure we did," he said, looking amused.

Then he shook his head and laughed a little.

"So Steph really *did* change her own mind."

"Evidently." Bobbie looped her fingers around the lapels of his thick jacket and tugged him closer. "So the kids will be here before Thanksgiving? That gives us about a week and a half."

"To do what?"

"Find a decent place to live. The carriage house is too small for all of us. It's too small even for the two of us." Though they'd been managing remarkably well since he'd been spending nearly every night with her there. "And your apartment is not exactly homey." In fact, she'd been appalled when she'd finally seen it. Which was why they were always at the carriage house. Even her hand-me-down furnishings were more welcoming than his nearly sterile place.

"Are you suggesting we move in together?" His hands linked behind her back. "I'm almost shocked." His lips tilted wickedly.

She laughed. "I seriously doubt that."

"Okay. We'll find a bigger place to rent until we decide on something more permanent. Maybe we'll find some land and I'll *build* us a home. Satisfied?"

She nodded. A home with Gabe? What more could she want? "Extremely."

"And in the meantime, since the kids will be back soon…how fast can you put a wedding together once they are?"

Bobbie looked at him quickly. "You want to get married right away?"

"A marriage *is* usually the end result of an engagement," he reminded her.

She smiled slowly, then turned around, only then realizing that nearly everyone in the office had been watching them avidly. "Cheryl, I'll be leaving now for the day, if anyone calls."

Her secretary looked surprised, then an indulgent smile crossed her lips. "Sure thing."

Bobbie turned back to Gabe, grinning. "Boss's prerogative," she whispered. Then she hopped off the desk, ducked into her office to grab her jacket and purse and raced back to the love of her life. "Come on." She pulled him out of the building and into the uncommonly sunny afternoon.

Gabe followed, his laughter low and deep. "Where are we going now?"

"To start the rest of our lives, of course."

He caught her around the waist and delight swept through her just as easily as he swept her right off of her feet. Sunlight shined across his face, turning his eyes even bluer. "That started the day we met."

She wrapped her arms around his neck.

Oh, how she did love this man.

"All right," she conceded. "Then we're going to go see Mom and call my sisters." She smiled mischievously. "Because if anyone can organize a wedding in a matter of weeks, it's the Fairchild women."

"Maybe we should take a quick detour along the way." He brushed his mouth against hers. "Because I'm feeling suddenly desperate for just one Fairchild woman in particular."

How easily he could have her blood rippling through her veins. "Maybe a quick detour. But then off to my mother's."

He nodded, looking amused and obedient and wholly sexy all at the same time. He set her back on her feet. "You think all of you can pull a wedding together before the end of the year and not be disappointed?"

Bobbie tangled her fingers with his. "Nothing about marrying you will ever be a disappointment," she promised quietly. And then she smiled brilliantly. "And yes. I'm sure that we can."

And they did.

* * * * *

We hope you enjoyed reading

ONE STEP AHEAD

by *New York Times* bestselling author

SHERRYL WOODS

and

ONCE UPON A PROPOSAL

by *New York Times* bestselling author

ALLISON LEIGH

Both were originally
Harlequin series stories!

HARLEQUIN®

SPECIAL EDITION

Life, Love and Family

NYTHSE1215

SPECIAL EXCERPT FROM

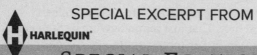

HARLEQUIN®

SPECIAL EDITION

*When tycoon Ben Robinson enlists temp Ella Thomas
to help him uncover Fortune family secrets, will the
closed-off Prince Charming be able to resist the charms
of his beautiful Cinderella?*

Read on for a sneak preview of
FORTUNE'S SECRET HEIR, the first installment in the
2016 Fortunes of Texas twentieth anniversary continuity,
ALL FORTUNE'S CHILDREN.

Ben figured it was only a matter of time before the security
guards came to check that he'd exited. But having gotten
what he'd come for, he had no reason to stay.

He went out the door and it closed automatically behind
him. When he tested it out of curiosity, it was locked.

"Crazy old bat," he muttered under his breath.

But he didn't really believe it.

Kate Fortune was many things. Of that he was certain.
But crazy wasn't one of them.

He looked around, getting his bearings before setting
off to his left. It was dark, only a few lights situated here
and there to show off some landscape feature. But he soon
made his way around the side of the enormous house and
to the front, which was not just well lit, but magnificently
so. He stopped at the valet and handed over his ticket to a
skinny kid in a black shirt and trousers.

He tried to imagine Ella dashing off the way this kid
was to retrieve his car, parked somewhere on the vast
property. He couldn't quite picture it.

But in his head, he could picture *her* quite clearly.

Not the red hair. That just reminded him of Stephanie. But the faint gap in her toothy smile and the clear light shining from her pretty eyes.

That was all Ella.

A moment later, when the valet returned with his Porsche, Ben got in and drove away.

Don't miss
FORTUNE'S SECRET HEIR
by New York Times *bestselling author Allison Leigh,*
available January 2016 wherever
Harlequin® Special Edition books and ebooks are sold.

www.Harlequin.com

Copyright © 2016 by Allison Lee Johnson

HSEEXP1215

HARLEQUIN®

SPECIAL EDITION

Life, Love and Family

Save $1.00

on the purchase of

FORTUNE'S SECRET HEIR

by Allison Leigh, available

December 15, 2015, or on any other

Harlequin® Special Edition book.

Available wherever books are sold, including most
bookstores, supermarkets, drugstores and discount stores.

Save $1.00

on the purchase of any Harlequin Special Edition book.

Coupon valid until February 29, 2016. Redeemable at participating outlets in the
U.S.A. and Canada only. Not redeemable at Barnes & Noble stores.
Limit one coupon per customer.

52613281

Canadian Retailers: Harlequin Enterprises Limited will pay the face value of
this coupon plus 10.25¢ if submitted by customer for this product only. Any
other use constitutes fraud. Coupon is nonassignable. Void if taxed, prohibited
or restricted by law. Consumer must pay any government taxes. Void if copied.
Inmar Promotional Services ("IPS") customers submit coupons and proof of
sales to Harlequin Enterprises Limited, P.O. Box 3000, Saint John, NB E2L 4L3,
Canada. Non-IPS retailer—for reimbursement submit coupons and proof of
sales directly to Harlequin Enterprises Limited, Retail Marketing Department, 225
Duncan Mill Rd., Don Mills, ON M3B 3K9, Canada.

U.S. Retailers: Harlequin Enterprises
Limited will pay the face value of
this coupon plus 8¢ if submitted by
customer for this product only. Any
other use constitutes fraud. Coupon is
nonassignable. Void if taxed, prohibited
or restricted by law. Consumer must pay
any government taxes. Void if copied.
For reimbursement submit coupons
and proof of sales directly to Harlequin
Enterprises Limited, P.O. Box 880478,
El Paso, TX 88588-0478, U.S.A. Cash
value 1/100 cents.

5 65373 00076 2   **(8100)0 12120**

® and ™ are trademarks owned and used by the trademark owner and/or its licensee.

© 2015 Harlequin Enterprises Limited

Let #1 *New York Times* bestselling author

SHERRYL WOODS

sweep you away with the soul-stirring story of a beloved O'Brien family member claiming the life she always dreamed of living.

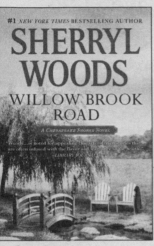

Spirited, spontaneous Carrie Winters has grown up under the watchful eyes of not only her grandfather Mick O'Brien, but the entire town of Chesapeake Shores.

Now that she's home from Europe, a glamorous fashion career behind her and her heart broken, there seem to be far too many people watching to see if she'll live up to the expectations her family has for her. As if that weren't enough pressure, Carrie finds herself drawn to sexy, grief-stricken Sam Winslow, who is yearning for someone to help him raise the nephew who has unexpectedly come into his life after a tragedy.

With her own life in turmoil, is Carrie really ready to take on a new career and a new man? Or is Sam exactly what she needs to create the strong, loving family she's always wanted?

Available now, wherever books are sold!

Be sure to connect with us at:
Harlequin.com/Newsletters
Facebook.com/HarlequinBooks
Twitter.com/HarlequinBooks

www.MIRABooks.com

MSHW1766

Turn your love of reading into
rewards you'll love with

Harlequin My Rewards

**Join for FREE today at
www.HarlequinMyRewards.com**

Earn **FREE BOOKS** of your choice.

Experience **EXCLUSIVE OFFERS** and contests.

Enjoy **BOOK RECOMMENDATIONS**
selected just for you.

PLUS! Sign up now
and get **500** points
right away!

Earn **FREE** REWARDS
HarlequinMyRewards.com
Join Today!

MYR16

HARLEQUIN®

A *Romance* FOR EVERY MOOD™

Stay up-to-date on all your
romance-reading news with the
Harlequin Shopping Guide,
featuring bestselling authors, exciting new
miniseries, books to watch and more!

The newest issue will be delivered right to you
with our compliments! There are 4 each year.

Signing up is easy.

EMAIL

ShoppingGuide@Harlequin.ca

WRITE TO US

HARLEQUIN BOOKS
Attention: Customer Service Department
P.O. Box 9057, Buffalo, NY 14269-9057

OR PHONE

1-800-873-8635 in the United States
1-888-343-9777 in Canada

Please allow 4-6 weeks for delivery of the first issue by mail.

THE WORLD IS BETTER WITH

Romance

Harlequin has everything from contemporary, passionate and heartwarming to suspenseful and inspirational stories.

Whatever your mood, we have a romance just for you!

Connect with us to find your next great read, special offers and more.

f /HarlequinBooks

🐦 @HarlequinBooks

www.HarlequinBlog.com

www.Harlequin.com/Newsletters

Ⓗ HARLEQUIN®

A *Romance* FOR EVERY MOOD™

www.Harlequin.com

SERIESHALOAD201